Plantation Secrets

A Novel by

James W. Ridout, IV

PILOT BOOKS

WASHINGTON, DC

PUBLISHED BY PILOT BOOKS
WASHINGTON, DC

PO Box 817
Vienna, VA 22183-0817

Library of Congress Control Number 00-090492
Ridout, IV, James W.
    Plantation Secrets; a novel / James W. Ridout, IV. – first Edition.

    1.   Fiction, Gay and Lesbian 1. Title.

ISBN 0-9678838-0-6

Printed in the United States of America

First Edition

June 2000

10 9 8 7 6 5 4 3 2 1

This book is dedicated to

Julia S. Carson

A special thanks is given to God

For his gentle spirit and subtle sense of humor

CHAPTER 1

It was a hot and sunny day. Sweat covered the young man's clean shaven face and streamed down his smooth chest. He could feel the trickle of liquid running between his shoulder blades. There before him, the woman whom he had adored ever since he could remember, was being lowered into the ground. A preacher was noting some phrases, quoting from the Bible. A sweet voice asked him if he would like to shed his black worsted wool jacket. Without saying a word, he removed the garment and handed it to the person with the sweet voice. As the casket was lowered into the vault, it was sealed and placed into the ground. He could feel a tightening in his chest. The sealed vault would never let anything inside it to harm the body or cause it to decay. It would be preserved forever unless somebody chose to open it, to violate what should stay untouched. Finally, the dissension was complete and the tightening in his chest relaxed. *It is done,* he thought.

The people beside the grave started to engage him in mindless chatter and condolences. However, the young man said very little in response. He removed himself from the gathering and began to reflect about this recent death and the events that lead to this day. The pain was intense. Then a light breeze came, just long enough to cool the sweat that covered his body. It was almost pleasant. He began to walk along the road that ran along side the cemetery. Nobody seemed to miss him, so he kept walking. The breeze touched him lightly again and he felt another refreshing sensation. He looked up into the tall oak trees that lined the side of the road. The broad leaves were fluttering just so lightly. Perhaps it was the squirrels playing or gathering acorns. *Their lives seemed simple,* the man thought. They labored just to feed and to provide themselves with shelter. With these thoughts, the man continued his walk down the road.

The afternoon sun was beginning hide between the trees. It was no longer so hot. His walk led him to the center of town, where the road stopped in front of the bus station. He saw a water fountain and hastened toward it, as he had worked up a good thirst. Next to the water fountain, a middle-aged man was standing at the ticket window. The older man said a few words to the woman on the other side of the ticket window.

The woman asked, "Where to?"

The older man answered, "Atlanta one way." They exchanged some cash, then he received his ticket and proceeded to the direction of the buses.

"May I help you?" asked the woman as she gave him a little smile.

After a brief hesitation, the young man answered, "Yes, Atlanta one way."

"Okay, that's $33.00. It seems to be the popular ticket at the moment," the woman responded with a smirk.

The young man nodded gently, handed the woman a few dollars from his money clip, obtained his ticket, and proceeded to the row of buses.

CHAPTER 2

He stepped from the *Greyhound* bus. He observed his surroundings while feeling the hot humid air. The sun was scorching the earth. Sweat poured from his thinning blond hair, across his reddened face, flowing over his entire body.

The coat that had draped his broad shoulders had long been discarded. *Where was it?* He had forgotten. The white broadcloth buttoned down shirt had lost its starch. It was now pressed to the skin of his body, as the sweat acted as an effective glue agent. The color of his flesh glimpsed through its threads, revealing the contours of his muscled body. His black trousers and tie acted as a magnet for heat.

He stood, surveying the landscape around him, searching for a direction to follow. *Where to go to?* The bus had deposited him in front of a lime-green, boarded up old dime store that possessed a sign stating "White Only" above the front door. On top of the store was an old faded

Coca-Cola sign, which read "Coke Sold Here." The store was overgrown with trees and other shrubbery.

As the sweat continued to flow, the young man walked forward, pushing his body in an unmapped direction. *Shade*, he thought. He noticed some trees. As he walked along the white washed ground surrounding the store, he came to the trees. Beyond the trees he could see some people. Better yet, it seemed to be a small community. Instantly, he was aware that he was not in the middle of an isolated area but had been let off in some town. He started toward the town line.

As he stepped from the trees, he recaptured the asphalt road, where he had been left at the front of the old green dime store. Approaching the town, the first building he saw was a weather worn structure with a sign that read, "Lou's Restaurant" over the front entrance.

The young man climbed the few steps leading into the building. When he entered the restaurant, he could see a counter with several stools along the perimeter. Two stools down from where he sat, an older gentleman was sipping some hot soup. A big burly man with black hair pressed to his skull shoved a menu in front of him. Startled as he was, he stared straight into his black eyes in almost utter horror. The burly man asked, "What will it be, mack?"

After a pause he asked again, "What will it be? Cat got your tongue?"

"Ice water, please," the young man finally replied.

The burly man placed the glass of water on the counter next to the unopened menu. "I don't recall seeing you around in these here parts before today. Are you just passing through?"

"I don't know," answered the young man.

"My name's Lou. Welcome to town." Lou stretched out his hand to shake. With a slight hesitation, the young man responded by gently placing his hand inside the extended grip.

"I didn't catch your name."

After a brief pause, the young man answered, "Matt."

"Well Matt, how do you make your living?" Lou inquired.

After a pause Matt answered, "I don't have a job. I don't have any money. I'm sorry I can't pay you for the water."

Lou waved his hand in front of his face and replied with a chuckle, "I guess you aren't going too far with no money. Your best bet is to work in the fields of one of the farmers because folks aren't apt to hire a stranger into their stores. You seem a bit on the shy side, makes people wonder what you're thinking. Not too many white folks work the fields, but there's a few. It ain't easy work for a city boy like you."

Matt nodded. "Field work is fine."

"Those fancy black britches and nice shirt will get dirty awful quick," Lou shot back.

"Field work is fine," Matt answered a second time.

Lou smiled at Matt as if to say, *Take it light.* " Well, this is the center of town, about a couple hundred miles west of the nearest big city in Louisiana. I'll tell you what. Since you're new around here, I'll give you directions to the Pilot plantation. You probably should wait until after the afternoon sun goes down to take to the road because it's a good way. It will take hours for you to reach it. You probably could hitch a ride with someone."

Matt nodded as if to thank the big burly man as he took the small piece of white paper. He looked at it momentarily and then stuffed it into his soaked shirt pocket. He then turned to exit the store. He could hear the old thin man speak for the first time. "Peculiar boy. Think he's running?"

"No. I suppose he's never wandered too far from home before. He can't be more that 25 years tops. I don't think the sheriff would be looking for him. He doesn't seem the criminal type and he's old enough to leave his mama and daddy. I guess he's just peculiar."

"Hmmm," replied the old thin man, thinking it over.

Matt stepped off the porch of the small restaurant and walked toward the rest of the town. There were stores lined up on each side of the town's main avenue. There was the post office, the nickel and dime, the barber, the fire department, and the church on the end of one row. On the other side of the street, there was a co-op that was bigger than the dime store and a couple of buildings that looked like they were no longer being used. The windows were boarded up. As he reached the end of the avenue, he looked and saw a row of houses with about a hundred yards between them for as far as he could see. As he gazed down the road, the preacher came out of the white board structure with the towering white steeple. He looked to be middle aged with salt and pepper hair. As he headed down the steps, he took notice of Matt. "Howdy son, you lost?"

"No, sir," Matt replied

"My name's Reverend Samson. I don't believe I've seen you in my church before. You passing through?"

Matt took the piece of paper from his shirt pocket and looked at it, "I'm looking for the Pilot plantation, to get some work."

"Well, there's plenty of it, but it's hard work. It's several miles from town. It's straight down the road from here about 10 miles or so, and then there's a right turn at the fork, go a few more miles and then there's the drive to the house. The drive is a good many miles itself, as you pass some fields and such." The preacher paused and studied Matt more closely. His unusual clothes puzzled him. "Where you from, son?"

"Boston," Matt answered. He nodded to the preacher and started on his way toward the Pilot plantation. He walked about a mile when a red pickup truck stopped alongside the road. Matt kept walking. The man in the pickup rolled down his window and kept his truck at even pace with Matt. "Need a ride, buddy?" asked the man.

Matt paused briefly, opened the passenger door and climbed into the truck.

"My name is Jack," Jack held out his hand for Matt to shake. Matt reached across his body, took the hand and gave it a brief squeeze. Jack was about Matt's age, medium height with a stocky build, and red wavy hair.

"I'm looking for some work," Matt replied bluntly.

"My daddy does some hiring. There's plenty of work on our farm. We are always looking for people. The Pilot farm is one of about three of the biggest sugar producers in the parish. Daddy likes to employ as many as he can to do his share in keeping the local economy going. People in these parts need work. It's not the life for everybody. The folks here depend on the family to be there for them. Most of the folks live on the land. The men live in the barracks and the women have their quarters. Families have family quarters. Meals are provided in the big kitchen next to the barracks. You may lose some of the freedom that you're used to, but Daddy takes real good care of his people, treats them like his own family. He says without these folks, the farm could not run. He shows his appreciation for them and in turn wants their respect. The folks give it to him."

Matt listened carefully and considered the man's words. The situation seemed agreeable to him. "Is your daddy home?" Matt inquired.

"He gets home for supper, but sometimes he's there during the day. It depends on the schedule he's running. He likes to be accessible to everybody and tries attempts to be available," Jack answered.

As they approached the farm, they came to a fork in the road. Jack turned the truck to the right and shortly turned up a dusty dirt road. After a few miles, they approached what seemed to be a small town. To the left was a short road, which lead to a large house. To the right, a road stretched through a community of small buildings on one side. On the opposite side, three or four large barns lined the narrow lane. Straight ahead, the road stopped in front of a large fenced pasture. The buildings and grounds were impressively manicured. Dust stirred into the air as they continued up the road to the big house.

Jack stopped the truck and put it into park. He motioned for Matt to hop out of the truck and follow him up the walk to the big house. They opted for the back entrance to the kitchen. As they walked into the house, a woman stood in the kitchen slicing tomatoes. She was slender and rather tall as women go, but her bones were small. In her younger days, she must have been rather striking, for in her middle years she still sported a beautiful hour glass figure. Her face had light beads of sweat. Her blue and white checkered cotton dress was wet with perspiration. She turned as she heard them come through the door and wiped her brow with her forearm.

"Hi Mama," said Jack as he kissed the woman on the cheek, "This is Matt." He turned to Matt who was standing in the archway.

"This is my mama, Louisa Pilot," said Jack as he introduced the two.

Matt nodded toward the woman to acknowledge her.

The woman smiled as she further acknowledged Matt's presence. "You'll have to excuse my appearance. We've been canning vegetables all day and the big kitchen gets rather hot on a day like this one."

Matt gave a short nod of understanding, while Jack smiled at his Mama.

"Mama works as hard as anybody around here if not harder to keep the big house in order and keep the farm's women busy with their work." He paused and then asked, "Is Daddy around? Matt is interested in working on the farm. I thought he could talk to him."

"I expect him for supper. Why don't you show Matt the farm and explain the way things work, then bring him back so he can join us for supper."

"Sounds great. Can you let Marge know what I'm doing? She'll be wondering what I'm up to about now," Jack requested.

Louisa nodded to confirm his request and the two men left the house.

"Marge is my pretty little wife, We're expecting our first child in the next few months," Jack explained.

Jack got into the pickup, so Matt followed suit and entered on the passenger side. "Women work the vegetable gardens that are located close to the big house. These gardens produce enough vegetables to feed all the farm hands and their families for an entire year. In the summer, we eat fresh vegetables and fruit, while in the winter, we eat the canned food that the farm's women are now preparing. The canning is done in the mess hall, which Mama calls the big kitchen. That is where all your meals will be served." After a pause he asked, "You do plan to live on the farm don't you?"

"Yes," Matt answered quietly.

"If you don't mind me asking, is everything okay? You seem kind of quiet. Maybe you don't have much to say," Jack asked hesitantly. "After all this time, I really don't know anything about you. Why did you come to this parish? Where do you come from? And why do you want to work on a farm? Like I said I don't mean to pry, so if I'm out of line, you don't have to answer."

"I just buried my mother and thought I needed a new start," Matt answered briefly.

"It's just peculiar, 'cause we don't get to many white folks wanting to work the farm. Are you aiming to be an overseer or a barn boss?" Jack asked with more curiosity.

"No. Nobody's boss," Matt answered.

Jack felt more comfortable with his new mysterious friend now that he knew a little bit more about him. "Okay. Let's finish the grand tour,"

They drove along side the barns. Jack described the animals that lived in each of the barns. After a short time, they turned up the road that led away from the big house and ran deeper into the farm.

"This is what we call the Cattle Road, because the cow pastures border along this road. We have lots of Angus cattle. We breed purebred Black Angus. They are covered in black from head to tail. These cattle are an important part of the farm's operation, because they are a prime source of food and they produce fantastic fertilizer for our crops," Jack explained. He glanced at Matt to see if he was paying attention. The man with such a calm exterior seemed to be listening intently.

Jack, satisfied that he had a captive audience, continued his talk. "Further down this road, as we pass the cow pastures, the hay fields begin along to the curve to the left up here. On the right side of the road are the fields, where we grow feed corn. We harvest enough each year to provide food for the farm's animals. We must produce enough corn, oats, and hay to feed the animals all year long. Beyond the feeding crops, we have the sugarcane, which is our cash crop. This is what we produce to make the farm productive. This is where the greatest amount of manpower is used on the farm. We have some machinery that allows us to produce the sugar of a hundred farmers. This is a big farm. Only the big farms are making it these days. My brothers and my daddy run this farm as a business. I'm the only one of my brothers who actually lives on the farm. My oldest brother travels the world to explore new advances in farming, mainly sugarcane. My middle brother runs our office in New Orleans. I'm the youngest of the boys."

"I've done a lot of talking. Do you have any questions?" Jack inquired.

"No," Matt answered with little expression.

"Let's head back and drive down the Quarters Road. That's the road going directly away from the Cattle Road, running parallel to the Farm Road."

Jack pointed out the small cottages along side of the Quarters Road, which housed the farm's families.

"When a farm worker marries and decides to live on the farm, he or she is provided a house of their very own," Jack explained. "If there is not one available, one is built for them. Additions are provided if they need more room as children are born."

After touring the Quarters Road, they turned back toward the Cattle Road and the Main Road. Jack chose to drive down the Main Road, back toward the big house. He drove past the big kitchen. However, he stopped at the first barn. He decided to get out of the truck, so Matt followed suit and lumbered out to Jack's side.

"This is the horse barn. If you're going to have cattle, you need horses to work the pastures. We raise a few horses for our own needs, but we will sell a few yearlings each year." They watched as some of the geldings galloped along the fence to see what was approaching them.

"They are beautiful," Matt exclaimed in a gentle tone.

Jack smiled. He was pleased to bring some expression to this peculiar man's face. "Here is a couple of sugar cubes, you can feed them."

Matt took the sugar cubes and walked toward the fence where a couple of the horses stood. He gave each horse a couple cubes. When the other horses saw that Matt was feeding these two, they rushed over. Matt gave a short laugh as he said, "Sorry guys, all gone."

"You seem to have made a couple of new friends already," Jack teased.

"They seemed to like the sugar," Matt explained in a soft voice.

"I think we better get back to the house for supper as Mama will be waiting for us. I think Daddy should be home. He usually is pretty hungry about this time," Jack replied.

They arrived at the big house as the day's heat was beginning to cool. The man, who must be Jack's daddy, was conversing lightly with his wife as she made the final supper preparations.

She smiled at Matt, "See, I set an extra place for you at the table next to Jack."

"Thank you." Matt nodded and then looked at the giant mountain of a man next to the tall slender woman. His hair was turning blond from red instead of gray. His face had rugged canyons, more from the sun than age. All at once this brawny human presented his huge hand to Matt. He took it into his as they gave each other a relaxed and easy shake.

"The name is Pilot," the man introduced himself.

"Matt," Matt replied.

"Louisa says you are from out of town. Where are you from? Pilot inquired.

"Boston." Matt answered softly. "If you have some work for me, I'd be indebted."

Jack smiled as he could see his friend was beginning to relax. "I showed him around some parts of the farm, to give him an idea what goes on around here." Again he smiled at Matt, "I think he will fit in just fine."

"What type of skills do you have, Matt?" Pilot asked, "What did you do in Boston?"

"I went to the university," Matt replied. "I'll do anything."

Pilot smiled toward Jack, "I guess we can find something for the likes of somebody like Matt." He patted Matt on the back.

"I think we better sit down to supper, before Louisa shakes a stick at us," Pilot warned.

After supper, the three men walked to the front porch. The sun was disappearing behind the white puffy clouds in the west. As the sun set, it turned the overlying clouds orange with a little bit of yellow around the fringes. Matt stared and remarked with softness in his breath, "I don't think I've ever seen anything so beautiful."

"Yeah, I guess we don't have any of the smog you all have back east," Pilot explained.

As they sat admiring the sunset, nobody said a word, as they were so full of food that it was almost uncomfortable to move. After a time, Jack rose. "I guess I'd be better getting back to Marge, but first I'll show Matt his bunk," he said. "You ready?"

Matt nodded as he followed Jack down to the driveway. "Good night Daddy," Jack chirped as he bounded down the steps. Pilot gave them both a salute and then went back into the house to help his wife with the supper dishes.

They walked down the driveway toward the barracks where Matt's bunk would be. Along the way, there were fence posts strewn by the road with planks of wood in a pile not so neatly interspersed.

Jack pointed to the piles. "That will be your first job. You'll be replacing some of the fences on the farm. We'll get to that in the morning."

Neither one of them again spoke until they reached the building. They went inside and Jack showed Matt to his bunk. It was private. His room was the size of a closet. It was just big enough for a cot and a small chest of draws set against the wall with a tiny mirror above it. The walls, floor, and ceiling were not painted. Jack flipped the switch to a single over headlight bulb with no glass globe.

"This is it," Jack exclaimed, " I know it's not glamorous, but it serves its purpose."

Matt was expressionless as he entered the small room. The room would serve its purpose. It did seem crowded with the two of them standing in the center.

"I'll say goodnight. I'll be by early tomorrow to pick you up for breakfast. I'll bring a change of clothes for you. We'll go to town later to get some things as it seems you forgot to pack a suitcase," Jack kidded.

"Thank you," Matt said.

"Sure," Jack answered, then exited and closed the door.

Matt surveyed the room slowly, as if he may have missed something the first time he looked it over. Finally, he eased to the cot and sat on it. Slowly, he stretched his five foot, ten inch frame across the small cot. Just as his head hit the tiny pillow he was asleep.

When Matt woke, it was still dark outside. He had slept well through the night, but when he woke, he was wide-awake. His clothes were dried stiff with sweat and had become quite ripe. He was anxious to get started with his work, but he thought he had better wait for Jack. He sat on his bed and waited. As the commotion of men ended down the hall where the showers were, Jack appeared at his door. He knocked lightly and walked into the room.

"I see you're up. I figured you might have wanted a little extra rest. You looked as though you hadn't slept in 3 days." Jack said.

Jack stepped a few more paces into the room and threw some clothes onto the cot. "I brought these old clothes of mine for you to wear. They'll do until we can get some others when we go into town. The guys usually do their personal shopping Saturday afternoon. In season, we work Saturday morning then have the afternoon and all of Sunday off." Then he added, "Here. Take these. Have yourself a shower and get out of those stinking clothes."

Matt took the towel and wash cloth and proceeded down the hall to the shower room. Jack went to wait in front of the barracks. When Matt finished changing, he met Jack outside.

"Are we ready to start work?" Matt asked.

"Hold on just a minute! We still have breakfast to get," Jack replied. "Aren't you hungry?"

Matt shrugged, "A little bit."

They went to the big kitchen, which was across the dirt road from the barracks. There were about two hundred people, mostly men and mostly black. "Most of the guys here are single. The married ones have their wives to cook them breakfast and supper, but just about everyone on the farm comes here for the mid-day meal. Lunch runs in shifts. You can eat it whenever you want between 11 and 2 o'clock."

Matt nodded as he listened. There was a long line at the table, where the food was being distributed. Although it was long, it moved rather briskly. The servers were all black women. They were spooning eggs and grits on plates and sassed the men if they happened to take too long to walk through the line. The men sassed back but moved just the same, so that the ladies could serve the other hungry farm hands.

As they approached the serving line, Matt could see Louisa going from the stoves to the counter tops, ensuring that everything was running smoothly. She had a very gentle spirit about her. As hectic as things were, she breezed along without getting excited or angry. She never raised her voice.

He took the plate that was offered and followed Jack to the long tables with seats attached to them. It seemed like he was sitting a great distance from the table and had to reach for his food. Jack engaged in conversation with the other men seemingly ignoring the presence of the females. The women kept to themselves, away from the men. The men hardly acknowledged their existence. Matt noticed that the big kitchen was getting crowded and the men were later forced to sit with the females. Still the men sat and talked among themselves, while the women engaged with each other. This seemed peculiar to Matt, but it did not seem to bother anybody.

Matt sat silently and picked at his food. All at once Jack stood up; his plate having been cleaned, and said, "Time to go."

Immediately, Matt stood to follow. Before he could reach to pick up his full plate, a small black woman grabbed it from the table and scurried to remove plates from the other settings.

Outside, the sun was getting stronger. Immediately, a sweat a broke on Matt's forehead. He noticed that Jack's tanned skin began to glisten with perspiration. It was going to be a long, hot day. Jack led Matt to the pasture just in front of the big house.

"This is where you will begin work. The old fence has been taken up already. The holes where the old posts were have been filled with dirt,"

Jack explained. He then pointed to the fresh soil areas marking the positions of the old posts. It was easy to determine how the old fence may have looked. The grass was tall where the old posts stood, because the mowers were not able to cut around them.

Jack began to demonstrate exactly what he wanted done. "First, you use the digger to drill the hole about three feet into the ground." The post hole digger was powered by gasoline and vibrated violently as Jack proceeded to dig two holes. He placed a post in each of the two holes he dug. He then filled earth between the posts and the ground to close the distance between the enlarged holes and posts. He demonstrated how to pack the dirt using a metal pole with a blunt end to make the fresh dirt hard.

"Go ahead and put a few posts in the ground and I'll come get you around lunch time. After we eat, I'll show you how to put the boards in place to complete the actual fence," Jack ordered.

"Do you have any questions about what you are supposed to do?" Jack asked.

Matt shook his head "No." He proceeded to lift the heavy machinery to the next marking to dig the following hole.

Jack gave a half smile and said, "You're on your own. I'll see you in a few hours."

Matt did not give a reply and immediately started his work. He dug the next hole and put the post into it. He covered the gaps around the post as Jack had directed. After completing the first installation, he stepped back a few feet to compare his installation with Jack's. He noticed his post was slightly higher than Jacks were, so he lifted it out of the ground and dug a few inches deeper. After he placed the post into the ground for the second time, he noticed that his was perfectly erect, while Jack's swayed ever so slightly to the right. He thought he should adjust Jack's two posts to make them stand straight but decided Jack might not be happy with the corrections.

Shortly before noon, Jack appeared. He asked, "How are things going?"

Matt noticed that he looked neither impressed nor unimpressed with his work for the morning.

"Don't worry. You'll pick up a lot of speed once you get the hang of it. Come on. Let's get some lunch," Jack said.

Matt was astonished that Jack did not comment further upon his work. Were his posts straight enough? Were they the correct height? He figured that Jack would have said something if he wasn't pleased.

As they crossed the Main Road to the big kitchen. Matt noticed an older black man doing the same fence installations. However, this man would drill a hole, quickly place a post into the hole, and then pack it hastily with dirt. Immediately he would proceed to the next marking. The posts were lined in a perfect row, exactly the same height.

Jack saw Matt eyeing this man. "That's Tim. He's a good worker. He has been mending fences, since I was a little boy," Jack replied. He gave Tim a friendly wave and the gesture was returned with a flash of white teeth.

Matt saw that he was going to have to improve his production if he expected Pilot to let him stay at the farm. "I really don't need lunch. I could go back and finish the posts," said Matt.

"Finish!" Jack exclaimed, "There is a good amount of work there for a few weeks. There's plenty of time. Besides, you hardly touched your breakfast. You need to eat and drink to keep your strength in this heat."

Matt nodded and proceeded to follow Jack to the kitchen.

After lunch, Matt returned to the field where he had been working. He skipped supper and worked on the fence until it was just about dark. His hands were blistered, bloodied, and very sore. The physical pain did not seem to bother him. He believed he put in a good day's work and he was exhausted. Too tired to eat, he lumbered to his little room inside the barracks. Once he lay on his bed, he put his head on his pillow and fell instantly asleep.

The summer passed quickly. On most days, Matt worked from sunup until sundown. He labored to get the fence project completed. He could see the results of his good work. After all, the man Pilot did not order Matt to leave the farm for his poor workmanship.

Every couple of days, Jack would give instructions for the next fence layout. Eventually, Matt had his responsibilities increased. Now, he was removing the old fence posts and boards. Also, Jack gave him instructions on how the new layout would differ from the old one. Matt made the actual measurements and locations of the new fence posts. He thought his job was safe as long as Jack did not ask him to redo any of his installations. Pilot's son never commented whether or not he was pleased with his work.

After a few weeks, Louisa started sending one of her servant girls to the barracks with a small bundle of food. These were the only meals Matt managed to eat. As a result, he was becoming quite slender. His muscles had become more compact and hardened from hard work. Gone was the gym body, which consisted of the fleshy soft tone that he had when he arrived on the farm.

Soon after arriving at the barracks after a hard day's work, he would eat the food the Louisa would sometimes send him. While getting ready for bed, he would assess his aches and would delight in them. He rendered these pains as signs of accomplishments for the day's completed tasks. He would then fall fast to sleep on his pillow in his little closet of a room. Some nights he would not even undress for bed or eat his dinner.

Saturdays were a happy time on the farm. Everybody would work half a day and quit after lunchtime. This gave the farm's people a chance to do personal errands not easily done during the course of the week. Many of the farm's workers went into town to shop. The single folks would prepare for dates and a night of fun, while families planned their time together.

Some Saturdays, Matt would work clear to sundown. However, he too needed time to tend to his errands. He took little interest in this needed time. Jack would occasionally prompt Matt to go with him into town to purchase clothes and toilet items. This was not altogether necessary, as Pilot provided largely for the farm's workers giving them clothing for work, along with soap and towels for bathing. After spending some money in town, which was very little, Matt would give his leftover sum to Jack for safekeeping. He, in turn, would give it to Pilot. There were farm workers who did not need to keep their entire wages, so it was customary to give money to Pilot for later use. Pilot was generous, as he paid interest for wages saved.

Many of the farm's single men would leave the farm on Saturday nights to drink and have a good time. Alcoholic beverages were not permitted on Pilot's plantation. Those who wished to enjoy that type of merriment found alternative places. However, most of the farm's people stayed on the farm Saturday nights and provided their own sources of entertainment.

Matt was never invited to go out with the guys for fun and games, but he was pleased just the same. He would watch the sunset from a favorite perch located on some feed drums lined against the fence of the pasture along the little dirt road from the main house to the barracks.

Sundays were very somber on the farm. The farm's people were only permitted to speak in whispers. All of the meals were prepared in advance and served cold. Pilot required everybody to go to church. This included the people of color. However, they prepared their own church service. The whites went to the church in town. Pilot had to fight tooth and nail for the blacks who wanted to go into town to church, to be allowed to go to Reverend Samson's Baptist church. The town's people eventually agreed that every person, black and white, needed spiritual guidance. However, a compromise was reached to allow the blacks to attend only the early service.

Pilot would not tolerate anybody skipping church. However, a valid excuse was usually acceptable. For some folks who had enjoyed too much merriment the previous night, church going was sometimes difficult. Oddly enough, everyone was usually accounted for and present for the ride to town. All of the farm's pickup trucks had been cleaned the day before to carry loads of farm workers to church and back without soiling their clothes.

Matt opted to go to the early service. There were no rides provided for the late service, since there were very few white workers on Pilot's farm. Matt would ride in silence to church, sit on a pew with the rest of the folks, listen intently to the preacher, and ride in silence back to Pilot's farm. The rest of the day was spent resting, or reading the Bible. Since Matt did not carry a Bible, he spent his time resting in his room.

On one Sunday evening, Matt started to feel restless. He could feel the perspiration begin to bead on his body, but it was not due to any physical exertion. He went outside to get some fresh air and decided to go for a run. He broke into a jog. After loosening up his body parts, he increased his pace. After a distance, he broke into a full sprint. His muscles started to ache, but he did not let up his unwavering pace. After a short distance, he let up on his speed, while his breathing did not decrease. He continued to run briskly until his breathing returned to a steady rhythm. He finished his run with a light jog for a couple of miles. When his run was finished, he was near exhaustion.

He found himself in the moonlight surrounded by trees and black pavement. When he stopped in his tracks, he looked up into the stars. *Where am I?* He thought. He could hear rustling in the trees. It was the squirrels. They were working fervently, relentlessly to move their food from one place to another. As hard as they worked, he could see that they were happy. They worked for a reason, to survive the winter. He yearned to be like the squirrels, to have a simple life with the plain rewards of survival. He looked down at the road ahead and started the long walk back to the farm.

CHAPTER 3

November arrived in time for the sugarcane harvest season. The 8-month growing season was coming to a close. Sugarcane was the farm's cash crop. It was transported to the main farm from the fields by carts pulled by horses, as well as large trucks with big tires forming lines coming down the Cattle Road to the Main Road, and leaving down the Farm Road.

Many of the farm's workers left their primary jobs on the main farm to bring in the sugarcane. The atmosphere created by the big harvest intrigued Matt. He hoped soon to be able to work the sugarcane fields.

One day, Jack caught Matt standing outside the big kitchen watching the trucks come in from the fields. The trucks were moving one at a time down the Farm Road. As they arrived, men were quickly unloading the freshly cut sugarcane from the small trucks onto bigger trucks to transport the sugar to the mills along the Mississippi River where it would be refined.

Jack explained to Matt how the Pilot farm worked its sugarcane crop. Many sugar producers use heavy equipment to harvest their sugarcane. While machinery is an efficient means of harvesting sugarcane, the quality of the sugar crop suffers through this method of harvesting. Mechanical harvesting mixes trash and dirt in the harvested cane, which has bad effects on the refining process. Matt listened intently as Jack started to ramble through the history of the Pilot farm. He was quickly developing a desire to become a part of the tradition of sugar growers.

There had been a few generations of Pilots, since the early 19th century, when the sugar industry was starting to flourish in Louisiana. A young Travis Pilot decided to break tradition with the farmers of northern Louisiana and set out to the Mississippi River delta region to start producing sugarcane. After a few short years, there were some prosperous harvests. In years to come there would be devastating floods, diseases, and pests in the river region, where the Pilots founded their plantation in the southern parish.

The sugar business became lucrative for the Pilots. To build the business, Travis took daring risks. He invested most of the family's assets in land claims surrounding the southern delta region of the Mississippi River. Although the family owned many slaves, Travis had to convince many of the black male slaves to journey with him to the river region to start a new and prosperous life. Many of the black slaves did not want to leave their families, but Travis convinced them it was in their best interests to the join the new adventure. He promised a better life for the slaves. If the sugarcane was successful, he promised their children would learn to read, write, and gain their freedom. The slaves trusted Travis, because he had always respected them as human beings.

Travis held to his promise. After the farmhouse, barracks, and barns were built, the Pilot family along with the rest of the slaves arrived on the farm. Travis continued to treat his slaves with respect and gave them continued praise for their hard labor. He built comfortable living quarters with running water for their families, and later his grandson, Travis III, provided them with electricity when it first became available. Travis eventually gave those slaves who helped build the farm their freedom, but most continued to stay and work for wages as they enjoyed their quality of life.

Most of the farm's families have lived on the farm since that first founding generation. John Pilot continued the tradition of those before him, treating the farm's black people with respect and dignity. He never hesitated to lift a helping hand to assist those who wished to leave the farm to pursue their dreams and happiness. Some blacks left the farm to pursue college education, art careers, and other interests with John Pilot's financial support.

The Pilot Plantation continued to be successful. Labor costs weren't so high to spur the need for machinery. While other sugar producers complained of labor shortages, the Pilot plantation continued to have loyal field workers. The farm produced sugarcane second to no producer. The

Pilot family stayed loyal to the founding families who still lived on the farm. They always had a secure place to live while the Pilots operated the plantation.

The sugar harvest brought excitement to the farm. Finally, the last big truck of cut sugarcane rolled away down the Farm Road. It was another superb year for the sugarcane. Cooperation from Mother Nature along with good luck produced a banner sugar yield.

On three occasions, Matt asked Jack to be placed with the sugarcane field workers. With reluctance, Jack approached Pilot of the subject. Jack reported to Matt that Pilot promised the matter would be discussed again in the spring when the sugarcane would be planted. Matt was disappointed not to get the response he wanted, but accepted the answer with quiet grace.

"Why do you want to work in those fields?" Jack would ask and then would add, "That's such grueling work. Pilot would give you a pleasurable job, like working the horse barns. Your living quarters would dramatically improve. You would have your own shower and toilet, along with a room with space for a couch, television and other amenities."

One Friday evening sunset near the end of the harvest, Jack again questioned Matt's desire to work in the sugarcane fields. They were sitting on Matt's favorite perch on the feed drums.

"I don't need easy jobs. I just want to earn my keep," Matt explained with his eyes pointed to the ground.

"You have to stop worrying about being kicked off this farm," Jack exclaimed warmly but firmly. "My mama and daddy have taken a liking to you, so you really have it made pretty good."

Matt said nothing but continued to look at the ground while Jack spoke.

"Tomorrow, we'll move your things to the horse barn. You're to start working the horses beginning Monday morning," Jack instructed and then asked, "Will this be satisfactory?"

Matt moved his eyes in line with Jack's and answered, "Until the spring."

Jack shook his head in disbelief as he walked toward his pickup truck. He started the motor and drove away without another word to Matt.

After a few minutes, Matt walked toward the horse barn. He slipped through the door at the north end of the barn. A dimly lit aisle with horse stalls on the left and right flowed to a narrow point to the far end of the barn. The horses began to rustle as they could sense somebody coming into the barn. Slowly, he walked down the barn aisle, listening and watching for anything strange. After a few moments, he relaxed and looked more closely into the stalls to see the horses. All of the stall doors were securely closed, with the exception of the top door of the corner stall on the far-left end. The horse in this stall was a dark brown animal with a black mane. As Matt approached the stall, the horse pinned its ears against its head and gave him a mean look. Matt decided that he would continue to explore the barn. At the south end of the barn, an open set of doors led to an outside pasture on the left-hand side. Running directly along the west end of the barn, a series of rooms lined the perimeter. There was a bathroom, a tack room containing saddles and bridles, a feed room, a room with a desk, and two locked rooms. On the south side of the barn, was a second aisle lined with stalls. They bordered both sides up to the east end.

Matt returned to the stall with the door that was open on the top half. Once again, the horse pinned its ears against its head. Matt said some gentle words to it and rustled his hands into his pockets, as if he had some food for the horse. Instantly, the horse's mood changed to that of curiosity. Matt came closer and the horse nestled his shirt. Once it realized that he did not have any food, it turned away towards its feed bucket. Matt smiled as he started to leave.

"Hey there young fella," said a voice.

Startled, Matt looked behind him and saw an older black gentleman.

"Hi," Matt said in a gentle voice.

"I see you've come to take a look at your new bunk," the old man said.

Matt nodded in affirmation and looked over at the horse that had shunned him.

"That's Betty. She's a skittish old mare," the man exclaimed.

"She is pretty," Matt said.

"That she is. She's a bay who's given us several nice babies," the man explained, "I can show you where you will be bunking up if you'd like."

"Okay," Matt answered.

Matt followed the old man, as he unlocked one of the locked doors. "I just keep this locked, since nobody is living here for the moment. I cleaned it real nice and didn't want anyone to mess it up. You don't really have to keep it locked up around here," the man explained.

Matt nodded as he eyed his new quarters. The room was bigger than the one where he had been staying. On the far wall, there was a private bathroom and shower, just as Jack had said. The room had a single window with a pull down shade on the left wall. A bed, neatly made, ran along the same wall. On the right side of the room, a rust colored couch, a matching chair, and small table stood on a dark area rug. The room was luxurious compared to the barracks.

"Very nice," Matt commented.

"I'm Bill," the old man introduced himself without offering his hand, "Folks call me Old Bill."

"I'm Matt."

"We're to be working together for a while. I'll show you what you need to know," Old Bill explained.

Matt gave a simple nod.

"Stay as long as you like. I need to be getting back," the old man said. He did not elaborate where back was.

"Close the door on your way out. When you stay here, we'll keep the doors open. For now it would be better to keep them closed," Old Bill said.

He did not say why the doors needed to be closed. Matt obliged and secured the doors as he left for the barracks.

Early Saturday morning, Matt was all packed and ready to move. All that he owned, he could carry.

This job just doesn't end," Old Bill said, while shoveling manure into a wheelbarrow. "I guess I'll be able to keep up with you helping."

Matt nodded.

"You'll need to keep the barn clean; keep the stalls clean; groom the horses; have the horses ready to ride at a moment's notice; keep them fed; keep the equipment clean. If everything sparkles, then we're doing all right," Old Bill explained.

Again, Matt nodded.

"I'll be the one to show you around. Somebody's got to show you. You can't show yourself," Old Bill said simply.

"How are the stalls to be cleaned?" Matt inquired.

Old Bill grabbed a pitchfork for Matt and demonstrated how to use it. When all of the old straw and manure were removed from the stall, he showed Matt how to apply new straw and how much was needed.

"When you run out of straw, there is more and bails of hay in the loft above," Old Bill said, "The steps are over there by the tack and feed rooms. You put the manure in the pile outside the barn. Somebody will come pick it up to use real soon."

Matt nodded, "I'll finish these."

"No, No, no reason for that," Old Bill said.

"How many are left?" Matt asked.

"We got these whole two rows left. If we're lucky, we'll finish mid afternoon." Old Bill explained.

"I got it covered," Matt urged.

"If it means that much to you, I guess I could go on back," Old Bill conceded.

Matt picked up his pitchfork and started working. Old Bill left him there to finish the stalls, which suited Matt just fine.

Matt liked handling the horses. He would talk gently to them, as he moved them from the stalls that he was going to clean, into vacant stalls. Then, he would return them to the original stalls.

"Now you have a fresh bed," he said to a chestnut mare as he returned it to her home stall. He liked the horses. He was able to lead them around the barn without fear of being hurt. He spoke softly, ending any initial jitters the horses may have had about a stranger tending to them.

It was well into the night when Matt finished cleaning all of the stalls. He figured he would have to work faster to make time for other responsibilities. He took a break to give the horses some hay for supper and fresh water in their buckets. Matt then realized he was tired.

When Matt reached his room, he saw that he was covered with dirt and manure. Once inside his room, he stripped his clothes and showered in his own private stall. Once he toweled himself, he crawled into his new bed and fell fast asleep.

The next morning, Matt awoke with a bad headache. He then remembered he had not eaten the previous day. He got himself dressed into some clean clothes, so that he would be ready for breakfast prior to leaving for church.

Matt was always glad when Monday returned, as he was eager to get back to work. It was okay to work along with Old Bill, because the two men liked to keep to themselves to do their work without getting in each other's way. Most nights, Matt would send Old Bill home early to his family. Then, he would finish the chores himself.

One day for lunch, Matt received his plate from the serving line and went to sit down at the corner of a table by himself, as was always the case. People would usually fill in around him as the lunch crowd thickened. Before he was able to sit, he heard a voice.

"I hear you have that barn looking like a spiffy hotel," the sarcastic voice said. "Don't you know that this is a farm, and farms have dirt?" The man shaped like a fireplug was named Oscar.

Matt stood with his plate in hand, did not say a word and just looked Oscar in the eye. This response annoyed Oscar. "Don't you ever talk? I demand you give some indication that I even exist."

Matt stood there and continued his silence, looking Oscar stonily in the eyes.

"Say something, punk," Oscar said, giving Matt a punch in the face.

As Matt swayed back from the force of the blow, a tall slender black man caught him. Then the man then stood between Oscar and Matt.

"Out of my way black boy," Oscar said in a nasty low tone.

By now all eyes in the big kitchen were focused on the three men. The room was in complete silence as the entire crowd waited for the dreaded outcome of this event.

Oscar made a slight step toward the young black man. A group of a dozen black gentlemen stood up from their meals to address the situation.

"I guess you need to have the blacks fight your battles for you, punk. You're a sorry excuse for a man," Oscar replied, as he sat down to finish his lunch.

Without saying a word, Matt moved to the next row of tables quietly. He sat and ate his lunch without lifting his head to look around the big kitchen. Soon, the normal commotion resumed as the lunch period continued as usual.

That night, Jack paid Matt a visit to the horse barn. Matt was chopping some of the mane from one of the mares.

"I heard what happened at lunch today," Jack said, "I immediately made a report to Pilot."

Matt stopped his work on the horse and looked at Jack without emotion. He waited until Jack continued to speak.

"Oscar has just come from a meeting with Pilot. He was told to pack his belongings and leave the farm first thing in the morning. Pilot gave him a few dollars and suggested he stay in the hotel in town until he was able to make some plans," Jack explained.

Matt looked down to the ground with one hand on the mare's withers and the other dangling to his side. After a moment, he looked back up to Jack.

Seeing no immediate response from Matt, Jack continued to speak, "I don't know what drove the man to hate you. I suppose he blames you for taking his room here at the horse barn. He had other responsibilities, and he did a satisfactory job tending to those. The agreement was for him to live in this barn and to help with some of the upkeep for the horses. He also was supposed to keep watch on them at night. He wasn't helping with the chores like he was expected to do. Old Bill and the others had to shoulder 100% of the work. He wasn't expected to do much, but he didn't do anything for the horses," Jack explained.

Matt was watching Jack as he was explained the situation. As Jack talked, he shifted his position to give him his full attention.

"He was sore at having his room moved to the barracks. He was forced to share bathrooms, showers, and living space with the blacks. He was rather nonplussed at having a closet for a room," Jack explained and then added, "He blamed you for taking what he thought was rightfully his. Every day he spent in that barracks, he became increasingly bitter. Pilot told him he had himself to blame, because the job was only his to lose."

As Matt continued to stand there without saying a word, Jack asked, "Are you okay with everything? Are you upset or worried about this situation?"

"No. I'm okay," Matt answered with a half smile.

"Good. I'll let you finish your work. Don't stay up too late working. It'll still be here in the morning," said Jack with concern in his voice.

Matt nodded a reply, as Jack left for the door and exited the barn. He picked up the clippers and resumed the mare's haircut.

At breakfast the next morning, Matt received his plate of food and turned to find a quiet place to sit. On the far end of the table, in a corner of the big kitchen, he saw the tall slender black man who had interceded on his behalf yesterday. He looked to be in his mid-twenties with light brown skin and a full head of hair cropped to his scalp. His white buttoned down cotton shirt seemed to make his skin glisten in the light produced by the overhead lamps. After a short moment, Matt strode over and put his plate on the opposite side of the table.

"'Mind if I sit here?" Matt inquired.

The young black man continued to stare at his food and shook his head. He looked up at Matt briefly as he sat down.

"Thanks," was all Matt said.

"Sure," the man replied.

Throughout the entire meal, the two ate in silence. The black man finished his meal first since Matt ate slowly and also got a later start. He waited for Matt to finish. When Matt completed his meal, the two got up and headed outside. A few feet out the door, the black man nodded to Matt, bidding him good-bye as he headed toward the Cattle Road. After a moment's pause, Matt crossed the Main Road and went to the horse barn to continue his work.

At lunch, Matt got his plate of food and once again saw the slender black man at the far right corner of the big kitchen, sitting by himself at the end of the table, facing the door at the opposite corner on the left side. Matt strode over and put his plate opposite the man as he did that morning, except this time, he did not ask to sit with him. Midway through the meal, an older black man finished his meal at a neighboring table. He waved to the slender black man.

"Hey, Billy," the older man said. The younger man sitting across from Matt waved back without saying a word.

After lunch, Matt and the young man named Billy left as they did at breakfast, with Billy giving Matt a nod and then headed for the Cattle Road. Matt continued his trail back to the horse barn.

As the supper bell rang, Billy appeared inside the barn. Matt was faced away from him, cleaning the hooves of one of the horses. When he felt Billy's presence behind him, he turned to look.

"Supper?" Billy asked.

After thinking a moment, Matt answered, "Yeah." It was unusual for Matt to have three meals in one day. He put the horse in its stall and washed his hands in a nearby faucet. Then they walked together to the main kitchen.

The two men became friends. They always ate their meals together in silence. On Saturdays, they would go into town to get the odds and ends they needed. On Sundays, they would ride to church together and later hang out together in Matt's room. They said very little to each other. They just enjoyed each other's company. Eventually, Billy became Matt's running partner.

As the weeks continued to pass, it was almost Thanksgiving. The air was no longer hot but actually pleasantly warm. A warm breeze could be felt at most any point of the day.

Billy invited Matt to spend Thanksgiving dinner with his family. They lived down the Quarters Road. Billy still stayed with his mama and daddy in one of the modest homes, much smaller than the big house. A few days before Thanksgiving, Billy wanted to show Matt where he lived, so he would know where to come for supper. When they arrived at Billy's house, there were a couple of surprises. First, Old Bill was there in the house. He had come from the barn after finishing his day's work. Billy did not introduce Old Bill to him, since he figured Matt already knew him from the barn. However, he did introduce him to his mama. She was a rotund browned skinned woman with a piece of cloth in her graying hair. The small kitchen area seemed to suit her, as she did not have to move very much to tend to her cooking. She smiled brilliantly as Matt was introduced to her.

"I've heard so much about you from Daddy," she boasted. "I know you like working the horse barn."

"Yes ma'am," Matt answered.

Billy's mama rambled about how glad she was that Matt and her son had become such good friends. She said Billy was shy and did not hang around too much with the other boys.

After a few minutes, a pretty young black woman bounded into the house and said, "Hi Mama."

The young woman saw Old Bill sitting in a chair in front of the TV set. She went to give him a kiss on his cheek. Then she saw Matt and Billy sitting in chairs in the living area. "Hi," she said.

"My sister, Lisa," was all Billy said, not bothering to give Matt's name.

"These are the last of my babies," Billy's mama reminisced, remembering the day they were born. "Most of my other children have gotten themselves husbands."

Matt was invited to stay for supper and he accepted. The cooking turned out to be much better than the food prepared in big kitchen. He heard Old Bill refer to Billy's mother as Jeannette.

Shortly after supper, Lisa excused herself and went out the back door. It was getting dark early these days, so Matt thanked Billy's family for the meal and got up to leave.

"You sure you know your way for Thanksgiving?" the rotund woman asked with a smile.

"Yes ma'am," Matt answered and made his way to the door.

Outside the house, Jack was talking with Lisa. The two were giggling about something together.

"Hi Matt," Jack said.

Matt nodded to Jack in acknowledgment.

"Did you have a good dinner?" Jack asked.

"Yes," Matt replied quietly.

"The cooking is almost as good as my mama's," Jack said with a smile and giving a wink of the eye toward Lisa.

Matt nodded a good-bye toward the couple and started walking up the Quarter's Road to return to the horse barn. He could hear Jack and Lisa giggling as he made his way up the road.

Thanksgiving had come and gone. Billy's mama had cooked a huge dinner with turkey, stuffing, greens, cranberry sauce, and pumpkin pie. Matt did not think that he would able to eat for another week. Friday was quiet. There was not a lot of work to be done on the farm, since the sugarcane harvest. This was the time of year for farm maintenance, equipment overhaul, painting of the buildings and fences, and getting the farm in shape for the spring. Matt and Billy would go for their runs frequently, since there was more spare time.

Saturday afternoon, an order from the big house came with instructions to get three carriages ready, each teamed with two horses, for the evening. It was the Saturday night after Thanksgiving and the Pilot family was going to a ball. It was rare that the horses were used for anything. Matt was pleased that tonight these handsome animals would be employed.

Three of the farm's black men were assigned to be drivers for the evening. They were dressed in black tuxedos and white shirts with starched collars. Their shoes were spit shined black patent leather. Matt and Old Bill brought carriages from the wooden shed next to the tractor cover. They harnessed six horses, two to each carriage, and brought them to the lane in front of the big house. There, the three drivers waited by the carriage to seat their passengers. Matt and Old Bill were finished with these horses until the family returned home.

From the horse barn, Matt watched as the family boarded the carriages. He thought how handsome the horses were in their harness attire. They stood still even with the commotion surrounding them. Matt saw Pilot and Louisa leave the house with Jack, accompanied by a small woman with short-cropped auburn hair. The men had black tuxedos and the two women wore long evening gowns. Having seen enough, Matt returned to his work in the barn.

After a couple of hours, Jack came into the barn with his sleeves rolled up and black bow tie loosened.

"Back so soon, young fella?" Old Bill inquired.

"Marge wasn't feeling good, so we got a ride back early," Jack said and then added, "I just wanted to let you know that the carriages will start coming back about 11:00 PM and the other two about a half an hour apart."

"Okay, we'll take care of it," Old Bill replied.

"Thanks, I'll see you guys later. Good-night," said Jack.

Matt looked toward Jack as he left the barn, and gave him a nod. He looked at the clock on the wall above he tack room and saw there would be a couple of hours before the first carriage returned.

A little after 11:00 that evening, the first carriage returned. Matt and Old Bill watched as three couples exited the carriage. After the couples reached the steps of the front porch of the big house, Old Bill went to relieve the driver and to bring in the horses and carriage. Shortly after the horses had been groomed and put in their stalls, the next carriage returned to the farm. It was Pilot and Louisa. Again, Old Bill went to retrieve the horses and carriage.

Enough time had elapsed since the second carriage had returned to the farm that Matt and Old Bill were able to groom the horses, clean the harnesses that were used, and return the two carriages to their shed. They waited outside the barn for the last carriage to return. It had been a long day and the two men were getting tired and sleepy.

Finally the last carriage returned. There was just one couple that disembarked from the carriage. They were a strikingly handsome couple. Matt stared at them, as they walked to the front porch of the big house. The man had jet-black hair, parted and slicked to the right side of his head. He was tall and slender with long arms and legs. His smile was brilliant as he spoke with the woman accompanying him. She was a beauty as well. She wore a long cream dress filled by her beautiful hourglass figure, which looked familiar to Matt. Her long wavy brown hair was arranged in a stylish fashion. The couple looked stunning together.

"Who are they?" Matt asked in a whisper under his breath without expecting an answer.

From behind him, Old Bill answered, "That's Pilot's daughter with her young beau," Old Bill replied. He then moved forward ahead of Matt to relieve the driver of this last carriage.

As the couple stood on the front porch in front of the door, the man tilted his head forward to kiss the woman. Matt stood and watched as the couple entered the house.

CHAPTER 4

The day after Thanksgiving, it seemed like the farm's people were getting ready for the Christmas holidays. The sugarcane harvest was complete, and the winter sugarcane planting had been finished.

Matt was becoming a familiar face at Billy's house. Often, he would stop by to fetch Billy to go running with him. At times, things were slow at the horse barn, and with Matt and Old Bill doing the work, it did not take long for the chores to be done. Matt had accomplished all the special projects to be performed for the horses. The barn was clean enough for one to dine on the barn floor. The horses always had immaculate beds of straw in their stalls. The horses were seldom used, so they did not require frequent grooming and shoeing.

On several occasions, Matt came to Billy's house and Jack would be talking to Billy's sister on the front porch. Whenever Matt approached, their conversation ceased, until he entered the house or was coming out from the little cottage. Matt would feel embarrassed to see the two together. The three would exchange pleasantries and go about their business.

Christmas day passed quickly. Matt got several nice gifts from Billy's family. Billy's mama had knitted him a light cotton sweater, "For cool nights, for when he sat on his perch," she said. Also, he received a fruitcake and a can of nuts to take back to the barn. Matt was very thankful but embarrassed that he did not bring any gifts for the family.

When Matt had returned to the barn Christmas evening, he noticed a short red-headed female leave the big house in great haste. She climbed into Jack's pickup truck and sped down the Farm Road, leaving in a hurry. Jack came dashing out from the big house calling after her, begging her to return. He waved his arms above his head, signaling her to return to the big house. Seeing his attempts were hopeless, he went back into the big house. Thoughts about Jack's visits to Billy's sister flashed through Matt's mind. He quickly decided to dismiss any reasoning of ideas causing this domestic feud. Instead, he opted to go to his room. He was so full of Christmas dinner that he wanted to lie down while his food digested.

A few days later, Jack paid a visit to the horse barn. Matt was busy cleaning stalls, but decided to take a short break, as he sensed Jack wanted a few minutes to talk with him.

Jack sat in a nearby chair and cradled his face in both hands and then ran both of them through his light red hair. He leaned back into his chair, placing a palm on each thigh. "My marriage is in bad shape. Christmas day, Marge and I had a big argument at Mama and Daddy's house. She had been lying about her pregnancy. She was never pregnant. She said she had to lie to me, because I was pressuring her to have children. She makes it sound like I'm committing a crime, because I want kids. We've been married for 3 years and no babies have been born. She stormed out of the big house on Christmas saying she never wanted to have kids. To tell the truth, I would settle for having a wife at this point. She's never home. She's always off to some class or high society political meeting,"

Matt nodded in understanding. He stared at the floor for a brief pause and then looked to Jack.

Jack paused a few moments, taking a few breaths to regain his composure "She was raised as a simple country girl. That's what I loved about her. She thinks she needs to prove herself. I guess she married me because I was from a good family and had gone to college. I always wanted to come back to my daddy's farm to work with him and my brothers. Maybe she didn't believe me when I told her this before we were married, or she thought she could change my mind and live in a big city. She says farm life is boring. She wants to be a society business women," Jack said with a defeated look.

"There is no divorce in the Pilot family, so that has never been an option. Pilot would never accept me divorcing her. She wants to keep the Pilot name, so being married to me is part of her plan," Jack said with great thought.

"Maybe one day when she makes it big, she will leave me for good. Maybe one day she will come to her senses and will want to be my wife again," Jack said skeptically.

Matt continued to watch Jack while he spoke, giving him his full attention.

"What do you think of all this?" Jack asked.

Matt shook his head and replied, "It looks pretty bad."

Jack invited Matt to supper up at the big house.

"Sure," Matt replied with his usual shrug.

When they arrived, Louisa was busy in the kitchen. "I thought you may come over, so I fixed you a plate. There's plenty left for you, Matt," Louisa said with a broad smile.

Louisa prepared two plates of food and put them into the oven to warm for a few minutes. When the oven timer chimed, she removed the two plates and placed them on the table.

"Mama, go ahead with your chores," Jack said.

"I still have to get your silverware. It will just take a minute," Louisa responded.

"I'll get that. We're not totally useless without you," Jack teased with a smile. "Go on. You and Daddy deserve some time together."

"You're sure?" Louisa hesitated with a look of concern.

"Sure," Jack responded, still smiling warmly.

Louisa left the kitchen. Jack got the silverware and napkins from one of the counter drawers and handed a set to Matt, as the two men sat to eat their supper.

"I guess I thought every man had a wife like my daddy has," Jack said sadly. "I can really appreciate my mama working as hard as she does to make this house a happy home."

After a few moments had passed, Jack added, "They will only be home for a brief time. They usually take a long trip this time a year, but return to the farm periodically if Daddy has some business that needs some attention."

The two finished their dinner and went their separate ways. Matt trotted to the horse barn to relax for the rest of the evening, while Jack left in his pickup truck.

Matt found himself feeling sad about Jack. When Matt felt upset or anxious, he would have trouble sleeping at night. Unpleasant dreams left him waking up with perspiration pouring from his body. The nights were getting chilly, but when he would wake, it seemed like he had come from a sauna bath. When he first came to the farm, bad dreams were infrequent, as he would be exhausted from working on the plantation's fences.

Sunday nights were the hardest to get sleep, because of the inactivity of Saturdays and especially Sundays. To use his excess energy, Matt would go for long runs. Sometimes Billy would accompany him, but Matt was running most every day, since the horse barn did not always require much work. He found the work in the horse barn to be far less taxing than installing fences.

Matt felt real comfortable with the horses and became especially fond of a young gelding Palomino. Its name was Butch. This horse was big and strong, with a sweet and curious disposition. Matt would bring him special treats from the big kitchen, usually a sweet sugary dessert. Butch always looked forward to seeing Matt. He did not get ridden much, but loved to run through the pastures with the other geldings.

The Thursday after Christmas, a call came from the big house. Young Miss Emily and her beau Mr. Robert would be going for a ride shortly after the noon hour. Matt got Butch ready for the ride, since he was big enough to handle Mr. Robert's long frame. For Miss Emily, Matt readied a slender black mare named Kelsey. Matt thought the two handsome horses would match perfectly with the two equally fashioned couple.

"Hi," said a gentle voice.

Matt was giving Kelsey a few last minute adjustments to the mare's bridle outside her stall. The voice was soft, but he was not startled after being caught by surprise.

"Hi, Miss Emily," Matt replied as he looked from the other side of the horse. He released Kelsey from her lead rope and went to the other side of the horse to approach Miss Emily.

"I have a horse ready for you," Matt said in a serious tone.

"That's very nice," Miss Emily replied. "How did you know that this one was my favorite?" she asked with a gentle smile.

Matt smiled slightly embarrassed. "I can saddle another horse for you if you'd like. They are all freshly groomed," said Matt.

"No. This horse is fine. You picked the one I want to ride today," Miss Emily replied, as she gave the black mare a pat on the neck.

Matt seemed pleased. He immediately went to fetch Butch. When he brought him from his stall, he was already wearing his saddle. Matt began to put on the horse's bridle.

"He may not want that horse," Miss Emily remarked in a gentle voice.

A concerned look came over Matt's face.

"I'm just teasing. I'm sure this one will be just fine," she said with a smile.

A few short moments later, Mr. Robert entered the barn. He looked at Miss Emily. "I'm sorry if I kept you waiting too long. The time seemed to get away from your daddy and me."

"No bother," Miss Emily replied. She then turned to Matt.

"This is the stable man. I don't think I know your name," Miss Emily said as she turned to face Matt.

"Matt," Matt replied nervously without offering his hand.

"I'm Robert Lamond from the Lamond Plantation. I'm sure you are familiar with the place," Mr. Robert said, extending his hand.

"No sir," Matt replied, placing his now sweaty hand into Mr. Robert's grip.

Mr. Robert tilted his head slightly toward Miss Emily with a half smile as he released his grip. Matt let his wet hand fall to his side.

"Matt fixed this pretty horse up for you," Miss Emily stated. "Will it do?" she inquired.

Mr. Robert looked over at the other stalls, craning his neck to inspect the other horses. Matt figured he could not get a good look at them from where he was standing, but Mr. Robert still chose another horse.

"I'll ride that one over there," he said, pointing to a stall three doors to his left.

Without a word, Matt placed Butch back into his stall. Then he removed a handsome bay gelding from its stall.

"What's its name?" Mr. Robert inquired.

"Pat," Matt answered in a relaxed tone. He attached Pat to a lead rope outside the stall that secured the horse from moving about the barn. He then went to the tack room to fetch the gelding's saddle and bridle.

"He's a bit lively," Matt stated as he placed the saddle on top of the horse's back.

"That's okay," Mr. Robert replied.

"I'll finish this up," Mr. Robert offered, taking the bridle from Matt's hand.

Matt nodded toward the couple and went into Butch's stall to remove the gelding's saddle. The couple talked softly to themselves, giggling in the same way Jack and Lisa did when they were together.

"Sorry buddy. No ride today," Matt said very softly to the horse. He returned the leather gear to the tack room and placed it neatly on a holder attached onto the wall.

When he left the tack room, Miss Emily and Mr. Robert were mounting their horses outside in the pasture lying in front of the big house and barns. Matt waited by the tack room door, so as not to invade their privacy. Soon, they rode off toward the trees to the west end of the pasture. As they rode, Matt watched them as they disappeared into the trees. The sadness left him that had been present since Saturday, when he spent some time with Jack. It pleased him that the handsome couple was enjoying themselves together.

When Miss Emily and Mr. Robert returned to the horse barn, Matt was finishing making new beds of straw for the horses. Both of the horses were drenched in perspiration, while their riders had pink in their cheeks from the wind. Instantly, Matt placed his hand on the horses' breasts just between their front legs to check if they were cool. Satisfied, he placed lead ropes on each horse and led them into the barn.

The couple followed slowly, talking about their ride, describing the details of their adventure. Once in the barn, Matt began to remove the saddles from the horses.

"Thanks so much for your help," Miss Emily said with a light smile. Matt noticed she was like her mother in her gestures as well as her beautiful figure.

"Sure," Matt replied and then continued his work. He stopped when Miss Emily continued to speak.

"We will not be riding again for awhile. I go back to college the day after tomorrow. I'm sure we'll ride again, when I come home for the Easter holiday," she said, inflecting some promise.

Matt again nodded giving her a half smile. Mr. Robert gave a saluting gesture as the couple left the barn.

Once outside, Robert and Emily started their walk to the big house to change for supper.

"Why were you so friendly to him?" Robert asked her.

"He is one of the workers on the farm," Emily answered and then added, "From the time I was born, Daddy taught my brothers and myself to treat the farm's people with kindness and respect."

"Okay," replied Robert softly with a smile.

"Does it bother you, for me to be nice to him." Emily inquired with a light smile.

"No. Not at all," he answered. They continued their walk to the big house and spoke of other things.

Matt finished his business in the horse barn in time to watch the sunset, sitting on his perch on top of the feed drums, just off the Farm Road. With his back leaning against the top board of the fence, he thought how early the sun was setting these days. He looked forward to the beautiful summer sunsets coming in the approaching months. After the sun had set, he sat awhile longer to ponder the next action on his agenda. He felt relaxed, so he did not feel the need for a run. He thought about fetching Billy to go with him to the big kitchen for supper, but figured he had eaten with his mama and daddy. Slowly, he bounded off the drums. He hoped to catch the last part of supper.

The next couple of months moved quietly, with little excitement on the Pilot Plantation. The emphasis of farm activity was placed on getting the plantation ready for the spring season. All of the farm's buildings were painted a luminous white. The roofs of some of the older structures were replaced. Repairs and overhauls of machinery were done. Decisions on purchases for new materials and machinery were made and executed. Pilot was conservative with his investments in heavy equipment and improvements to the plantation. He would not jeopardize the future of the plantation by over investing in high priced items, but would not refuse purchases if they greatly enhanced the future of the farm. Purchases were not made on credit, as everything was paid in cash. These were the topics of conversation among the overseers at mealtime. They generally talked amongst themselves, while Matt listened.

It was the first week in March, when Jack approached Matt about working in the sugarcane fields.

"Do you still want to leave this cushy horse job and work in the treachery of the sugarcane fields?" Jack asked with a touch of sarcasm.

"Yes," Matt replied evenly, as he continued to brush a chestnut mare.

"Well, it's time to start the spring planting. You might as well learn from the beginning. The sugarcane stalks need to go into the ground this week. Some were planted last fall. There will be plenty of guys to show you how it will be done," Jack said.

"Okay," Matt answered.

"Fine. You can start this afternoon," Jack stated.

"Sure," Matt said with a nod

"You can catch Silas's truck after the first lunch shift. You'll be working with his crew. He brings his men back and forth from the main farm to the fields." Jack said.

Matt nodded

"Pilot wants you to continue living here to help tend to the horses. You can feed them breakfast and supper can't you?" Jack inquired.

"Sure," Matt answered.

"Good," Jack said with a smile. "I wish you luck, buddy. I sure hope you know what you're doing."

After the first lunch shift, Matt waited outside the big kitchen for the man named Silas. After a few minutes, Matt noticed several pickup trucks parked across the Farm Road. He had seen them before, but never gave much attention to their presence. He thought perhaps they were the trucks going to the fields. Matt crossed the Farm Road to where several men were waiting around the trucks. He lingered quietly with the men while they spoke with one another.

"Hey, what's going up?" a sweaty black man asked as he noticed Matt standing alone.

"I'm waiting for Silas," Matt answered without much expression.

The man pointed to Silas. Matt gave the man a friendly nod and walked over to meet his new boss. Silas was a balding man with gray hair and a big belly. He was talking to one of his men about some of the events that took place in the field that morning. Matt waited patiently until he was finished with his conversation. After a few minutes, Silas let out a gentle laugh, generated because of a humorous comment his friend had made. As he laughed, he turned to look at Matt as if he was just noticing him for the first time.

"What's up?" Silas asked.

"I'm Matt. I'm supposed to go with you to the fields this afternoon," Matt stated in a less than firm voice.

"Is that right? I guess I can always use a new hand," Silas commented.

"Who sent you?" Silas asked.

"Jack," Matt answered.

"News to me," Silas replied and then added, "Hop up into the truck with the other boys and I'll show you around."

Matt did as he was told and moved to climb into the back of Silas's pickup truck with several other men.

When they got to the field, there were already dozens of people working. The land looked barren as far as one could see in all directions, except for some mounds of dirt on the ground. When the truck stopped, all of the men got out and seemed to know what they were supposed to do. Matt went to the front of the truck to wait for Silas.

Silas got out of the truck, barked a few orders to some of the men and then turned to Matt.

"I'll explain things as quickly as I can. You can ask any of the guys for help while you're working. They'll be glad to help," Silas explained. He started moving toward the field, so Matt walked beside him to be sure not to miss any instructions.

"Sugar needs to be replanted every 4 years. The fields produce 3 years of sugarcane, and 1 year of corn, oats, or soybeans. We plant other crops on the 4th year to replenish the fields of nutrients soaked up by the sugarcane. The plantation's fields are all on a rotation, so each year 25% of the fields are planted with something other than sugarcane. This field and others like it, we did not use to grow sugarcane last year. They have been freshly plowed in the last couple of months," Silas explained as they walked through the fresh dirt of the sugarcane field.

"Do you follow me so far?" Silas asked.

"Sure," Matt replied.

Silas began to talk once more about the sugarcane process, "We do not use seeds to plant sugarcane. A sugarcane stalk is planted into the ground, like a seed. After a while, sugarcane shoots sprout through the soil from each of the joints of the planted sugarcane stalk. Each planted sugarcane stalk produces between twelve and eighteen new sprouts."

"Each year, we select the best sugarcane stalks from the current harvest to plant that fall or the next spring. It's best to plant in the fall, but sometimes frost will kill some of the young sprouts, so we plant both in the fall and later in the early spring. A long time ago, planters used inferior or the worst stalks from the harvest, but that would produce a poor crop. On this plantation, we use the best looking stalks to plant."

"That's farming sugarcane in a nutshell," said Silas.

"I'm going to show you what I want done in this part of the field. I'll fetch you some tools. We plant in six-foot rows. There needs to be good ditches around these rows to let the water drain off the mounds. I'll show you where I want this done and you can see how the others are doing this," Silas instructed.

"Do you understand?" Silas asked.

Matt nodded his head. Silas gave him the needed tools to complete these tasks.

It was early in the spring, but Matt was already able to feel the humidity in the air. Although the air was not hot, the sun was causing him to perspire.

Matt took a few minutes to observe how the other men were creating mounds of dirt in six-foot long heaps. Shortly after the men fixed these mounds, others came with sugarcane stalks and gently placed them underneath some dirt on top of the mounds. Once he got the picture of how it was done, Matt began to create his own mounds of dirt.

By the end of the day, Matt's hands were swollen with bloodied blisters, mixed with dirt. Most of the men used working gloves and wore straw hats to protect them from the strong sun, so he would have to remember to bring those items the next day.

The humidity and heat exhausted Matt rather than the work. The weather was cool compared to the heat in the summer. Soon, the rains would be frequent, mixed with the heat. It was important to drink plenty of water while working in the fields, for it was easy to become dehydrated.

Matt understood why Pilot would not let him work in fields last summer, as getting used to the weather was a gradual process.

Silas's pickup truck returned the men to the main farm. However, a stop was made at the top of the Quarters Road to let off those who lived in these houses with their families. Matt returned to the barn to feed the horses. After this was done, he crashed into bed and fell fast asleep.

During the next couple of weeks, Matt became used to the life as a field worker. He was content with the hard work, which always made him tired by the days' end. Usually by the time the horses were fed, he was ready to go to sleep. He was up early the next morning to tend to their needs. Weekends were pleasant, as he was able to rest his aching body.

One Friday evening after eating supper at the big kitchen, Matt saw somebody in the small paddock, just off the horse barn. He recognized the figure instantly as Kelsey, the black slender mare. Miss Emily was running her horse over a series of jumps set up inside the small fenced area. The horse and rider seemed to glide gently over each jump. Matt stood at the barn door, while he watched Miss Emily guide her horse effortlessly over the jumps.

Emily saw Matt watching her out of the corner of her eye, as she approached the next jump. Distracted, she slowed her horse from a canter to an even posting trot. She circled her horse to see who was watching her. When she noticed the person was Matt, she smiled in his direction.

"How long have you been standing there?" she asked.

"Not long," Matt replied, slightly embarrassed.

"I don't mean to interrupt you, I'll let you alone," Matt said with little emotion. He turned to go to his room.

"No, I don't mean to shoo you away," Miss Emily said, "I was just surprised to have somebody watching me."

"You ride very well," Matt commented gently.

"Thanks. Do you ride?" Emily asked.

"No," Matt answered with a little anxiety.

Emily dismounted the horse and opened the gate as if to leave the paddock.

"Do you want to give it a shot?" she asked with a small smirk.

"I really don't think I should, Miss Emily. It might not be right for me to ride the horses," Matt replied.

"Nonsense. The only time these horses get any exercise is when I'm home," she said, "Besides. It's only fair that I get to watch you ride, since you were watching me."

Emily held her hand out with the reins, as a gesture for Matt to grab them.

"It'll be okay. I know you're not afraid of the horses. You're so good with them," she said with encouragement.

Matt nodded, submitting to Emily's request to take the reins. He stepped forward and took the reins from her. He whispered a few encouraging soft whispers to the black mare. He placed his foot into the stirrup and mounted the horse with little difficulty. A bright smile instantly emerged on Emily's face.

"You're going to be just fine," Emily stated with promise.

Matt shortened the length of the stirrups, as he was not quite as tall as the slender Miss Emily. Once he was comfortable in saddle, he moved the horse to a working walk around the circled shaped paddock. Feeling more comfortable, he moved Kelsey into a posting trot, rising and falling in the saddle, keeping time with the horse's rhythm. After a couple exercises around the paddock, he sat hard in his saddle, pushed his hips forward, signaling Kelsey to move into a working canter. Riding in a slight rocking horse motion, Matt felt as if he was riding on a magic carpet. Feeling the horse beginning to tire, he slowed into a gentle posting trot and moved to where Miss Emily was standing. By the time he reached her, he had Kelsey moving at a working walk.

"You ride like a real pro," Emily said with an excited smile. She pursed her lips playfully. "And you said you didn't ride."

Matt smiled back at her without giving a verbal reply, but it was evident to Miss Emily that he thoroughly enjoyed himself.

"You'll have to take her for some jumps after I return to college. She really likes to jump," Emily said. "Or you can saddle up Butch and take him for a ride. He loves to run on open grassy fields."

"He's a good horse," Matt replied pensively. "I like to watch him run with the other horses."

"I could tell he was your favorite," Emily said. "Robert usually likes to ride him. I was surprised that he chose another horse to ride, when you had Butch saddled and ready to go."

"It's okay," Matt said with a quiet half smile.

"Well, I guess I'd better get Kelsey cleaned up before it gets too dark," Emily said with a light sigh.

"You go ahead, Miss Emily," Matt offered. "I'll take of this."

"I do have to meet Robert at the big house shortly. I'll repay you the favor," Emily replied sweetly.

Matt shook his head slightly. "That's not necessary. Kelsey is fine with me."

"Thank you, Matt. You have a happy Easter this Sunday," Emily said warmly.

Matt nodded and began to lead Kelsey into the barn, as Emily made her way to the big house.

The next Monday brought heavy rains. By early afternoon, they subsided to a gentle sprinkle. Silas said that most days would have rain. Once in the field, Matt made sure the rain drained properly through the ditches. It was important to keep the water moving, to save the fields from flooding. Shortly before mid-afternoon, the rains subsided for about an hour, before the downpour resumed. Jack paid Matt a visit in the field. Jack usually drove his pickup truck back and forth across the plantation each day, using a two-way hand held radio to communicate with his overseers. Jack was Pilot's information source and mouthpiece for the plantation.

"How do you like this stuff?" Jack asked in full raincoat attire.

"It's okay," Matt replied, climbing out of a ditch to greet him.

"You still could come back to the farm to work if you'd like," Jack offered.

"No. This is fine," Matt declined.

"I didn't think so," Jack replied with a grin.

"I haven't had any problems with the horses since you've been there. It's been kind of nice to have it that way," said Jack.

Matt smiled gently; appreciative of the praise Jack gave him.

"You're doing really good work here from what Silas tells me," Jack commented.

"Thanks," Matt replied.

"I understand you went for a little ride the other night," Jack said.

The smile slowly disappeared from Matt's face as he nodded affirming Jack's inquiry.

"If I'd known earlier you'd rode, I would've encouraged you to give those horses some work outs. Feel free to do it anytime. They need the exercise," Jack encouraged, slightly animated.

"Are you sure?" Matt asked in a surprised tone.

"Yeah. Didn't Emily tell you to ride anytime?" Jack asked.

Matt nodded.

"By the way, my little sister got engaged last night," Jack beamed.

A small look of surprise registered on Matt's face as he looked at Jack.

"Yeah. Robert popped the question last night and even asked my daddy's permission."

"That's good news," Matt said softly with a half smile.

"Yeah. They haven't set a date yet. The wedding will be sometime this summer, after Emily graduates from college," Jack said.

Jack looked at his watch. "It's time for me to go. Besides, I don't want you to get in trouble with your boss," Jack teased with a broad smile, as he trotted toward his truck.

Matt watched him drive away and then went back into the ditch to resume his work.

The next Sunday after a brief storm, Matt went to sit on his perch, as he often did after eating supper at the big kitchen.

"Hi," said a familiar soft voice.

"Hello, Miss Emily," Matt replied as he began to come off the drum where he was sitting.

"Oh no, don't get up," she seemed to beg.

Matt stopped his progress and resumed his original position.

After a brief pause, Emily said, "I can see you sitting here each day, when I look from my window."

"It's peaceful here," Matt said with a shrug. "Nice."

"I'm on my way to the barn to say good-bye to my horse, since I leave to go back to school tomorrow," Emily said. "I saw you sitting here, so I'd thought I'd say hi."

Matt quietly nodded to Miss Emily with a half smile, to thank her. After a moment, she asked, "Would you care to keep me company on my walk over to the barn?"

After a short moment, Matt gave a shrug and answered, "Okay."

Emily smiled lightly, as Matt bounded off the drums to her side. As they walked to the horse barn, a ring on Emily's left hand caught Matt's eye. It was set with a big diamond.

Aware that Matt had seen her ring, Emily brought her hand in full view for both of them to see. "I guess you may have heard the news by now?" Emily said, half questioning.

"Yes," Matt said, "Congratulations."

"He's a real good man and he seems to love me very much," Emily said.

Matt nodded, confirming her belief.

"We are to be married at the end of the summer, just before the harvest," Emily explained.

Matt nodded, listening to her plans.

"I understand you are working the sugarcane now," Emily stated.

"Yes," replied.

"You seem to get along with the horses so well, I was surprised when Jack mentioned it."

"I still like the horses," Matt said a little defensively, but smiling.

"I guess it's a macho thing, to want to get your hands dirty," Emily teased.

"Maybe," Matt answered with a shrug.

"Well, I'm sure the horses miss you very much," Emily said.

Matt responded by smiling, as they reached the barn. They walked inside together as the barn doors had been left open. It was getting too warm to keep them closed, but the storm had cooled the air, leaving the weather pleasant. They sauntered down the aisle to see Kelsey, the slender black mare.

"How did you know that it was Kelsey I liked to ride that time you saddled her up for me?" Emily inquired with a smile.

"I just knew," Matt responded.

Emily shook her head slowly, as she turned to get Kelsey's attention. Finishing her supper, Kelsey turned away from her feed bucket and moved to greet Emily. They were glad to see each other. Emily gave the mare some affectionate pats. Kelsey responded by nuzzling Emily's pockets for some special treats.

"She looks for you to come see her each day," said Matt. "I took a guess it was you that she was waiting to see that day you came to ride with Mr. Robert."

"Really?" she replied with surprise.

"Yes," Matt answered.

She gave her horse a big hug around the neck. "It's nice to be missed."

Matt sensed that horse and owner wanted some time to spend together, since Emily would not see her again until the summer.

"I'll say good evening, Miss Emily," Matt said with a nod.

Emily looked outside Kelsey's stall toward Matt and answered with a smile, "Thanks for the company. We'll have to go riding, when I return from school in June. That is if you're not too tired from that messy sugarcane."

Matt gave her a nod, as he walked toward his room at the end of the barn.

CHAPTER 5

By the time summer came, the air seemed thick enough to able to cut with a knife. The rains usually waited until the late afternoon when fierce thunderstorms would hit the Pilot plantation. The field workers always returned to the main farm by the time the storms actually hit. This gave Matt a chance to help move the horses into their stalls and secure the rest of the barn, by closing the stall doors to the outside.

With the changes in weather patterns and his new field duties, Matt found plantation life exciting. For him, there was never a dull moment, except Sundays when the farm was quiet. The slow moving winter a few short months ago were after thoughts, when the farm came to a virtual standstill. These days, time seemed to be moving fast. Matt learned to be a good sugarcane field worker, while keeping many of his duties at the horse barn.

Great attention was given to the sugarcane by Jack, the overseers, and the field workers. When heavy rains poured through the fields, emphasis was placed on the field workers moving the water through the ditches, away from the sugarcane to prevent flooding. There was a constant watch for rodents, insects and disease. These were the nuisances associated with growing sugarcane. The crop needed to be frequently monitored to guard against these potential hazards.

Pesticides were largely used to counteract some problems. Poisons had to be used carefully, so as not to endanger the health of the field workers and neighboring wild life. The government placed restrictions on the type of chemicals used to protect the environment, including the area's water supply.

After thunderstorms moved swiftly through the parish, Matt found time to sit on his favorite perch. He watched the sunset and the wind move through the trees on the western horizon. His seat was usually wet, but that did not seem to bother him. Sometimes after he had been sitting awhile, Billy would come to join him and keep him company. It would be rare for Billy to come after a thunderstorm, because he did not like to get his clothes wet from the damp drums.

Matt would have another visitor come to see him, while he sat on his perch. Miss Emily would ride her horse shortly before dinner and take a walk after helping her mother with the dishes at the big house. While taking her walks, she would see Matt sitting on his perch, staring into the wind. Emily liked his calm exterior and felt comfortable talking about a wide variety of subjects.

"I'm glad we've become friends," she said to Matt one day, while sitting on his perch. She was too late to horseback ride before supper, so she took her walk early this day.

"Why?" Matt asked.

"Because you don't care about the way I act or what I say," Emily replied.

Matt nodded slowly, trying to follow her train of thought.

"What I mean is," she started to explain, "It's not easy being Pilot's daughter. I've always felt like I'm supposed to act a certain way. The way of some aristocratic family."

Matt nodded, looking at the ground, concentrating on Emily's words.

"Take for example my wedding," Emily started again, "I've been working on the arrangements since I've returned from school. I find myself wondering if this wedding is for me, or the important people from all over the state that I'm supposed to invite. Some of these people are mere acquaintances."

"It doesn't have to be so hard, Miss Emily," Matt said quietly.

"What's that?" Emily asked in response.

"Life," Matt said simply.

"Life?" Emily sighed. "Try being Pilot's daughter."

Matt smiled lightly at Emily, then returned his gaze to the trees.

"Do you want to go riding?" Emily asked. "We have so much daylight now and it will be cool enough for the horses."

"Okay," Matt answered.

"I'll meet you at the barn later," Emily said with a smile.

Emily walked toward the big house to help her mama prepare supper. Louisa insisted on running her own kitchen without the help of any of the farm's women. She enjoyed taking care of her family and created her own warm atmosphere in the kitchen. She allowed her daughter to help her. Emily cherished her mama. They enjoyed each other, while preparing meals for whatever family members would be present. Sometimes special guests would dine with them.

Matt left his perch shortly after Emily departed to eat supper at the big kitchen. As he bounded off the drums, he saw Billy approaching the perch to fetch him for supper. Matt smiled as he joined Billy to walk to the big kitchen.

Usually the two men said very little to each other, as they enjoyed each other's company without making too much conversation. This day was different.

"You best stay away from the boss's daughter," Billy said to Matt as they walked.

Matt had his head pointed to the ground as he listened to Billy. A slight nervous feeling came over him, like a child realizing for the first time that he had done something wrong.

"What did I do?" Matt asked.

"People like us have no business with people like them," Billy said anxiously.

"I don't understand," Matt said, confused.

"Miss Emily is to be married to a man that her daddy wants her to marry. He's a man of different breeding from us. We are workers. We will always be workers," Billy explained.

Matt started shaking his head in disbelief.

"If you do anything to confuse that girl, Pilot will send you away from here. Do you understand?".

"We're just friends," Matt said defensively.

They came to the door to the big kitchen. Billy went to enter first. He looked back to Matt. "I'm telling you. Keep on," Billy said with a nod. "You'll see where it gets you."

The two men sat and ate their supper quietly. This was not unusual, but a tension was resting between them. This made Matt feel uncomfortable. After Matt finished eating, he and Billy got up to leave. Once outside, Matt started to go in the direction of the horse barn, but stopped an looked at Billy, "Hey," Matt said and paused until he had Billy's attention. "Thanks."

"Sure." Billy returned with a nod and the two men parted company.

Emily came to the barn a short time after Matt had returned to his room. She knocked gently on Matt's door and waited for him to answer. Matt answered his door and made a point not to invite her inside.

"I can't ride tonight," Matt said gently. "I have some work here that I must get done tonight. I'm sorry."

"Oh. Okay," Emily said with disappointment. After a moment she regained the small amount of composure she had lost. "I don't want to get you into trouble."

Matt shrugged and shook his head with a smile.

"I guess then I'll see you later," Emily replied.

Matt nodded, "Good night Miss Emily." He closed the door as she walked over to see Kelsey. Relieved, Matt put on his boots to get ready to feed the horses and refresh their water. He waited until Emily had left the barn with her horse before he came out of his room to begin his chores. He was sorry he did not offer to saddle up her horse, but she didn't ever seem to mind doing it herself.

Matt made himself scarce when Emily returned with Kelsey to the barn. When he saw she had left, he returned to his work. He was in the middle of fixing the hinges of one of the stalls.

Matt changed his routine of sitting on his perch until Miss Emily had returned to the big house following her late afternoon ride with Kelsey. Instead, he and Billy would go for a light run before supper. They would be tired from a day's work, but both still enjoyed the exercise. This was different from the laborious exertion required in their jobs. Matt figured Miss Emily would forget about him soon and he would not have to be concerned about coming in contact with her. He was sad to have lost a friend, because he did not have any except for Billy. He liked life on the plantation. He wanted to continue living in the horse barn and working in the sugarcane fields.

After a week had passed, Matt heard a soft knock on his door one Saturday afternoon. He recognized the gentle strike instantly and hesitated before opening the door. It was Emily.

After he opened the door, he could see Emily was not pleased about ﾏething. It was one of the few times he saw her not smiling. As usual, vas wearing a pair of blue jeans and a white cotton blouse, as if she ady to go horseback riding.

tt met her in his doorway without offering to invite her inside his Sensing she was not going to get an invitation, she asked softly,

"Do you mind if I come in to talk with you for a few minutes? I won't take too much of your time."

After a slight pause, Matt moved so she could enter. He wondered if it would be wise to close the door behind her or to leave it open. He sensed Emily might be insulted by such as gesture, so he chose to close it. Emily walked to the cushioned rust colored chair facing the door and sat down gingerly. It seemed like she was trying to keep her movements from making noise. When Matt sat on the adjacent couch, she began to speak.

"Is there something going on that I should know about?" she asked softly, "Have I offended you?"

Matt could see her face was furrowed with concern. "No," he replied softy with concern.

After a short pause, Emily took a deep breath and said, "You're avoiding me. Why?"

Matt sat silent for a few moments. "I don't want to displease your daddy by being friends with you. I don't have anywhere else to go if he ordered me to leave."

"Where did you get an idea like that?" she asked in surprise.

Matt gathered his thoughts to speak as truthfully as he could. He looked at Emily and said, "It's not so easy, when you are not a Pilot."

She started shaking her head. "I don't understand."

"I'm just a worker here. I have no business associating with a fine lady as yourself, Miss Emily," Matt explained quietly.

Emily sat still for a few moments, while she gathered her thoughts to speak. She had a troubled look on her face and Matt could see she was disturbed by his explanation. Still, he waited patiently for her response.

"My daddy sent me, as he did my older brothers, to college to get a fine education and experience the world. We don't live in a society anymore where women are repressed; to answer to every desire that men have for us. I can't, in good conscience, accept that my daddy would send me away to gain this knowledge and then return to the plantation as a subservient female, not capable of running her own life," Emily said, finishing her speech.

"I wasn't finding fault with you, Miss Emily. You will always be fine here on the farm. My future is never as certain," Matt replied.

Emily looked into space, compiling information in her head to understand Matt's attitude. She placed her mind in line with Matt's, attempting to understand what was troubling this man.

"I don't know too much about from where you came. I do know that you have found a home here with us and keeping it is your greatest priority. If I'm ever to cause you misfortune here on the farm, I will se that you are reimbursed with good fortune and security," Emily promised as she smiled.

Matt smiled faintly without looking at her. Emily sensed he was still troubled. "You know you can tell me what it is that's bothering you," she said with a light smile of concern.

"Your daddy is a fair man. His word is the final say around here," Matt said solemnly.

At once, Emily realized what Matt was thinking. She said, "He is a fair man. He is not rigid in his reasoning. To you, he is a big man with enormous power. He has to be strong willed to operate a farm with hundreds of people working on it. But Matt, he listens and is not afraid to admit when he's made a mistake," Emily explained.

She could sense Matt relaxing, as he looked at her while she explained her reasoning. "It's seems he runs all of our lives to his content, or to his liking. Daddy is very opinionated and is not afraid to exert his influence upon his children, or any of the other people from the farm. He does let us have free will, to do as we choose. As much as he wanted you to continue to work with the horses, he gave in to your desire to work with the sugarcane."

Instantly, Matt felt a tremendous weight come off his shoulders. He gave Emily a light smile.

"Are you interested in riding today?" Emily offered gently.

"Sure," he responded.

Matt saddled up Butch while Emily got Kelsey ready to ride. Once the horses were ready, the tandem made their way to the grassy fields, beyond the trees in the west. Once they reached the first plain, Emily pushed her horse into a full gallop. Instantly, Butch chased the black mare without so much as a nudge from Matt to catch the speeding horse. As Butch blazed forward in an attempt to overtake the streaking Kelsey, Emily slowed the mare as Butch moved close to end the race.

"I knew he would do that," Emily said of Butch as the two horses slowed to a brisk walk. "That's why I did it," she added with a smirk.

Matt smiled gently as she spoke, breathing heavily himself. This was a much fun as he'd had since coming to the farm.

Later, Emily returned to the big house. She had a concerned ensemble 'ting, as she was an hour late meeting Robert for a date.

'm sorry about this," she gushed to Robert. "I'm so embarrassed to kept you waiting. I apologize for being so rude." Pilot and Louisa aited on the front porch with her beau, for her return.

m just glad you're okay. It's not like you to be late," Robert replied.

Slightly agitated, Emily replied, "I'm going upstairs to freshen up real fast, I'll be right back. I promise." She then went briskly up the wooden steps to her bedroom.

When she returned to Robert and her parents, she sported a pink and white sundress and her nerves calmed.

"Where were you?" Robert asked with concern. Pilot, Louisa and he looked at her waiting for a reply.

"I convinced Matt to take Butch for a ride with Kelsey and me in the western plains. The time got past us," she replied lightly.

"He's such a nice boy," Louisa said warmly with a smile, "I'm so glad you and Jack like him so much." She was uncomfortable with her remark and looked toward her husband.

"Nice fellow. He doesn't have a whole lot to say," Pilot added.

"I talked to a friend of mine who is about the same age as Matt who must have attended the same college as he did about the same time, but he doesn't recall a Matt Smith. I thought it was odd since the school was so small. I then talked to the dean who's another friend of mine and he said a Matt Smith never graduated from the school. I just thought it to be strange," Robert said slowly, rubbing his hands together.

"I'm sure there is some explanation," Emily answered quickly and pursed her lips. "It's getting late. Good night Mama, Daddy," she said, giving them both kisses on their cheeks. She grabbed Robert's hand and they bounded of the porch and headed for Robert's sleek forest green sports car in the driveway.

"I get the feeling something weird is going on," Louisa said suspiciously to her husband, after the young couple drove off into the distance.

"I felt it too, but Emily can take care of herself. She is the most level headed of all our children." Pilot said as he headed back into the house.

Matt became a favorite among the overseers of the sugarcane fields, because he learned his duties quickly and accomplished a great deal of work each day. There was never a complaint about Matt slumping on the job or hiding as some of the hands were known to do. Consequently, Matt's name was called when special tasks and chores needed attention from the oversees. It came to be known if Matt was asked to accomplish a special task, it would be done without worry.

Robert came to realize that Emily and Matt spent time together each week, as friends will usually do. He was clearly dismayed.

Most of the time, the pair went riding in the early evenings to practice their riding skills. Emily liked to participate in state shows with he favorite horse, Kelsey. Robert would prefer Emily to go riding with him, but his business usually kept him from pleasures such as horse back riding. This left him spending time with Emily solely on the weekends.

Robert spent a good deal of time with Pilot discussing their sugarcane business. They were two of the largest planters in the parish. When smaller planters would go out of business, it was usually Pilot or Robert's family who purchased the land. It would come cheap from the mortgaging lenders or the former planters themselves. It was hard for small sugarcane planters to be successful. The majority of successful planters were large corporations. The Lamonds and Pilots were always trading the newly acquired parcels of land. The deals involved the land that would fit better geographically in connection with their respective plantations.

Young Robert had to take over the family business after his father passed away just a few short years ago. He died shortly after his wife passed away due to cancer. Robert's remaining family was a sister living in Chicago with her husband and two children.

Under Robert's control, the family's plantation flourished. It held titles to the most sophisticated machinery in the sugarcane business. The Lamond plantation employed workers solely to operate this machinery, whereas the Pilot family used a mix of field workers and machinery where necessary. Very few of the Lamond plantation's workers lived on the farm itself, as Robert encouraged them to seek shelter in the neighboring communities. The two families had different philosophies constructing successful businesses, but had been equally profitable.

It was in the middle of the summer when Pilot and Robert concluded a deal to trade a couple of parcels of land that the two had worked together to purchase from a bankrupt planter. The two men went out on the front porch of the big house, while Robert waited for Emily to return from a ride with Matt. The two chose to ride later in the evening, because the heat of the day was cooled by this time. The daylight allowed them to take longer rides, which did not please Robert.

"Do you think it such a good idea for Emily to spend so much with that field boy?" Robert inquired of Pilot, as he sipped a glass of iced tea.

"Why is there a need for concern?" Pilot asked as he leaned back into ʼs wicker rocker.

"Well," Robert replied dolefully, "It's approaching later in the summer ∣he hasn't committed to a wedding date."

∣thought it would be sometime later in the fall," Pilot replied. "There's ∣me."

"Emily and I have a dream to run our sugar business together, much like you and your wife. I'd just like to get started with it. It's hard for me sometimes, doing things myself," Robert explained.

"There's still time for you to do that," Pilot answered, "I wouldn't push that girl. She does have a mind of her own. You'll just upset her if you force her to a decision before she is ready to make it."

"I think that boy distracts her from thinking about things which need her attention," Robert said, taking another sip of iced tea. "The man has already lied about attending that college. I think she needs some protection. What about his violent streak and propensity to get in fights?"

Pilot felt uncomfortable with Robert's remarks. After thinking a few moments he said, "It's true we don't know a whole bunch about that boy. I'm sure there is some explanation about that college thing. I get glowing reports about his work with the horses and in the fields," Pilot responded, still pondering a solution to satisfy his business associate and future son in-law. "I don't like meddling in other peoples affairs, but she is my only daughter. Let me give it some thought and I'll see what I can do."

"That's all I can ask," Robert said, rising from a wicker chair. He set his glass on the iced tea tray. "I think I'll pay a visit to the horses to see what's keeping this lovely lady." He smiled and gave Pilot a salute as he bounded from the porch to head for the horse barn.

Matt and Emily were finishing their horse grooming when Robert entered the barn.

"Hi guys," Robert said walking toward Emily. He gently kissed her cheek. "How was the ride?" he asked.

"Great!" Emily said as she smiled with brilliance. "You should come with us some time."

"Maybe I will," Robert replied. "Can I walk you home?" he asked.

"Sure," Emily answered a little tentatively.

As the couple started their exit, Robert turned to Matt who was closing a stall door. "By the way. A friend of mine is a dean of your college in Boston. He said he never knew a Matt Smith graduating from his school. I figured he may know you, since you two are about the same age. After he couldn't remember, he checked you out and said you weren't in any graduating class."

Immediately, Matt responded, "I did not graduate. I attended two years there before a bad car accident." Matt stared at the ground; "I never went back after that happened." Matt turned and went to his room.

When Robert and Emily left the barn, she asked, "Why did you bring that up?"

"I figured we deserved the truth. He told your family that he graduated from a place I'm sure he never attended," Robert explained.

"He never said he graduated." She added, "No more mention of this subject. You could see it upset him. It probably brought back bad memories. Besides, it is none of our business. You promise to leave him alone," Emily demanded protectively.

Robert smiled and put his arm around her waist. "I was just trying to help," he said unconvincingly.

"I know," Emily smiled lightly. "I just respect the man's privacy. He does good work here and he's been a good friend."

"I'll respect your wishes," Robert promised. "It's my curiosity. I like him too. I just naturally want to know about people I like." He squeezed Emily a little harder and smiled his most handsome smile. "I want to know all about you."

Emily relaxed and smiled. "Is that so?"

"You bet," Robert replied.

The next morning, after Matt and Billy left the big kitchen after breakfast, Jack intercepted Matt as he was walking toward Silas's truck to go to work in the fields.

"Hey, guess what?" Jack asked with a smile.

"Yes," Matt answered with curiosity.

"You get to have today off with pay," Jack replied.

"That's not necessary," Matt said with discomfort.

"Wait 'til you hear the rest. We've decided to move you to the west end of the plantation. It's sort of like a promotion. Those fields are too far away to operate from the main farm, so they have their own headquarters out there. It's a plantation we've recently taken over. Your quarters are much nicer there than they are here. You'll be sleeping in air conditioning every night and you can cook your own meals if you'd like."

"I really don't cook much," Matt responded.

"That's okay. The house kitchen is in the same place where you sleep. There's fewer people to cook for, so the food taste much better than the big kitchen," Jack explained. "We don't use as many people on that part of the plantation. Machines do most of the work. You will learn to operate all those machines. An instructor will teach and certify you in no time. It's more responsibility and more pay. Pilot is really counting on you." Jack said with a smile.

"Okay. When do I leave?" Matt asked, still surprised.

"I'll come get you tonight, sometime after supper," Jack replied.

After Jack left him, Matt returned to the horse barn. Billy met him at his door. "What happened?" Billy asked with concern.

"Jack says I've been promoted," Matt answered without expression.

"Promoted?" Billy asked with a confused look.

"He said Pilot wants me to work on the west end, so I'll be moving," Matt explained as he looked at Billy sadly.

"It's because of that girl. You know that don't you?" Billy responded.

"It's okay," Matt replied. He smiled at Billy and went into his room to get ready to move to the west end.

Matt wasn't hungry, so he skipped supper and opted to sit on his perch. After a short time, Emily found him sitting on the drums.

"Hey there," she said with a light smile. "You're out here early today."

"Good evening, Miss Emily," Matt replied easily.

"Do you mind if I sit with you a while?" she asked.

"Sure," he responded as he moved to make room. Emily usually stood next to Matt while talking to him as he sat on his perch.

"I've got troubles on my mind, Matt," she deadpanned.

"What's wrong, Miss Emily?" Matt asked with concern.

"I'm not so sure I want to get married now," she answered with a solemn face.

After a few moments of silence, Matt responded, "Okay," and waited for additional troubles.

"Okay? That's it?" Emily said quickly.

"What seems to be the problem?" Matt asked with a confused look. He brought his knees to his chest and wrapped his arms around as to hug them.

"It's not so simple, Matt," she responded almost impatiently.

After a few awkward moments, Matt took a deep breath and said, "Well Miss Emily, if you're not so sure what to do, maybe you should not do anything for awhile, until you're sure."

"It's not that easy, Robert wants to set the date right now," she said, slightly agitated.

"What do you want, Miss Emily," Matt asked patiently.

"I don't want to make a decision right now," she answered.

"It looks to me you may have solved your problem," Matt said with a half smile.

"I guess so." She sighed with light skepticism. "I've got to be my own woman."

Matt gave her a light shrug accompanied with a light smile.

"Thanks," she said as she got up to leave, "I'll let you alone."

"I'm moving tonight," Matt said gently.

"Where are you going?" Emily asked without concern.

"I got a promotion. I'm going to work and live on the west end."

"That's good news," Emily said without much conviction.

"Thanks," Matt replied quietly.

"I guess I better get going," Emily said. She turned and walked quickly to the main house. Matt turned his head and resumed his stare into the trees in the west.

When Matt arrived at the west end, he could see a big difference from the main farm. The buildings were much more modern than the ones on the Pilot plantation. The atmosphere was quiet compared to the hustle and excitement of the big kitchen and barns. There were no horses and livestock. There was a big warehouse containing tractors and other machinery. Matt had a carpeted air-conditioned room with nice furniture and a TV set. He merely had to go down the stairwell for his meals. In addition, each floor had just a few rooms and their own washrooms. Matt felt he was going to be very comfortable, but his thoughts were on other matters. He looked forward to learning to work the new machinery.

After a few weeks, Matt was growing familiar with his new arrangements. He was driving tractors, pulling manure and other fertilizers to nourish the sugarcane. He seldom had conversation with anybody else but never felt lonesome. He liked having fewer people on the farm, because the quiet atmosphere was pleasant. Jack would visit every couple days to see how he was doing. Sometimes he would lounge in Matt's room and watch TV with him.

"There is nobody at home to worry about me being late," he would say. Jack's marriage did not seem to be getting any better. He still talked of Lisa, so Matt figured he was still giving her a good amount of attention.

One evening while they were watching a horror movie that Jack had wanted to see, he mentioned that Emily had canceled her engagement.

"She said she doesn't want to get married. I don't blame her. I think marriage stinks. I guess it does work for some people," Jack said without remorse.

Matt nodded his head

"Needless to say, the man is not taking it very well," Jack said with hidden sarcasm.

Matt shook his head slowly, as if he had a hard time believing this latest news.

"He's a good man. He just happens to be as stubborn as she is. Robert wants things done properly and orderly, while Emily has her own way of leading her life," Jack explained.

Finally, it came time for the sugarcane harvest. In past years it had been called the time of the grind. This term was still used on some plantations. In years past, the plantation's sugarcane was cut and transported directly to a sugar mill on the plantations' site. Later, it was transferred off site by rail. Today, the Pilot plantation used trucks to transfer the sugarcane from the farm to the local refineries. Most plantations sent their cut sugarcane to refineries along the Mississippi River.

Matt assisted in handling the machinery that actually did the cutting of the sugarcane. The other workers removed the leaves on the stalks and placed them in trailers pulled by tractors. By Thanksgiving, the harvest would be completed.

When Thanksgiving arrived, Matt was invited to come with Jack to the big house for the holiday dinner. Jack was almost certain Marge would find a way to exclude herself from the holiday feast. Matt was concerned he found disfavor with Pilot, because of his friendship with his daughter. After thinking a bit, he decided he was happy with his new environment and no longer considered his promotion banishment. After some initial resistance, Jack persuaded Matt to come to the big house for the holiday meal.

There were a lot of people at the Pilot dinner table at the big house on Thanksgiving Day. Matt stuck close to Jack and kept a good distance from most of the guests. Jack's wife Marge was with them, but she seemed aloof from the rest of the group. Emily talked to most of the guests as she made a point to visit each person. Matt managed to avoid her through the entire dinner, except to say good night, as they left through the back door leading to the Main Road.

"I'm sorry I didn't get to visit with you, Matt. It's been such a long time since we've seen each other. You'll have to make it up to the main farm some time, so we can ride or something," Emily said with a warm smile. She stood at the door and gave her brother Jack a hug. Then she placed her arms half way around her sister in-law in a strained embrace.

"Sure, Miss Emily, you have a good night," Matt replied as he stood awkwardly in front of her at the door.

"Well partner. Let's go," Jack said as he gave Matt a pat on the back.

The three walked out to Jack's pickup truck in silence. As Jack opened the passenger door for his wife, Matt said, "I'm going to walk over and see Billy before I go back." His faced reddened as he was not sure of what Marge's reaction would be to him mentioning Billy's family. She appeared to have the same stolid appearance as she had the rest of that day, so he relaxed his muscles and started to walk toward the Main Road.

"Okay," Jack replied, "I'll give you a lift over. Hop in."

Reluctantly, Matt entered on the passenger side, which left Marge sitting between the two men.

When they arrived, Marge remarked, "Why don't I just let the two of you all off and I'll drive myself home."

Matt flushed, while Jack looked over at his wife. "What's that supposed to mean?"

"I know you'd much rather be here than at home with me," Marge said sarcastically.

"That's just not true," Jack answered patiently. He glanced over to Matt. "I'll check you later. You have a way home tonight?" Jack inquired.

"I'll manage," Matt answered quietly. "Thanks for the ride." He let himself out of the pickup truck and made his way to Billy's front door. His mama answered his knock.

"Matt, it's so good to see you. We sure miss you around here." Jeannette said as she put her arms around Matt and gave him a tight squeeze. Matt gave her a half smile as she released him. Old Bill, Billy and his six sisters were watching the television in the living area. All had babies in their laps, taking naps quietly. Billy got up to greet Matt.

"You need something to eat, Matt" Jeanette asked as she went into the kitchen.

"No ma'am. Thank you," Matt answered as he followed Billy to the living area to watch a football game. Before they sat, Matt asked Billy, "You need some air?"

"Sure," Billy answered. The two men went outdoors to take a walk along the Quarters Road going toward the woods.

"Pilot wants me back to the main farm," Matt deadpanned softly.

After a pause, Billy asked, "What'd you tell him?"

"Nothing. I just said okay," Matt answered.

After another pause, Billy asked, "When?"

"I don't know. Maybe he'll forget." Matt replied with disappointment.

"You don't want to come back?" Billy asked with surprise.

"Things are good on the west end. Why would he want to move me again?" Matt wondered.

"Everyone knows you're a good worker. It takes three men to do all the work you did when you were living with the horses. Naturally, he wants you close by the main farm," Billy explained. His English was better than his daddy's was, but he still was difficult to understand at times. Some of his words had the same accents, as the old man's had.

"He said sending me over there over was a mistake. He says his daughter was cross with him for sending me," Matt said thoughtfully.

"Can't you see?" Billy replied. "The man Pilot is giving you another chance. You got it real good. You probably will be an overseer someday. Don't mess it up with that girl."

"I'm sure she's forgotten about me. I'm just going to do what I'm told. I can't worry about all that," Matt replied, slightly irritated.

"That's fine. But I'm telling you. Stay away from that girl. She's trouble to you," Billy warned.

"I know," Matt answered gently, "I just don't have a good feeling about all this. I wish I could be sure why he wants to move me again." He looked over to Billy and quickened his pace. After a short while, they turned back toward the house.

When they arrived at the house, Jeannette was seated in a chair with her legs sprawled on the floor. She had finished cleaning up after the family's Thanksgiving dinner. All of Billy's sisters had gone home with their babies.

"You can stay here tonight if you'd like. You'd have to sleep on the couch," Billy offered.

"Thanks." Matt nodded, accepting his invitation. After everybody had gone to bed, Matt lay his lean frame across the long couch and fell fast asleep.

In the morning, Matt opened his eyes to see Jeannette shaking him to wake. He was covered with sweat.

"You was a movin' and twitchin', so much I could hear you in the other room. Going to bed with a full tummy probably made you have some bad dreams."

"I guess," Matt answered. He was exhausted as if he had been awake all night.

"What did you dream about?" Jeannette asked as she moved toward the kitchen stiffly, stretching from a night's sleep.

"I don't know," Matt answered, "I feel okay now."

"Get some clothes from Billy. You'll catch cold being wet like that," Jeannette ordered.

Matt went to Billy's room and got some clothes. Billy gave him a bath towel from a hall closet and directed him to the washroom. "You oughta' wash that stuff off you. You'll feel better."

When Matt finished his shower, he came to the kitchen after dressing. He could hear Jeannette telling her husband, "I've never seen anybody sweat like that before. Soaked." She looked up as she saw Matt coming to the kitchen. "Feel better? Sit down here and I'll get you some coffee."

CHAPTER 6

"You don't have to move if you really want to stay. Pilot just asked if you would be willing to come back to the main farm," Jack explained as he watched Matt pack his few possessions.

"I see," Matt replied quietly, as he continued to stuff his duffel bag. He did not mind moving back to the main farm, but just the same, he was feeling settled at the west end.

"I know it's nicer here with all the modern conveniences," Jack said as he pondered the situation. "You'll do fine back at the farm, trust me."

"What about the sugarcane? Who will take my place?" Matt inquired.

"Boy, you sure don't miss a beat. Just dive right into work," Jack commented with a slight grin. "You'll be with the sugarcane workers," he answered, "Probably not so much working with machinery as you will be planting and cutting."

Matt nodded.

"You'll probably learn a little bit about cutting with a machete. It's an art you know," Jack explained.

"Really?" Matt looked up at Jack from his packing.

Jack noted his sudden interest. "'Like I told you. Sugarcane wasn't always cut with machinery. It all was cut with machetes until a few years ago. If sugarcane doesn't lie just right, it can't be cut with machines.

Sometimes it has to be cut by hand. Some of the other planters ignore that sugarcane and plow over it. Pilot still has many cutters who can still cut with hand held machetes. Not many other planters have guys who can cut by hand."

"Okay, I'm ready," Matt said and pushed his duffel bag over his shoulder. Jack opened the door and they left for the main farm.

At the main farm, Matt settled into a room at the barracks. It was a typical Saturday afternoon on Thanksgiving weekend. Most of the guys were doing personal errands. Matt decided he would go for a run, mostly to relieve some of the stress he was feeling. He started walking slowly toward the Quarter's Road where he and Billy used to run. *Could Billy be right about Pilot giving me another chance?*

"Hey stranger," said a familiar voice. Matt turned and saw Emily coming from the big kitchen.

"Miss Emily," Matt nodded toward her as he stopped walking to wait for her to approach him.

"How are you doing, Matt," she asked in a broad smile. She looked the same as always in blue jeans and light cotton blouse. Her brown hair tied to the top of her head, like the way her mother wore hers.

"Fine," Matt said. He sounded less than convincing.

If she seemed to notice his apprehension, she looked past it and instead asked, "Where are you headed?"

"Taking a run." Matt nodded toward the trees bordering the Cattle and Quarter Roads.

"It's nice to see you again, Matt," Emily replied. "It seems ages since we talked, rode, or did anything."

"I'm living back on the big farm now," Matt explained, but he figured she might already know.

"I thought maybe you were coming back," she confessed.

"Yes," Matt said quietly, "I guess I need to be getting on to the run. You take care, Miss Emily."

"Matt, wait. I wanted to say something before you go. I don't blame you if you're mad at my family and me. I know why you were moved to the west end in the first place. I guess I knew at the time but didn't want to admit it to myself. I had my mind on a lot of things, you know, about breaking my engagement. What I'm trying to say is that I didn't want to believe that Daddy would do what he did. I mean move you for what he thought would be for my benefit. I finally asked him about it Thanksgiving Day, and he admitted he was pressured by Robert to get you away from me. I was very angry with him and demanded he undo what he did. He said you were very happy where you were and probably wouldn't want to move again. I just felt you deserved a choice in the matter, so I assume you wanted to move back here."

Matt blushed, as he gave a slight smile. "It really doesn't matter Miss Emily. I just hope your daddy is happy with me. He gave me a place to work and live, so I do as he wishes."

Emily smiled. "I made him promise me that he would leave you alone and never manipulate your situation again."

Matt had his doubts as to whether she would be able to keep that promise to his daughter. "Really everything is fine, Miss Emily." He nodded to her and proceeded to walk toward his running course. As he approached the trees, he began to stretch his legs and abdominal muscles to limber up for his run. In an odd sort of way, he decided it was nice to be back on the main farm. As he started a light jog, his mind cleared the pressures of his relationships with people.

By April into the new year, life for Matt resumed quietly as it had been several months earlier on the main farm, when he was living in the horse barn. Once again, meals were usually spent with Billy. He was still working as a mechanic, helping to maintain the plantation's vehicles. He seemed to like his work, because Matt never heard him complain about it. He worked faithfully until all his tasks were completed.

Matt became relaxed in his friendship with Emily, despite the warnings that he received from Billy. The rest of the Pilot family seemed to like Matt. Louisa once again on occasion would have one of the farm girls leave a small plate of brownies or cookies on his bunk in the barracks. Jack would spend some evenings with him, watching television in the barracks recreation room. Most of the time, they were the only people in the small room, as most tended to stay in the privacy of their own quarters.

Since the work in the fields was still light compared to the drudgery the summer would bring, Matt had extra time to horseback ride with Emily. They worked dressage, as Emily wanted to compete in the coming summer in the local state competitions. This was her hobby and she loved to perform with her black mare, Kelsey.

After one of their rides, Emily asked, "You seem to have such great experience. Where did you learn to do all this?"

Matt fidgeted with his hands, then looked up and smiled at her. "I can't really say. After riding awhile, I had these images and ideas come into my head." He thought a bit more. "I just know how they move and how they think." He smiled, "With that in mind, it's quite simple."

"I don't think it so simple," Emily replied. "Have you ever competed?"

Without expression, Matt answered, "I don't like to compete. I just like working with the animals."

Suddenly Emily felt a little bit uncomfortable. With furrowed brow she asked, "Do you find fault with me for wanting to show my horse?"

"Oh no," Matt replied, "They love the excitement. The competitiveness is their nature with most of them. They don't even have to win. The horses just love the sport of it all."

"I guess us humans could learn good sportsmanship from them," Emily mused.

Matt replied with a nod.

Night had long since come. They reached the big house. "Goodnight, Matt," Emily said with a smile.

Matt gave her a gentle wave.

"We'll ride again after supper tomorrow?" Emily asked.

"Sure," Matt answered.

As it got later in the spring, the temperature started to rise and the days were getting hot. The work in the fields was more taxing on the workers. These days, Matt would not ride with Emily every evening, as he was sometimes too tired by the end of the day. He needed his rest to be able to get up the next day to work in the blistering heat.

"I'll make you a bet," Emily challenged one day when she was able to convince Matt to go for a ride.

"A bet?" Matt answered.

"Let's race a course and if I win, you have to take me to the 4th of July fireworks celebration in town."

"Okay," Matt said. It sounded easy enough. "What do I get if I win?"

"You won't have to take me to the fireworks," Emily answered in a sweet voice.

Matt gave her a stern look and broke into a grin. "That sounds fair, I guess."

"I tell you what," Emily offered, "You get to set the course."

"Fair enough," Matt answered

"Do you really think that you can win?" Emily inquired with a competitive spirit.

"It's quite possible," Matt replied in a serious tone.

On the 4th of July, Matt accompanied Emily with the rest of the Pilot family to see the fireworks demonstration. Joining them was Jack without Marge, Pilot and Louisa. When they arrived into town, they took their share of blankets, chairs, food and other items to set up a place. They covered the ground with blankets to position themselves to watch the fireworks.

After settling with the family, there was some time to kill before the sun would set. The fireworks were scheduled to begin shortly after dark. Jack decided that he would take a look around to see who else had come to the splendid event.

"You want to come along for a few minutes? " Jack inquired of Matt.

Matt looked toward Emily and was getting ready to decline, when she said, "Go ahead. See what's going on."

"You sure?" Matt asked with light concern.

"Sure. Go ahead," She waved them off.

"Okay," Matt replied and left to walk along with Jack.

"I thought we'd go look for Old Bill's family," Jack explained.

"Sure," Matt replied as they scoped the grounds.

When they found Old Bill and his family, Matt saw Billy along with his sisters. They were eating some good food. Billy's mama had fried up some chicken with mashed potatoes and gravy, biscuits, collard greens, and thick apple pie made with molasses. Jack and Matt knew better than to sample some of her cooking, because they would get in trouble with Louisa if they failed to eat the picnic dinner with the Pilots.

Matt visited with Billy while Jack spent time talking with Lisa. After a short while, Jack signaled that it was time to return to the Pilot picnic.

After walking a short distance, Matt spotted Robert Lamond. Instinctively, he tried not to catch Robert's gaze, but it was too late.

"Fine day for fireworks," Robert stated to the two men as he quickly approached them.

"Sure is," Jack replied, "I just hope it will cool down a little bit more."

"I don't think there is too much hope for that happening," Robert said with a forced chuckle.

"You should stop by and see the family tonight. They'd love to see you," Jack said as Matt stood silently by his side.

"Maybe I'll do that," Robert replied with a light smirk.

"Well, we've got to be getting back," Jack stated.

"Sure," Robert replied and after a short hesitation, he looked toward Matt. "Would you mind having a word with me for a few minutes? I won't keep you too long."

Matt looked toward Jack for help, but Jack failed him. "You two talk, I'll tell the family you'll be with us shortly." Jack said quickly as he gave Matt a pat on the arm and left the two men to talk. Matt stood silently as he waited for the tall, dark haired, handsome man to talk.

"I'm a little bit concerned about Emily. I understand you two have become quite good friends," Robert said with exaggerated concern.

Matt nodded to confirm Robert's assertion.

"Emily is a bit confused right now. It wasn't too long ago that she graduated from college, she needs a little time to set the direction of her life," Robert stated.

Matt was not sure he agreed with Robert's logic, but he nodded just the same to show that he was listening to the man's declaration.

"I don't see that the time you spend with Emily is to her benefit. I believe you put ideas into her head that tend to sway her judgment," Robert accused.

This time, Matt did not acknowledge Robert's contention, but stood motionless, hoping this situation would soon be over.

Robert moved closer to Matt and grabbed his right arm. In a light but firm whisper he said, "I'm warning you. Stay away from Emily or you will very sorry."

Matt felt a burning sensation from Robert's grasp, The feeling sent Matt's mind racing into a dizzy state. Satisfied that he made his point clear, Robert released his grip. Then, he turned and walked off into the opposite direction that Matt was going. Once Matt regained his composure, he made his way back to the Pilot picnic.

"There he is," Emily said as Matt approached. "Everyone is ready to eat. Do you want some chicken?"

"Sure," Matt replied as he sat on the big picnic blanket.

"Jack said that you guys ran into Robert," Emily stated as she prepared his plate.

"Yes, we did," Matt answered unwaveringly.

"I understand he wanted a few words with you. Did everything go okay?" After a short pause, she added, "It is not my intention to pry, but I was just concerned."

"He said he was concerned as to how you were doing. He wants to be sure you're doing well," Matt replied.

"How sweet," Emily said with modest relief. Matt did not give a reply and started to eat his supper.

After a short while, Robert appeared to give his greetings to the whole Pilot family.

"Hi Robert. It is so very good to see you, " Louisa exclaimed as he approached the Pilot camp.

"Hi Louisa. You look just as lovely as you always do," Robert replied with a big plastic smile. "Pilot," he acknowledged the patriarch with a big handshake.

"Robert, it's kind of you to stop to see us," Emily said with Matt by her side. The two had just finished eating their supper.

"I would not have done otherwise," Robert answered with a softer, more genuine smile. He looked straight into her eyes, completely ignoring Matt who was standing at her side.

"Robert, can I fix you a plate or a piece of apple pie?" Louisa inquired.

"No, but thank you kindly just the same," Robert answered with forced warmth. "I really must be going," he replied with a touch of discomfort.

Jack rose from the blanket from an intense conversation with his older brother Victor, who had come to join them. "We need to get together to discuss business," Jack said, wiping his mouth with a napkin.

"I'll phone you in the next day or two," Robert replied. "You all have a good 4th of July," he said in a loud enough voice for all to hear. He then gave Matt a slight sneer out of the corner of his eye as he departed, but only Matt seemed to notice.

After Robert left, Jack took Matt to the side and said in a whisper, "I caught that look he gave you as he was leaving. Do you need to tell me something?"

"No," Matt replied, slightly shaking his head.

"That's good. Lamond is one man that you would not want to cross. He has lots of money and lots of friends, all of which he uses very well," Jack warned.

"I'll remember that," Matt replied with little conviction.

CHAPTER 7

Matt became a regular for Saturday night supper at the Pilot house as Emily's guest. The Saturday supper was a big occasion, because little cooking was done on Sunday in respect for the Sabbath. Since Matt was included with the family's church attendance, the feeling was that he should join in the big meal on Saturday nights. At first, he felt peculiar eating with the head family, but they made him feel comfortable. Actually, not much was made of his presence, which suited him.

One night after Saturday supper, Matt was fixing to go back to the barracks. Oddly, Pilot said that he some business out the same way, so he would accompany Matt on his way to his room. They walked by Matt's perch.

"Isn't this where you spend some of your time?" Pilot inquired as he pointed to the empty feed drums lined against the pasture fence.

"Yes sir," Matt answered calmly.

"Well, let's go over there and have a look," Pilot suggested as he turned slowly to the perch. The two did not speak for the next few steps until they reached their destination. Matt could sense that Pilot had something on his mind.

"Let's have a seat Matt, there is something on my mind I'd like to talk with you about," Pilot said in a serious but friendly tone.

"Sure," Matt replied as he bounded up on his familiar perch.

"I try not to meddle in my children's affairs, but as a father, it's sometimes difficult to refrain," Pilot said and then paused.

Matt started feeling anxious. Suppose he had overstepped his boundaries with Pilot's daughter? He should have listened to Billy. Why didn't he? Emily could be so sweet and friendly. Matt did not have too many friends. Sometimes it was hard to be alone.

"I think they need a little help sometimes. After all, why else would God have made daddies?" Pilot mused.

Matt offered no response, but did manage to smile lightly to keep from being rude.

"I realize that you and my daughter have gotten to be special friends. I was curious as to how close the two of you really are, " Pilot asked directly, as he looked toward Matt.

Surprised, Matt still managed to keep his composure. He looked directly into Pilot's eyes. "My intentions toward your daughter have been honorable. I will abide by your wishes if you want me to spend less time with her," Matt replied.

"On the contrary, my boy," Pilot retorted with animation. "You must understand that I want the best for my daughter. Her long term happiness is of utmost importance to me."

Matt did not understand Pilot's response, but he knew the man was not angry with him. He paid close attention to him as he continued to speak.

Pilot furrowed his brow and looked at Matt with a very serious expression, "Have you ever considered marriage, son? Every good man needs a wife. It's something you should give considerable attention when thinking about your near future."

Matt thought Pilot was being gracious by advising him to marry soon, so he would have less time spend with Emily. As a result, she would forget him forever.

"I haven't thought about marriage. I don't know that I'd make a good husband," Matt replied with little enthusiasm.

"Nonsense!" Pilot exclaimed, "My daughter may not know it yet, but I know she's very fond of you. The two of you would make a fine pair."

"Emily?" Matt said in disbelief, "and me?"

"I can see you are surprised by this matter," Pilot observed. "Give it some time and thought. The two of you have been good friends. Friendship could lead to a marriage. Couples have to be friends to live together peacefully for a long time. You can take my word on that."

Matt was speechless, as he kept still on his perch. Pilot rose to leave. "You have my blessing if you should decide to take my suggestion to heart. My family would welcome you with a wide embrace. I think they already have to some degree." Pilot smiled and gave Matt a salute with the brim of his hat. He then proceeded to make his way back to the big house.

The night was dark and the sky full of stars, as Matt gazed up into the big sky. When he was sure Pilot was out of hearing distance, he took a deep breath of air to clear his mind of the confusion he was experiencing. He was remarkably calm for the surprise Pilot had presented to him. Although he could not reason why the man would want him to marry his daughter, he knew he could not refuse him.

The next day, Matt and Billy were walking toward the big kitchen for lunch.

"How do you get someone to marry you?" Matt asked Billy as they walked.

Billy answered, "Who wants to know?"

"Me," Matt answered, "I have to do this."

"Are you sure?" Billy asked with confusion. "Who have you been courting'?"

"Nobody," Matt answered.

"How are you going to get somebody to marry you if you hadn't been courting them?"

Matt opened the door for Billy as he walked into the big kitchen.

"You have to first court somebody if you want them to marry you," Billy stated as they entered the building.

The two ate in silence, which was not unusual, but both were intense in thought throughout the meal. They finished and got up to leave.

"How do you go about courting somebody?" Matt asked.

"First you have to find a girl to court," Billy replied.

"And then what?" Matt asked.

"Then you bring her candies and flowers from the field. After that, you take her on long walks," Billy explained as they left the building.

"Okay, thanks," Matt replied, as they were ready to part ways.

"Sure," Billy said as he turned to walk to the tractor barn.

She was on her way to the horse barn when he jumped from behind the bushes.

"Oh Matt it's you." Emily was a touch startled. "I thought for a minute it was a ghost sneaking behind me."

"I am sorry for scaring you," Matt replied awkwardly. He presented a bouquet of freshly cut flowers to her. "I picked these from the field after work today for you. Would you like to go for a long walk?"

Emily smiled graciously as she accepted the flowers. The bouquet consisted of daisies, violets, heather, and lilies; all arranged neatly and tied by a thin vine. "Okay, I guess Kelsey can wait a bit longer until we return."

The two walked a good distance before Emily asked, "Matt, is everything okay today? Is there something you want to tell me?"

Matt thought for a minute. He figured the courting should take longer than one night. He had not given any candies to her. Still, he did not feel comfortable with the process and thought it was better to tell Emily the truth.

"Miss Emily, I would like to marry you," Matt answered.

Emily smiled as they continued a slow walk into the woods. "Is that what these flowers were about, to convince me to marry you?"

"They were for courting," Matt replied.

"Matt, the time we spend together is fine with me. I enjoy it so much. You don't have to ever impress me. Let's always be good friends and keep it loose. I think that's more our style," Emily said with sincerity.

"I'll have to think about marrying you," she said as they started their return to the main farm. "I must admit that I'm surprised you asked. I didn't think you could see me as your wife. I'm a bit confused about your feelings for me. Marriage is a serious matter. I thought about it once, but this time is different."

As they walked, Matt noticed a strain between the two of them that had not been present in the preceding months, when they were getting to know each other. As they were saying good night, Matt instinctively took her hand and gave it a light squeeze. It could have been considered a romantic gesture, but Matt did this out of concern for Emily, as she seemed troubled.

"Good night," Matt said with concern.

"Good night," Emily replied with a smile to cover her now heavy heart.

As Matt walked to his perch to relax before bed, he sensed that things had not gone as they should have tonight. He could only hope that things would work out for the best.

As Matt sat on his perch and gazed into the woods, he felt relieved of Pilot's task. What more could he do? He had done what Pilot requested. Hopefully, he believed that his daughter had the final say on the matter. Surely Pilot would know that he at least tried to marry Emily. Matt knew that he did not have the charm of a Robert Lamond. He had the uneasy feeling that his relationship with Emily had changed that night. Maybe Pilot would change his mind now those things were out in the open.

After awhile, Billy made his way to Matt's perch.

"Hey," Billy said, as he leaned against the fence post.

Matt nodded to acknowledge his presence.

"Pilot asked me to marry his daughter," Matt stated point blank.

After a brief period of silence Billy asked, "What are you going to do?"

"I asked her and she said she would think about it," Matt replied and added, "I don't think she will do it."

The two were silent for a brief period.

Billy seemed puzzled, "What else did she say?"

"She didn't think I saw her as my wife," Matt replied

"She's a smart lady," Billy stated and then asked, "Do you?"

Matt paused a moment and turned to his friend. "Do I what?"

"Can you see her as your wife?" Billy asked gently.

"Yeah, I was surprised as she was by this, but it seems it's what her daddy wants," Matt explained.

"That's just it. She wants you to marry her, because it is what you want to do, not because it is something you are supposed to do," Billy commented.

"I don't think Pilot would have informed her of his discussion with me," Matt replied.

Billy tried a different approach, "She wants to know if you love her," Bill explained.

"Are you sure?" Matt asked in surprise.

"Yes. That's how women are. They need to know they are loved," Billy said with a smile.

Billy left. Matt was more confused than he was before Billy's visit. There seemed to be truth in what he said. Emily was a smart woman. Pilot was a smart man. Matt believed himself to be a hard worker who wanted to keep life as simple as possible. He was not the romantic courtier or the love stricken suitor. He decided to keep Emily's advice to his heart and not try so hard. He set himself to let things happened naturally. He would try to do what was right, when the time came for decisions. For now, he decided to wait and see what the future would bring.

"Are you getting married?" Billy inquired as he and Matt began a light jog.

"I haven't seen her," Matt responded quietly.

"At all?" Billy asked.

"I haven't seen her since I asked her to marry me," Matt explained, as they picked up the pace to their run.

"That's been a couple of weeks," Billy observed.

"It will work out," Matt said as he pushed into his working pace.

When the two men had come to the end of their course, they slowed to a walk to cool themselves before going to wash for Sunday supper.

"You have to show her that you love her," Billy said with as much emotion as Matt had ever seen in him. Matt knew that when Billy spoke, he had something worthwhile to say. It was the bond the two men shared that kept their friendship comfortable.

"Whenever I try to force her to do anything, it messes things up with us," Matt tried to explain to Billy. "Maybe it's not meant to be."

"You can try the candies," Billy offered.

"I think you are right in what you say, but I don't think it's candies she wants," Matt replied.

"Maybe a little kiss?" Billy offered again.

"That probably would work if it was someone other than me," Matt answered with seriousness.

Billy shrugged and turned to go down the Quarters Road. "I'll see you later."

Matt nodded and headed toward the barracks. When he got there, he found a visitor waiting for him, sitting on his bunk.

"Hey Matt," Jack greeted him as he entered the room.

Matt nodded to return the gesture.

"The family knows about your proposal to Emily," Jack said.

Matt again nodded, so Jack would know that he had heard him.

"The family is 100% behind you, Matt," Jack said, rising from the bed. "We try to steer her in the right direction and say that you are a decent guy. She does want to hear from us, but she also wants to be left alone. I would think this would be a happy time, but she seems to be in a funk these last couple of weeks."

Matt went to his bed and sat down, putting his elbows on his thighs as he stared straight at the wall ahead of him.

"You may want to talk to her. I think she would like that," Jack suggested.

Matt nodded to confirm that he had heard his suggestion, but continued his stare into the wall.

"Call on any of the family at whatever time. We are always here on the farm."

"Okay," Matt managed to say.

When Jack left the small room, Matt got himself together and headed toward the shower room. He made extra sure his face was cleanly shaven, and his hair, bleached flaxen by the sun, was neatly groomed. As he looked in the mirror, he could see his tanned complexion. He usually did not pay so much attention to his appearance. Emily would comment how she liked his deep tan and sun bleached hair, so he took extra time to try to look handsome this evening.

After eating his supper, Matt waited a while to give the folks at the big house ample time to complete their meal, before making his way to visit Emily. After enough time had passed, he started on his way. He did not feel nervous about seeing Emily. She was easy to be with and he did miss her company.

"Good evening, Missus. I've come to call on Miss Emily," Matt said when Louisa answered his knock on the kitchen door. The farm's people always entered through the back door of the house and so did anybody else who was familiar with the Pilot home.

"Sure Matt, come on inside. Sit down here and eat some apple pie. I'll get Emily for you," Louisa said with a big smile. Matt did as Louisa had instructed. Her apple pie was impossible to resist, so he sat at the kitchen table while she put a plate with a piece of pie in front of him. When she returned from fetching Emily, his pie was just about gone. Shortly, Emily followed behind Louisa. Her mother continued fussing in the kitchen.

"Hi Matt," Emily greeted with a smile.

Immediately, Matt got up to greet her.

"Oh no, don't get up. Finish your pie," Emily exclaimed.

Matt took the remainder of the pie in his mouth and swallowed it instantly.

"All finished," Matt said as he moved closer to her direction.

"I thought we could visit for a while," Matt said.

"That would be nice," Emily agreed. "Let's go to the front porch. The others are watching TV in the great room."

They went to the porch. The air was still warm for it was getting later in the fall. Soon it would be time to bring in the sugarcane. Talk of courting and such would have to wait until the winter months. They both sat on the floor with their legs hanging over the edge of the porch.

"It's good to see you, Emily," Matt said.

"I want to explain why I have kept my distance of late, Matt," Emily said.

"It's not necessary unless you feel the need for explanation," Matt replied. Emily looked away from him to search for words in the darkness beyond the porch.

"I am not a man of many words. When I try to do things that aren't natural to me, I mess things up. You always seem like you know what I'm thinking."

"I think you're right in what you say, but I don't seem to know what you're thinking about me and that frightens me," Emily explained. "Why do you want to marry me?"

Matt stood up on the ground in front of the porch. For a moment he stared into the darkness, before he turned to face this fine lady. In a light gesture, he took her hand. "A very wise person told me that a man should have a wife. If I'm ever to have a wife, you are only woman I could ever want."

Emily stood up and drew close to him. Matt moved his head to kiss her gently on her lips. She was taller than he was, so she had to move her head to join her lips with his. After a short time, they embraced. Finally he let her go and stepped back a few inches to examine her. She smiled ear to ear, while he gave her one of those half smiles of his.

After a moment, Louisa popped her head from the screen door. "Can I interest anybody in some iced tea?"

Matt looked at Emily for a sign or a hint of desire for a drink. She merely grinned and gave a little shrug.

"Sure, that would be nice," Matt replied.

"Great, I'll be back in a jiffy," Louisa said as she closed the screen.

"Do you mind?" Emily asked with a slight smile, because she realized that Louisa meant to join them.

"No. Not at all," Matt answered as he gave his head a small shake.

The two made their way back up onto the porch, where they sat on the comfortable porch chairs. After few moments, Louisa brought a pitcher of iced tea on a platter with three large glasses. She sighed heavily after setting them on a small table and then she reclined into a large cushioned chair. Matt was glad that she had joined them, so he could visit with her, as she relaxed from a day of laboring.

They talked about the farm, mainly of the coming weeks, when the sugarcane was to be cut and trucked off the farm to the refineries.

After a short while, Matt said that it was time for him to leave. The two ladies thanked him for his visit. They said it was good of him to have stopped up to the big house and should do so again very soon. Emily offered to walk him up the back lawn to the Main Road, as he made his way to the barracks. He obliged and they started a slow stroll up the walk.

"I am really glad, you stopped to see me tonight, Matt," Emily said as she took hold of his arm.

"Good," Matt replied as he smiled lightly and glanced sweetly into her soft brown eyes.

"I promise I'll have an answer for you soon, Matt. I have to give it some more thought."

"You are kind for giving my proposal any thought. For that, I'm grateful," Matt replied with affection.

As they reached the Main Road, Matt turned to her and looked into her eyes. "Don't feel pressed for time. Take all you need. There's no hurry," he said.

"Thanks, I appreciate that very much," Emily replied. After a short pause, she said, "Well,..Good night. I'm sure I'll be talking to you soon. Maybe you could take me to church Sunday."

"Okay," Matt answered with a nod and waited for her to turn to leave. Out of courtesy, he waited until she entered the big house before he turned for the barracks.

A few days later, Matt was working in the sugar fields, moving water through the ditches. The weather had been dry, and there was concern the sugarcane would have to be brought in sooner if some rain did not arrive soon. The sky looked as though it promised rain, so there was hope the crop could stay in the field a while longer as scheduled. However, water was being pushed over the sugarcane to prevent the varmints from contaminating the crop.

As he was working, he heard a motor wining through the sugarcane. As the noise came closer, Matt was surprised to see the truck this far into the sugarcane. It was Jack's truck. The four-wheel drive could easily make it through the mud, but trucks did not usually come this far into the sugarcane as a precaution to prevent damage to the crop. Matt stopped his work and looked up from the ditch. Jack lowered the truck window as it approached, only it was not Jack. It was Robert Lamond.

"I see you didn't take my advice and keep your nose out from where it doesn't belong," Robert sneered as he set his elbow on the window ledge. He was wearing a nice suit, so Matt doubted he would get out of the truck.

Matt stood and looked straight into the angry man's face without saying a word.

"I warned you, but you didn't listen," Robert raged. "I can't believe that the likes of you would actually propose marriage to a fine sophisticated lady such as Emily Pilot. A stable boy! A field hand!" Robert was now laughing as he bellowed.

"What have you got to say for yourself, boy?" Robert asked with sarcasm.

"Nothing," Matt answered. The man did not affect him as he had on the 4th of July.

"That's shouldn't be surprising. A low life like you really knows his place in life. You are taking advantage of this woman's feelings," Robert exclaimed with obvious concern. "Someone's got to make her see what's she's doing."

"Maybe it's you," Matt responded.

"She won't see me, you fool! You've been able to poison her against me," Robert said, building into another rage. "I'll get you for this. You just wait." Robert attempted to drive the truck away. The truck spun its wheels, flinging mud in all directions. Matt was now completely covered with filth. In an instant, the truck caught some flattened sugarcane and was able to drive off through the crop.

Matt washed himself to remove the mud. Field workers were filthy by day's end, so Matt was not so concerned with being covered with mud. Matt figured Mr. Robert had his reasons for behaving the way he did toward him. However, it bothered him that he had acquired an enemy. Was that what the lanky man was, he wondered? An enemy? Should he be concerned about Lamond? He figured that he did not have a work affiliation with Lamond, so he would try to engage less with the man. He was careful not to take too much time pondering the situation, so he quickly returned to moving water through the ditches.

Matt bathed and dressed for Saturday night supper. It would not be for a while longer, but he wanted to be ready to leave for the big house early. He thought about visiting with the horses to kill some time, but thought the barn dust might soil his fresh clothing.

There was a light knock on his door. Matt rose from his bunk to answer. It was Billy. Immediately, Matt revealed a box of candy.

"It's nice," was all Billy said.

"Your mama tied the ribbon," Matt informed.

The two men stood in the room, as there was not much room for both to sit.

"Well, I best be going," Billy said as he turned to leave.

"Your mama says I need a ring for Miss Emily," Matt said flatly.

"Yeah?" Billy replied as he turned his head back toward Matt.

"What should I do?" Matt asked.

"Wait," Billy replied, "Things will fall into place."

"Wait?" Matt said with light surprise and then shrugged, "I can do that."

After Billy left, Matt sat and waited until it was time to go to Saturday night supper. By and by, he rose from the edge of his bed and headed for the big house. When he arrived, Louisa, Emily and one of the farm's ladies were still preparing supper.

"Well, hello Matt," Louisa said with surprise as she answered his knock. She was slightly embarrassed with her appearance, because she had not yet changed for supper. Emily soon took time out to see who was at the door. She too was slightly embarrassed by her appearance, but Matt did not seem to notice the difference. He was too wrapped up with the task at hand.

"Hi, Matt," Emily said delicately as she sauntered behind her mother.

"Evening, Miss Emily," Matt said, "I brought you these." He thrust the package toward Emily.

"Well," Louisa started, "I'll let you two be, while I finish up here." She then went to the stove and removed a couple of pots from the heat.

"Thank you, Matt," Emily said, accepting the gift.

Matt nodded with a half smile.

"We still have some finishing up to do, so why don't you go to the TV room for a while," Emily offered.

Matt, wondering if he had overstepped his boundaries said, "I can come back a little later."

"Nonsense!" Emily replied with animation. She smiled, "I won't be too long. I just need to freshen up a bit and I'll be right back."

Again, Matt nodded. He walked into the TV room and sat on the overstuffed green sofa. The TV was already on as if somebody had recently been watching. After a short while, members of the family and invited guests started to appear in the TV room. Soon, Louisa announced that there were appetizers in the main parlor for everyone to sample. Supper would be served in the dining room.

Matt felt a little more at ease when people started to arrive. Usually, he did not like to be in the midst of a group of people, but he found it awkward being the only guest for a long period of time.

Emily came into the room, arm in arm with a lady seemingly to be the same generation as Louisa. "Matt, I would like you to meet Candace. She's a dear friend of the family. She's also the first lady of our state and the governor's most cherished. She makes her way through the parish, visiting different planters, but she spends extra time with us. I've known her just about all my life. She's a second mother to me," Emily said proudly.

Matt nodded as he took the lady's hand into own.

"So," Candace began, "This is the stable boy you've been telling me about for all these months?"

Emily pursed her lips and then smiled quickly. "Matt is a very valuable part of the farm. He sets a good example for all to follow with his good work."

Matt gritted his teeth, feeling slightly nervous.

"How nice," Candace said with a less than sincere smile.

Finally, supper was over. Matt could go back to the barracks. He was concerned because Emily did not offer the candy to any of the guests. Maybe because there was already so much food available. She had talked among the guests, while he entertained himself, which suited him fine. However, he found himself looking for signs from her to indicate her intentions toward him.

I just can't worry about things, Matt said to himself, as he sat on his perch. After a short while, Billy came to join him.

"How'd it go?" Billy asked.

Matt shrugged despondently. He was clearly pouting.

Billy shrugged in return and sat for a while next to Matt. The two sat in silence, relaxing with the light breeze.

"I'm sorry," Billy said after a long time.

"It's okay," Matt said with a light smile. He continued his stare into the top of the trees in the far end of the front pasture.

"What next?" Billy asked.

"Nothing," Matt replied, "Wait and see."

CHAPTER 8

Sunday church came and went with the main family. Matt sensed Emily was her usual self with plenty of smiles. The folks were generally quiet on Sunday, but Louisa, Pilot, and Jack all seemed happy. Only Marge did not seem so content with herself. She did not seem friendly, but Matt still felt at ease with her. Perhaps this was due to the fact that they were both from outside the family.

About mid-week, Marge paid Matt a visit one late afternoon, while he was sitting on his perch.

"Hi," Marge said as she approached. The breeze was light, so she buttoned her sweater.

"Hi," Matt nodded to her. He looked away into the fields. He figured she could sit if she chose.

"Mind if I sit for a minute?" Marge asked.

"Sure," Matt replied.

"Seems I always see you here, when I come by the farm," Marge observed and then added, "And that, my friend, is not too often."

Matt was surprised to learn he had another friend. "It's nice here," he answered.

"Can I ask you something personal?" Marge inquired as she looked at the side of his face.

"Sure," Matt answered without turning toward her.

"Why on earth would you want to get mixed up with that family?" Marge asked with disbelief.

"Why not?" Matt replied with a question. This time he looked at her momentarily.

"You know you'll end up giving them your life and soul," Marge warned.

Matt shrugged.

"You just seem like the type who likes to keep to himself. Others say you may have a stiff-necked attitude with a lot of haughtiness, but I think you're more like me. We keep to our own business," Marge observed a second time.

"Why would others care?" Matt asked with concern.

"Because you are different," Marge explained, "Like me."

After a pause, Marge expounded on her viewpoint, "I'm not exactly a high society babe and neither are you. I want to be, but on my own terms, not as somebody's wife, hanging on my husband's arm. I married into this family and I guess I have to live with it. I come from humble beginnings, like you." Matt turned his head and looked at her again momentarily.

Marge continued, "I have to fight, tooth and nail, for my own space. You know, they'll try to dominate your life on their terms. I wasn't about to work in some hot kitchen, telling people the proper way to can vegetables, or manage the food consumption on the farm. I want my own life. Is that so bad?"

Matt slowly shook his head, but Marge didn't seem to notice. She was on a roll.

"Jack thought he was marrying a sweet little county girl." Marge laughed with disbelief. "I've sure showed him what sweet can be."

Marge rose from the drums and brushed herself as if she had dust on her clothing. "I figure I can use the Pilot resources to become what I have always wanted to be; a learned woman, not some dangling wife. You better come up with a motive for involving yourself with this clan if you want to keep your sanity. They'll take that away from you, if you let them." She turned to leave. "Good luck. I really wish you well."

Matt nodded and then turned his head away from her. He returned his gaze to the trees. After a short while, he once again heard footsteps approaching his seat.

"Hi, Matt," Emily said as she came near to him. She was wearing a light cotton dress underneath a brown knitted sweater.

Matt nodded and doffed his cap.

"How is everything going?" Emily asked.

"Okay," Matt replied. After a short pause he added, "You?"

"Okay. We're trying hard to finish the vegetable harvest, so we can be done before the sugarcane comes in from the fields."

"It should be any day," Matt replied.

"There's a strong rumor at the big house that it will start a week from Monday," Emily reported.

Matt nodded and acknowledged her statement.

"I was wondering if you were busy next Saturday afternoon?" Emily inquired as she climbed up on a drum to sit next to Matt.

"Nothing planned," Matt replied in return.

"Would you be interested in a picnic with me? I'll bring the lunch. We can take the horses," Emily said with a big smile.

Matt smiled, "Sure."

"I'll look forward to it," Emily replied.

"I'll get the horses ready and bring them up to the big house," Matt offered.

"That's great. Is the lunch hour an okay time?"

"Sure," Matt replied.

The two sat for a while. They didn't say much. At times Emily said something that entered her mind. She liked to talk and Matt did not seem to mind listening to her. He decided that it was nice to hear her talk.

After Emily left the perch, Billy came for a visit.

"Hey," he said as he climbed on the metal drums.

Matt nodded. After a short time of silence, he remarked, "I'm going on a picnic on next Saturday."

"With who?" Billy asked.

"Miss Emily," Matt answered lightly.

"You're learning to court," Billy observed.

Matt turned his head to him slightly and frowned. He shook his head slowly.

"Ladies like picnics," Billy remarked, "It's a good idea."

"It was Miss Emily's idea," Matt informed.

"Are you still going to call her Miss Emily when you're married?" Billy asked.

"I don't know," Matt answered with his forehead slightly furrowed, " I may not have to worry."

"You will," Billy said quickly.

"Why?" Matt asked.

"My mama said so," Billy explained.

Saturday finally did come. Matt had the horses, Kelsey and Butch, saddled up for the ride. He brought them up to the big house and waited at the back door until Emily appeared with the lunch. After a while, she came out with a couple of sacks with the lunch. The food was not in a basket, as one would imagine. That would not have been practical, since they were riding on horseback. The sacks would fit nicely inside the saddle pouches.

"What do think of the apple orchard on the far end? Do you know which one I'm talking about?" Emily asked, as Matt gave her a leg lift onto Kelsey.

"Yes," Matt replied, "The horses will like it too."

Emily smiled, "There may still be a few apple left here and there."

They plodded along the Main Road, past the big kitchen and barns. They entered the woods where the Cattle and Quarter roads met. Along the beaten path, the aspen trees were tall, shading them from the sun's rays. Shortly, they came to a large creek.

"Have you ever fished along here?" Emily asked.

"No," Matt answered.

"My daddy used to take my brothers down here when they were growing up," Emily remarked. "There are a few pools along the bank where fish like to feed. The water runs slower, so they don't have to work hard to swim."

Matt nodded

Emily suggested they cross the creek at a shallow point and ride along the bank for awhile. Matt said that would be fine. They eventually reached a section of the creek where it widened into a small lake. The water was calm. They could see ducks and geese swimming along the banks. Soon, they came across the apple orchard, which was close to the creek.

"How is this spot?" Emily asked.

"It's fine," Matt responded.

When they dismounted the horses, Matt attached lead ropes to both of the horses and tethered them to a nearby apple tree. The horses had enough slack in the line to be able to graze and search for apples that had fallen from the trees. After securing the horses, he removed the sacks full of lunch and a blanket. After the blanket had been spread across the ground, they sat down and Emily started removing items from the sacks.

"I would have prepared your favorites, but I don't know what they are," Emily said while making the place settings.

"This looks just fine," Matt replied with a half smile.

"What are your favorite foods?" Emily asked.

"I like everything," Matt responded.

"No favorites?" Emily asked in disbelief while she smile.

"Well, maybe two," Matt admitted.

"Yeah?" Emily said almost eagerly.

"I like your Mama's brownies and cookies," Matt replied.

"Guess what I brought?" Emily said as she retrieved some brownies and cookies from a sack. "Except I made them myself."

Matt smiled. Emily could tell he was pleased.

The food tasted real good and Matt ate hungrily.

As they were nearing the end of their meal, Emily asked, "So, when do you want to get married?"

Matt's chewing slowed to a near halt. Could this mean she wanted to get married? Or did her decision depend on when they would get married?

After a couple of moments, Matt chewed the rest of his food and swallowed. "Soon," he finally replied.

"Well, when's soon?" she asked lightly.

"We'd have to get a ring for you first," Matt said knowingly.

"That would be fine," Emily replied, "I'd wear it proudly."

"Does this mean we are getting married?" Matt said with a calm half smile.

"Yes," Emily laughed, "It does."

"Good," Matt said as he gently laid his hand on hers. She responded by reaching over to embrace him. *He's so shy*" she thought to herself, *It's quite charming.*

They kissed lightly for a moment.

"Are you ready for dessert?" Emily asked with a giggle.

"Congratulations!" Jack said. He had taken Matt aside after the church service. "And I thought that all you were interested in was sugarcane and horses," he beamed.

"Thanks," Matt replied, as they stood outside of the church. Robert Lamond walked past them and gave Matt a wicked scowl. It was rare that he attended church, since Emily would decline his invitations to sit with him. She never used Matt as an excuse for refusal. After all, he was her escort. She would always find a gracious way to say "No."

"I think you got the best girl around, but I'm biased," Jack gushed with a short laugh.

"Yes," Matt agreed. After a short moment, he asked, "Do I have enough money saved to buy a ring?"

"My friend," Jack replied, "You have enough saved to buy ten rings, that is if you intend to spend a reasonable amount."

"What is reasonable?" Matt asked. "How do I pick one?" Billy had said one should buy a ring that came inside a black velvet box. The gentleman then would present it to the lady over a romantic supper.

"If I were you and this is what I did for Marge," Jack started slyly in a hushed tone, "I'd take her to the jewelry store and let her pick the one she wants." He added with a laugh, "You'd be taking a big risk on your wallet, but I think Emily's a sensible woman."

"Thanks," Matt replied almost graciously. He liked Jack's idea better than Billy's.

"No problem," Jack said with a smile and a headshake. "I guess we better find the ladies and the family," he added.

As suspected, Monday was the start of the sugarcane grind. It was midweek when Jack approached Matt in the barracks during early morning. "Why don't you take the day off and take your lady to get her ring."

"It's time for the cutting," Matt protested.

"You'll just be a few hours,"Jack replied, "Besides, it's not good to keep a lady waiting on her ring."

"I'll need some money," Matt said as he decided to take Jack's advice to heart.

"Tell the jeweler to bill Pilot for it and he'll take it from your savings," Jack said. "He'll be expecting you."

Matt and Emily drove into town in one of the farm's cars and picked out a pretty little ring. Emily's fingers were long and slender, so she was more concerned with the way it looked on her hand than the size of the diamond. Matt didn't care. He only wanted a ring that would please Emily.

"Isn't it beautiful," Emily said to her mama as she showed off the ring on her finger. She and Matt stopped at the big house for lunch after shopping in town.

"Yes it is," Louisa replied as she took her daughter's hand and smiled while she examined the ring.

After releasing her hand, Louisa asked, "Have you set the date?"

"No," Emily replied, "What do you think, Matt? Name a date."

"How about next week?" Matt responded. The sugarcane should be cut by then, he thought.

The two ladies giggled. Louisa said lightly, "It takes a good 6 months to plan a wedding, but it's nice to see you're so eager."

"6 months it is then," Matt replied with a half smile.

"That's sounds good to me," Emily agreed. "That should put us close to the second Saturday in May."

"Sounds like it's been settled, " Louisa said, rather pleased. "Oh," she said, almost startled, "We have to plan an engagement party."

"Yes," Emily agreed, "I want to show off my new ring, as well as my fiancée." She put an arm around Matt's waist for emphasis.

"Who should we invite?" Louisa asked, "Do you want it small or large?"

"I don't know," Emily said, "What do you think Matt? Who do you want to invite?"

Matt pondered for a moment. He had a very short list. "I guess any of the farm's people who would want to come."

"Oh, then you want a big party, "Louisa said with a deep smile. "That will be good. Everybody will be in good spirits with the sugarcane being in and the holidays coming."

This surprised Matt. He could not imagine many people would want to come on his behalf, but maybe they would come to see Emily.

"That would be dandy," Emily responded with excitement, "Do you reckon it would still be warm enough to have it outside?"

"It might be a little cool, but we'll see," Louisa promised.

"Why don't we have campfires!" Emily suggested. "We could roast hot dogs on sticks!"

"Now there's a clever idea!" Louisa replied with a big grin.

Matt smiled at the two ladies. He was pleased.

The sugarcane was cut quickly as most of it stood just right for machinery to cut it and lay it up onto huge tractors. Still, Matt was able to learn the art of cutting the sugarcane by hand using a large machete. It was mostly old men cutting with this method, as the younger men opted to run the big tractors. Matt stood with Tim as he learned to cut low and carefully. This technique was many times slower than the high powered tractors. The cutters were able to get down into crevices, where the big machines could not reach. Using the cutters saved a good amount of the sugarcane. Besides claiming sugarcane otherwise ignored by the tractors, the cutters sliced lower, getting more of the sugarcane. This prevented some of the damage to the sugarcane incurred while cutting with tractors.

Finally, the last of the sugarcane left on a truck down the Farm Road bounded for a refinery along the Mississippi River. The timing was good for the night of the engagement party had come. The dress would be casual, since it was an outdoor affair. Children were welcome as the event turned into an outing for the entire plantation. The farm's people were taking well to Matt. Emily made sure all knew it was he who wanted them there to witness the special event. As groups of people roasted hot dogs, potatoes, and marshmallows over the fires, Matt, with Emily on his arm, made sure to visit with everyone to thank them for sharing this special time. This event turned out to be important, since many of the farm's workers were leery about one of their own becoming a member of the big house. Many still didn't know Matt even though he ate with them, worked alongside with them, and kept his quarters close by to them. They knew him as a silent man who kept to himself and never shied from a day's work. In regular fashion, he still spoke few words to them, but his gentle smile was able to warm their hearts.

Several days after the engagement party, Robert Lamond paid Matt a visit at the horse barn.

"Hello," said an animated voice. Matt could not see to whom the voice belonged to on the other side of the mare that he was grooming. In an instant, he knew who its owner was. For a moment, Matt stopped brushing the tan mare, but then began the stroking once more without returning the greeting. After a few more moments, Robert quickly appeared. Matt kept his stoking rhythm, still not uttering a word or acknowledging his visitor.

"I can understand your coolness, but I've come to make up. To make amends," Robert said, even toned with a smirk.

Matt stopped brushing the mare and dropped the currycomb to his side. He stood and looked right into Robert's eyes. His appearance was different than usual. His flowing black hair was disheveled. He wore a loose white cotton, buttoned down shirt, tucked into a blue pair of dress slacks. His shoes were a pair of loafers instead of the spit shined laced variety.

Pleased that he got the reaction he wanted, Robert moved closer to Matt. "I lost," Robert said with a wide grin, holding both hands from his hips with his stretched palms facing Matt. His voice reflected a forced despondency.

"What did you lose?" Matt inquired, standing in front of the illustrious planter.

Robert brought a hand to his chin and crossed his free arm over his chest to support the weight of his elbow. "Well, let see..." He said with a pause, "For starters, Emily."

Matt resumed his grooming.

"What's the matter?" Robert asked slyly, "I'm trying to be nice."

Again, Matt stopped his grooming and looked Robert straight in the eyes. "I didn't take anything from you," he said with little feeling. He finished grooming the mare, then unfastened the lead ropes from each side of the aisle and led her into a nearby stall. Robert moved quickly to avoid the mare's hooves from stepping on his feet.

"Look," Robert began sanguinely with a relaxed smile and said, "I didn't come to argue. I mean to call a truce."

"A truce?" Matt replied, coming from the stall.

"Yes," Robert nodding his head, "A truce."

After moment of silence, Robert held out his hand. "Let's shake on it and be done."

Matt met the hand with own and clasped it securely. Robert's hand was large, soft and warm. He could feel his own rough callused hand against the tender pliable skin. Robert held Matt's hand longer than was customary. Matt sensed it was a subtle sign of warning.

Robert smiled. "There. Now that wasn't so bad. Was it?" he said, releasing Matt's hand and cocking his head slightly to one side.

Matt pursed his lips and gave the handsome man a short nod.

Robert turned and gave Matt a little smirk from the corner of his mouth accented with a twinkle in his eye, as he left the barn. Matt sighed and then resumed his work.

After a short time, Jack came to the barn. "Was that Lamond I saw leaving?" Jack asked with concern.

"Yes," Matt replied lightly, continuing his work.

"Did he give you a rough time?" Jack inquired as he stopped in front of Matt.

"No," Matt answered as he stopped to look at Jack. "We made a truce."

"A truce?" Jack asked with disbelief, his brow furrowed.

"Yes," Matt assured.

"That's odd," Jack said, tilting his head to one side. "He had just got done pleading with Pilot to do everything he could to stop your engagement. Pilot adamantly refused, but Lamond kept trying to call any possible favors that Pilot might owe to him. Pilot still could not be swayed. Finally, he told Robert that he had work to do and could he excuse himself. I guess he headed straight here."

Matt looked away and resumed his work.

"Don't let him get to you, Matt," Jack said soothingly but then added firmly, "Just watch him, Matt, watch him."

Thanksgiving passed and so did Christmas. Matt spent these holidays up at the big house. Louisa insisted he spend the holiday nights in one of the many empty bedrooms in the big house. He reluctantly obliged. He thought he had better get used to it, since Emily and he agreed to live in the big house with Louisa and Pilot once they were married. They would have their own rooms on the west wing of the house on the floor below Louisa and Pilot. The rooms on that floor were currently not in use. Emily had decorators visit the big house to choose window treatments, wall and floor coverings, and such to modernize the west wing. This set of rooms, on the second floor, was remote from the rest of the house, suitable for newlyweds' privacy.

The idea of living in the big house seemed awkward at first for Matt, but he realized he couldn't have Emily live in the barracks and thought she may not be comfortable with a house on the Quarters Road. After a short time, he came to an understanding with himself that he didn't care where he lived as long as his fiancée was happy. Besides, he enjoyed spending the holidays up at the big house with the family. With this in mind, he started looking forward to living with Louisa and Pilot, with Jack stopping by daily.

The wedding plans started to progress quickly after the first of year. Matt did not have any living relatives, so Emily and Louisa decided to make the bridal party small. Surprisingly, Pilot had some ideas for the wedding. He was excited to have his only daughter wedded to the man she loved. It was Pilot who suggested Billy and his family take part in the bridal party. He was very interested in the details of the ceremony, since Emily decided she wanted to have the wedding outside.

Matt left most of the planning to the ladies and Pilot. Instead, he offered his services to run errands for the ladies when needed. Emily did give him the task of choosing a best man to stand with him. Naturally, he chose Billy.

"Would you stand with me in my wedding?" Matt asked Billy one day on his back porch.

"How's that?" Billy asked, looking away from Matt.

"I'm asking you to be my best man. You know, for my wedding," Matt said with greater emphasis.

"I don't see how I can," Billy said, looking down at his feet.

"Why not?" Matt inquired lightly.

"Those people at the big house won't want me standing up there," Billy replied.

"Pilot suggested your family be involved," Matt advised.

"I don't think it would be right, Matt," Billy said sadly, "I have to live with these folks here and I can't be getting uppity."

"Uppity?" Matt asked, confused.

"Yeah," Billy responded, finally looking at Matt, "Those folks up at the big house live differently than we do down here. We keep to ourselves and they keep to themselves. It's always been that way."

"You're mad at me," Matt accused with disappointment.

"No, I ain't mad," Billy said, smiling with reassurance. "We all think a lot of the man Pilot. His family has always been good to us. Why don't you ask his boy to stand with you? He'll jump at the chance."

"Okay," Matt resigned. After a short moment he added, "I'll sure be lonesome without you, your mama and daddy."

Billy understood Matt's plight. He had no other family. He knew once he got to know the Pilots living up at the big house that he would be fine. However, he did not want him to be lonesome on his wedding day.

"I'll do anything to help," Billy offered, "And so will Mama and Daddy."

This did not seem to cheer Matt.

"How about if I help seat people?"

"Seat people?" Matt asked, bewildered.

"Yeah. Like usher or something," Billy explained.

"That might be okay," Matt responded hopefully.

"Then it's done," Billy said relieved.

"Do you think your mama and daddy will sit in the front row?" Matt said feeling he was pressing his luck. "I sure would be grateful."

"I'll see what I can do, if it means that much to you'" Billy said, aware that this would take some convincing.

"Thanks," Matt said quietly as he beamed from ear to ear.

"That's great news," Emily replied as Matt told her Billy and his family agreed to be in the bridal party, "I know how much that means to you."

Matt smiled.

"Can we arrange a time for Billy to come up here to fit for his tuxedo?" Emily asked.

"Tuxedo?" Matt said with surprise.

"Yes silly," Emily teased lightly, "You and all the men in the bridal party have to wear those monkey suits."

"Hmm," Matt said thinking out loud, "Would you mind if we went to his house?"

"Sure," Emily replied slyly, curious of his motive.

"Thanks," Matt said gratefully, "It's important."

As Billy had suspected, Jack was thrilled to be Matt's best man. Everybody now seemed happy with the wedding plans. At last, Matt felt things were falling into place. Emily suggested they take a riverboat cruise for their honeymoon. Matt thought it was a good idea. At mealtime, the farm's people often talked about the beauty of the Mississippi River.

The wedding date was nearing and most of the plans had been made even though the wedding was still two months away. The spring planting had to be done, so there would have been little time to plan for the wedding during this season.

Candace was very helpful picking up the loose ends, while Louisa and Emily supervised the breaking of ground for the year's vegetable crop. She had many contacts for the necessary vendors, tailors, and seamstresses to produce a fine wedding.

One factor not planned for the wedding was the weather. Rain could not be averted, but canopies were made for adequate protection for the outside event if necessary. The problem was that torrential rains swept through the delta region for most of the spring after the planting was done.

Most of the farm's people were used to help move water through the ditches to prevent harmful flooding to the sugarcane. As the day of the wedding came closer, it became a daily struggle to save the sugarcane from washing out. Vegetables already would have to be replanted once the rains dissipated, but this did not spell disaster as there usually was enough time for a second crop during the year. However, this was not the case for the sugarcane. It needed a full season.

Matt and Emily considered postponing the wedding until the weather stabilized, but Pilot would not hear of it. "You two have waited long enough and so have your mama and me," Pilot said firmly one day. All that was left was the hope that the day would not be spoiled. Pilot had the loft in one of the barns cleared out to hold the reception. This would allow for plenty of room and would keep everybody dry.

The day of the wedding finally came. The rains slowed significantly by luck. This allowed for some of the farm's people to rest from working the fields and others to help with preparations. Canopies were being set up on the front lawn of the big house to protect the wedding party and its on-lookers from the rain. Workers were busy placing chairs inside the canopy tents.

It was still a few hours before the wedding was to take place at 2:00 in the afternoon. Robert Lamond was watching in the background, while the crew from the big kitchen was placing an ice sculpture on a large table. Other workers were securing lines to hold the canopy structures upright.

"I'm really surprised to see you here," Jack said to Robert as he approached from the big house. He was still dressed in casual clothing and was carrying a warm cup of tea with him.

Under the canopy where the onlookers were to sit, Robert replied, "This should be quite an event. I surely wouldn't want to miss it."

"Were you invited to this?" Jack asked suspiciously.

Robert responded calmly with a sly smile, "Well, I know I'm a special friend of the family's, so I assumed that the invitation must have been lost in the shuffle before it reached me."

"You aren't planning to upset anybody are you?" Jack asked impatiently.

"Of course not!" Robert replied defiantly, "I've made up with your boy. I think we're even starting to become friends."

"Is that why you tried everything to convince Pilot to disrupt this wedding?" Jack said acidly.

"Well that is true," Robert admitted. "But I think your father helped me see the light."

"I sure hope so," Jack replied with disbelief.

"Trust me," Robert assured with a smile.

Jack warned, "If you do anything to upset anybody or interrupt this event, you will be very sorry."

"Well then, you can sure rest assured that I won't try anything," Robert replied with slight mockery in his smile and voice.

"Good," Jack said, with a pleasant demeanor, "I best be getting cleaned up." He turned and walked quickly to the big house.

Robert carefully scoped all the preparations. He noticed that two canopies were joined together exactly above where the bride and groom were to stand. Once Pilot had given his daughter away in marriage, the bride and groom would join together, while they exchanged their vows.

He studied the two canopies and how they were supported. A thick strap with plastic stripping sealed the two canopy pieces together to make one large non-leaking piece. There was a rope coming from the canopy to a stake that was driven to the ground that kept the canvas taut, allowing for the water to drain off the edge. Robert thought if there was some slack in the rope that the canvas would not be so taut, causing a puddle of water to build where the two pieces were joined by the strap.

"Hey boy," Robert called to a young worker driving in canopy stakes and attaching lines of rope to them and the canvas. "Yeah, you. Come over here."

The young man came over to Robert to be addressed, "Yes sir?"

"Move this stake over here and leave some room in the line. It's going to tear the canvas."

The young man looked at Robert awkwardly.

"Do as I say, boy, I'm in charge here," Robert bellowed with a nasty stare.

The young man took up the stake and positioned it how Robert requested. As Robert had suspected there was some give in the canopy where the two pieces of canvas met. Water immediately started to collect. If the rope were given more slack, even more water would collect, causing the strap's seam to burst due to the induced weight. A light breeze made ruffling noises from the canopy sides, so a slight shift in the canopy would go unnoticed. Most peoples' attention would be placed on the bride and groom since this would be the crucial moment in the ceremony. Robert smiled as he reserved his seat of choice to carry through his plan.

Billy along with Emily and Jack's two older brothers began to seat the guests. They were dressed in fine gray pinstriped tuxedos with white starched shirts, black bow ties and cummerbunds. Their shoes were spit-shined patent leather black.

First, Billy seated his mama and daddy. They were in their Sunday best clothes, except his mother was wearing a beautiful hat, a gift from the bride. Billy had a few moments to gaze at his surroundings. There were plenty of flowers. Most of them were white. Along with his mama and daddy, the rest of the wedding party wore white flowers.. Everything was so beautiful. The only people sitting so far were his parents and the Lamond man that always gave Matt such a rough time. Matt never spoke poorly of the man, or even mentioned him, but he knew that man was not in his corner. More people wanted to be seated. Soon the event would begin.

"Is Matt ready?" Emily asked her mother and Candace. She was putting the final touches on her makeup in front of her mirror.

"Don't worry about him dear," Candace said. "He's in good hands." She brought the veil over for Emily to put on her head.

"Thanks so much for helping me," Emily gushed slightly. "Mama is a bit nervous."

"That's all right. I'm helping her get ready too. Actually, she's left to be seated," Candace announced.

"I was hoping to see her one more time," Emily said disappointedly.

"Everything is going to be just fine," Candace assured, placing her hand on Emily's forearm.

There was a knock on Emily's door.

"Darling, it's me," Pilot said in a low serious voice.

"Come in," Emily said brightly.

Pilot opened the door and stepped into the room. "Well, sweetheart, it is just about time," he said with a smile, clasping his hands together nervously.

Emily rose from her vanity. "I'm ready."

Pilot gasped with a low chuckle. "You are beautiful. The spitting image of your mother 35 years ago."

"That's quite a compliment," Emily said with a bright smile, "I'm glad you're with me on the happiest day of my life." She kissed him lightly on the cheek.

"I'm very proud of you," Pilot said with emotion, "But I guess you already know that."

Emily smiled.

"Let's go be in a wedding," Pilot said opening the door. "Are you ready?"

"Oh yes!" Emily replied with vigor.

"Are you sure you know what to do?" Jack asked.

"Yes," Matt said calmly with a half smile. It was time for the two to stand before the preacher, Reverend Samson. Matt's tuxedo was a solid black, which was different than his groomsmen. His shirt was white, starched so stiffly that it cut sharply into his neck when he moved, but he did not mind. It was what Emily wanted. His hair was still bleached by the sun and shortly cut to a half inch from his scalp. His skin was slightly tanned from working in the fields.

The music started and soon after, Emily came walking down the aisle with Pilot. The people sitting in the folding chairs were now standing with their gaze on her. With good reason; she was beautiful. How proud he was of her! She had a long flowing dress and her face was covered with a veil. Her face was radiant behind it. She seemed to float down the aisle. He stopped hearing the music as he stared intently into her eyes. They were like cool pools of blue, which seemed to help him relax.

She stood in front of him. Matt continued to examine her. Jack had to nudge Matt for him to turn to face the preacher. Still he could not hear what was being said, but he managed to go through the motions. Soon, Emily was joined to his side. She took his arm, while they stood before Reverend Samson.

The time had come. The breeze was ruffling the canvas. Robert reached his foot over to the stake from where he was sitting on the end of his row. His used his foot remove the rope line from the stake. The canopy sagged low just above the bride and groom. Luckily, nobody seemed to notice. It seemed the swelling was growing larger by the second. He started to smile broadly, but everybody had smiles on their faces. He had to clear his throat quietly to suppress a laugh, until the water burst through the straps joining the seams. The bride became drenched like a wet dog. Robert was no longer able to contain his laughter and he roared. Nobody heard his laugh, because they were gasping and screaming in horror as Emily sunk to her feet. Matt instantly went down with her to make sure she wasn't harmed. Slowly, she rose back to her feet and Matt followed. She removed the veil from her face and started to laugh lightly. Seeing she was not harmed, the audience gave a sigh of relief as they smiled in return.

"Sweetheart, are you all right?" Pilot said as he held her steady.

"Oh yes Daddy," "Emily said, catching her breath, "Nothing can ruin this day. Let's continue." She straightened her veil and collected her composure.

Matt looked at her doubtfully.

"Really I'm fine," she said, touching his hand with hers to give assurance.

Matt nodded his head and turned to face the preacher.

"Okay, let's take our seats ladies and gentlemen, and let's have some quiet," Reverend Samson ordered. After a moment he resumed, "Where were we? Oh yes. Do you, Emily, take this man........."

After the wedding was over, torrential rains returned to devastate the delta region. Guests were urged to leave the reception early to beat the flood that was threatening to wash out the roads. Pilot said this could be record rainfall accumulation for this time of year. Emily and Matt decided to postpone their honeymoon until the rains subsided. First of all, riverboats were not likely to risk the Mississippi. Second, their help was needed to save the sugarcane.

On their wedding night, Matt and Emily were finally able to relax. After the wedding festivities, they sauntered slowly to their newly renovated rooms in the west wing. They were drenched with rain. Umbrellas had failed to keep them dry coming to the big house from the barn where the reception took place. Individually, they bathed to warm and to cleanse themselves. After Matt had finished his shower, he came into their bedroom, wrapped in a beige terry cloth robe. Emily was already in the bed, relaxing with the lamp on the nightstand illuminating the ceiling above the bed. She opened her eyes.

"How do you feel?" Emily asked as Matt entered the bedroom.

"Okay," he replied with a half smile. He sensed that she was naked under the cover. Shamelessly and without modesty, he shed his robe and gently climbed into bed underneath the cover beside her.

She turned herself to him and they kissed lightly. The intensity of their petting picked up slightly, but still there was the awkwardness that occurs with two new young lovers.

After a few minutes of kissing and heavy petting, Matt could feel that he was still flaccid and not aroused. Surprisingly, he hadn't thought much about their wedding night. Perhaps it was just part of the chain of events taking place. First the engagement, then the wedding, and then the wedding night.

He stopped the kissing and paused. Emily looked at him with a smile and gentleness in her eyes. "I've never done this," Matt said quietly.

"Relax," Emily said smiling. She turned to lie on her back and then closed her eyes. Placing her forearm just above her forehead, she said, "We have the rest of our lives to learn how to do this. No hurry."

Matt felt relieved as he sunk back into his pillow. He thought about the terrific woman he had married. He knew he was lucky to have such an understanding wife. *Look at the trouble Marge gives Jack*, he thought. Matt understood that Emily would do anything she could to help him be a good husband. Perhaps it was at this time that he knew that he loved Emily.

Turning on his side, he faced her body. Her face looked so peaceful, with that smile that never seemed to disappear. Slowly, he touched her body, just under her breast. She felt warm to the touch. Gently, he ran his hand down her body against her thigh. He moved closer, so quietly as if not to disturb her stillness.

She let him explore her body, not interrupting by making any gestures or sounds. His breathing increased as he lay against her. She felt his breath against her neck and breasts. Feeling him close, she began to want him, to need him. She knew he must have sensed her craving, because he moved delicately on top of her, between her legs with his arms straddling her body as if he was conscious that his weight would crush her. As he glided gently into her, she beckoned him close to her, so she could feel his weight.

When it was over, they laid on their backs quietly as they waited for their breathing to steady. Still, there were no words. He felt a physical release, which was pleasurable. However, the rest was still a mystery. *Had he pleasured her?* Did he do it correctly?

"How do you feel?" Matt asked with a serious tone.

"Marvelous," Emily said as she turned to face him, smiling broadly.

"Did everything go as it should?" Matt asked with greater hope.

"I should think it did!" Emily exclaimed as she playfully pinched his breast.

He smiled. He could tell she was happy. After a few moments, he drifted off into a sweet slumber.

Early the next morning, Emily opened her eyes to the new day. It was still dark and still too early for the rest of the house to be awake. She did not wake on her own. She turned on her side to face her new husband. He was twitching ever so lightly, but the jerky motions had startled her in her sleep. The sheets were soaked with the sweat pouring from Matt's body. Was he having a bad dream? Should she wake him? After a few moments, she pushed several times against his shoulder.

"Matt, honey, wake up," she said lightly, still coming from the night's sleep. "You're having a bad dream, sweetie, you need to wake up."

Slowly Matt opened his eyes. He propped himself on his elbows and tried to catch his breath. After a few moments, he looked over to her. "I'm sorry. Did I wake you?"

"That's okay, but I'm concerned about you," she said with a worried look on her face. Are you okay?" she asked.

Matt nodded, finally catching his breath.

"What in the world were you dreaming about?" Emily asked. Her worry had turned to curiosity.

After a moment, Matt responded, "A lady I don't recognize."

"Do want to tell me about it?" Emily asked gently, cradling her head in her hand, with her elbow supporting her weight on the mattress.

Matt slumped back against his pillow and sighed. "I have this dream all the time." After a few more moments he added, "I dream about terrible things happening to her. I see them and they frighten me."

"What kind of things?" Emily asked, giving him her full attention.

Matt stared straight ahead, but he was looking into his thoughts. After a moment of thinking he said, "I must be a little boy, at least I think it's me. I'm holding this woman's hand. We're standing at an air strip in the middle of a stormy night, except there is no rain; just thunder, lightening, and strong winds. We both look up and see a plane fly over us. It crashes on the airstrip. The woman is greatly pained, but she remains motionless. I feel her pain as I know that someone who was special to her was in that plane and surely didn't survive. Still she remains expressionless, just standing there, not doing anything."

After a moment of silence, Emily asked, "Is there anything else?"

"No," Matt responded, shaking his head. "I dream that over and over, like there's something wrong with the dream. I want it to change, but it never does."

"You've dreamed this dream on other nights?" Emily asked with surprise.

"Others like it. The same woman. The same little boy," Matt explained. "Sometimes the woman is being attacked and all I can do is watch. She is always expressionless, but I know she hurts. I feel the hurt."

"Who do think the woman can be?" Emily pondered.

"I've never seen her before," Matt said, shaking his head slowly. "Only in my dreams."

"Do you have dreams every night?" Emily asked raising her eyebrow.

After a moment, Matt responded under his breath. "No, just some nights." After a moment, Matt added, "Other nights I dream of my mother, but they aren't bad dreams. I don't want to forget her, I'm glad I dream about her."

"She must have meant a lot to you," Emily said warmly.

"Yes," Matt replied quietly. "I have a picture of her. I'll show you." He got up out of bed. He went to his tuxedo jacket that was hanging in his closet. He reached into the inside pocket and retrieved a small photo. He brought it over to Emily.

Emily took the picture into her hands as she sat up in the bed, propped against her pillow. The woman was handsome, but older than Emily had expected. It was difficult to see the resemblance to Matt, so she figured he must favor his father. She did detect that they had the same smile, but that was all she could determine. "She is rather striking in a gentrified way," Emily mused. After a moment, she came up with an idea. She got up out of bed and pulled a picture frame from their stash of wedding presents.

"Why don't we put the picture in here and put it on the dresser? That way you can look at her the first thing every morning." Emily offered.

"Are you sure? " Matt responded with surprise.

"Oh yes," Emily replied. She could sense he liked the idea. She put the picture in the frame and set it on the dresser.

"What do you think?" she asked as she stepped back to view it.

"Good," Matt replied, "Thank you."

Emily smiled in return while the two looked into each other's eyes.

After a moment, Matt observed, "It is getting to be time to go to the fields. They're going to need all the help they can get."

"Okay," Emily responded, satisfied. This was by far the most Matt had ever shared of himself. She felt warmed by the intimacy. The last 24 hours brought a new closeness to them. *It must be what it means to be husband and wife*, she thought.

CHAPTER 9

It was soon after the wedding that Emily started feeling sick in the mornings.

"I can't imagine that you would know you are pregnant, so soon after the wedding," Louisa mused while sitting with her daughter at the kitchen table. "We've barely cleaned up from the wedding."

"I'll call the doctor in town for an appointment. It is probably just a bug," Emily replied.

Louisa laughed, "A bug that only acts up in the morning? I have had enough babies to know when it's the flu or when a new bundle of joy is on the way."

"Are you ready to be a grandmother?" Emily teased.

Louisa got up from the table to pour some coffee. "What does Matt think?"

"I didn't mention anything to him. He's been working so hard to save the sugarcane that I think he hasn't noticed my behavior being any different," Emily contemplated.

"Dear, you've still been a perfect angel. Why would he notice anything different?" Louisa replied lovingly.

Emily stood up from her chair quickly and then slowly removed her apron. "We still don't know for sure, but I think...I think, I hope it's true."

Louisa stood while taking a last sip of her freshly poured coffee. "You know if it's not...It's only been a short time since the wedding. The two of you have plenty of time."

"Well, the suspense is killing me. I'm going to try to get an afternoon appointment," Emily exclaimed, and then gently asked her mother, "Would you drive with me? I'm sort of nervous."

"Sure," Louisa replied, "I can't wait to hear the news myself."

The farm's people united to save the sugarcane from the impending floods. Matt helped in the fields from sunrise to sunset to move the rising water in the trenches away from the tiny sugarcane stalks. It was estimated that 25% of the crop was lost and the remainder was in poor condition. Pilot said he doubted whether the sugarcane would ever stand properly, meaning machinery would eventually have trouble cutting it. The last 2 days brought good news as the rains finally subsided.

When Emily and Louisa returned to the farm, it was time to get supper ready. Louisa went to the big kitchen to check the progress for the evening's meal. Meanwhile, Emily was preparing the meal at the big house.

"Hi sweetheart," Pilot addressed Emily, as he came through the kitchen door.

"Hi, Daddy," Emily replied with a big smile. She resumed her singing as she moved back and forth between the sink and stove.

"Is this just honeymoon joy, or is something special going on?" Pilot asked.

"What do you mean?" Emily answered with a question.

"Never mind. Your husband will be in shortly. He caught the last truck back to the farm. I saw him cleaning up, as I was driving around checking on things," Pilot said as he moved toward the stairs. "I'm going to get ready for supper, honey, I'll see you in a bit."

"Okay," Emily replied and kept singing as she prepared the family meal.

Matt came through the kitchen vestibule. He sat down before entering the house to remove his boots. Emily recognized his heavy thuds hitting the wooden floorboards and knew he would be inside shortly.

After removing his boots, he opened the kitchen door. He looked to see who was in the kitchen. When he saw it was just Emily, he addressed her.

"'Evening," Matt said as he moved toward her to observe what she was cooking.

"Hi," she replied as she resumed her cooking. Then at once, she grabbed his hand a placed it on her stomach.

"In 9 months, we're having a baby," Emily said with a smile and then returned to the cooking.

After a brief pause, Matt asked with a confused look. "How?"

Emily blanched quickly and moved a pot from the stove to the sink. She poured some hot liquid down the drain and placed the pot on a hot plate.

"I know it happened quickly. Mama and I confirmed it with the doctor today," Emily explained.

Matt looked straight into her eyes and said, "It's good." and gave her a half smile and turned toward the stairs to get ready for supper.

"Matt!" Emily said sharply.

Matt stopped and looked toward his wife.

"Are you really happy about this?" she asked as she touched her stomach.

Matt nodded once and then continued up the steps.

Emily sailed through pregnancy without much difficulty. Even the morning sickness went away a short while after the first visit with the doctor. She was able to continue her normal activities all the way up to her 9th month. She did not show much. The baby lay nestled in her wide hips, allowing her great mobility. However, in her 9th month, the baby decided it was really time to grow 2 weeks before the due date and she found it a challenge to get out of an easy chair.

Finally, the baby was born. It was a boy! He was named Jesse Pilot Smith. Emily noticed Matt came alive when he held the new baby. Much in the way he came alive when handling the animals. He made little baby sounds to entertain the newborn. Jesse smiled brightly when his daddy picked him up to be held. Could he really tell who was who at this age, she wondered?

"Well son, you look tickled pink to be a new daddy," Pilot quipped as he entered the bedroom where Emily lay with Matt sitting at her side holding the infant.

"Yes sir," Matt replied, looking up to Pilot. Then he looked down at the baby's face, while he slowly raised to his feet as not to disturb the infant. Then, he gently moved Jesse to his grandfather's big chest.

Pilot was beaming as he cradled the baby close. "It is amazing how small they are this young and then how fast they grow from this point," he said as he looked at his daughter.

He held the baby a while longer and gently lay him into his mother's arms. "Well, I best be moving on now," Pilot said with a smile. "I am so proud of the both of you. You will be fine parents." Pilot then left the room before the couple had a chance to reply.

It was not long after baby Jesse was born that Emily was back on her feet, bustling around the house, helping Louisa with the household chores. She had one of the farm ladies help with Jesse, so she could assist her mother with farm responsibilities.

The family business continued to grow as small planters gave way to the larger ones. There would be more farm hands to feed and house.

Just shortly after Jesse's birth, Emily began feel an upset stomach in the mornings. This time Emily knew she did not have to go to the doctor. She was pregnant. Matt took the news in stride, with little reaction when Emily informed him of the latest event to be. She pressed, "Are you disappointed that it's so soon after the first one?"

"It's good news," he replied and gave his wife a short nod.

Louisa was not so easygoing with the news. "It's mighty hard on a woman to go through it again so soon. I'm worried about you," she said with furrowed brow.

"No need to be," Emily retorted, "I hardly knew I was pregnant the last time until just before the baby was born."

"I find that hard to believe," Louisa replied with a smile.

"It's these wide hips," Emily said, as she patted her pelvic bones, "By the way, from whom did I get these cow birthing things?"

Louisa answered with a chuckle, "If you haven't noticed, mine aren't so narrow, but you are built a little bit bigger than me."

It was true. Emily was a larger and younger version of her mama. Both women were strikingly beautiful. Louisa had small streaks of gray running through her thick golden brown hair and Emily carried a youthful glow cast from the same mold.

Just under 10 months from the day that baby Jesse was born, Emily gave birth to baby Jay. His given name was John Pilot Smith.

Emily did not get pregnant so soon after Jay was born. Instead, it was three months from his birth that Emily again announced that she was with child.

"You are just a regular baby machine," Jack teased as Emily informed the family of the news. "But you better start having some girls, or you'll get a reputation for being partial to little boys."

"Just as long as she or he is healthy," Emily quipped in response. She was clearly happy.

"Being with child sure seems to make that girl happy," Pilot observed with amazement.

Matt said it was good news. Like his wife, he seemed to get great joy learning that he was going to be a daddy again.

"Matt, are hoping for a little girl this time?" Jack asked.

Matt shrugged, "Either is okay."

The baby again was a boy. Emily wanted to name him Matt after his daddy, but Matt wasn't so agreeable for a change.

"One Matt's enough," was all he said. Emily did not press him. She wanted the baby's daddy to be pleased. She named him William Pilot Smith. This seemed to make her husband happy.

A year later, baby boy number four was born. His name was Louis Pilot Smith. The year after Louis was born, Matt and Emily celebrated the birth of their first daughter, Candace Pilot Smith. Shortly after she was born, Emily began to call her Sally, because family members kept referring to the baby, as "Candy" which did not please the once again new mother. However, Candy was the nickname that stuck, so Emily finally gave in and agreed to refer to her daughter as "Candy."

"She just doesn't look like a 'Sally', she is just the sweetest thing," Pilot would say.

After 5 years of marriage, Emily and Matt had five small children. Both parents were pleased. The big house was a very lively place these days.

CHAPTER 10

Pilot was showing Robert to his car after the two were through conducting business in Pilot's office in the big house. His grandchildren were on the back lawn with their mother, enjoying the late afternoon sun. Robert stopped and turned to look at the little ones playing gently with their mother.

"They are a beautiful sight, aren't they?" Pilot commented as he stopped beside Robert to share his gaze.

"They should have been mine," Robert replied in a low hushed voice.

"Pardon?" Pilot replied.

"I said, as they should be. They have a beautiful mother." Robert said with forlornness.

"That, she is." Pilot agreed.

The two men shook hands one last time and Robert drove off to his own plantation headquarters.

A few months later.

"Haven't you found anything yet?" Robert bellowed to the man sitting in front of his desk. "Where has all of my money been going? Why can't you find any information about this little hick farmhand."

"As a matter of fact," Oscar mused, attempting suspense, "I may have something for you."

"Well, what is it? Out with it!" Robert exclaimed.

"I kept coming up with dead ends, when I had the farms in the area checked out," Oscar started to explain.

"Out with it!" Robert shouted.

"So I started looking beyond our backyard," Oscar said, keeping his composure. "Our boy is from back east."

"You idiot!" Robert swore, "That's what the punk has said all the long! Tell me something I couldn't have figured out myself."

"I found his mother," Oscar stated.

"Well, that's a good start," Robert responded. Then he reached and grabbed the notes from Oscar.

"It will be quicker to read your report than to listen to you babble all night." Robert said, irritated with his subordinate.

Robert sat at his desk and began to read. After a short while, a smile began to appear on his face. "Good work," he said as he leaned back into his chair. "I think it would be a good time for a mother-son reunion."

"It will be arranged," Oscar assured.

"I want you to keep on digging. I don't care what it costs. I want to hang this man by his toenails! Do you understand!" Robert said, regaining his foul mood.

"Yes sir. I'll get right on it," Oscar replied, as he left his office.

He was being paid handsomely by this guy Lamond to lead the investigation to dig up anything in Matt Smith's past. Oscar was to be the man responsible for ruining Smith. It would be logical, since everyone knew that he hated the man for stealing his cushy high paying job with the Pilots. He did hate Smith, but he didn't think he hated him as much as Lamond did. Oscar preferred to settle things man to man, not in the sneaky manner in which Robert Lamond was getting his revenge. However, Oscar wouldn't complain, because he was being paid well for hiring the best detectives in the parish. The job was easy and profitable; two things Oscar could not resist.

At the big house, the children had been put to bed for the evening. The rest of the family, Pilot, Louisa, Jack, Emily and Matt were relaxing in the TV room after one of Louisa's delicious suppers.

There was a knock at the front door. It was unusual for guests or any of the farm's workers to knock at that entrance. People who knew the family were accustomed to using the back door, as was the norm.

"I wonder who that could be?" Louisa questioned as she rose from her needlepoint to answer the caller.

When Louisa opened the door, there stood a woman, 5'8" with dark brown hair tied behind her head in a neat bun. She wore a dark blue suit, black low-heeled shoes with a small matching purse. The woman looked behind her as she saw a dark sedan drive down the Main Road toward the State Road. Quickly, she returned her attention to Louisa.

"May I help you? I don't think we have ever met," Louisa said with a friendly smile.

The woman returned her smile, which looked familiar except it was steely cool. "My name is Elizabeth Steele. I am here to see this young man." She thrust forward a picture for Louisa to regard.

Louisa gushed lightly with a smile, "Sure, you came to see Matt. Come right inside."

Louisa led the woman to the TV room. She started to introduce the woman to the family, but the woman would not wait.

"Julian?" the woman whispered, as she gazed at Matt.

At that moment, Matt rose from his place on the couch next to Emily and stood speechless. The woman started toward him slowly, but Matt retreated toward the back of the room.

"Get away from me!" Matt shouted in a whisper.

By this time, all the family was alarmed and on their feet.

"What's the matter Matt?" Emily asked with concern.

"Please. Get her away from me!" Matt retreated further from the woman, backing into a nearby chair, knocking it over on its side.

"She's the woman from my dream." Matt whispered as his gaze left the woman for the first time and went to the floor. Quietly, Matt slid down the back wall until he was sitting. Bewilderment and horror were on his face as he stared hard into the floor.

"Maybe you'd better go," Emily said to Elizabeth as she knelt by her husband's side.

Louisa lead Elizabeth to the kitchen as Jack, Pilot, and Emily tried to console Matt. Their efforts were futile. Matt continued to stare at the floor and seemed unaware of their presence.

"I think we better get him to bed. He doesn't look well," Pilot directed.

The three helped Matt to his feet, but they had to carry him to the bedroom where they promptly laid him into bed under the spread.

"I'm going to call the doctor," Emily said as she picked up the receiver next to the bed. She phoned the doctor and urged him to come immediately. She apologized for the late hour, but this was an emergency.

"The doctor said he would come right away," Emily said as she set down the phone onto its cradle. "Can you two stay with him? I'm going to see who this woman is."

"Sure, sweetie. We'll be right here if you need us." Pilot assured.

Emily went down stairs to the kitchen. Louisa and Elizabeth were seated at the kitchen table, when Louisa rose to greet her daughter.

"Sweetheart, I think you better sit down with Mrs. Steele and I to talk," Louisa said with grave concern in her voice.

"It's Elizabeth, please," Elizabeth replied with an icy half smile.

Emily took a seat across from Elizabeth. "Who are you?" Emily demanded evenly.

Without missing a beat, Elizabeth replied, "Julian is my son."

"His name is Matt. Besides, Matt has a picture of his mother on our bureau. That woman is slightly older and doesn't look like you."

"Is that so?" Elizabeth answered evenly.

"I'll go get it, so you can see for yourself," Emily said with conviction. Still, she had a sick feeling in her stomach, as she rose to fetch the photograph.

When Emily returned. She placed the picture in front of Elizabeth to view. Elizabeth glanced at the picture and smiled fondly at it.

Quickly she reported, "This is my mother in-law. She and Julian were very close. The last time I saw Julian was at her funeral. She died very suddenly."

"This can't be," Emily said. Then regaining her composure, she asked, "Why would he tell us his name was Matt if his name was really Julian?'

Elizabeth smiled with ice on her breath; "Matt was my mother in-law's favorite son. He died in a car accident just before Julian was born. My mother adored both Matt and Julian. It was as if Julian took his place."

"Why would Matt deceive us like this? It just does not make sense." Emily said perplexed.

"I don't think he set out to do it on purpose, dear," Elizabeth said, "A lot of terrible events transpired in Julian's life before he left. It is my guess the stress of it all got to him and then took the best of him."

"How can you say that? Are you saying my husband is crazy?" Emily gasped with irritation.

"No. Not crazy," Elizabeth started to explain, "Perhaps confused. Yes, I should say that's a better label for it. Let me explain the events that happened in Julian's life before he left."

"I think that might help, sweetheart," Louisa said, trying to comfort her daughter.

"Okay," Emily sighed, "I'll try to keep an open mind."

"Very well," Elizabeth continued, "Julian and I were close in an odd sort of way, but in a different relationship than he had with my mother in-law. His father and I divorced when he was fairly young and my job took me away from him. My mother in-law, along with a slew of nannies, raised him to be a fine young boy. She was with him almost from the first day he was born, so they developed a certain fondness for each other. When he was older, he went away to the finest boarding schools. I think he may have resented me for sending him away. However, I believed it best for him.

After college, he joined a company and quickly became a buyer of investments for them. He was very successful and widely respected. He and I would do business together on many occasions. I'm a stockbroker with a large firm. Things were going well for him. Later, I accepted a job in St Louis. It was a good opportunity for me. My other son and family lived in St. Louis, so that made the decision to move more attractive. About the same time, a relationship of Julian's went sour. He was saddled with a huge mortgage and car payments. That would not have been so bad except the stock market took a big dive and Julian's company's investments went south along with his own portfolio. Needless to say, his superiors were not happy and they needed a scapegoat, so Julian was fired.

"It wasn't long before the bank was ready to foreclose on all his assets. The night before Julian was to lose everything, we got the call that my in-law mother suffered a massive heart attack and died."

"That sounds so awful," Emily said disbelievingly.

"You see, in just a short period of time, Julian went from prosperity and happiness to being broke, alone, and ruined," Elizabeth explained.

"I guess it would be similar if I lost the farm and my family," Louisa commented, "That had to be a lot for a young man to handle all at once."

"Shortly after my mother in-law's death, we had a graveside service and Julian disappeared soon after she was laid to rest," Elizabeth said. Emily thought she almost detected sadness in her voice.

"I hired the best professionals to find Julian. After two years, I gave up the search. I thought he might be dead. You know now that he is legally dead, he's been missing for so long. That's the story."

"Well, he's not dead. He is very much alive," Emily replied. "Tell me what he was like back in those days."

"Julian was lively, he enjoyed life so immensely. He was extremely animated, quite charming, and ambitious. Everyone liked him," Elizabeth answered.

"That doesn't sound like Matt. He's quiet and sweet. He's devoted to the children and me. He thrives on hard work and exercise." Emily replied.

There was a knock on the kitchen door. It was the doctor.

"I'm sorry for the delay. I was sound to sleep when you called and had to dress," he said with a low chuckle.

"Thanks so much for coming. I'll take you to Matt," Emily said, leading him past the kitchen to the steps.

Louisa stayed with Elizabeth in the kitchen.

"You know you have grandchildren, don't you?" Louisa said with an awkward smile.

"Grandchildren?" Elizabeth said with surprise.

"Why yes, five," Louisa answered holding up five fingers.

"Umm," Elizabeth said contemplatively.

"You don't seem pleased," Louisa said with concern.

"Oh yes, I am. I'm just surprised. I didn't know what to expect coming here. I guess I didn't expect grandchildren or a wife for that matter, but it's just fine, I assure you," Elizabeth said without fluster.

The doctor came from examining Matt and summoned the family with Elizabeth to the main parlor.

"Matt has suffered some sort of breakdown. He will need to be taken to a facility up state tomorrow morning, so he can get the help that he needs to get well. The doctors there will need to ask you questions about his recent behavior and history," the doctor explained.

"I give the family my deepest apologies," Elizabeth said, addressing the family.

The doctor turned to Elizabeth. "Please don't feel responsible. If you didn't trigger this something else would have. Let's just be thankful it happened at home with loved ones. He was just a time bomb waiting to go off. Now he can start his road to recovery."

Emily and Pilot showed the doctor to the door, thanking him for making the trip.

The family was still in the main parlor talking amongst themselves, when Pilot and Emily returned. Elizabeth moved to address Pilot and Louisa.

"I'll need a taxi to get to a hotel in town. Can you help me get one?" Elizabeth inquired.

"Don't be silly," Louisa retorted, "There's more than plenty of room here. You're welcome to stay as long as you like. After all, now you're family."

"I must admit that I'm exhausted and I graciously accept your invitation," Elizabeth replied.

"Good. I'll show you to your room" Louisa replied.

The next morning, Matt was transported to a mental hospital in northern Louisiana. It was a long trip from the farm. Matt made the trip with Emily, Pilot and Louisa. Elizabeth went along in a separate limousine. It was a long trip with little conversation.

The hospital was hidden in a suburb of a good-sized city in a neighborhood of modern homes. The institution was seen tucked in a large grouping of trees that bordered the grounds. On top of a knoll, a single story building sat along a comfortable stretch of greenery and flowerbeds. It looked restful and peaceful.

Matt was placed in a room by himself. He remained dressed in city clothes and was seated in a chair by a window overlooking a grassy hill. However, Matt didn't seem to notice. He was as despondent as he was the previous night.

The family met with Dr. Hopkins who would be Matt's presiding physician. Dr. Hopkins had a technician show the family the premises, so they would have a better idea of where Matt would be living for the near future. The doctor asked to meet with Emily and Elizabeth privately to discuss Matt's history and probable causes that brought him to the hospital. The two discussed the past several years with Dr. Hopkins, while Pilot and Louisa walked along the hospital grounds.

When the interview was completed, Dr. Hopkins walked the two ladies outside to meet Pilot and Louisa. While Emily went to join her parents, Elizabeth took Dr. Hopkins aside.

"Excuse me for doing this, but I did not feel comfortable discussing this with my daughter in-law present," Elizabeth said in a low tone.

"Sure, I understand. What is on your mind?" Dr. Hopkins asked.

"This may not make a difference and I'm inclined to think Julian's new family may not know this," Elizabeth paused for a short moment, "My son Julian is homosexual. At least he was before he came to the Pilots."

"I see," Dr. Hopkins answered, without much surprise.

"I don't think that would change, would it?" Elizabeth inquired.

"It is extremely doubtful, unless he had leanings to change before he became ill." Dr Hopkins explained.

"I know for a fact that he did not have those leanings," Elizabeth replied, "We had many discussions on this very subject."

"If this is true, then your family is in store for some great pain," Dr Hopkins surmised.

CHAPTER 11

Pilot, Louisa, Emily, and Elizabeth stayed in a nearby hotel for the night after leaving Matt at the hospital. Shortly after breakfast the next morning, they went back to the hospital to see Matt. However they were advised that he wasn't to see visitors until some time of observation was completed.

"Do you want to stay a few more days, sweetie?" Pilot asked his daughter.

"I want to, but I have to get back to my baby. It's too soon to be away from her too long."

"We will come back real soon if Dr. Hopkins agrees," Pilot assured.

From the farm, Emily called several times daily for the next week to check Matt's status. Still, there was no change in his condition.

After a week, Dr. Hopkins telephoned to speak with Emily. "I'm concerned that there hasn't been any change in his condition. However, I am reluctant to use any strong drugs at this point to accelerate his progress."

"What do you suggest we do?" Emily asked.

"I'd like for you and his mother to come for a visit in the next week. Perhaps being with the two of you, he'll feel safe enough to come back to us," Dr. Hopkins said.

"We will be there tomorrow," Emily answered.

Pilot drove the two ladies up state the next day. Again, the long trip was marked with silence, as each person had dread and hope on their minds.

When they got to the hospital, they were seated in the lounge until Dr. Hopkins could see them. Shortly, he invited his guests into his office.

"I'd like for you, Mrs. Smith, to see him first," Dr. Hopkins said, "I'm trusting that he will be glad to see you."

"Sure," Emily agreed.

"We will see how it goes and then we will plan our next step," Dr Hopkins explained.

Emily knocked lightly on Matt's door. After a short pause, she gently opened it. As she entered, she could see that Matt sitting by the window in a chair. He was staring at the floor and not through the window.

"Matt, honey, it's me," Emily said with her sweetest voice. She entered the room and pulled up a chair and seated herself beside Matt.

"Matt, can you hear me sweetheart?" Emily asked.

Silence. He did not acknowledge her presence.

"Matt, I know things are tough, but we can get through it, dear," Emily offered.

Silence.

"Matt, we want you to come home sweetie, but you have to get better first," She paused. "You know I love you. The children love you. We're all waiting for you."

Matt continued his stare at the floor, expressionless. After a few more minutes, Emily got up to leave.

"I'm going to say goodbye for now, but I'll be back. I promise," Emily said as she kissed his forehead. Then she left.

When she got back to Dr. Hopkin's office, she sat down next to Elizabeth. Dr. Hopkins entered the room.

"He did not respond to me, doctor. It was as if I wasn't there, " Emily informed.

"I know. We were observing him. I'm quite disappointed as I know the two of you are," Dr. Hopkins said as he sat at his desk.

"I want to bring the mother into his environment. It was her shock that spurred his state. Perhaps she is the catalyst to his recovery." Dr. Hopkins explained, "We can't begin any treatment until he starts to talk. If the mother does not have any effect, we will have to try something more aggressive."

"I'm ready at any time," Elizabeth offered.

"Okay, let's go," Dr. Hopkins said, rising to his feet.

"Would it be okay if I observed with you, Dr. Hopkins?" Emily asked hopefully.

"I don't see why not," Dr. Hopkins replied.

The three walked to Matt's room. With confidence, Elizabeth crossed the threshold. She stopped when Matt turned his head to look at her. Instantly he rose to his feet.

"Keep away from me!" he shouted in a hoarse whisper.

Matt scurried to the furthest corner of the room. "Go away!" he cried.

He threw a pillow in Elizabeth's direction. Briefly, he searched for something else to hurl at her. When he went to grab a nearby chair, the nurses came to restrain him. Dr. Hopkins came into the room and quickly lead Elizabeth into the hallway. Almost instantly, Matt became limp and gave up his struggle. Restraining was no longer necessary.

Dr. Hopkins ushered the two women back to his office. "We will check on him later, but I think he will be fine. Are you okay?" Dr Hopkins asked Elizabeth.

Emily was not interested in consoling Elizabeth. "Doctor, is this a set back for Matt?" Emily asked.

"No, not necessarily. He responds to his mother which is better than what he was doing," Dr. Hopkins said. "I believe he will come out of this. He just needs to feel safe enough here to do it. It's my guess he's terrified to face the reality of his pain."

"I guess that's good news," Emily said hesitantly.

"Julian will fight," Elizabeth deadpanned.

"We have some sweet and charming men and women on our staff. They will work with him this week to assure him that this is a safe place. I believe he'll start to listen," Dr. Hopkins explained. "I want you, Mrs. Smith, to come next week for a visit. Bring some of his favorite cookies or some sort of gift that he would appreciate. Mrs. Steele, it may be a little while before you should see him again, but I assure you that day will come."

Dr. Hopkins showed the ladies to the door when the phone rang. After a few quick words, he said, "Mr. Smith is fine. He is seated in his chair as he was earlier."

"Thank you, Doctor," Emily said.

"Yes, Doctor, keep in touch," Elizabeth said as the two left his office.

The week after seeing Matt wore slowly for Emily. She remained agitated as something was on her mind. She went to Elizabeth's room where she was making her bed one morning.

"Why did you come here?" Emily asked.

Sensing confrontation, Elizabeth still easily kept cool. "To see my son, dear," Elizabeth replied.

"Did you ever think that he may have not wanted you to see him? If he did, I'm sure he would have contacted you." Emily said, starting to pick up steam.

"Surely, being a mother yourself, you are constantly concerned for your children," Elizabeth answered. "I did what any mother would do to see that her child was safe."

"I learned that being a mother means putting my child's interests ahead of my own. Clearly you have not. He can't stand the sight of you. You should not have come, your intentions were purely selfish and you've ruined everything. I just hope things can be repaired," Emily said with hostility.

"Dear, your life with him was meant to be a brief destiny. It was only a matter of time before it was to end. You will see," Elizabeth answered with coolness.

"What can you possibly know? You know nothing of my life with Matt," Emily replied tartly.

"That may be true, but I do know my son." Elizabeth smiled a half-icy smile. "I didn't want to be the one to tell you this, but you are going to find out soon nonetheless. Perhaps the sooner you know, the better." Elizabeth sat on her bed and patted a place next to her for Emily to sit.

"I'll keep standing. Say what you want to say," Emily demanded.

"Very well," Elizabeth said. Without pause she started her explanation, "My son is a homosexual."

"Ha! That's a good one," Emily snorted, "Just look at his five children and you can really tell he is a homosexual."

"Let me finish," Elizabeth challenged coolly. "Julian lived with a man he met in college for several years before he left. The man dumped him for a young female, his boss's daughter, to further his career. That was one of the things that drove Julian to the edge. Before this young man, Julian had one or two other boyfriends. He had always been comfortable about his sexuality. He told me many times that he no interest in females. I spoke with Dr. Hopkins and he said that he did not expect that to change once Julian got better."

"You told this to Dr. Hopkins?" Emily asked in disbelief.

"I felt obligated to tell Dr. Hopkins all the facts, so Julian's progress would not be impeded," Elizabeth explained.

"What you say may or may not be true, but I know my husband loves me and our children. We had a good life until you intruded on us," Emily said as she started to leave.

"For your sake dear, I hope you are right and Julian will want to come back to be with you and the children," Elizabeth replied.

"You can count on it," Emily answered. As she exited, she turned. "By the way, his name is Matt until he says differently. He was Matt before he went into the hospital."

After she left the room, she went downstairs into the kitchen where she found her mother, tending her chores.

"I thought I heard loud voices, or at least one," Louisa inquired.

"That woman is a vindictive witch," Emily replied.

"Mrs. Steele? I don't know about that but she sure is on the house line a lot," Louisa commented.

"Who is she talking to, when she's on the line?" Emily asked.

"She says she is talking to her office. If she's not calling them, they're calling here. She also is tying up your daddy's other line," Louisa said accusingly.

"Do you want me to talk to her?" Emily asked. "We have real honest relationship," she quipped.

"Oh no, dear," Louisa said, retreating, "Remember, she is your mother in-law, so she is family. We should give her what she needs if we can."

"I'm not sure I agree with that, but that's fine for now," Emily said. "I have to check the baby, she will want to be fed." She kissed her mother's cheek and went back upstairs.

Pilot sent the limousine for Emily to make the trip to the hospital. Dr. Hopkins wanted her to bring a gift for Matt, but she couldn't think of what he would want. Matt was not impressed with gifts. She did think he might like to see the baby, so she brought Candy along on the trip. Perhaps it would give Matt some joy to see one of his children. She did not want to subject her other children to the hospital, fearing it may frighten them. The children and the horses were the only things she knew that consistently brought a smile to his face.

When Emily and the baby arrived to Dr. Hopkins office, she could see he was surprised to see the infant.

"This is Matt's gift," Emily explained.

"Very well," Dr. Hopkins replied, "Let's hope this cute little thing makes an impression on him. There still has not been any change."

When Emily and the baby entered Matt's room, he was sitting in the same chair, but staring out of the window instead at the floor. She sensed that he was growing more comfortable with his surroundings.

"Matt, I brought somebody here to see you," Emily said brightly. "She has missed her daddy very much."

Matt did not respond to their presence. Emily took a chair beside him with the baby cradled in her lap.

"Matt, please talk to me," Emily pleaded. "The only way you can come home is to respond to us here at the hospital. The children really miss you and they need you very much. I want this baby to know her daddy. She has only been with us for a short time. Please Matt, talk to me."

Slowly, Matt turned his head to face her. His eyes moved gently down to where she was holding the baby. Tears started running down his face and he began to cry softly.

"Oh sweetie, everything is going to be alright," Emily assured, "There is nothing we can't get past."

Quietly, Matt raised his face to meet her eyes. His sobs had stopped.

"I'm so sorry," he said.

"You don't have to be sorry," Emily replied, "I understand, really."

"Thank you," Matt said, wiping his tears.

"I brought you a gift," she said, gently offering him the baby to hold.

He took the baby and said, "She's beautiful. She lessens the pain."

"Are you okay? Do you feel pain?" Emily asked with concern.

Matt answered, "I am so very tired." He handed the baby carefully to Emily.

"We should let you rest," Emily said as she rose. Matt slowly nodded his head and looked over to the bed.

"Matt, I'm very proud of you," Emily said beaming. Matt gave her a weak smile and got himself up to go to bed.

Emily headed for the door.

Matt called quietly, "Come back soon." Emily smiled in response and left the room. Dr. Hopkins led her back to his cluttered office.

"I still haven't gotten my new secretary," Dr. Hopkins offered to explain the mess. "I see we had some good luck. You know your husband well."

"I'll be staying a the hotel not far from here. I don't know how long I can stay. I have small children at home," Emily said as she found a spot to sit.

"It won't be necessary for you to stay after tomorrow," Dr. Hopkins advised, "Mr. Smith has a lot of work to do to get better. You might be a distraction. However, there will be a time in the near future, when he could see you more often."

"Are you sure this is necessary?" Emily asked with disappointment.

"Your husband his been under enormous pressure. Although families are a great source of love and support, they can be a source of pressure," Dr. Hopkins explained.

"I think I get the picture, you mean his mother," Emily said with disgust.

"Matt isn't able to make decisions for himself at this time. When he can, he will decide when and who he will see," Dr. Hopkins ruled.

Emily had something on her mind. "Doctor, I'm going to be direct with you. I insist that any visiting rights his mother has be revoked until he asks to see her. I am the legal party responsible for my husband and I'm holding you responsible for his emotional safety."

"I understand, Mrs. Smith," Dr. Hopkins answered. "I am well aware of the recent impact she has had on him. We will keep him safe, I assure you. That's what this hospital is all about, keeping its patients safe, so they can get well."

"Thank you, Doctor," Emily said as she rose to leave with the baby who was sound asleep. "I will return in the morning, before I leave for home. I promised him I'd come back soon."

"That will be fine," Dr. Hopkins replied. "Good-day."

After Matt slept a few hours, Dr. Hopkins paid him a visit. He knocked on his patient's door and entered. Matt sat up in his bed.

"I hope you had a nice nap," Dr. Hopkins said in a pleasant tone. "Let me introduce myself. My name is Dr. Hopkins."

Matt nodded to affirm his presence.

"Why don't you come sit down with me for a little chat," the doctor said, pulling two chairs across from each other.

Slowly and carefully, Matt got out of bed and sat across from Dr. Hopkins.

"Do you know where you are?" Dr. Hopkins asked.

Quietly, almost in a whisper Matt answered, "I assume I'm in some hospital from the looks of this place."

"You are in a mental hospital in upstate Louisiana, just outside of a large city," Dr. Hopkins informed him. After a short pause he asked, "How do you feel?"

After a few moments Matt answered, "I feel a lot of pain. It hurts to talk. Things seem jumbled in my head."

"Where is the pain?" Dr. Hopkins asked with concern.

Matt put his hands on his chest, just underneath his breast. "It's burning. My feelings hurt," Matt tried to explain. "I'm really tired."

"Okay, let's just talk for a few more minutes," Dr. Hopkins said. "Do you remember your name?" he asked.

"I'm not sure," Matt said, "It hurts too much to remember, but I don't think it's what that woman called me...Matt."

"Very well. While you are awake, try hard to remember your name for when we talk tomorrow," Dr. Hopkins prodded. "You'll be getting some medication for the pain. It will start to lessen over the next couple of weeks. The nurse is also going to give you something to help you rest."

"Thank you," Matt said. Dr. Hopkins got up to leave.

"I'll see you tomorrow," he said with a smile.

After the doctor exited, Matt got back into bed. A few moments later, a nurse came in with a pill. As the doctor promised, he relaxed and faded off to sleep.

"How was he?" Elizabeth asked when Emily came through the door.

"Better," Emily answered as she handed the baby to her nurse. "He actually spoke some."

"Really?" Elizabeth responded with surprise. "Why did you leave so soon? You had the baby with you."

"The doctor said he wasn't to have anymore visitors until he gave the 'Okay'," Emily answered.

"Well, this is good news, "Elizabeth said smugly.

At that moment, the phone rang. It was for Elizabeth.

"Your work sure keeps you busy," Emily commented, "Even a few thousand or so miles from home."

"Yes. Most of my work is phone, so I have been lucky not to miss too much; perhaps just a few luncheons and cocktail parties," Elizabeth said with a cool smile.

"You can call the doctor," Emily offered. "I'm sure he could give you better details than I could."

"Thank you," Elizabeth said. "I think I will call."

"I'd better check on the children," Emily said as she headed for the stairs.

Elizabeth made a couple of short phone calls. Then, she went to check the mail for her latest documents.

The next day, Matt showered and was dressed when Dr. Hopkins came to visit. The male nurse insisted that he start a daily hygiene routine.

Dr. Hopkins stepped into the room. Doctor and patient sat in the same chairs as they did yesterday.

"How do you feel today?" Dr. Hopkins asked with a smile.

"The same as yesterday," Matt answered. "I slept good."

"Good," Dr. Hopkins replied. "Did you think about our little assignment?"

"Yes," Matt answered, "My name is Julian; Julian Smith."

"Very good," Dr. Hopkins replied. He was very pleased. "What else do you remember?"

"That sweet lady yesterday with the baby, she called me 'Matt', " he explained, "It's rather confusing."

"How is it confusing, Julian?" Dr. Hopkins asked with interest.

"I am not sure. I think she is close to me and that was my child," Julian answered and then added, "I'm really tired."

"I think this is enough for today," Dr. Hopkins decided.

"Doctor, am I crazy?" Julian asked, perplexed.

"No, not in the least," Dr. Hopkins assured him. "You are a very confused man. The reason you're so tired is your mind is working very hard to keep you from remembering your past. It is protecting you. It will have to work extra hard to let you remember a little at a time, so you will have fatigue. When the medicine starts to work, the pain will lessen and your mind will feel less panicked about you remembering the past."

"Maybe I don't want to remember," Julian said sadly. "Were things really that bad for me?"

"From what I understand, the last few years were pleasant, so we will concentrate there first," Dr. Hopkins replied. "Nothing is insurmountable. You will get past all of this trouble."

"I hope so, especially if I have a small child waiting for me," Julian said.

"Where is Elizabeth?" Emily asked. "I've been taking phone messages for her all morning.

"I don't know," Louisa answered as she finished making a sandwich for lunch. "She rode off in a limousine, just before breakfast this morning."

"She didn't mention going to town?" Emily asked as she started to make her own sandwich.

"I doubt it," Louisa replied, "She wouldn't need a limousine just to go to town."

"You don't think she went to the hospital, do you?" Emily asked as she paused from making her sandwich.

"I couldn't tell you," Louisa replied. "But that woman does live by her own rules."

"Well, I'm going to phone the hospital just in case she decides to pay a visit," Emily said as she rinsed her hands.

She dried her hands and then picked up the receiver to call Dr. Hopkins. When Emily had him on the line, she was brief and to the point.

"Doctor, I have reason to believe that Matt's mother is on her way to see him," Emily warned. "She should be arriving after supper some time."

"We'll be ready for her," Dr. Hopkins assured her. "This sort of circumstance is not unusual."

"Fine. I will check with the night nurse this evening to see how Matt is doing," Emily said and then hung up the phone.

"Are you going to worry about this all day?" Louisa asked as she bit into her sandwich.

"Probably," Emily said as sat down across from her mother.

Candace came in without knocking.

"Hi dolls," she said, "Why so glum?"

"Oh it's nothing. I'm just being silly," Emily said and then asked, "Can I make you a sandwich?" She rose from the table to wait on her.

"I guess now that you're up that would be dandy," Candace said as she sat next to Louisa. "And an ice tea would be delightful."

"Sure," Emily replied.

"How is your husband?" Candace asked.

"He's doing better, thanks for asking," Emily answered.

"Will he be coming home soon?" she inquired.

"Oh, I think it will be quite a while," Emily replied. "He's dealing with some weighty issues."

"Such as...?" Candace prodded.

"For one thing, dealing with his mother," Emily quipped, "He's scared to death of her."

"Is that so," Candace pondered, squinting her eyes.

"Matt is going to be just fine and he'll be back with us before we know it," Louisa concluded.

"I hope you're right, Mama," Emily replied. "I hope you're right."

"How are you today, Julian?" Dr. Hopkins asked.

"Miserable," Julian answered.

"What's making you miserable?" the doctor asked.

"It hurts to remember," Julian replied.

"What have you remembered?" Dr. Hopkins inquired.

"I remember a big white house," Julian started, "I remember the woman who visited me in the big house as my wife, Emily. There are small children. I know each of their faces." Julian paused.

"That wasn't so bad, was it?" Dr. Hopkins encouraged with a smile.

"No, but its seems strange to me," Julian said with his head in his hands.

"Yes," Dr. Hopkins prodded.

"There was this nurse who helped me make my bed, sort my laundry, and a few other little chores," Julian said as he sat back into his chair. "He was very sweet and I noticed him as handsome. This was a slight surprise."

"How was it a surprise?" the doctor asked.

"Well, I realized I was gay, but it wasn't earth shattering," Julian replied, "It was as if I really didn't forget. It is sort of like an old shoe. I didn't think about it so much, because it has always been a comfortable fit."

"But you did forget," Dr. Hopkins commented and then asked with a confused expression, "How do you feel about being a homosexual or gay as the term you used."

"I feel comfortable with it," Julian responded, "I suppose I always have. It seems strange," he added after a few minutes of thinking.

"What seems strange?" Dr. Hopkins asked.

"How does being married with a child fit in with me being gay?" Julian asked, looking to the doctor for insight.

"I suppose you might have put it aside for while," Dr. Hopkins offered.

"I find it hard to believe that something so inherent as sexuality is something you can just put aside for a while," Julian said, not comfortable with the doctor's suggestion.

"Well something of that nature must have happened." Dr. Hopkins pushed the issue. "Unless you and your wife had some sort of arrangement, because I think that would be hard to keep secret very long."

"You said the past few years have been pleasant for me," Julian remembered. Then a very sad expression came over his face. "Dennis," he blurted.

"Dennis?" Dr. Hopkins asked.

"Can we stop now?" Julian asked, "I suddenly don't feel so good."

"Just a few more minutes," Dr. Hopkins insisted. "Who is Dennis?" he asked.

"Dennis hurt me very badly," Julian said sadly. A tear rolled down his cheek.

Sensing that Julian had enough for the day, Dr. Hopkins decided that it was time to wrap things up. "I can see why you would put sexuality to the side if remembering a failed relationship brought that much pain. I want you to sit with this a few days. Talk to the nurses about it, if you wish. You're making great progress, Julian," Dr. Hopkins finished with a smile.

"I demand to see my son, now!" Elizabeth said firmly.

"I'm sorry Miss, but there are strict instructions that he have no visitors," the desk nurse repeated.

"But I'm his mother," Elizabeth said with conviction, "Get me your boss."

The desk nurse went to seek the hospital administrator on duty. A man accompanied the nurse back to her station.

"May I help you?" he asked.

"Yes. I'm here to see my son. I just spent 10 hours in a car to see him."

The administrator read Julian's file. "There are specific instructions that you are not to see him. This file says specifically that today you are not to see him. Perhaps you can come back tomorrow, when the doctor is here."

"This is absurd," Elizabeth said unrelenting, "Get the doctor immediately. I know you can page him."

Reluctantly, the administrator paged Dr. Hopkins and handed Elizabeth the phone, when he was on the line.

"What seems to be the problem, Mrs. Steele?" Dr. Hopkins asked pleasantly.

"They won't let me see Julian, Doctor," Elizabeth said coaxingly.

"I'm afraid that is not possible at this time, Mrs. Steele," Dr. Hopkins replied.

"Doctor, I have waited for years to talk to my son, surely you can understand my position," Elizabeth said, stating her case.

"Yes I understand, Mrs. Steele," Dr. Hopkins said with sympathy, "Try to hold on a little longer, until Julian is strong enough to have visitors. A few more weeks is not much longer, considering the amount of time you have already waited."

"Can these people ask Julian if he will see me?" Elizabeth, trying to strike a compromise.

"Ordinarily, we ask the patient if he will accept a visitor. However, his wife has strictly ordered that you are not to see him. We have to abide by her wishes, as she is his legal guardian, unless, of course, you get a court order to change her status."

"I see," Elizabeth said, realizing she had lost the battle. She hung up the phone and abruptly left the hospital.

"Why would you not let me see him?" Elizabeth demanded to know.

Emily was sitting with Marge and Louisa in the kitchen, when Elizabeth entered the big house.

"Because he has not said he wants to see you," Emily answered, unflustered.

"I rode all the way out there and it was your order that prevented me from seeing him," Elizabeth accused.

"Had I known you were leaving, I would have told you not to waste your time," Emily said in defense. "I have to do what I think is best for my husband, until he can decide for himself. My intention was not to hurt your feelings."

Elizabeth decided to take a different tack, which she hated, "When will I be able to see my son?"

"I tell you what," Emily said in an effort to quell her mother in-law, "I'll ask him if he will see you the next time I visit him. That should satisfy you."

"No, but I guess it will have to do," Elizabeth replied. She went in to the parlor to make some calls.

After a few minutes, Marge wandered into the parlor. Elizabeth set down the receiver after checking for messages at her office.

"I have been wanting to meet you," Marge said, sitting in an adjacent chair from Elizabeth.

"Is that so? Why?" Elizabeth asked, as she checked her makeup.

"Is it true you are an important business woman from back east?" Marge asked in slight awe.

"I guess I'm important to my clients," Elizabeth replied.

After a few moments, Marge said hesitantly, "I'm sorry about your son. It must be hard for you."

"Well, thanks for your concern," Elizabeth said in response.

"I like Matt. He's one of the few people here that I feel comfortable being around for any length of time," Marge explained.

Elizabeth smiled.

"I can't understand why she won't let you see your own son," Marge commented.

"I suppose she thinks she's protecting him from big bad Elizabeth," Elizabeth said jokingly.

"I can see why you would be angry with her," Marge said meekly.

"Well, it's been rumored that I have been known to eat my young," Elizabeth said matter of factly. "I'm not really mad at her. I believe she has Julian's best interests at heart. I just did not get my way. I'm not used to that."

"You don't seem so scary," Marge said.

"Well, I am," Elizabeth said with a smile. "I must get back to my calls," she added, picking up the phone.

"Can I come visit you some time?" Marge asked as she got up to leave.

"Anytime, dear," Elizabeth replied as she dialed.

"I'm a sugarcane cutter," Julian told Dr. Hopkins one day.

"Is that right?" Dr. Hopkins replied with a smile.

"Yes. My family and I live in a big white house with my wife's mother and father, Pilot and Louisa," Julian added.

"It sounds like you've broken a lot of ground," Dr. Hopkins said rather pleased.

"I suppose," Julian replied. After a short pause, he added, "I still am confused how I came to be married with five kids."

"Perhaps that memory will come in time," Dr. Hopkins advised. "We have to be patient with ourselves."

"Do you suppose she knows I'm gay?" Julian asked his doctor.

"Who?" Dr. Hopkins asked, stalling for a little bit of time.

"Emily," Julian responded, "Do you think she has any idea?"

"Well, I don't know," Dr. Hopkins answered, sounding perplexed.

"I need to find out," Julian announced. "I'm going to ask her when she comes to visit."

"Are you sure that's a wise idea?" Dr. Hopkins asked calmly.

"She has to know at some point if she doesn't know already," Julian replied. "I don't remember a lot of things, but there is one thing that I do know. I am not a deceiver or a liar."

"How have you been doing?" Emily said as she entered Julian's room.

"I can't really tell," Julian replied, "I feel so drugged."

"I suppose the drugs are to help you get better," Emily said, trying to sound encouraging.

"You are right as usual," Julian said, smiling lightly.

"You seem talkative," Emily commented as she pulled a chair next to Julian's.

"Really?" Julian replied surprised.

Taking on a different note, Emily asked, "I promised your mother to ask you if she could come to see you."

Julian paused and started to fidget. "I want to wait until I remember her."

"I see," Emily replied. She decided to change the subject, as she noticed Matt feeling a little stressed.

"Tell me about the progress you've made," Emily said to regain the light mood.

"I'm remembering things; especially about life on the farm. Beyond the past few years I remember bits and pieces," Julian replied, relaxing into his chair. He then asked, "We were happy, weren't we?"

Emily smiled, "Yes we were."

Julian nodded reflectively.

"I will be moving to a different ward soon," Julian said, "I'll have a roommate and start group therapy."

Emily imagined that this would be tough for her husband. "What do you think about it?" she asked.

"I'm nervous, but Dr. Hopkins believes it will help in my recovery," Julian answered.

"I noticed your name on the door says Julian Smith," Emily said awkwardly. "Do want to be addressed as Matt or Julian?"

"It doesn't make a difference," Julian replied, "At this point, I remember more about myself as Matt." Julian paused. "Whatever you feel comfortable calling me suits me fine."

"It seems strange after all these years to think of you as somebody other than Matt," Emily said as she shifted her weight in her chair.

"There is something I want to ask you," Julian said gravely and then paused.

"What is it Matt?" she asked, but she somehow knew the dreaded question he was going to ask.

"This may surprise you or it may not, but I don't remember how we dealt with this," Julian said, trying hard to concentrate. "Did we ever address my homosexuality? I can't seem to remember how we handled our intimate moments."

"We handled it well," Emily replied tensely.

Julian seemed to relax. "I wasn't sure you knew about that part of myself. I don't know if I used to keep things from you, but I feel compelled to be as honest with you as I can."

"You always did your best to be honest with me, Matt," Emily replied with a tear running down her face. "Your fine, quiet character attracted me to you, as we got to know each other."

"I remember clearly life before we were married, but the last few years are not so clear," Julian stated, still concentrating.

"Do you remember our wedding day?" Emily asked softly, trying to keep her composure.

After a few seconds, Julian responded. "It rained," he said and laughed lightly.

"Yes," she said, joining in on the laughter.

After a few minutes, Julian said, "We get along pretty well, don't we? Did we always get along so well?"

"We did, but it was different," Emily replied quietly. "You were always so quiet and sweet. I think it was impossible not to like you."

"I guess I haven't been so quiet today," Julian said with a light smile. "I suppose it's the drugs."

"No, I don't think so," Emily said somberly.

Emily and Julian talked awhile longer, mostly about the children and what they had been doing. Then Julian was tiring, because he fought so hard to remember things. The last few years seemed to have been pleasant and Julian was anxious to remember them.

During the next few weeks Julian worked hard in individual and group therapy. He liked having a roommate and the opportunity to talk to other patients on the ward. Julian started to smile more often and he became relaxed enough to tell some jokes, dated as they were.

Visits from Emily were frequent. On one trip she brought their oldest son, Jesse. Julian shed many tears as he hugged and kissed his son. Mother and son knew that his daddy was a different man, but then Matt was more animated with the child than at any other time. Emily was afraid this might frighten her son, but he was happy to see his daddy.

"You've remembered a great deal the last few weeks, Julian. You should be proud of yourself," Dr. Hopkins admonished.

Julian was pleased with the praise.

"I am concerned that you've remembered very little before the Pilots came into your life," Dr. Hopkins said gravely. "Why do you think this is the case?"

Julian's mood turned somber. "So far, what I have remembered from that earlier time period is pain," he said.

"You look really sad now," Dr. Hopkins observed. "How come?"

"I don't want to remember life before the Pilots," Julian explained. "Why is it so necessary?"

"It was your efforts to forget that brought you to the hospital," Dr. Hopkins said gently. "Do you agree covering up the past was no longer working for you?"

"If I want to leave this place, I have to remember," Julian agreed.

"I can understand why you would like it here," Dr. Hopkins surmised, "It's a safe place. There are caring people around you. The amount of attention you receive has to feel good."

"I eventually want to leave the hospital," Julian exclaimed. "I think most of the patients want to be able to leave some day."

"Then why the resistance to uncover the past?" Dr. Hopkins asked.

"I am afraid of it," Julian said coming to tears, "I know it was painful. I'm terrified of facing the pain."

"You have taken the first step in recognizing that there was a lot of pain," Dr. Hopkins encouraged. "You are a strong man, Julian. Your will to survive, your fellow patients' support, and the staff are all here to help you."

Julian was bawling. "I know these things. It's just hard to do."

"You can do it," Dr. Hopkins admonished, "Remember that you are in a safe place."

"I promise to do the best I can," Julian said, wiping his eyes. He continued to cry for a few more minutes. Then he stopped. He knew what he had to do.

CHAPTER 12

It was several weeks before Julian would see any family members. He fought through the pain and depression. He did not want anybody to see him in such a weak state. He would not accept any phone calls. He did develop several friendships with patients who were also dealing with their own traumas. Julian discovered he was not alone anymore and could trust other people. His new friends and he shared a common bond, which was to heal past mistakes and experiences. Together, they chose to move on with their lives. He realized he would never see any of them again once he left the hospital, but for now he depended on them for their deep and caring support.

After a long time period, Julian remembered his past. However, the pain would not go away quickly. He remembered losing everything in his life and then fleeing the pain to live on the Pilot Plantation. Now, his two pasts, the life before the Pilots and life with the Pilots fit together. However, it would be some time before he could figure how the future would bring together his pasts.

"Julian," Elizabeth said as she entered the ward meeting room.

"Hello, Elizabeth," Julian answered as if he had just seen his mother last week. He got off the couch to greet her. He gestured for her to walk with him down the corridor.

"How are you?" She asked.

"Fine. This is my room. I have a roommate," Julian replied as they entered his room, "Have a seat," He gestured to the desk chair, while he sat on the bed.

"It's definitely not luxurious," Elizabeth remarked.

"It's not what you are used to, but maybe you should try it sometime," Julian said evenly.

"I've waited a long time to see you," Elizabeth said.

"I couldn't see you while I was weak," Julian said. "I wouldn't have been a formidable opponent for you. It just wouldn't have been a fair match."

"I didn't come here to fight with you, Julian," Elizabeth said with a half smile.

"Why not?" Julian asked. "Fighting is what we do best."

"Why do you have to put me through such misery?" Elizabeth asked staring intently at her son.

"Oh come off it, Elizabeth," Julian replied. "It's not as if you have ever used kid gloves with me. Besides, you know I adore you nonetheless."

"I see you've softened these last few years," Elizabeth responded.

"Don't get used to it," Julian warned with a little smile. "Remember, I am sick."

"Why did you keep me away so long?" Elizabeth accused. "You must have known that I've been waiting for you."

"It was enough to see you this time, dear," Julian replied. "The doctors must have been scared to death of this meeting. I'm drugged up, I know I won't remember this visit."

Elizabeth bristled softly. "And I was prepared to be on my best behavior."

"You've never been one to care too much about how you behave," Julian replied.

After a moment, Elizabeth answered, "You are probably right."

"Have you worn out your welcome at the Pilot's" Julian asked.

"I am sure I did after the first week," Elizabeth said seriously without smiling.

"I see it hasn't kept you from staying these past months," Julian replied.

"No," Elizabeth answered. "I see it as my son's home, so I figured I could stay as long as I'd like."

"What do you think of my wife?" Julian asked coolly.

"She's fine," Elizabeth answered. "A bit protective, don't you think?"

"It is her motherly instinct," Julian replied. "Maybe you could learn something from her."

"I'm sure I have some other redeeming qualities," Elizabeth answered, unashamed.

"What do you think of your grandchildren?" Julian asked with a sly smile.

"They seem to be sweet little things," Elizabeth answered, disinterested.

"Do you know them by name yet?" Julian chided.

"Of course," Elizabeth answered with a half smile. "Name recall has always been one of my strengths."

"When are you leaving this cheery place?" Elizabeth asked as she looked at all four green bare walls. "You seemed to have regained your memory."

"I have to mourn the loss of my lover, my adoptive mother, going broke, losing my home, most of my worldly possessions, and lack of family life," Julian answered matter of factly. "Then, I'm free to go."

"It happened so long ago," Elizabeth commented. "Can't you just get over it? Why the fuss?"

"Because it's unfinished business," Julian explained.

"Well you don't have to worry about being broke or losing your little love nest, thanks to me," Elizabeth said with a light smile. "You had options on all your stocks and they came back after the crash a few short weeks after you left. They turned a handsome profit. You had so much red tape at your office; they could not easily sell the stock and options you bought for them. This in turn, made a nice lump sum for them."

"The red tape was in place, so not just anybody could trade their investments," Julian explained.

"It was a smart move, for their sake," Elizabeth said. "They looked for you for months after you left, because they wanted to dump those stocks. By the time they gained court orders to trade them, their value had skyrocketed." Elizabeth shook her head. "God must watch out for fools."

"Who cares?" Julian said, disgusted.

"Well, your penthouse is paid in full, just waiting for you to come home," Elizabeth said. "And you have a good chunk of cash in the bank." She turned her head and stared into her son's eyes slyly and smiled. "I guess I'm not such a bad mommie after all."

"You can have all that money for all I care." Julian turned away from her. "Second thought, keep it in the bank. My children can use it for college some day."

"As you wish," Elizabeth replied.

"Are you going to still be at the farm when I get home?" Julian asked.

"You are not seriously considering staying there, are you?" Elizabeth said in disbelief.

"Why not?" Julian asked, puzzled.

"Julian, that place is barbaric," Elizabeth said seriously. "I came here to bring you home. Our home. Our city. Civilization."

"I have a family waiting for me," Julian said defensively.

"Dear, I know what you like and it sure isn't her type," Elizabeth said smugly. "Besides, those little children will grow up fine. They are always so giggly and happy."

"Save it, Elizabeth," Julian said, staring into the wall.

"We can discuss this at a later date," Elizabeth said, rising to leave.

Julian turned and looked hard at his mother. "I will make up my own mind," he said slowly and succinctly.

"I cannot understand why I have to live in a half way house before I can go home," Julian argued.

"Julian," Dr. Hopkins answered, "You suffered a major breakdown, which has taken months for you to recuperate."

"But, why?" Julian started.

"Please, let me finish," Dr. Hopkins said firmly. "You have not experienced the outside world for some time. It's not unusual for patients to forget the pressures of everyday life. Try to think....try hard to think of the hospital as a haven that protects you from the harsh world. You have to make a gradual transition to normal life. In your circumstances, you have a lot of responsibility to consider. I want you to ease back into it. Also, you will be returning to a small town that has different feelings toward homosexuals than this big city."

"But nobody knows I'm gay," Julian replied.

"You may choose to keep it that way, but these are the choices you will have to make," Dr. Hopkins said with concern. "When you return home, it will essentially be the end of your treatment. You won't have the resources you have here. Of course, you can always telephone me."

"I like to think I'm a reasonable man," Julian replied. "I am just afraid my children won't remember me."

"Then just think how much fun it will be for them to meet their father all over again," Dr. Hopkins answered with a smile.

Julian returned the smile. "I will do as you ask. You know I trust you with my life and I respect your advice. I look forward so much to going home, it's hard to always listen to reason."

"You won't be disappointed," Dr. Hopkins assured him. "Look at it as a continuing step in your progress."

After a few weeks of living in quiet quarters, Julian was ready to go home. Pilot, Emily and Elizabeth brought him back to the farm.

"Welcome home," Emily said as they got out of the car.

"Where are the children?" Julian wondered out loud as he looked toward the house.

Emily smiled at him. "I'm sure they're inside playing where it's cool."

Julian moved quickly toward the big house, forgetting his belongings. Pilot smiled as he watched him go inside the kitchen door. He took the suitcase from the trunk of the car and went with the others toward the big house.

"Matt!" Louisa exclaimed. "It's so good to see you home." She gave him a quick embrace.

"It's good to see you to, Louisa," Julian said, returning her hug.

"I know you must be anxious to see the children, so I won't keep you," Louisa said, sensing his urgency.

"Where are they?" Julian asked.

"They're in their playroom with the nanny," Louisa replied.

Instantly, Julian moved toward the hallway and up the stairs. When he came to the playroom, he could hear the quiet play of his young children. Careful not to startle them, he opened the door quietly. He went in the room slowly. The oldest boy Jesse, sitting on the floor, turned and faced his daddy.

"Daddy!" Jesse exclaimed with great surprise. The boy jumped up from playing and ran to his daddy. Julian lowered himself, so he could meet the little one's embrace. After a short moment, Jay and William ran to greet him. The boys tackled him and soon Julian found he had three boys sitting in his lap. Louis, sensing being left out, came toddling over to be with his brothers. Julian swooped him up into his arms and gave him a sloppy kiss on the cheek. The little boy squealed with delight.

"It seems you have quite the welcoming team," Jack said, entering the playroom.

"And a welcoming party it is!" Julian exclaimed as he gently tickled little Louis.

"It's good to have you back, Matt," Jack said seriously. "We've all missed you, though maybe not as much as the boys did." He gently lowered himself to his knees to be with the boys and their daddy.

"Uncle Jack, Daddy's home," Jesse exclaimed, falling into Jack's lap.

"I see," Jack replied. "I guess you are glad to see your daddy."

"Yeah, he had to go away for awhile, but now he's here to stay," Jesse said with glee.

"Is that so?" Jack replied, looking over to Julian.

"You bet!" Julian said, "Daddy's staying right here with his boys and little girl."

He rose, gently shedding the boys from himself. He wanted to see his daughter. The nurse sat quietly in a rocking chair, with baby Candy in her arms asleep. How she had grown, he thought. His boys must have grown several inches. Suddenly, he mourned the time he had missed with his children. The nurse, sensing his remorse, stood and handed the baby Candy to her father. Julian carefully took her into his arms as not to wake her. Gently, he lay her head on his shoulder, while she continued to slumber.

Jack presented some toys to the boys to keep them occupied, as he stood up to walk over to where Julian was standing with the baby. In a quiet voice he started, "You know, Matt, you may have a little talk with Emily to let her know what your plans are."

"What do you mean?" Julian asked, patting the baby on her back as she started to stir.

"Well, you've changed, Matt. It's obvious to me just spending the last few minutes with you. You are not the same person that came to this farm a few years ago," Jack explained.

"Sure I am," Julian argued. "I'm just not as confused as I was."

Jack paused a moment before continuing, "You had a whole other life before coming to us. It was completely different than life here on the farm. Your mother hasn't been waiting for the past several months to see you come back here to live with us. She came to take you back home."

Julian turned and looked Jack in the eyes. "This is my home; here with my children and my wife. I'm not going anywhere."

"Well, you may want to convey that message to your mother and the family," Jack advised.

"Okay," Julian replied, nodding his head.

After spending some time with the children, Julian left them to their playing and made his way to the front porch where he assumed the family would be. As soon as he opened the screen door to the porch, a man came flying into his arms and heartily embraced him.

"Oh, Julian, you're alive!" the man said, hugging him and sobbing on Julian's shoulder.

"Papa, it's okay, I'm fine," Julian said, assuring the man.

"Bernard, stop blubbering over the boy like a fool, he's just getting home," Elizabeth scolded.

"It's okay Elizabeth, I'm fine," Julian interjected, releasing his father.

"How could you not tell me that you found Julian!" Bernard accused Elizabeth.

"That's just it," Elizabeth explained. "I found him, or was led to him. I figured Julian had his reasons for privacy and that he would let you know where he was, when he chose to tell you."

"He obviously was not capable of notifying me," Bernard bellowed. "You should have let me known."

Before Elizabeth could retort, Julian interrupted, "Enough, you two!"

"Why don't we leave father and son alone to get aquatinted," Candace said, putting her arm around Elizabeth to steer her away from the confrontation.

"Excellent idea," Bernard agreed. He took his hands and joined them with Julian's. "Oh Julian, you don't know how I waited for this day," Bernard said with tears streaming down his face. "I was so worried...."

"How did he find where we were?" Emily asked, facing Elizabeth, "It didn't occur to me that Matt's father would want to come to see him. Surely you must have had some idea."

"I just didn't think it was my place, dear," Elizabeth explained, "Bernard and I haven't spoken in years. I don't think I even know where he's living at the present time."

"Well, surely somebody had to inform him," Louisa said with shared confusion with her daughter.

"The situation does seem peculiar," Pilot agreed. "Tell us again how you came to find us, Mrs. Steele."

"This man came to my office and handed me a packet with Julian's picture and a plane ticket. He said a limousine would be waiting for me at the airport to take me to Julian," Elizabeth explained. "That's all I know."

"That's exactly what happened to me." Bernard said, joining in the conversation.

"Didn't you two think to ask any more questions?" Pilot inquired.

"The man seemed hurried and I was stunned to say the least," Bernard replied. "All I could think about was finding my Julian after all this time."

Julian was tiring. It had been quite an eventful day with plenty of excitement. "I think I'm going to take a nap," Julian said, intending to make a graceful exit.

"That's a good idea. I'll walk up with you," Emily said, making her way quickly to the screen door.

"I hope you are not too overwhelmed," Candace said with concern.

"No," Julian replied. "I just all of the sudden I feel very tired."

"Well that's understandable, sweetheart, " Louisa said. "I know it's been a big day for you."

"Trying is probably more like it," Elizabeth interjected.

The two made their way up the steps of the big house to their bedroom. It appeared the same as Julian had last seen it before going to the hospital. The room was bright with sheers draping the windows, letting in the sunlight. The bed was neatly made with a fresh white bed spread. Emily looked at the floor, then gazed up into Julian's eyes.

"I thought it would be better for you to have your own room for a while until you got yourself in the swing of things. I will stay in one of the other rooms," Emily said with little expression.

"That's really not necessary, Emily," Julian replied, returning her gaze. "This is your room as well as mine."

Emily gave no reply and let her gaze fall on the bed.

"I want to stay here with you and the children," Julian stated with concern. "You do understand that, don't you?"

Emily sat on the edge of the bed where she usually slept. "Let's see how things go," she said cautiously.

Julian sat on the edge on his side of the bed. "You do want me to stay, don't you?" he asked with a touch of surprise in his voice.

"Of course," Emily smiled. "It's just that so much has happened and I want to take things slowly. We should give each other plenty of space. I don't want to complain, but this whole situation has been hard for me, although I can imagine it has been harder for you."

"I understand," Julian said, getting her meaning. "Forgive me for not being more sensitive."

"I don't expect you to read my mind, dear," Emily laughed. "I just needed to tell you."

Julian nodded with a smile.

After a brief pause, Emily asked, "Were you and your father close? He seems awfully glad to see you."

"No, not really," Julian replied, looking into her eyes. "He gets emotional. Then it leaves his mind, as quickly as it came. It is kind of like the situation never happened. I'm sure he did not think much of me the last several years, until the man met with him. Then it became a crisis."

"That seems strange," Emily mused.

"It is, but both my mother and father are a bit on the unusual side," Julian smiled. "Papa is much like Elizabeth, when it come to his work. It has always been priority in his life to be the most successful financier."

"Did you want to follow in their footsteps?" Emily asked and then added, "You too were a successful financier."

"Yeah, but my motivation was different," Julian replied thoughtfully. "I got a big high from making a big score. I did it to have fun and then I'd party to celebrate. They just want to make more money than anyone does. It is all ego related for them."

Emily thought for a moment. "Why do you call your mother Elizabeth?"

"As opposed to Mama, or Mother?" Julian laughed.

"Something along those lines," Emily replied, waiting for a response.

Julian thought for a moment and then smiled. "After a very brief time of motherhood, Elizabeth grew wary of having children. She clearly was not happy being saddled with two children. She hated the stereotype of being a woman with children. I guess she had my brother and I call her by her first name, so as not to be reminded of what she was. However, as my brother got older, he started calling her Mommie. She hates it. I think he does it to get under her skin."

"You seem to like to get under her skin in your own little way," Emily teased.

"One has to keep Elizabeth in check or she will eat you alive," Julian defended. "You don't seem to have any trouble with her."

"No. However, I'm somewhat more direct with my feelings toward her," Emily laughed. "I guess she doesn't particularly like me."

"That is certainly not the case," Julian smiled. "If she didn't like you, she would simply ignore you. People are competition in her eyes. She must see you as a formidable opponent. That's how you can tell she likes you."

"So people are combative with her, because of her whim?" Emily asked in disbelief. "What if people don't want to play her games?"

"I think you have to be God to have her insults produce no effect upon you," Julian explained. "Most people want her held accountable for what she says and does. If she is not held accountable, she feels she has won."

"Won what?" Emily asked, "So what if she thinks she won by getting no response or a poor retaliation from people."

"You are correct, of course," Julian agreed. "But most people don't take to being humiliated without some sort of retribution."

"You are right," Emily smiled. "Why is your last name different from Elizabeth's last name?" She asked, changing the subject.

"Elizabeth is not her given name. She was born with the name Emma Jones, which she changed when she divorced Papa." Julian smiled as he explained, "Elizabeth Steele sounds more impressive than Emma Smith or Emma Jones according to Elizabeth."

"Why Mrs. Steele instead of Ms or Miss Steele?" Emily asked.

"Again, it's the image Elizabeth is trying to portray," Julian explained. "Mrs. is more distinguished, mature, and reliable than Ms or Miss."

"What happened to her to make her the way she is?" Emily asked with concern, "You said you used to dream about terrible things happening to her."

"The explanation comes from my grandmother and parts come from Elizabeth herself. When she was a very young woman, Elizabeth was quite a beauty. I think she is still very pretty to this day, but not in a feminine sort of way, as she was earlier in her life. Now she is handsome, I think. Anyway she had long flowing brown hair, darker than yours and your mother's. The color now comes from a bottle and has changed as a result. She wore cotton dresses and deep red lipstick. All the boys wanted a date with Emma Jones."

"One day, she fell in love with her high school sweetheart. She was very happy with him, happier than she had ever been. They got married and lived in the country. He decided to fly airplanes for a living and was excited for her to see him fly a plane. So, one day after he got a job flying planes for an airline, he invited her to come to the airstrip. She came to the airstrip only he was already up in the air flying a plane. Another aviator pointed to a plane in the sky. He told her that was her husband flying that particular plane and that he would be landing shortly. As the plane approached it started to malfunction and it crashed on the airstrip right before her very eyes. Needless to say, the sight was devastating. Something changed in young Emma. She didn't grieve with a whole heart. She wanted to be loved again like her husband had loved her. She wanted it desperately, but Emma must have figured she did not deserve it, because she chose mates who were physically abusive. She spent a tremendous amount of time recovering from bruises and would refuse to leave her home. Finally, she decided it was time to make another change in her life. This was the time she met my father. They struck a deal for marriage. He agreed to pay to educate her at any university she chose. He wanted to move up the corporate ladder and a pretty wife on his arm would charm his superiors. Emma was perfect. She was to provide him with two children, hence my brother and I came along soon after they were married, while she attended the university. Also, he insisted she change her first name, so she chose Elizabeth."

"They both kept their ends of the deal. Elizabeth did charm many businessmen into doing special favors for my father, while making future contacts for her. Elizabeth became happy with her newfound success, but she had also hardened as result of past pain. She thrived on her work, but marriage and child rearing got in her way. She considered them tedious responsibilities. She became an overnight success and so did my father. They both got what they wanted. He did not object when she hit him with a divorce. She sent my brother and me off to boarding schools and expensive summer camps. Papa was less than thrilled with the responsibilities of marriage and child rearing himself. The divorce did not cost him anything financially, so he said for her to do whatever she wanted, as long as he wasn't bothered. As she became more successful, she also became more belligerent. That's the Elizabeth Steele story."

"That all sounds so pathetic," Emily responded with a look of horror. "You seem so unmoved by it."

Julian instantly became depressed. He looked longingly out the window from the bed. "I think I'm ready for that nap."

"I'm sorry," Emily said with regret. "That was insensitive of me. Of course it bothers you. It bothers me and I wasn't involved in that part of your past."

"Dr. Hopkins says I should talk when I get in these moods," Julian said slowly, looking forlornly at the spread on the bed, "However it hurts to talk, when I feel this way."

"You can talk to me, Matt," Emily replied with reassurance. "It may be good for you to learn to express yourself."

"Yeah, I know. I just hate it," Julian explained. "I just feel like I missed out on having parents, or some semblance of normal parents. I try to love them for whom they are, but I sometimes wish they could have been different. That's one of the many reasons I love this place so much. I feel your parents have adopted me and it eases that pain. I also want our children to have the kind of parents I never had; the kind you have. I don't have much expertise in that area, but I feel I'm learning from Pilot, Louisa and especially you."

"You are a wonderful daddy and I think it comes very natural to you," Emily replied proudly. "All it takes is a loving and willing heart. The rest takes care of itself. We still won't be perfect parents and we will make mistakes. We can only do the best we can."

"I love you, Emily," Julian said with mist in his eyes. "I hope you believe that."

"I do," Emily answered, standing up from the bed. She came over to his side of the bed and kissed the top of his head. "I think you need your rest. I'll leave you alone. Are you going to be okay?"

"Yeah," Julian replied softly. "I am very tired. I'll have supper in my room when I wake. I've had enough socializing for one day." Then he added before she left the room, "Wake me before the children go to sleep for the night. I'd like to play with them a bit before bed."

"You bet," Emily replied with a smile and then left the room, closing the door behind her.

CHAPTER 13

"Have you heard from that hospital yet?" Robert asked.

"Well, they are just not going to hand over the information," Oscar responded. "There are laws of confidentiality."

"I don't care about those details," Robert bellowed. "That's your problem. I just want the results."

"I understand, but these things take time," Oscar said defensively. He was tiring of his boss's constant tirades.

Robert stood up from behind his desk. He walked to the back of the overstuffed leather chair where Oscar was sitting. The office was grand. It sat in the rear of Robert's family plantation mansion. He lived there alone with a modest staff of servants to tend to the upkeep and cooking. However, only one maid lived in the house. Her quarters consisted of a room off the kitchen. The office was decorated with heavy mahogany paneling to each side of the desk, which sat in the middle of the room towards the rear. A large picture window was the backdrop shaded with white silk sheers. The floor was dark wood, matching the paneling, but was mostly covered with expensive Persian carpeting. The paneling, though very grand, did not take up very much of the wall space. Heavy matching bookcases lined most of the walls except where a wet bar stood against the wall to the left of the door. A camel back sofa covered with material the color of cream was situated against the wall. A bear claw mahogany cocktail table was parked to the center, in front of the sofa with matching ends tables to each side. Several feet between the cocktail table and the desk sat two tufted ox blood leather wing chairs. A swivel high back chair, which matched perfectly with the other two chairs was placed on the other side of the desk. All tables and the desk had heavy brass lamps and very few knick-knacks sitting on their surfaces. A modest crystal chandelier hung from the center of the high ceiling.

This room was where Robert spent 90% of his time when he was at home. He always wore a dark suit and a tie in the winter the months. In warmer times, he would wear a light cream colored suit and a matching tie. Sometimes in the evening, he would dress down to casual attire. He rarely entertained and he seldom did business outside his home.

"The daddy apparently did not create the kind of stir the mommie did. It was more of a mushy reunion," Robert reported.

"I think we hit the jackpot with Mrs. Steele," Oscar agreed. "I don't think anybody else will cause him to return to the crazy house."

"That may be true, but it's worth a try," Robert replied, calmly mulling over his thoughts.

"Don't you have other things to do like making money, instead of concocting ways to ruin this kid?" Oscar asked with defiance.

"I have plenty of money," Robert defended. "Besides, it is none of your concern. You are paid very well to do what you are told."

"You called it looking after your interests," Oscar said, smoothing slightly ruffled feathers. "That's all I'm doing."

"That's true, but it's me who decides what my interests are, not you," Robert said, returning to his desk. He sat in his chair and glanced at some papers.

"Very well," Oscar said, resigning himself to more unpleasant work. "What area do you want me to concentrate on or what direction should I be taking?"

Robert paused a moment before responding, "Get the hospital records. I suspect there will be some useful information in those."

"That will be time consuming," Oscar stated. "I really can't be gallivanting across the country looking for missing relatives if you want me to break into the file cabinets of that institution."

"We'll put your gallivanting on hold for now," Robert responded with his impatience growing. "Just get the records. Can't you slip it to some secretary and get into the necessary office?"

"I'm glad to see you have such confidence in my charms, but I think it may take a bit more than that," Oscar replied with a wide grin.

"I did not mean that, you idiot, use cash if necessary. That's what makes the world go around. However, I don't mean to undermine your prowess if it could be of some assistance," Robert said with slight mockery.

"I'll find a way to get what you need," Oscar assured him. "I always do."

"I don't care what you do. Play every dirty trick you know. Spend the money you need to get me results. Even whore your wares if need be. Just get me those records!" Robert ordered, pounding his fist hard on his desk.

"Good morning, Julian," Bernard said from the breakfast table in the kitchen while sipping some coffee.

"Good morning, son," Elizabeth said, looking from her morning coffee and a two day old *Wall Street Journal*. The parents were both dressed for big business. Bernard, in a three-piece suit with a tie, Elizabeth, wearing her standard blue blazer, matching skirt and hat. "I trust you rested well?" she asked.

Julian did not look rested and he was agitated. "When are you two leaving?" he asked.

Bernard feigned hurt feelings, while Elizabeth took the inquiry in stride. "When you've made your decision, of course dear," Elizabeth answered with a pasted smile. "You need time to get yourself together. There is certainly no hurry."

"I've spent the last 7 months getting myself together and my decision has already been made. There is no need for the two of you to hang around. I appreciate your concern, but I'm fine now. I know the two of you have your lives waiting for you back east," Julian said, unloading the frustration he felt for his parents.

"Perhaps it's best for Julian to come back with me," Bernard decided. "I'll see to it his recuperation is successful. I'll take good care of him."

"That's not necessary, Papa," Julian objected.

"It's amazing after 32 years that you would be so concerned with your son's well being," Elizabeth hissed. "I guess the old saying is not true after all. It is possible to teach an old dog new tricks."

"It was you and that man he was living with that drove him to insanity in the first place," Bernard accused. "Do you really think you know what is best for our son?"

"Enough you, two!" Julian growled. "I am a big boy and all grown up. It seems to have happened when I was at some Swiss boarding school or summer camp in the south of France. Maybe it was Oxford. Whatever the case, I'm staying here with my wife and children, so feel free to pack your bags and scoot."

"Whatever you feel, Julian, you have to admit I have always seen to it that you had the very best. I gave you the finest clothes, food, schooling and everything there was for you to be a successful young man. There was no expense that I shied from to make sure you had all of these things. I cannot leave this place, until I know you are truly safe and have everything you need. It's my duty as a mother," Elizabeth said with forced pride.

"The same goes for me, Julian," Bernard agreed, "You know we only want what is best for you. That has always been the case."

Elizabeth rolled her eyes. "Bernard, please hush up. Your sudden concern for our son is repulsive."

"Elizabeth, please," Julian pleaded.

"Thank you, Julian," Bernard said, coming to near tears. "I agree I wasn't the model parent, but I always had your interests at heart."

"I know, Papa," Julian said, trying to prevent his parents from killing each other. "Stay as long as you wish, I guess," he added, resigning to the stress. "Just please, try to stay out of trouble. And stop fighting!"

"Julian, your father and I disagree. We don't fight. We wouldn't do something so barbaric," Elizabeth calmly corrected her son.

"Certainly not!" Bernard agreed.

"Fine," Julian conceded. "I'm going to bed."

"You just got up!" Bernard exclaimed.

"I have a headache," Julian explained and then left.

After a few moments, Louisa came into the kitchen door. "Is everything okay this morning?" She asked.

"Oh yes," Elizabeth smiled, getting up from the table to refill her coffee cup, "We were just chatting with our son."

"I know you must be thrilled to have him back in your presence," Louisa said with a bright smile.

"Oh yes," Bernard replied, "Julian is the apple of our eyes."

"You're new around here. Aren't you?" Oscar said.

"Well, not exactly. I've been here a few months," the woman answered.

"Gee. I guess it has been a while since I've visited with Dr. Hopkins," Oscar exclaimed, sporting a white coat and donning a pair of big black spectacles resting on his nose.

"Still, I don't believe we've met," the woman replied suspiciously.

"I agree. I certainly would not have forgotten a glamorous woman such as yourself," Oscar said with a mushy smile. He proceeded to sit on the edge of the secretary's desk.

"Doctor, eh....., you are a doctor?" the woman asked with discomfort.

"Yes, Dr. Rogers. And I'm most pleased to meet your charming acquaintance," Oscar replied.

The woman blushed. She shied away from the side of the desk he was occupying. She rolled her chair backward slightly. "Doctor, your mood is hardly laudable. God only knows that I am far from eh...glamorous. You shouldn't humor me so," the woman said with nervousness.

"Ah but you have been misled. Each finds beauty in his own unique way," Oscar boasted, touching the lady's hand.

"You shower all this attention upon me and you don't even know my name," the woman cried, withdrawing her hand.

Oscar suppressed a gasp of irritation, both with himself and with this homely woman. Instead he smiled and gushed, "I was so overtaken with your presence, that I dismissed such shallowness as names." Again he took her hand.

"I must admit, I'm suspicious of your brash romantic inclination, but for the life of me, I can not figure what you could possibly gain from being so nice to me," the woman said bluntly, again withdrawing her hand.

"Well, let's start with names, dearest," Oscar said smugly. "My name is John Rogers, Dr. John Rogers. And yours?"

"My name is Joan Miller," Joan said, looking at her hands in her lap. She was a young woman, but she had an old appearance. She wore spectacles with a costume leash around her neck. Her hair was a short dark brown combed back off her forehead, thick with spray, pasting the curls, which lined her neck. Her face was plastered with makeup, which made one think she was trying to hide something, like acne scars from her youth. She wore a cheap suit, purchased from a local thrift department store.

"Well, Joan......You don't mind if I call you Joan, do you?" Oscar asked. Without waiting for a response, he continued, "I have to admit, I am very lonely. When somebody nice comes along who's friendly, I'd have to be a fool to let that someone get away," Oscar explained, putting his hands in his lap.

"You think *I am* friendly?" Joan asked with disbelief. "I have only rebuffed any overtures you have presented"

"Well, eh...your aura gives off friendly vibrations, I guess," Oscar replied.

"Aura?" Joan asked, wrinkling her forehead. Oscar could swear that her makeup cracked.

After an extra moment he answered, "Yeah, aura."

"Hmmm," Joan said contemplating the situation. "Okay. What do you want?"

"What do you mean?" Oscar said with guarded nervousness.

"I confess I do not have much practice with this sort of thing, but I know enough that you probably are looking for some end to a means. Unless of course, if you intend to flirt here all day long. If the latter is the case, than my boss will be unhappy, because it will be hard to complete my work," Joan said, gaining some unfamiliar confidence.

"Oh, I see," Oscar started. "How about lunch for openers?"

"Okay," Joan said with controlled excitement. "There are several nice little cafes..."

"I thought we'd try the cafeteria," Oscar interjected.

"Here at the hospital?" Joan said, again wrinkling her forehead, which made Oscar wince. He was sure a piece would fall off her face if she moved her skin another millimeter.

"Eh...yes. I hear the food is excellent and I have never had the opportunity to try it," Oscar explained.

"Okay," Joan agreed with caution, " I have to say you are the most peculiar..."

"Are you ready?" Oscar asked as he stood up from the desk.

"Why yes," Joan answered with a small tone of reluctance.

"Great!" he replied as he reached to grab her purse for her.

As they made their way down the hall, Joan commented, "I get the feeling we're in some sort of rush."

"Not at all," Oscar said with a forced smile. "It may take a few minutes for me to settle down...you know...since I'm used to hurrying between appointments."

"That's understandable," Joan replied with a nod. "Then I'm sure you won't mind if I go to the ladies room."

"That's fine," Oscar said, trying to conceal his impatience. "I'll go get us a table."

"Very well, but do you have a pass card?" Joan asked.

"No, why would I need one....What I mean is being staff, wouldn't the clerks know to let us inside?" Oscar inquired.

"Now Doctor, you should know about hospital security," Joan admonished with a quizzical look.

"Well, my hospital is different, I guess. Why don't you give me your pass card and I'll have everything ready."

"Well, I have it attached to my purse, so I won't lose it." Joan said with some agitation.

"I'll keep your purse safe," Oscar said with a broad smile, putting his arm around her.

In an effort to relieve his anxiety, she had him carry her purse with the pass card attached. After she went into the ladies' room, Oscar quickly retracted their steps back to her office. He found the key she used to lock the doctor's office and quietly slipped inside the room. There were several cabinets in Dr. Hopkin's study area. None of her keys worked to open file cabinets. He cursed. He knew he had to find an inconspicuous way to get in the cabinets without the doctor knowing he had penetrated them. "Time for another plan," he thought.

"I'm sorry to have kept you waiting, my dear. I got lost," Oscar said, gushing with regret.

"Doctor, we were only feet from the cafeteria, when I went into the rest room," Joan said accusingly.

As he guided her through the assembly line to get their food, he retorted, "Well doll, it's just that I am a doctor and not a very good navigator."

"You are the strangest man," Joan replied, pushing ahead.

"It took you long enough to get these," Robert sneered as he opened the file.

"I trust you will see that it was worth the wait," Oscar replied with irritation.

"I don't need that tone from you," Robert said, as he sat at his desk. He was grouchy.

"You got what you wanted," Oscar said evenly.

"We will see about that," Robert replied. After a few moment of reading, he smiled. "So our boy is a homosexual. This could not be better."

"Evidently, he's reformed," Oscar retorted.

"It doesn't matter if he is or not. You know what to do, don't you? I'll take care of the rest."

Oscar nodded without a word and left the room.

"I never can get over how long it takes to get the family loaded up," Emily said with a sigh, wiping her brow with her forearm.

"It always takes awhile with small children, dear," Candace responded as she seated herself in the front seat of the station wagon.

"Yes, I know, I really am not complaining, as much as making an observation," Emily explained.

"Well, where is your husband?" Candace asked with a trace of mock irritation. "Shouldn't he be helping?"

"He's inside changing the diaper of your namesake," Emily replied sweetly.

"Shouldn't it be the other way around? You know, you change the diaper and heeee... load the little ones into their child seats?" Candace asked with a little more edge.

Emily did not seem to notice. "Well, he has missed so much with the baby, that he's afraid she'll never bond with him, so he's been spending extra time getting to know her." Emily added, "I wish you would grow to like Matt."

"Whatever do you mean dear?" Candace asked with embellished disbelief.

"Sometimes I feel you don't care for him," Emily explained, as she strapped in the last child.

Candace adjusted her seatbelt. "Remember, I was there with you at the wedding to help you get ready. I was there when each of your babies was born. He seems to be a good boy. Although I hope he realizes how lucky he is to have married you. After all, he was just a worker boy."

"As it comes to be, he probably has bluer blood than we do, coming from high society back east," Emily reminded her.

"Oh, those parents of his are just well dressed snobs," Candace replied with disgust. "They won't even be joining us for church."

"Okay, I have the last one," Julian said, coming out of the big house with baby Candy. "Is everybody ready?" he asked as he handed the baby to Emily. After seeing all were strapped into their seats, including Candace, he got behind the wheel.

"I think we're all set," Emily answered as she took her place in the back seat with the children.

Satisfied the family was secure, Julian made sure all of the doors were locked. With the start of the engine, he put the old Ford station wagon into gear and headed off to church.

The 40-minute ride along the winding country road brought Julian and his family to church for the early service. The churchgoers left behind at the big house would be coming to the later service. The ride was pleasant enough, with both parents working to keep their children happy, and Candace instructing them on the correct parental procedures.

After the family alighted from the station wagon, Robert Lamond went out of his way to greet Emily and Julian. They were getting the children together to put them in their respective Sunday school classes.

"Well, how are you today, Matt.....That is still your name, is it not?" Robert greeted as he graciously shook Julian's hand. Before Julian could reply he moved to Emily, "I know you must be very happy to have your husband back with you after...what 5, 6 months," Robert snorted with a big open smile.

Again, without waiting for response, Robert tousled with the children a moment. "Well, I best be getting inside. I have to get a good seat," Robert said, as he made his way to the front entrance.

"I didn't know Robert went to church," Julian commented quietly.

"I agree. I haven't seen him here in some time," Emily replied while taking the baby up in her arms. "However, the Lord does work in mysterious ways," she added with a smile.

Julian returned her smile, while taking one hand of both Louis and William. Candace had Jesse and Jay within her sight. With everybody set, the Smith family made their way into church.

After putting the children into Sunday school, Emily and Julian, along with Candace, ventured into the sanctuary to be seated for the Sunday service.

"Why don't we sit in one of the middle pews, since it's seems we have our pick today," Candace said decidedly, as she picked the pew she wanted.

"Matt?" Emily inquired as she followed Candace.

"Sure," Julian answered, as he followed his wife.

After the congregation settled into theirs seats, the organ sounded to indicate the commencing of the procession. The choir began singing the opening hymn as they marched down the isle toward the altar. Rev. Samson trailed slightly behind, clutching his Bible with both hands. Julian noted the preacher's white knuckles as he passed by the family's pew.

After a few incidentals and hymns, Rev. Samson settled in behind his pulpit to begin his sermon.

"I start today's message, keeping in mind our responsibility to our church family. When one or more of us has gone astray, it is up to the family to bring this fallen member back. However, first we must send this person away to reflect upon his sinfulness and then welcome him back after he has truly repented of his wrongs," Rev. Samson preached with solemn concentration. He paused briefly to take a long swallow from his glass of water.

"In the book of Corinthians, the apostle Paul stated that there was a great deal of immorality which was poisoning the church. The great apostle was not concerned with so much with the indecent acts. No, he was grieved with the church's growing lack of credibility for spreading the good news. The reputation of the house of God was becoming soiled because of the despicable behavior of some of its members. Paul, in his efforts to cleanse the weakened church, instructed the elders to 'expel the immoral brother." Rev. Samson paused once more as he gazed over the congregation, aisle by aisle. Convinced he had all eyes centered on him, he moved forward with his monologue.

"This is what we must do. When we have somebody within our family who has sinned and who continues to sin, what we have to do is 'expel the immoral brother.' Brethren, we have somebody in our midst who requires this strict church discipline," Rev. Samson proclaimed. He took another gulp of water, while quiet whispers echoed through the sanctuary.

"Matt Smith, please stand," Rev. Samson said with even cadence.

Slowly, Julian began to rise from his pew. Instinctively, Emily rose with him and went for his hand. She squeezed it tightly. A look of shock registered on her face. Candace shook her head slowly in silent disbelief.

Rev. Samson began gently, but with great volume, the explanation of his address. "Matt, as of today, you are no longer to be associated with this church family. Your past behavior proves incompatible with the laws of our church. It has come to the church's attention that you are a homosexual. You have been an active participant in this deviant and sinful lifestyle. I must ask that you leave at once and not return until the church's decision has been appealed and your status reinstated."

The congregation was now in an uproar. Several gasps rose, as Matt, Emily and Candace made toward the exit of the sanctuary. The shock among the church was severe. There was denial among the members. Something this crude could not possibly happen in their church.

In an attempt to regain order, Rev. Samson began to speak. "As you know, normally at this time, we break into a hymn to close the service. However, in light of today's sadness, I am going to ask for all of us to pray for Matt and his family, along the spiritual health of this church. Grief is to be expected when a family member has been stripped from us. Please have faith that God will use all of this sorrow for his useful purpose. Now, let us bow our heads."

After closing the church doors behind him, Julian took several deep breaths, trying to recapture his composure.

"Are you okay?" Emily asked, as she placed her arm around his waist.

"Yes," Julian said, nodding his head. He then looked toward his wife. "How about you?"

"Well, I was a little embarrassed by the attention, but I want you to know how proud I am of you," Emily said with a light squeeze.

"Thanks," Julian replied with a smile, as he placed his arm around her waist.

"I guess you feel humiliated by those awful lies," Candace said with an attempt to console.

"That's the thing, Candace," Julian replied with a chuckle, "They were not lies."

Candace had a slight look of surprise and bewilderment about her.

"The thing that bothers me about all of this is that I feel like am the target of something evil and bad here," Julian said thoughtfully. He then turned to Emily. "Come, let's get the children and go home."

Rev. Samson always greeted his members following his services at the rear of the sanctuary, as they made their way through the doors. Today, most members had something to say to him as they made their exit. Some commended him for his action, because poor character was not acceptable in the church. Others offered their support, with promises of prayer. The last member to shake the preacher's hand was Robert Lamond.

"I most enjoyed your service today, Reverend. It was a job well done," Robert said with a smug smile.

"You got what you wanted, so why don't you leave for another several years," Rev. Samson replied quietly through his gritted teeth.

"I don't know. I feel I may have experienced a rebirth today," Robert mocked with a solemn expression.

"God will get you for the evil you subjected to his children today," Rev. Samson warned.

"Moi," Robert feigned, taken aback by false insult. "It was you, my dear padre, who sent the man out on his duff. I merely imparted my imperial wisdom to you for your taking."

"That was only because of your threats to have the building inspector close this fine structure and make public a few of my past indiscretions," Rev. Samson replied, while starting to turn red in the face. "I'm not stupid. I know what you are capable of doing."

"I always knew you were a smart man," Robert defended with a grin. "You have my word on my promise to keep quiet."

"Son, I will give you pastoral advice," Rev. Samson said in a somber tone. "If that boy has brought hurt to you, let it lie. Remember that vengeance belongs to the Lord alone. It is not up to us to make others pay for the sins that they have brought against us."

"Thank you Padre, for that morsel of thoughtfulness. I assure you that it will not go upon deaf ears. Surely somebody will take heed," Robert replied. He gave the preacher a slight bow of the head and then made his exit out of the church.

CHAPTER 14

After church, Julian and his family arrived back to the big house. There was a contingent waiting for them. Pilot, Louisa, Jack, Marge, Elizabeth, and Bernard were standing on the front porch as the old station wagon roared up the Farm Road.

"Are you ready for this?" Emily asked her husband, as they pulled into the lane that led to the big house.

"We will all be okay," Julian replied with a light smile, as he glanced at his wife.

"Well, we will have to see how the others handle all of this," Candace warned. "They might be concerned about a scandal erupting."

"Candace!" Emily exclaimed with quiet alarm.

"She may have a point, Emily," Julian said thoughtfully. "Tough times for us may just be getting started. Especially if somebody aims to make trouble for us...or for me."

"What do you mean, Matt?" Emily asked lightly, as she got out of the car. She then turned to retrieve the children from the back seat.

Julian lifted the baby from her car seat and replied, "I wouldn't be surprised if Robert had something to do with this morning."

"Matt," Emily replied in a tired, frustrated state.

"I can't believe Robert would do such an aberrant thing," Candace interjected.

"You have to admit," Julian explained, as they walked toward the house, "A lot of weird things have been happening with no explanation."

"What does that have to do with Robert?" Emily asked.

"Well, we both know he hates me," Julian started. "He said in so many words, that he would never let me forget how angry he was and still is that I married you."

"Don't you think he'd be over it after all this time?" Emily asked, now starting to get concerned.

Julian stopped midway up the walk to the big house. "Stop and think for a minute," Julian replied. His mind was racing. "Our wedding, with you getting mysteriously soaked with rain. Then, my mother and father show up here after all these years. He knows I crashed when I first saw my mother and hoped I would do it again when I saw my father. When I managed to keep intact, he was desperate to find something else, so he used his resources to get more information about my past...No, I think somebody at the hospital must have tipped him off."

"How can that be?" Emily asked in disbelief. "What happens there is supposed to be private."

"That's true, but I've been gone from back east so long, surely nobody would remember me. He would have to dig awfully deep to get any details," Julian said, waning in his thoughts. "I guess there is no sense worrying. We will have to see what happens. If it's him, I am sure we haven't heard the last."

As they reached the house, they walked around to the front porch to address the rest of the family. "Candace, would you mind taking the children upstairs, while Matt and I talk to the family?" Emily asked.

Candace hesitated momentarily before replying. "Why of course darling," she said with a smile. "Are you sure you won't need me down here.... I know you're upset."

Emily smiled. "Thanks dear, but I'm among family.... I should be fine." Julian gave the baby to Candace and then looked over the group of people waiting for an explanation.

"Can we all sit down?" Julian asked as he took a chair. " There should be no great cause for concern."

"Sure," Pilot replied as he gestured for the family to take to their seats. "I'm concerned for the two of you and your children."

"Why did that preacher say those awful things, Matt?" Louisa asked with impatience.

"Are you sure you wouldn't like to lie down for a while, Julian, and take up this conversation later? "Elizabeth asked lightly.

"Maybe that would be a good idea," Bernard agreed.

"I would like to know a little about what's going on," Jack said, irritated with the parents' interference.

"Why don't you all let him do what he wants," Marge deadpanned.

"I'm fine," Julian replied firmly. "Just let me get in a few words."

"He's right." Pilot agreed, "Let the boy speak."

After a short pause, Julian began. His eyes were faced to the floor. He looked up to the family. "What the preacher said is true. I have always considered myself to be homosexual. When I came to this farm, years ago, I didn't think about such things, or I didn't feel things. I was deeply depressed, the doctors say. Although I repressed all the hurtful feelings I had, I suppose I was aware of my nature. It was easier to forget everything, including who I was and the feelings I had inside me, as well as the place I came from back east. I remembered some things, but they were somehow mixed with fantasy and reality. Anyway, my time at the hospital helped me remember my background. I still love my wife and children. That much is still the same. I want to be a good father and husband. I am not ashamed of my past life and the one I am currently living. I think it will be better with everything in the open.... No more secrets."

"But these things are so private," Louisa exclaimed. "Why must they be brought out for the whole world to judge things it could not possibly understand?"

"I agree with you, Louisa," Julian replied. "Believe me, this was not my doing. I wouldn't want my wife, children, and the rest of the family to be hurt. I'm glad that you all now know the truth."

"It's just too bad that everyone else has to know, " Jack muttered.

"Let them judge as they will," Pilot retorted. "Who cares what others think? A man shouldn't hide behind secrets. It was not like the boy broadcasted his affairs. It appears someone wanted his business known. So be it. Like he said, he isn't ashamed of anything, so we shouldn't be either. We will stand by him and refute any gossip. Is that understood?" Pilot glared at each of the family members.

"Thank you for supporting my son," Elizabeth replied with a light smile to the patriarch. Bernard nodded in agreement.

"What about the rest of the people who work this place?" Marge asked with sarcasm. "Do you think they will want to leave well enough alone?"

"What do you suggest, young lady?" Pilot asked.

"Tell them the truth," Marge said offhandedly.

"Tell them the truth and surely we will have anarchy on our hands," Jack replied. "People are afraid of things they don't understand."

"I don't think people will ask too many questions," Pilot replied thoughtfully. "I think it would be a good idea for Matt to take aside some of those he's close to and explain his situation. For example, Billy's family. They will then tell folks what they need to know in their own way. Everything will be fine."

"We will see," Jack said, not totally convinced.

"I agree with Pilot," Marge said thoughtfully. "Take each situation as it comes and answer truthfully in a way they will understand."

"What it all comes to, is that Matt is with his family where he belongs," Louisa said firmly.

"He could still come away with us," Elizabeth said, absently nodding toward Bernard.

Julian glared at his mother. "We've been over this, I'm not going anywhere. Especially not to run away."

"Why not? You've done it once before," Elizabeth replied.

"Enough!" Pilot commanded. "You are not helping matters Mrs. Steele, your self interests are not welcome here."

"It was merely a suggestion," Bernard said meekly.

"I only want what is best for my son," Elizabeth replied stolidly, facing Pilot. "Can't you see that he has been through enough with you people? He has had nothing but grief since he arrived at this wretched place. He should return where he belongs."

"If I remember, it was his grief that brought him here in the first place," Jack defended. "The buck has to stop somewhere. I think Matt wants it to stop here. I support you Matt with whatever you want to do, but I do think your place is with your family." Jack reached and patted Julian on his back.

Julian smiled and said, "I'm staying."

"I never doubted it for a minute," Emily said as she glared at Elizabeth.

The next day, things started as they usually did on a Monday morning. Emily got the children ready for breakfast, while Julian dressed to go to work. Louisa fussed in the kitchen to make preparations for the first meal of the day. Elizabeth and Bernard were already dressed in their professional best. They were talking on telephones to their respective offices back east.

"You have a visitor," Louisa said to Julian, as he entered the kitchen. "He's in the side parlor. I'll bring the two of you some coffee and muffins, so that you can talk without missing your meal."

"Who is it?" Julian asked, lightly surprised with his eyes following his mother in-law.

"I don't know, but he is a rather dapper young man," she replied. "Dressed to the nines. I'd say he's come some way to see you."

"Another surprise from the past?" Julian speculated with a touch of sarcasm. Louisa smiled as she shooed him from the kitchen.

"Go on," she said. "See to your guest."

As Julian entered the side parlor, the man stood to greet him. He was just short of Julian's height with a medium build. He had big waves of auburn hair that was parted in the middle and covered most of his ears. His eyes were forest green and shined like marbles. His cheeks were flushed, but seemed to be the kind that were always rosy.

"Hi, my name is Adam Frank," the man introduced himself, as he took Julian's hand.

"Julian," Julian said in return. "Around here they still call me Matt."

"I guess you're curious about my visit," Adam said, as the two men seated themselves in two wing chairs around the large mahogany coffee table.

"I don't recall seeing you before now," Julian said, slightly bewildered, "Am I supposed to have known you?"

"No," Adam replied warmly. "I've only been around these parts a few short years. I'm a pastor of the town's community church just outside the main strip of town. I heard what happened to you yesterday at your church. I want to express my deepest condolences. This situation must have been very painful for you and your family."

"It definitely was not pleasant," Julian replied with guarded care. He was not feeling too comfortable with this visitor at the moment. "How can I help you? I know you must not have come out this way to offer just your kind words."

"Well, largely that is why I have come," Adam countered. "I hate to see God's words twisted in a way that hurts people like yourself. God wants to bring his people close to him, to heal their pain. I understand you have been through some terrific ordeals."

"Word sure gets around quickly," Julian replied absently. "How did your hear about yesterday so fast? How do you claim to know so much about me?"

"That's all people are talking about in town, yesterday and today," Adam explained. "I do try to keep from indulging in too much gossip, but

I need to know what's happening the community. What good is a minister if he doesn't know who needs ministering?"

"This is all private stuff," Julian said with disbelief. "How are people finding out about my personal life? I guess there's talk of my hospital stay."

"This is true," Adam agreed. He seemed perplexed. "Julian, I don't know if you've seen the morning paper from town, but your name is smeared all over the front page. I should say that people have some knowledge of your past life as an active homosexual."

"Why am I surprised?" Julian asked, as he fell back into his chair. "I'm not hungry, but go ahead and help yourself to Louisa's breakfast. She's a great cook."

"Thanks," Adam said, reaching for a muffin. "Like I said, Julian, I want to help. I want you to know that you have a place in our house of worship. Not all of God's people are so quick to judge you. Many want to help and offer support. Our members will support you and your family."

"What kind of church are you?" Julian asked, while he too reached for a muffin.

"We are a bible church, independent of any affiliation. New Testament passages give support to our thinking that churches can have different doctrine in each of the communities, where Christianity is present."

"The bible part makes me think that you people wouldn't be keen on having a homosexual in your presence," Julian surmised. "I'm still the same person I was before I came to this part of the country. I have no intention of changing. I could not change, even if I wanted to be different."

"I'm not asking you to be anything but who you are," Adam retorted. "There's much room in God's house for diversity. If God wanted everyone to be the same, he would have created us from the same mold. It is people who are more comfortable with things that are familiar. God treasures our differences."

"Why is it so important that I come to your church?" Julian asked with suspicion.

"First, to help you and your family in a time of need," Adam explained. "Secondly, and I might add almost as important, our members need to be challenged to accept people different than themselves. This will not be easy for some, but I believe even the skeptics will come around to see the light. It's easy to invite people to Christianity who are like ourselves, but that's not what God has asked us to do. For example, the great apostles had to be convinced to preach the good word to the gentiles.

They did not feel comfortable doing this, because these people had what the apostles thought to be aberrant customs. In short, they were not Jews. Their eyes had to be widened. God has plans for all his people, not just the ones within our circles."

"I believe what you believe, but do all your members accept your teaching? It has only been since yesterday that I was declared unfit to be a Christian. How can you know so soon the parish's attitude?" Julian challenged.

"Many sermons have been teachings about the subject of diverse cultures. There still is a lot of racism, anti-Semitism, and deplorable attitudes toward women. I believe your situation fits in with the subject of bigotry that I would like to see my members get past," Adam explained. He took a drink of coffee while collecting more thoughts. "The deacons and I got together last night. I want the opportunity to act quickly with your situation, for your sake and to take the opportunity to test my members. They all say they hail my teaching every Sunday after service. Will they say the same, when they have to practice what I preach?"

"Does this make my family and me guinea pigs of sorts? I can't put them through more rejection. Can you guarantee that we would be welcome?" Julian asked with skepticism.

"Of course there are always some risks, but I believe them to be small. Sometimes one has to take chances, but ones with favorable odds. When we get burned in life, we still have to fight the good fight and press on to the end. However, we should not be foolish in our judgements," Adam replied.

"I have to ask you again. Would they accept me for who I am without thinking I've been reformed? I cannot be part of a farce," Julian challenged.

"The deacons and I had to reach some compromises," Adam replied. "We will stress to the members to accept what you are. They may think you are reformed, since you have a wife and children and work every day to provide their support. The deacons will want to meet with you in private. Mainly to assure themselves that you are not involved in your previous lifestyle and that you plan to remain faithful to your wife."

"Of course I'd remain faithful to my wife," Julian replied with anger. "But what if I was not married and didn't promise fidelity to her? Would I then be an outcast all over again, if I would decide to court gentlemen over ladies?"

Adam said with a serious look, "I concede that this is a less than perfect solution, Julian. Still, it's great progress in this region if these people can look past your previous life. Your own congregation rejected you for something you were involved with years ago. My people would not only accept what happened during those years, but they will understand that you are still that man, and a very good man. Please be patient, Julian. Change happens slowly, but it still can happen in strides if we keep the pressure to continue to advance peoples' minds."

Julian thought for a few moments. "I'll have talk to my wife about all of this. I'm not sure I agree with all you've said. I have to think it through my mind. I would have to be 100% sure that this is what would be best for my family if I have any hope in convincing her to go to a new church. Her family has attended the Baptist church for many generations, but still I know she will never attend again. In a way, her heart has been broken. People she has known all her life have tossed her from their family. Still, I would like her to have faith in God. She has held so close to her religion all her life. She wants the children to share in her beliefs. Thanks for coming to see me. I hate to be rude, but I do have to get to work."

"Sure," Adam replied, rising to his feet with Julian following his lead. "I have to get going myself."

"Why are you so understanding of my plight?" Julian asked.

Adam slowly smiled and replied, "I have a brother who is gay."

As Julian was showing Adam to his car, he offered his hand in thanks. "I wish you and your members luck. I know they are lucky to have someone like you who is dedicated to their true spiritual growth," Julian said with sincerity.

"I wish you and your family peace and God's speed to heal yourselves. Remember, he was the greatest healer of all time, when he walked this earth," Adam said with a smile, as he closed his car door and fired the engine.

When Julian came home from work that evening, Louisa and Emily were in the kitchen. They stared at him without saying a word, but they had looks of apprehension on their faces.

"What is the matter?" Julian asked. He did not appear to have too much concern for their strange behavior. However, instinctively, he knew the attention to his entry meant for grave news concerning him.

"Nobody in the house has seen this yet," Louisa said, handing him the day's newspaper. "We thought you should read it before the others had a chance to see it."

"Sit down Matt," Emily advised, while she and Louisa each seated themselves at the kitchen table. Julian followed their lead and sat down, while gazing at the headlines.

In bold letters, the caption read, "Homosexual activist exposed at local church service."

"Doesn't that newspaper have anything else to print instead of this garbage?" Emily asked with anger.

"Yes," Julian sighed, as he gently placed the newspaper on the table. "I think they do."

"The rest of the family doesn't have to read this if you don't want them to see it," Louisa offered.

Julian smiled at his mother in-law. "It's okay, Louisa, they are bound to catch wind of it one way or another." He gently placed his hand on the newspaper, while a few thoughts crossed his mind.

"I think that it's time for all this nonsense to come to an end, " Julian stated evenly, gazing at the far wall. He then turned to his wife and said, "It's time I speak to Robert, to see if we can resolve this…" Julian shook his head warily. "This awful mess."

"Robert?" Emily said bewildered, "What's he have to do with all that's been going on with us?"

"Think about it," Julian started to explain. "All these coincidences and events happened at the same time. First, my mother and father appear from nowhere. Then my life story is made public. Then they print a ridiculous story on the front page of the newspaper, where it clearly does not belong. Somebody is out to get us, or me. I have no real enemies except Robert, who hates me."

"Yes," Emily sighed. "I know he hates you. I just can't make myself believe that he would go to these great lengths to hurt you."

"Maybe we should have your father have a chat with him," Louisa said to her daughter. "I know Robert has a great deal of admiration for him.'

"I think I'd better handle this myself," Julian replied. "I should have dealt with all of this hatred years ago." He stood up and said, "I'm going to clean up and change real quick. Then I'll head out to the Lamond place."

After Julian left, Louisa looked to her daughter with concern. "I don't know if it is such a good idea for him to go. He has been under a great strain since he's been back from the hospital."

"I know, Mama," Emily agreed. "But maybe the two of them can work out their differences. If Daddy gets involved, it might just make Robert angrier. We are not even sure Robert is behind all these dreadful occurrences. If he is not, perhaps he can help find out who is."

"That's true," Louisa replied thoughtfully. "I like to think that boy is not involved."

Julian arrived at Robert's house at sunset. He approached the side door. Emily had said that this was the door used by most people. He rapped on it with his fist, just loud enough for someone in the house to hear. After pausing for a few minutes, he knocked again. As he pounded the door, it opened.

"I wasn't expecting you to be the one answering the door," Julian said mildly.

"I gave the help the rest of the night off," Robert sneered, "What do you want?" He turned and walked into the bowels of the dark house. Julian hesitated briefly, then followed him through a long hallway. The house was dimly lit through the hallway, along with the various rooms and parlors. They reached a room at the end of the hall, where the lighting improved. Robert entered and Julian followed.

"Are you still here?" Robert asked in a monotone voice. "Get out of my house."

"We need to talk," Julian said, closing the door behind him.

"There is no one else here, so don't worry about the need for privacy," Robert said with sarcasm.

They appeared to be in an office or study. Robert sat behind a huge dark wooden desk and Julian sat in one of two wing chairs stationed close to the desk's front.

"What is it that you want, in order for you to leave my family alone?" Julian asked gently with little expression. He looked right into Robert's brown eyes.

"I don't know what you are talking about," Robert replied, as he looked away from Julian.

"Come now," Julian said gently. "Now is your chance to get everything you want. Just name your price."

Robert rose and turned his back from Julian. His face was shiny from perspiration. His thin white cotton shirt was beginning to stick to his lanky body. It seemed his black worsted wool pants, black socks, and shoes trapped all the heat from his body.

"Leave town," Robert said without expression. "But you can't take Emily and the children with you."

"Fair enough," Julian replied quickly. "I leave and my family stays, but you have to guarantee no more harm comes to them."

"You would leave just like that," Robert said, turning to face Julian.

"Yes," Julian replied sincerely, "I'm not fool enough to believe that you wouldn't find us if we tried to leave town in order to escape you."

"You give me a lot of credit," Robert smirked, seating himself again.

"You have proven to be resourceful," Julian stated mildly.

There had been a gun sitting on the desk to Julian's left ever since they entered the room. Julian eyed it, as Robert reached easily to pick it up. He pointed it at Julian.

"You know, you deserve to die," Robert said evenly, as he toyed with the gun. "There is one bullet in here. Perhaps it has your name on it."

Emily knew that she must hurry. She put a light bridle on Kelsey and then leaped on top of the horse's back. Instantly, they bolted into a full gallop, with Emily riding bare back. There were many shortcuts to the Lamond place. Riding on horseback would take less time than a motor vehicle. As a crow flies, the trip was much shorter than the roads from the Pilot farm to the Lamond place.

Emily had a sick feeling. She felt her family could be in some sort of trouble. She knew there had always been sparks between her husband and childhood sweetheart. They never had seen eye to eye. Robert was always pulling dirty tricks to make Matt's life miserable. As fate would have it, he never truly succeeded, but she knew the conflict ate at her husband. She did not know what she would do when she got there, but at the same time she could not sit still and do nothing.

As she arrived at the Lamond family mansion, both she and Kelsey were laboring in their breathing. Having grown up with the Lamonds so close by, she had spent a great deal of time playing with the children of the plantation.

Emily knew the place well. She turned Kelsey out to a small pasture close to the stable. Most of the help were in their quarters, so she probably would go unnoticed. However, most everybody knew her since childhood and would think nothing of the visit.

As Emily got close to the house, she felt silly for the rush to be at her husband's side. What if the two men were having a productive civilized conversation, working out their differences, while she came bursting in, perhaps ruining any chance of a truce? She thought about turning around and going home, but the uneasy feeling would not subside. Somehow, she had to be near the two men without being noticed. She would be available if things got out of hand.

She remembered a window in the basement that she and Robert used to sneak through to come and go from the house without being noticed. It was really silly in those days. The house had so many doors, surely they could have escaped through one without too much fanfare. However, the drama of it all was too much to resist. Despite the guilt of intrusion, she pressed on and went to the basement window. It was still kept unlocked! Slowly, she opened it, while it complained with a creak. She crawled inside; resigned to the idea that she would soil her slacks and blouse. Quietly, she made her way up the boarded steps to the main house.

She saw that the door to Robert's office was closed. The halls were so dimly lit that it seemed to be pitch dark all through the first floor of the house. There was a gleam of light coming from the bottom edge of the door. She edged closer to the office door.

"Shoot me if you must," Julian said without any touch of fear.

Robert tossed the gun on the desk and rose, once more facing the back window. Absently, he drew the blind to a close to erase the glare caused by the dark night and laminated study. "That bullet is not meant for you," he said quietly, "Perhaps it has my name on it." He turned to face Julian. "Why don't you use it.... Go ahead, I won't stop you. All your problems would be finished. Big bad Robert removed from your lives."

Julian started to rise. "Robert, I...."

"You stay right there," Robert shouted as he pointed to Julian. "I don't need any of your pious pity."

Dumbfounded, Julian stood without moving a muscle. He did not fear the man, but felt an inclination to listen.

"Emily should have been mine," Robert bellowed. "Those children...those beautiful children should have been born to me." He paused, gritting his teeth in anger.

"You...took....them...all...from....me." He shouted, pounding his fists on the desk. He moved and got into Julian face. "You will pay the rest of your life for this."

Julian replied quietly, "I said I'd give them back to you. Without them, I've lost everything. My life will have little meaning."

"No!" Robert screamed, "It's not supposed to be like this!" Tormented, he grabbed Julian's face between both of his hands and planted a kiss onto his lips. Robert pulled away and gave Julian a bewildered look.

Julian experienced a sense of shock. He felt his blood begin to heat. He found himself wanting to be touched again by this handsome man. The adrenaline that flowed through veins made it hard to temper the increase in his pulse and breathing.

Quickly, Robert pulled him close again and kissed him passionately, this time moving down to graze upon his neck. His long arms pressed Julian into a hard embrace that seemingly forced out what little breath his targeted man had left.

Julian recovered from being awe-struck. He started to return an onslaught of kisses of his own, while beginning to pant with desire. He folded his arms around the tall lankly frame and would not let go.

This man is incredibly hot, Julian thought. He knew this from the first time that he saw him just a few short years ago. *I must have him,* he thought, *I know I've waited for this for so long.* His heart started to race, while perspiration poured from his body. Instantly, the room began to feel like a furnace.

Emotions that were pent up inside their bodies were being forced to escape. Passion, compassion, frustration and plain lust started to crescendo between the two men.

Robert knocked over a table and lamp, as he drew Julian over to a space on the carpeted floor. The two men tumbled onto the floor, rolling on top of the other, with lips, legs and arms intertwined. More sweat poured from their bodies, while they shared breath with quick sharp gasps.

While inhaling and exhaling at a rapid pace, Robert sat up onto his knees and fought to remove his shirt by ripping the buttons. He steadied Julian into a sitting position and urgently assisted him in pulling off his shirt. After putting it aside, he reached for a pillow from a nearby couch and placed it under Julian's head. Frantically, he undid Julian's trousers. He slipped them, along with his shoes, off his legs and feet. With the force that was earlier displayed, he flipped Julian over onto his stomach. He started massaging Julian's rounded buttocks. He studied them quickly, as their shapes contorted with each fresh squeeze and then returned to their perky shape when released. After a brief pause, he stopped and undid his own trousers, pulling them down to his knees. With little fanfare, he placed his erect penis into Julian's fleshy bottom. A forceful push elicited a large painful groan.

"Easy, it needs to be slippery," Julian said while making a pointless attempt to temper his partner's enthusiasm. His efforts were ignored, as Robert was not to be deterred. A heavy body fell upon his back, as Robert mounted him. His faced was shoved into the small pillow. Julian tossed it away, so he could breathe more freely. He felt another sharp pain, as he received the onslaught of heavy thrusts. Apparently, sweat and a heavy desire for penetration were enough to supply him with the necessary lubrication for Robert to enter. Very quickly, the pain turned to a sense of pleasure, as Robert worked a rhythmic assault into Julian's bottom.

Robert forced himself as far as possible into his lover's body. He wanted to get deeper inside. He pushed as hard as he could. He pounded out frustration, while biting the back of Julian's neck, leaving slight abrasions. With a final thrust, he climaxed, then collapsed onto Julian's body. After he caught his breath, he withdrew gently out from Julian's parted cheeks and rested back on his heels in a kneeling position. He then signaled with a murmur for Julian to turn over onto his back. After he concurred, Robert took him into his mouth, moving his lips up and down along Julian's penis. In just a few strokes, semen came quietly with just a few short whimpers. Once again, Robert released him and rested on his heels. He drew Julian's body to his waist with his partner's bottom resting on his thighs. He ran his large hands over the tan, glistening, muscular body. His nimble fingers explored the ripples of this man's tight stomach and firm chest more in adoration than for Julian's pleasure.

After a few moments, Robert slid Julian's body from his thighs but kept his lover's heels elevated. He then positioned his body to put his once again erect penis inside Julian. This time, he was very gentle and deliberate. With an easy pace going, he grazed Julian's lips with his own, while they shared breath. As he was getting close, he drew back and took Julian into his hand, bringing them both into a quiet climax.

The two men looked into the other's eyes, as they took time to regain their breath. As they made their recovery, Robert asked, "Did I hurt you?"

Julian was not sure what to make of Robert just then, so he replied quietly, "Nothing that won't mend." And then with a smile he added, "There is nothing wrong with a little pain."

Robert grinned, "You're sure?"

Julian nodded. Robert then lay beside his lover. He looked into Julian's eyes with affection. Julian returned his gaze. Then a light sadness crept into Robert eyes.

"Julian, I'm so sorry…"

"No," Julian replied softly, as he put a finger against Robert's thin lips.

Robert collapsed further to the floor and pulled Julian close.

"I feel like what the angels must feel at this moment," Robert said as he gazed toward the ceiling. He turned to look at Julian and said, "I feel so much weight gone from my body. I feel as if I am floating."

Julian continued to listen.

"Has this been what has been wrong with me? I turned all my frustration toward you…. The one I truly love. How can this be?" Robert asked.

"Robert," Julian replied with an easy smile, "So much has happened. Don't feel like you have to digest it all at once."

"But things are so clear now," Robert said with a light laugh, "Things make so much sense. I've anchored myself to this life of mine, not to achieve prosperity, but to cling to fear. I was striving to live the life my father lived; the life he wanted me to live. It was killing me that I was failing. I blamed you, because you represented the truth I could not face. Julian, I loved my father more than life…he was my life. Today, I feel I've been set free. My grief for him is over. I can now live my life."

Julian took his hand into his own. "I'm glad to be here to share this with you. It makes me feel very special. Contrary to what you believe, Robert, you deserve to be happy. You can be if you shed your ghosts."

Robert clasped both of Julian's hands. "I will show you," he started with enthusiasm. "Today I am a changed man. Julian, I fell in love with you the first moment I saw you in that stable. I haven't been the same man since that day. It may sound trite, but I've been a fool for you."

Julian sat up with his arms hugging his knees. "Robert, I confess, the first time I saw you, you were with Emily on her daddy's back porch. You were both dressed in your Sunday bests. Well even better, you were just returning from a grand ball. I thought you two were the most beautiful creatures that God had ever put on this earth. I look at you and I still believe it's true."

Robert sat up and reached to kiss Julian lightly on his lips. "You are right about me having to conquer my ghosts. I think I'm going to travel about for awhile; see the world through a different set of eyes. I don't want to turn back into my old self. I'm afraid that if I stay here any longer, I'll revert to the same bitter fool. Will you go with me?"

"Robert, I believe you are the same beautiful man who is sitting here with me. You are coming to terms with your turmoil to a large extent. I agree that you have a lot to learn about yourself and the world that exist outside of this parish. I feel you should go…. Go to explore places and learn to dream. As much as I would love to go with you, I cannot. I have five babies that depend on me. You see, I have my ghosts. I can't leave them the way my mother and papa left me."

Robert smiled as he put both his arms around Julian. "I already knew this in my heart. I knew I would later kick myself if I didn't ask." He turned to look Julian in the eyes and asked, "Will you wait for me? I will come back someday. I don't know when, but this is my home."

"You don't have to make any promises now. You may never want to come back for good, but I would welcome a visit from time to time," Julian replied warmly.

"If I do eventually settle somewhere, I'd really like for you to come see me. Would you consider it?" Robert asked softly.

"I look forward to it," Julian replied, quickly applying a light pressure to his hand.

"As much as I would like to be here with you, the folks are bound to be past worrying now. If I don't go, they will be here soon enough to look for me."

"Can you imagine?" Robert said with a laugh.

Julian dressed himself as best he could to look presentable to the family. Robert pulled his trousers to his waist and redid his belt buckle. He let his buttonless shirt hang open. He shed his shoes and socks. "At least my feet will be cool," he said with a smile.

They walked arm and arm to the back porch.

"You keep in touch...don't forget about me," Julian pleaded, as he took Robert's hands.

Robert embraced him and said, "Julian, no matter where I am, know that I will always love you and I could never forget you. Remember, I have already tried and failed. I am the happiest and luckiest man alive now, in no small part due to you."

They held each other tight for a few moments. " I better leave," Julian said, choking away emotion as he turned to go.

Emily heard a loud noise close to the door. She thought that maybe they were finished their visit and preparing to come through the door. Quietly, she crept back through the door to one of the side parlors. There she waited. When she figured that too much time had passed, she decided to go back toward the office.

Emily started toward the office door, when she heard it creak open. She scurried back to the same side parlor. She could see Robert and Julian walking side by side down the hallway, making their way to the back door. They were laughing softly and engaging in light conversation. *It seems that they worked things out tonight,* she thought.

Emily watched the two men embrace. *Why are they hanging on each other so? It is good that they worked things out, but they sure are acting strange. What could have happened in that office for such a long period of time?* A sudden chill ran down her spine, as she sunk her back against the wall.

CHAPTER 15

Julian began his trip home. As he got into the truck, he paused for a few moments to reflect on what had happened the past few hours. *It seems much has been resolved,* he thought. Robert is at peace. The two men came to understand their feelings for one another. His family would no longer suffer the consequences of their passion.

Julian felt partly responsible for Robert's actions during the past several years. Perhaps he had been too passive in his behavior toward him, which had to further torment Robert. Doing nothing to responsibly resolve their feelings for each other had to contribute to the escalating tension between the two men. *Now we will both be honest. He will not have to hide behind his father's ghosts to avoid our passion and I won't have to hide behind the Pilots and my children. What's going to happen now?* He wondered.

Julian put the keys into the ignition and started the engine. That question would have to be answered at a later time. He had a family waiting for him at home. They would be worried by now.

"You and your wife missed supper, son," Pilot said as he looked up from his newspaper. He was sitting on the front porch, as Julian drove up the Main Road.

"Where is Emily?" Julian asked as he climbed the steps to the porch.

"Don't know," Pilot replied returning to his newspaper. "I haven't seen her since you left." After a pause he asked, "How did things go with the Lamond boy? Any trouble?"

"No trouble," Julian replied softly, as he glanced at his shoes. He turned his gaze to Pilot. "Things went well. I believe everybody will be happy."

"I see," Pilot responded as he turned a page, "You are in one piece."

"If you will excuse me," Julian said, looking toward the door, "I'm going to clean…to relax a bit upstairs until Emily returns."

When Julian got upstairs to his room, he closed the door and collapsed onto the bed. *The children will need tucking in soon,* he thought. He looked at the clock on the dresser; *they would have long gone to bed by now,* he thought again.

He lay there for awhile to sift through the day's events. After a time, he decided that he needed a bath, before Emily returned. He knew he must look ravaged, but he felt more relaxed. He was experiencing a sense of relief that he had not felt in a very long time. *It would just be nice to bask in this for a while,* he thought, as he fell back onto the bed. After a moment, he sat up and put his head into his hands; *I can't be the same after tonight. I feel things inside that had been asleep for a long time. What am I going to do?*

A light knock sounded at the door. "Matt?" Emily said lightly.

"Come in," Julian replied as he looked toward the door. He stood as she entered the room.

"I was curious to see how you were," she stated with unease.

"There is no need for worry," he assured. Julian sat back down on the edge of the bed. He patted a place for his wife to join him. No matter the future, he knew Emily always had a warm place in his heart. She joined him. He could tell she was nervous.

"Things actually went pretty well," Julian stated with a light chuckle of mock disbelief. He could feel Emily's eyes intently on him, as she awaited his next word. He returned her gaze.

"It was touch and go for awhile," Julian explained as he started to gain momentum. "There was some arguing initially, but luckily, we were able to move past it. We discovered that we really wanted the same things."

"You did?" Emily said.

"Yes. We both want the best for you and the children. I didn't realize how much he loves each of you," Julian replied.

"I can believe that about him," Emily sighed as she relaxed for a moment. She looked toward the mirror. "I think I still know his heart."

"He really is not a bad person," Julian said with conviction. "He just has been lonely for so long. He needed a little help to feel better. He feared being so vulnerable."

"How were you able to do that?" Emily asked slowly.

Julian thought for a few moments. "He decided that it was time to take some risks. He needed to be willing to grasp a friendly hand. It hurt him to see that our family cares about each other. He felt left out. He wants to be a part of us. I believe I convinced him that he could. I don't think anyone had given him a chance to belong somewhere that he wanted to be. He wants to have relationships with all of us. Perhaps someday he will."

"Does this include a relationship with you?" Emily asked with guarded surprise.

"Why....yes..." Julian replied. "We discovered that we had more in common than was first imagined."

There was a knock at the door. "Julian?"

"Yes Elizabeth," Julian replied loud enough to be heard through the wooden door.

"You have a visitor downstairs and I think you may want to come this moment," Elizabeth said in her controlled voice, free of any emotion. Yet Julian could always sense things about his mother. He was sure that he heard a smirk in her voice.

"Okay Elizabeth, I'll be right down," Julian answered with a light sense of impatience.

"Are you okay, Emily? I feel there's something troubling you," Julian asked with concern.

"You have to admit," Emily replied as she stood, "There was a good chance things could have gone poorly. I was concerned for my family....our family, as well as yourself."

"Everything is going to be alright," he replied as he gave her hand a squeeze. "We better head downstairs before Elizabeth comes back to herd us down herself."

As Julian entered the great room he saw a familiar man gazing through the window, admiring the star studded night. He turned as he heard Julian come through the door. Emily was not far behind. He stopped abruptly, as he saw the man.

The man smiled, "So, it really is you. Did you think you could hide from me forever?

"Don't flatter yourself, "Julian said as he stormed into the room. "Emily, this is Dennis," he said with a hand gesture, "Dennis, this is Emily"

Dennis was a tall brawny man about the same age as Julian. He was slender at waist and towered over Julian. He had rust colored hair with a disheveled look. His skin had a fair complexion with a few freckles. He wore a brown felted shirt and slacks the same color, which revealed his awesome figure. Julian had to admit; he still looked good after these past few years.

"It's nice to meet you," Emily nodded toward the man, as she kept her distance. She moved close to Julian, sensing a need to protect him.

"It seems marriage agrees with you, as you look as good as the last time I saw you...when you were married to me," Dennis said with wide grin.

"What?" Emily replied with a confused look.

"Leave her alone, Dennis," Julian commanded in a low firm voice. "Any business here is between you and me. Leave her out of it."

"Does she even know who I am?" Dennis asked as he paced the floor.

"I'm sure she does now," Julian replied in the same firm voice. "I'm warning you, leave her alone, or I'll gladly have you thrown out of here."

"Matt, who is this awful man?" Emily asked pleadingly.

"It is like I said, little lady," Dennis answered, "I'm his ex-husband."

Emily covered her ears and ran from the room. "Emily," Julian said, as he started after her.

"I'll attend her," Elizabeth said as she came suddenly from the other room. "You deal with him."

"What is going on here," Pilot roared as he came into the room. "Is this man making trouble, Matt?"

"Matt?" Dennis said, wrinkling his forehead.

"It's a long story," Julian replied.

"I'll handle this, Pilot....it's alright," Julian assured him. "Dennis is a little upset. I need to talk to him a bit...To explain how things have been. I'll tell you about it later, or my papa can tell you about it for now."

"I can't have him upsetting my daughter, who happens to be your wife," Pilot growled. "I think I'll have him thrown out right this minute."

Please," Julian pleaded, "Let me handle this and then I'll get rid of him, so he won't bother us anymore."

Julian shut the door, leaving him alone with Dennis. The familiar question was posed to the visitor. " How did you find me? Did Elizabeth call you?"

"Yes, she did," Dennis replied. "Julian, how could you do this? How could you knowingly marry that poor little thing? She doesn't deserve this mess you've made!"

"I find it odd that you are suddenly running to her defense, after you just tormented her," Julian growled as he walked across the room. He sat on the arm of the sofa. Then he stood and walked back across the room.

"It is as you said. My beef is with you, not her," Dennis exclaimed. "She just happened to be at the wrong place at the wrong time. I will plead for her forgiveness later. Can you blame me for feeling that she and her family have taken you away from me?"

"How dare you!" Julian snarled. "You were the one who left me! Left me when I needed you most!"

"I wanted to come back to you, but you had already disappeared," Dennis explained.

"You left! That's all that matters. I had less than nothing when I disappeared, except the stack of overdue bills you were supposed to have been paying!"

"I had only been gone 10 days, when I wanted to come back," Dennis pleaded. "I was young and foolish. I did a lot of growing up in those 10 days. I worked countless hours, as you did. I did not take the time to pay bills, nor could I keep a sane head. I could never have married that girl, when I was mad about you. When I came back to the apartment, I had resolved that I would give up my promising career if that's what it would have taken for you to forgive me. Then I found you gone. I was devastated. I waited for you. And then I waited for you some more, but you never came back." Dennis was now crying softly.

Julian stood still in his place. "You know," he said with a wistful smile, "When I was in the hospital, I often dreamed that you would say these things."

"Hospital?" Dennis asked bewildered, recovering from his tears.

"Elizabeth didn't tell you what has been happening these last years?" Julian asked with little surprise.

"She didn't tell me a thing," Dennis replied. "Except to jump on the next plane, that she had found you."

"She must be desperate to get me back to Washington, if she resorted to contacting you to entice me," Julian mused.

"Well, I regret coming now," Dennis said as tears welled in his eyes once more, "You have your life here, as screwed up as it seems to be. I have mine, as I was really picking up the pieces. I was moving on with life without you. All I had were good, no, fantastic memories. We had it so good, Julian. Now, it's like reliving the pain all over again and you don't seem to really be affected. Same Julian. Clean as the moonshine over a still lake, but at least you never became the ice princess that your mother is."

"You don't know how I've suffered these last several years....in no small part due to you," Julian replied with anger. "Not have I only made a mess of my life and Emily's life, but I have five other small innocent lives that depend on me. I'm determined for them to not have to pay the same price that the rest of us have had. Mind you, I don't put the entire blame on myself anymore. There is enough blame to go around for everybody involved, except for the babies. There comes to a point of time when blame is not important. There comes a time when we all have to just deal with it. It just so happens that I'm not very good at it. I may appear to be smooth as glass or as slick as grease, but you, nobody, and sometimes myself, knows what's happening inside me."

"You are right, of course," Dennis relented. "You always make so much sense, Julian. You should have been the lawyer. Incidentally, why was I the one with the bills? You were the financier."

"I was social director, remember?" Julian teased. "You had to do something."

Julian and Dennis looked toward the hall, as they heard loud voices coming toward them. "Surely, Pilot cannot still be upset," Julian wondered.

The door opened. The town sheriff entered the room. "Julian Smith, you have the right to remain silent. Anything you say can be used against you......"

"Sheriff, what is the charge?" Pilot demanded.

"The murder of Robert Lamond," the sheriff replied.

CHAPTER 16

Emily heard the knock at the door. "Who is it?" she asked tersely. She was sitting on the bed, her face toward the opposite wall.

Elizabeth opened the door and came into the room. "I came to see if you were alright."

"I find that hard to believe. Matt says your ways may be wicked but at least you are forthcoming." Still facing away from her mother in-law she asked, "What is it you really want? This has been a night of hell."

"I can imagine you would feel that way," Elizabeth replied as she approached the end of the bed.

"You know, it's best to have everything in the open. Secrets have tormented your family enough to divide it. Wouldn't you agree?" Elizabeth inquired with a sly smile.

"It was you that brought him here, wasn't it?" Emily stated. It was more of a challenge than a question. She still faced away from the other woman.

"I confess it was," Elizabeth sighed. "If Julian is going to stay here, he better be certain it is what he wants. As you may be aware, my son is not good at facing truths."

Emily turned to face Elizabeth. "Why do you act with such concern now? Where were you, when he was growing up? Maybe he can't face things because it was too painful to know his parents really didn't love him. He faces the truth well enough to know that his two awful parents only do things to please themselves. You both hide under the guise that you really care for him. What is with you? Why don't you just leave him alone and let him make his own choices?" Emily was angry. Her face was red with fire, as she was now standing in front of her target.

"I have stated many times that I was not the best mother, and I still am lacking in that area," Elizabeth answered coolly. "Perhaps I'm trying to make up for my past neglect. It could be guilt that drives me to try to help him. After all, I am still his mother."

"Guilt?" Emily's was voice starting to rise. "When have you ever felt a bit of remorse? You are the most selfish woman I have ever met. Just get out of here and let me be!"

"I will." Elizabeth turned to leave, "You may not believe this, but I do feel remorse for you. You are a sweet child and don't deserve the plight that fate has dropped on you. There are more secrets in this house that are bound to reveal themselves in time."

"What are you talking about?" Emily asked in a lowered voice. She was still seething under her breath.

"Oh, come now dear child," Elizabeth replied, patronizing her daughter in-law. "You know what really happened in that Lamond house. It was all over Julian's face the minute he came into the house, as he hurried up the steps. It was a look of obvious relief and contentment that I haven't seen, since…. well, let's just say it's been a long time."

Emily shivered slightly. "Get out of here, you evil woman. Get out of here!" She started toward Elizabeth to show her the door.

However, Elizabeth did not need any further encouragement, as she slipped out the door. She then ran into Louisa.

"Mrs. Steele. What is going on up here? I heard loud voices clear down into the kitchen," Louisa exclaimed with worry.
"That dear girl has been under such pressure, with her family in turmoil," Elizabeth explained quickly. "I tried to help, but what I think she really needs is her mother," she added as she made a quick exit.

"It looks like you're going to need a lawyer," Dennis said offhandedly. It was a surprised reaction of sorts, but enough to take the edge off Julian.

"I guess I will," Julian replied, as the sheriff applied the handcuffs to his wrists.

"Is that really necessary?" Pilot interjected, looking toward the cuffs.

"Standard procedure," the deputy replied, as he searched Julian.

"No weapons, sir," the deputy said to the sheriff.

"This is absurd," Pilot exclaimed, "That boy is no murderer."

"There has to be some mistake," Bernard said, coming into the room from behind Pilot.

"He was seen just before the crime was committed, just a few hours ago," the sheriff explained as he started to guide Julian out of the door.

"Where are you taking him?" Pilot asked gruffly.

"The parish jail," the sheriff replied.

"That's over an hour away," Pilot exclaimed. "Can't you keep him in town?"

"I'm just following orders, Pilot," the sheriff admonished. "I have a boss to please."

"Who wants him?" Pilot asked.

"The district attorney," the sheriff answered. "Lamond is a big name. He practically owned the parish. I'm glad I don't happen to be that boy."

"You tell that strapping politician that this boy is my son in-law and he better do right by him."

"Yes sir," the sheriff replied as he shoved Julian into the police cruiser.

"Don't worry Julian, we'll get you out of there real soon," Bernard assured him as the door closed and the car drove off down the Farm Road.

Pilot marched back into the big house. Bernard, Dennis, and Elizabeth were not far behind. Pilot went immediately into his study and shut the door behind him before the others could follow. Dennis opened the door quickly and shut the door behind him and locked it before the others could sneak inside with him. Pilot was already on the phone.

"I don't care what time it is, get him out of bed!" Pilot roared.

"Who are you calling?" Dennis asked as Pilot was holding the line.

"The governor. Who else would I be calling?" Pilot replied tersely.

Dennis waited until Pilot got off the phone.

"What did you find out?" he asked.

"Said he'd look into it," Pilot replied skeptically, "And he'd better. He owes me a favor or two."

"Do you know of a couple lawyers in town?" Dennis inquired with a calm voice.

"A couple?" Pilot said with a raised brow.

"What's that got to do with it?" Pilot growled, as he looked hard into Dennis's face.

"It would be my guess that these people in this fine parish do not take or should I say, have not taken to the likes of Julian, or myself for that matter," Dennis started to explain. "Let me speak candidly"

"Please," Pilot replied impatiently.

"I do not think Julian will get a fair trial here, if it comes to it. I sense he will be railroaded quickly into jail with little fanfare. A homosexual will be getting what he deserves."

"It will not come to that," Pilot answered as he turned toward the window. "But it does bother me that the governor seemed to have a cavalier attitude. He was very evasive about his method for taking care of this matter."

"Do you think it's politics?" Dennis asked.

"Possibly," Pilot sighed, "But Lamond and I have always backed him. Without us, it would be hard for him to win re-election. He's not very popular. There's always some air of scandal surrounding him. I suspect Lamond has bailed him out a half dozen times. I supply the big bucks to drive his campaign, Lamond supplied some money, but also the muscle."

"We will need his intervention to have any hope of acquittal," Dennis stated.

"Are you sure this will go to trial?" Pilot asked, rather puzzled. "He was just arrested."

"I have no doubt. I've seen this many times. There's someone behind all of this nonsense. The guy was just murdered a few short hours ago and they have already made an arrest," Dennis explained. "Doesn't that seem a bit odd to you?"

"I suppose." Pilot pondered the thought as he stroked his chin with one hand, while resting the elbow on the other folded arm. "What can you do?" Pilot inquired. "I'm assume you cannot practice law in this state."

"Not really," Dennis agreed. "I can play an advisory role, but I can also do the real work...find the real killer."

"You think you can do that?" Pilot asked rather surprised.

"Part of being a good lawyer is the leg work, the required investigation. It may be tedious and time consuming. Let's hope the killer did a sloppy job of hiding his tracks."

"I'm sure glad to see you're not lacking in confidence," Pilot commented.

"If I were not arrogant, I would be a poor lawyer," Dennis replied.

"I ordered the car, it should be here momentarily," Elizabeth told Pilot s he exited his study.

"I'm surprised he would work at this late hour," Pilot replied with ndifference.

"Believe me, he is well paid to do as I please. You never know when I nay have to leave in a hurry."

"Very well," Pilot agreed. "There should be plenty of room for all of us."

Dennis came out of the study and met Pilot at the door as they were getting ready to go. "I spoke to the lawyer that you recommended. We're on the same page. He'll be there before the magistrate."

"It seems we're getting everybody out of bed tonight," Pilot said grimly.

"He's being well paid," Dennis commented. "I told him to send you the bill. I presume that is satisfactory?"

"Of course," Pilot replied, "That boy is like my adopted son."

"I will see you all in the morning," Dennis said in earnest. "Tell Julian not to be concerned and to hang tight. Everything is going to work out."

"You're not going with us?" Bernard asked.

"No," Dennis answered. "I have to get on the killer's trail, while it's still hot." With that, he bid them goodbye and began to set the course of his investigation.

"Wake up! Somebody wake up in there!" Dennis shouted loudly as he rapped on the wooden screen door.

"Hush all that noise," Old Bill said, as he came to the door with a squint in his eyes. He adjusted to the light just after he flipped the switch. "I'm a coming. No need for the racket."

"I'm sorry to wake your family sir, but I really need to talk to Billy. Are you him?" Dennis asked with urgency.

"You probably want my son. I'll get him. Come in," Old Bill instructed. "By the way, there are no sirs here. You must be a friend of that other white boy, Matt."

"Billy! Get up! There's a white man here to see you!" Old Bill shouted as he went back into his bedroom and shut the door. In a short moment, Billy came into the living area with a blanket wrapped around him.

"Come on! Get dressed," Dennis prodded impatiently. "We've got to go!"

Quickly, Billy got dressed and the two headed through the door. When they were outside, Dennis ordered, "Get a truck or something, we got to get moving fast!"

Dennis followed Billy and they got into an old pickup and headed down the Cattle Road toward the big house. "Mister, where are we going?" Billy asked.

"The Lamond plantation," Dennis answered. "I was told you would be able to take me there and you were a friend of Julian's...I mean Matt's"

"Matt in trouble again?" Billy asked.

"He's been accused of premeditated murder and we got to help him out. Are you with me?" Dennis asked.

"Yeah, anything to help Matt. That boy stays in trouble. He can't seem to hide from it. It always seems to find him."

"Well, he's had real good luck or real bad luck with nothing in between ever since the day I fell...I met him."

"Who are you, Mister?" Billy asked as he looked over to Dennis and then back to the road.

"I'm an old friend of Matt's from back east, coming to pay a visit. And just in time, I might add. Lucky for him," Dennis snorted. He offered Billy his hand, "Dennis Jensen."

Billy awkwardly took his hand, "Folks call me Billy."

"Billy, do you always just go along with people you don't know, when you don't know where you're going?" Dennis teased.

"I do when a white man comes to call. Besides, I knew right away you were a friend of Matt's."

"How's that?" Dennis asked amused.

"Because, you act just like him," Billy stated, "There ain't nobody around here like Matt, so you must be a friend of his."

"I'm more like him than you think." Dennis smiled as he looked ahead.

"How's that?" Billy answered astonished.

"Because trouble always seems to find its way to me like it does to him. It just won't leave either one of us alone," Dennis chuckled.

"Ah goodness," Billy sighed as he drove on down the road.

"How far up the road is the house?" Dennis asked in a low voice.

"About a mile or so," Billy answered.

"Good, Let's ditch this truck in the bushes. We can walk the rest of the way." Dennis said as he pointed off the road.

"If we put the truck in there, we'll never get it out," Billy complained.

"Well, find a spot to park it, where it can't be seen," Dennis ordered.

They parked the truck in a path just off the road, where it couldn't be seen by anybody in passing.

"Who are we hiding from?" Billy asked, as they walked quietly.

"The police," Dennis answered as he pushed forward.

"The police?" Billy exclaimed with disbelief. "Maybe I should wait with truck....in case someone sees it."

"What good would that do?" Dennis asked seriously. "Besides I need you to guide me around this place. Remember I'm lost here without you."

Billy reluctantly bounded after Dennis. As they got closer to the house, they could see a police cruiser parked near the front door, with a sheriff's deputy asleep slouched in the front seat listening to all night radio.

"Do you know your way around this place very well?" Dennis asked.

"Yeah. My sisters and I used to play around here, while my mama used to bake pies for the old Mr. Lamond. He liked her pies best, so he'd have her up here, when it suited him."

"Is there an easy way to get into the house, besides the front door?" Dennis asked.

"There are lots of doors to this house, but it's probably best to go through the cellar, if you don't want anyone to see you," Billy answered.

"Perfect," Dennis said excitedly as he started to move forward. Billy stopped him.

"Why do we have to sneak? Won't those people just let us inside? It doesn't seem fair not to let us see what happened," Billy inquired.

"The parish goons probably got in and out of there quickly, so they could make an arrest on Jul...Matt," Dennis explained. "They'll be back later, further contaminating the crime site. Then they would let us in there after they take what they want or leave what they want for that matter."

"Why would they act like that?" Billy asked.

"Because there is likely someone who wants this case moved quickly and that does not bode well for our friend Matt," Dennis replied.

"Now let's go," Dennis urged. "I'll explain the rest later. I want to get in and out before sunup."

Dennis followed Billy toward the house. They crouched along the hedge leading to the house. They made quite a bit more noise than Dennis would have liked, but they seemed to have reached the cellar door undetected. He noticed that the deputy was still asleep in the front seat of his car. They paused briefly, when he shifted his weight to get comfortable by leaning further into the car door. There did not appear to be any other watchmen on hand. Dennis started to pull at the cellar door.

"No," Billy shook his head. "It will make too much noise and slam after we go in. We should go through the window here. It will creek and slam too, but not as much as the door."

"Isn't there a quieter way into the house?" Dennis asked slightly perplexed.

"Yeah. The front door. All the others are painted shut, since they are never used, except the kitchen door and there are all those yellow tapes around it," Billy answered impatiently. "Got to hurry before we get caught."

" I want you to find a place to hide out here. I don't want to risk getting you into trouble. If there is commotion, hide until everything has been quiet at least for an hour and then walk home. Don't go for the truck."

"Walk!" Billy protested. "Do you know how long that will take to get back home?"

"Not as long as you would be sitting in jail if you get caught," Dennis retorted.

"I'll walk," Billy agreed, "I'm not about to go to jail"

"Good," Dennis said as he looked out the window.

"I may be a while," Dennis warned, "Just wait for me and then we'll head back to the truck."

"Okay. I'll wait," Billy assured him.

Dennis crept through the window. As Billy had said, it creaked and slammed shut as he entered the house. He hoped that this did not attract attention, because he had a lot of snooping to do in a short period of time. He just prayed that Billy would be safe. He liked Billy. It was easy to understand how Julian could trust him as a good friend.

Billy described to Dennis a very quick layout of the house. Dennis hoped this would suffice, since it would be risky to snoop around the big mansion for any amount of time.

Each second was important. If he was going to find the murderer, the trail would start in this house. Mostly likely, he would find little else beyond the crime scene, since it was easy to assume that nobody outside the family would be sympathetic to Julian. *Why would Julian choose to live with bigoted people? Certainly, he could take his wife and kids and move to a more tolerant city or town where people would understand a little diversity. I will have to sit down with Julian when this is all over and talk all this over with him.*

The door to the main house from the cellar was locked, probably due to police paranoia that the scene could be contaminated. They must have some idea of Julian's resources, because people in these parts most likely did not lock anything much less a cellar door. *There must be some other way to get into the house. I regret not spending more time getting information from Billy. All I'm doing is wasting precious time and taking greater risks of being caught.*

Dennis surveyed the cellar. Just when he thought of going back through the window, he saw a glitter of light shine in a far corner. *It must be through the floorboards. The flicker must mean there is a flashlight. Could the killer be coming back to the scene? Maybe this means he left something at the scene after exiting quickly after the murder. If it were anyone else, surely they would use the light switch. Should I confront the intruder? What if it is the killer and he's armed?* He silently cursed the fact he did not come armed. However, after thinking a bit more, it was probably a good idea that he did not have a weapon. If in the off chance that he did get caught snooping, it might be difficult to explain. He decided it would be a better idea to frighten the killer away, to keep him from changing the crime scene.

Dennis decided it was worth the gamble to assume that there was nobody in the house except him and the intruder. He figured that this was a safe bet, because the killer most likely had a better idea of the house's layout. This could only mean the killer was sure nobody else was in the house, or thought that nobody was in the house. There was a lot of "ifs" in this theory, but he felt he had little choice. He would have to go with his gut feeling.

Dennis knew he had to act quickly. He tiptoed gently over to the window. It creaked as it opened. *This could only startle the killer if he heard the noise,* he thought.

"Billy!" he shouted in a loud whisper. He had to shout a couple of times before he could see some of the bushes move. Dennis beckoned him over to the window. Reluctantly, Billy scampered over to his new friend.

Dennis stuck his head out of the window, as he held it open. "There's somebody in the house," Dennis informed him. "I need to get him frightened, so that he'll leave in a hurry."

"Who do you think it is?" Billy asked.

"No time to explain," Dennis answered.

"I need you to make a lot of noise out here, slam a couple of things against the house, while you stay hidden. Throw a few rocks at the police car to wake up the deputy. When he hears the other noise, he likely will check the house. This should spook the intruder into leaving," Dennis instructed.

Billy did what Dennis asked. He made enough noise to awaken the sleepy deputy. Still half asleep, he strode from his cruiser to check the house. He slipped underneath the yellow crime scene ribbons to enter the house to make sure all was secure.

Dennis noted that there was a quick shuffle of activity, as the intruder was probably aware that someone else was in the house. Perhaps he did know it was the deputy, or thought it could be somebody like himself, who was curious enough to make an unauthorized visit. *Would the intruder confront the deputy? Would he be hostile? Maybe he would try to make a quick escape.*

Dennis' thoughts were interrupted when he heard a short series of quick footsteps hurry across the floor above him. He heard a rattle against the wall upstairs. The intruder was probably trying to escape through a window and it appeared that he was having some problems with it. After a short time, he heard a noise coming from just outside the cellar window.

Could the intruder be thinking of hiding down here? Dennis moved quickly to hide behind some wooden barrels. When he was sure that nobody would try to come through the cellar window, he gently opened it. He noted the oil tank below the above window. The intruder likely bounded clumsily off the oil tank to hit the ground. He could vaguely see a slender figure running quickly toward a cluster of trees. It was odd that he did not try to seek cover while he trotted into the distance. To Dennis's immediate surprise, this person led a horse that was tethered in a small group of high trees to a clearing and quickly mounted it. This person was clumsy. The horse had started off, while he tried desperately to position himself in the saddle. As the horse bounded off, it amazed Dennis that he was able to stay on top of its back.

Dennis thought about what he had just seen. If this intruder was indeed the killer, he was by no means a professional. A professional would be better prepared and not have taken so many risks. Soon, he would know if it was the killer, he thought. If there was some lingering trail at the scene, Dennis was confident he would find it.

He waited a good little while after he was sure the deputy had left the house. Dennis was hoping the deputy would return to his cruiser and fall back asleep. However, this was not completely necessary, as long as he was able to keep quiet. His only concern was to finish his exploration before the sun started to rise. The risk for slipping off the plantation unnoticed would greatly increase in daylight. He was more concerned about Billy than himself. Billy had more to lose in this backward parish, where blacks were still second class citizens and gays simply did not exist.

He crept out the window of the cellar and bounded up the oil tank, as the intruder must have done earlier. Soon, he was inside the house. Billy said that Lamond spent all of his waking hours in his study. There was a good chance that this was where he was murdered. There was a door with plenty of police tape glued to it. It would be tough getting through it without somebody realizing that the scene had been tampered with.

Carefully, he entered the office. The study was slightly disheveled with cushions on the floor and the cocktail table pushed away from the ox blood leather couch. However, there did not appear to be signs of any struggle. Perhaps it was just sloppy housekeeping. There was no broken glass or evidence that items had been strewn through the room in attempt for Lamond to escape.

The desk was orderly except for a stain of blood on the blotter. A pencil holder, a matching paperweight and a small notepad were still perfectly aligned along the edge of the desk. There was no sign of a letter opener that sometimes came with such a set. Dennis thought that Lamond might have been taken by surprise by the killer. He must have been sitting at his desk when he was murdered. There was little mess from the fatal wound. Perhaps he was stabbed. If this was true, the killer must have been lucky with the first strike. A crime of passion? Most likely.

Dennis looked along the desk. He thought it strange that it did not have a middle drawer. The drawers along the sides were of course locked. Anticipating this, he had brought a set of picks to open the locks on either side. In a short moment, all the drawers were open. He surmised that there had been files in the lower two drawers, however they had been removed. There was no doubt the police would remove any evidence pointing to the murderer. Perhaps that was why the letter opener was missing. If it was covered with blood, maybe the medical examiner thought it to be significant. Certain steps had to be taken if the police planned to make a conviction stick. However, if the police took the files, why were the drawers locked? Maybe it was the killer who took them all in haste to get away. What was is it that he left behind that he came back to get?

There seemed to be enough depth in the desk to have room for a middle drawer, but there was not one to be found. There had to be one. Dennis moved his gloved hands along the edge of the desk, looking for some indentation that would signify an opening. Frustrated, he leaned on the top of the desk to think of what to do next. He thought he felt the surface give just a little bit. He ran his hands along the edge and lifted up on it. Instantly the top opened up like a lid of a box. The paperweight, notepad, other things cluttering the desk went crashing to the floor. Undeterred by the noise, Dennis looked intently into the compartment. It ran the length and width of the very large desk. The depth of it was about six inches. Inside, there were two manila folders, an appointment book stuffed with notes and a stack of legal pads. Dennis figured he had another hour before daylight. The tabs of the folders were labeled GW and the other Smith. He briefly sifted through both folders and then started taking pictures. Luckily, he had brought several rolls of film with him, because he was going to need them all. He photographed the entire appointment book and notes. When he finished, it was pitch dark outside. He put everything back in its original position and then made his way to exit through the window. Immediately, he jumped out the window. He had to hastily find cover. Another sheriff's deputy had pulled up in another police cruiser and was chastising the one keeping guard for sleeping on the job. The latter sneered at the new deputy and got into his cruiser and sped down the lane. The remaining deputy looked Dennis' way and appeared to catch him hiding behind the oil tank. Dennis did not know if he should make a run for it or stay still. If he ran, he surely would be seen and possibly caught or shot. If he took the chance he wasn't seen, he would risk being a sitting duck, when the deputy came to investigate.

About the moment Dennis decided to make a run for it, he saw Billy dash across the lane toward the trees along the dirt road.

"Hey, wait a minute!" shouted the deputy. However, by the time the deputy got into his cruiser and started the engine, Billy was gone.

Gee that guy is fast, Dennis thought. He quickly took the opportunity to make his own escape, while the deputy was distracted. Dennis made for the woods on the other side of the house. He ran hard until he was far away from the house. He trotted gingerly down the lane, leaving the house behind and keeping a lookout in case the deputy returned.

The sun was starting to warm up the morning. Dennis began to realize how tired he was from the last 24 hours. Just this time yesterday, he was leaving his townhouse in Washington to board a plane to this backward part of the country. It seemed a lifetime ago. *Enough reflecting,* he thought. He had to be careful not to make anymore mistakes.

When Dennis returned to the truck, he found Billy asleep on the ground, leaning against a rear tire.

"Aren't you taking it a little too easy?" Dennis asked with concern as he gave Billy a light kick on the side of his butt.

Billy sighed and then answered, "I worked all day yesterday and haven't gotten any sleep."

"What if the deputy caught you here napping?" Dennis said with panic.

"That lazy boy isn't going to get out of his car to come looking for us," Billy answered. "He must have ridden up and down this lane 5 or 6 times looking for something."

"Great!" Dennis replied, exasperated. "How long are we supposed to wait to leave before he decides he's had enough cycles?"

"We don't wait," Billy said, getting to his feet. "We leave as soon as he makes another pass up toward the house. He probably has already called for his buddies for help."

"How many of them are there on the force?" Dennis asked as he got into the passenger side of the truck..

"Oh, about three," Billy replied as he got into the driver's side.

"Only three?" Dennis asked surprised.

"There's not too much crime around these parts," Billy explained, "Usually, they're bored, with nothing to do except pay social visits to folks to make sure things are okay."

"This is likely the most excitement this place has seen in a while," Dennis agreed.

"There has been more excitement, since Matt came around here. He gives folks something to talk about, besides sugarcane and babies," Billy added.

"I'm sure he has," Dennis said with a smirk.

Billy looked over to him. "I'm sure you're not much behind him."

Dennis continued to look straight ahead toward the road. After turning onto the main avenue away from Lamonds, he asked, "Why did you run across the field like that? You could have been shot."

"Because you would have been caught," Billy replied with conviction and slight exasperation.

"You think?" Dennis asked meekly.

"Yeah," Billy replied, "While you were thinking of what to do next, that boy was half way up the yard getting ready to draw his pistol. I had to do something to distract him." And then Billy smiled. "Besides, I'm as fast as they come."

"I know, I couldn't believe how fast you moved," Dennis agreed. "Hey, thanks for doing this. You really took a chance."

"Yeah," Bill replied as he drove down the road.

CHAPTER 17

"I know you must be hungry," Louisa commented, as Dennis descended the stairs to the kitchen. "There is always plenty of food around here. I'll get you a plate"

"Thanks," Dennis said as he sat down to the table. "How is Julian, or Matt, as you call him?" Dennis virtually collapsed into bed as soon as Billy dropped him off at the big house.

"Fine," Pilot responded, as he joined him at the table. "He's still upstairs asleep. He didn't get much rest either last night. I have to admit, it was a trying night for the family. Everybody has slept past lunch."

"Was he released?" Dennis asked, "I knew he was here when I got back, but I didn't catch the whole story. I couldn't keep my eyes open."

"Not entirely," Pilot sighed as he poured himself a cup of coffee. "Want some?"

"Sure," Dennis replied, sliding a cup across the table. "So what's the story?"

"He has been charged with capital murder, with premeditation," Pilot replied.

"What!" Dennis exclaimed, "How is it that he was released?"

"Well, there are two things," Pilot started to explain. "There really wasn't any evidence pointing him to the murder, other that he did not like

Lamond. The DA's office could not even produce anything to that effect. He never had done anything or said anything about Lamond, other than he wanted to make peace with the man. What's strange is that Lamond had a ton of other enemies and it's assumed that Matt was the biggest."

"You said two things," Dennis blurted.

"The other is that I was due a favor," Pilot replied softly.

"So why charge him? What grounds?" Dennis asked upset.

"The DA dropped the fact that Matt was a former homosexual," Pilot explained. "Unfortunately, in this parish, that's enough to convict anybody. You got your work cut out for you, boy."

"How can he be charged or convicted with no evidence? That's ludicrous," Dennis questioned with disbelief.

"Things are different here than in the big city," Pilot explained. "Folks are afraid of things they haven't seen. The church here speaks volumes and it says homosexuals are evil from head to toe. So what are they supposed to think? He's a logical target."

"I should have guessed as much," Dennis mused.

Louisa joined them at the table, as she set a plate in front of Dennis. "I don't suppose you can help Matt, can you?" Louisa asked with worry. "I know he didn't kill that boy."

"Oh don't worry," Dennis said with a lawyer's arrogance. "He will not spend another night in jail."

"What did you find out last night?" Pilot asked, "I assume you were out and about searching for answers, since you got home after we did."

"I don't know what I have exactly," Dennis said vaguely. "We should go into your office in a moment to look at what I got."

Pilot understood Dennis's request for privacy. "Well, why don't we go ahead into the study, then," Pilot said, getting up from the table.

"I need to develop a few pictures, but it shouldn't take long," Dennis explained, "Why don't you go ahead and I'll catch up with you shortly."

"I'll be making some calls. Take all the time you need," Pilot said as he left the room.

Dennis made to leave the kitchen himself, when Julian came down the steps.

"Julian," Dennis said with surprise.

"Are you shocked to see me sprung so soon?" Julian asked with a smirk and yawn.

"I'm glad to see that you didn't leave your sense of humor in jail," Dennis retorted. "Grab a donut and some coffee then come into the next room," Dennis ordered. "We have some talking to do."

"Right now?" Julian complained.

Dennis replied testily, "Do you want my help or not?"

Julian nodded, picked up a couple of donuts and a cup of coffee that Louisa had set for him. "Let's go into the front room; we can have some privacy to talk." The front room was a reading room divided from the great room.

As they walked into the parlor, Dennis asked, "When did you start eating those things? You would never have gone near anything with so many calories a few years ago."

"I don't eat much anymore, besides the work here keeps me fit and I've taken up running," Julian answered, taking a bite from a sugar donut.

"Running?" Dennis said in disbelief. "I could never imagine you doing something more tiresome than a few weights."

"People change," Julian said with nonchalance. "Back home, people exercise and lift weights just enough to look good. We were the same; the pretty people in our society to gain status."

"Oh, Julian," Dennis said, exasperated "That had more to do with youth than any kind of status. After a certain age, we do things for different reasons, like to prevent heart attacks and to stay healthy."

"I run because I feel like it; not to answer to some medical journal," Julian said with distaste.

"I was not knocking you. I think it's great you're taking care of yourself. You could stand to gain a couple pounds, although you are as handsome as ever," Dennis said with a smile.

"Let's get to matters at hand," Julian said, changing the subject while sitting on the sofa.

"Okay, Julian, but you have to tell me everything you know about this man and your involvement with him," Dennis instructed.

"Where do I start?" Julian asked with unease.

"Relax," Dennis consoled. He patted Julian's thigh. "It's just me, remember?"

Julian nodded.

"I understand that he was horrible man. For some reason, this family had some affection for him," Dennis said to give Julian an introduction.

"He really wasn't that horrible," Julian said softly.

"Julian! The man tortured you. How can you say that he wasn't horrible?" Dennis replied with an astonished look.

"We came to an understanding," Julian answered as he shifted his weight uncomfortably.

"What?" Dennis said with a puzzled look.

"Why are you so willing to help me after all these years?" Julian asked with impatience. "Do you feel there are still issues between us?"

"Yes. We have some unfinished business to attend to, but that will have to wait, Julian. Let's just put all of that aside," Dennis prodded patiently. After he a few moments of silence, he asked, "Julian, what happened at that house last night?"

"What do you mean?" Julian asked as he looked away from him.

"Come on, Julian," Dennis demanded, losing patience. "What happened!"

"I went to Robert's house with the intention of resolving our differences. We made up and then I came home."

"From what I understand, you were there a long time," Dennis pushed.

"I was?" Julian answered with disbelief.

"Julian!"

"Okay, okay," Julian, replied gathering his thoughts. "I felt the turmoil between Robert and myself had to come to an end, because it was affecting my family. I was determined to do what was necessary to work out an understanding between the two of us. When I arrived at his house, I had to insist to have an audience with him. He seemed disgusted to see me. He did not invite me into the house, but he did not refuse me. He just walked away from me, retreating inside. I decided quickly to follow him. We got into his office and began to argue." Julian paused and took a deep breath and with a gulp, continued his monologue, "After a few terse exchanges, we resolved our differences and then I came home."

"How did you resolve your differences?" Dennis asked softly, trying not to smile.

Julian squirmed. "Well….."

"Go ahead," Dennis prodded.

"We….uh…..we….uh," Julian shrugged. "Made love on the floor of the study….that's all," he said matter of factly.

Dennis could no longer hold his amusement and burst out laughing until there were tears coming out of his eyes, "That is one heck of a way to call a truce, Julian. I have to hand it to you. You used the oldest trick in the book and it worked."

"It's not funny," Julian replied, not amused. "You haven't heard the whole story."

"I'm sorry," Dennis apologized. "It's just so unlike you to do something like that. I guess you have changed from a few years ago. You were always such a good boy." Dennis entered into another fit of laughter.

"Dennis, knock it off, or I'm going upstairs to try and think of a way to break this news to my wife," Julian said with frustration.

"Julian, you must be crazy," Dennis said, regaining some of his composure. "You can't do that to the woman. She adores you."

"At some point, I will have to tell her the truth," Julian explained, "One thing that hasn't changed through the years is that I do my best to tell the truth."

"Another discussion for later," Dennis decided. "Now. Let's hear your story from the very beginning, so I can understand the ending."

"Okay," Julian replied, inhaling a deep breath. "Some of this is still fuzzy, while other things are more clear. Life here in the parish has been basically good. I know you would find it hard to understand this, but I have always felt that I belonged here from the minute I landed on this property. At first, I guess it was an escape, like I was born to another world. You have to admit, it is a lot different than the place where we lived." Julian smiled faintly and Dennis returned it with affection.

Julian starred off, while trying to recapture the time of just a few short years ago. "You know, I continue to think about the past several years, as I try to put together my life to make it work. However, the part of Robert Lamond, I always left it out of my plans." Julian looked into Dennis's eyes. "I think it drove him into madness." A tear streamed down Julian's face. "Dennis, he really wasn't all that bad. He just had some things about himself that he did not understand. I did nothing to help him until…..Well, I guess it was too late."

"Julian, I'm not understanding you," Dennis said with confusion, "Start at the beginning….again. You came to this place and it felt like home. Forget about putting life back together for now. Let's go through this slowly."

"Alright," Julian replied, while he tried to concentrate. "This is hard Dennis, bear with me. I really am supposed to be taking things light for a while, but I guess it's long past time for recovering from a breakdown of sorts." Julian sighed.

"I was here working for the Pilots for a little while. Things were calm….well relatively speaking….. calm as far as I saw it. I saw them together one night from a distance, yet I felt so close to both of them. It was as if I was there with them. I could look into their eyes and see the most beautiful things. Their faces seemed to be the ones of angels." Dennis was getting ready to speak, until Julian put a finger to his lips.

"I fell in love with both of them that night," Julian deadpanned. "I loved them both in different ways. I somehow believed that both of them fell in love with me that same night, even though they could not see me. They just knew something had evolved that night and none of us knew what was born."

Dennis still looked astonished.

"Let me finish this," Julian said, asking for patience.

Dennis nodded.

"Of course I'm talking of Emily and Robert," Julian explained, "They became engaged that night."

"Interesting." Dennis nodded pensively.

"Well, very soon after that, I met the both of them," Julian continued. "Emily and I became fast friends. I really just liked to hear her talk about things. I was quiet in those days. It was good. I learned to listen, instead of being so glib, as I had been in the past."

Dennis smiled.

"The depression had really overtaken me, at that point. I felt some of the burden released when I overdid some things. For example, working until exhaustion; running until I dropped; fasting unnecessarily and being with Emily, while driving Robert crazy," Julian mused.

"Why did driving him crazy earn you some release?" Dennis asked.

"You have to realize," Julian explained, "I was repressing any real feelings I had inside myself for him. At that point, I could not have possibly dealt with the feelings of intensity which I held for this man. This sounds absurd, but for me to passively make him behave with some passion, gave me some release by seeing him so distressed."

"I take back about what I said about him being horrible," Dennis said soberly.

"I am not proud of the way I handled him," Julian demurred. "We really treated each other badly....until the end."

"The end?" Dennis replied.

"Yes. The end," Julian said softly. "You see, this story had a happy ending. At least I thought it did. You will see. Let's not get too far ahead."

"Okay." Dennis began to concentrate on listening. "You were not concerned with what you were feeling in those days, when you saw them together."

"Exactly," Julian agreed. " I really did not care about anything, except keeping the world around me in one stable piece. I was an active volcano inside, but I felt if the outside world was in harmony, my insides could contain my turmoil. So that was my life's goal; keeping the world, as I knew it. Emily and Robert would get married. That was okay, as long as I could be safe here on the farm. But it would not be that way. The three of us were drawn together. Emily and I got to be better friends. As our friendship grew, so did my involvement with the Pilot family here in the big house." Julian paused a moment.

"You know Dennis, I never really had a mom, dad, brothers, and sisters. I always wanted to be in a family like that, so naturally, I was drawn to the Pilots through Emily. I grew to love Pilot, Louisa, Jack and the other siblings, when they came back home for visits. This was more stability in the outside world to support the one crumbling inside of me."

"I will always remember you being so disappointed in having Elizabeth and Bernard as parents. Anytime we had other than phone contacts with them whatsoever, it was a constant reminder to you. Yet, you talked with Elizabeth every day."

"You know that was business," Julian replied defensively. "The only thing she ever mentioned that was personal was her distaste for you."

"How could I forget," Dennis said with mockery. "Let's get back with the story. While you gained a girlfriend, you gained the family you always desired. What about Robert? Where did he fit in this mess?"

"To everyone, it must have seemed he was jealous of my relationship with his fiancée and later his ex-fiancée. I think to some extent, this was true. Marrying Emily was all part of a great plan of his and his late father. He was to continue the great family legacy with a fine family such as the Pilots. Robert had deeply loved his father and would have died rather than disappoint him or go against his wishes," Julian explained.

"So you both were torn between the truth of your feelings for each other and the world in which you both lived," Dennis replied pensively.

"I suppose," Julian mused. "I wanted to be left alone to guard my safety net of the Pilots, while he wished to continue his father's legacy. We both decided that marrying Emily would seal our ambitions."

"Did you ever seek out to marry her?" Dennis asked.

"No," Julian replied. "I got lucky I guess."

"So did she," Dennis said warmly. "I imagine you were a better choice than he could have ever have been."

"Thanks," Julian frowned. "But she really deserved a lot better than the both of us."

"Perhaps," Dennis agreed and then added, "Finish."

"Okay. Without Emily, the man thought he had nothing else to live for in order to exist. The idea of a homosexual existence was not a concept he really understood, besides the fact it was something his father would have never accepted," Julian replied thinking while he was speaking.

"How did you come up with all these conclusions in such a short period of time?" Dennis inquired.

"I suppose I knew all these things, but never got around to putting words to them," Julian explained. "I'm just sorry it's too late."

"What are you saying, Julian?" Dennis asked.

"Dennis, I can't help but feel somewhat responsible for his death," Julian answered with guilt.

"Go ahead with the story," Dennis prodded.

"Robert made it his ambition to take back what was rightfully his family's destiny to carry the family name into the next generation," Julian reiterated. "He felt Emily truly belonged to him along with any children she birthed. I was branded as the bad guy. Not only did I possess the wife and children he coveted, but I ignited feelings inside him that did not conform to his destiny."

"This poor man was clearly tormented," Dennis agreed.

"But not in the end," Julian insisted.

"You keep saying that," Dennis replied, losing patience. "Let's get to the point."

"When I went into the house and followed him into his study, I closed the door behind us. We got into sort of a heated, emotional discussion. Once again, he was the expressing party, while I felt release during his tirade," Julian explained. "For some reason, I was willing to give him everything he seemed to want. My wife. My children. The promise to leave town and never to come back."

"Why did you do that?" Dennis asked gently.

"It got so I could not bear to see him tormented. I would have done anything at that point. He was so desperate; the end of his rope," Julian said with tears flowing from his eyes. "I would do anything for my wife and children to make sure they were safe. I felt the same for him. I wanted his suffering to end."

"Julian, what about yourself?" Dennis asked incredulously. "You are sounding overly dramatic and sanctimonious."

"Probably," Julian answered, "But don't you see, Dennis, it is the same thing all over again. I make a mess of everything to the extent that I feel overwhelmed. It was just easier to leave. Like, everyone would be better off without me."

"I understand," Dennis said, taking his hand. "So, what happened?"

"I thought he lost total control, but no," Julian struggled to understand. "He was released from a stronghold. He took me into his arms and we made the most passionate love….maybe I should not call it love. Whatever it was, does not have a name. Also, as wonderful as it was, I never want to experience it again."

"That seems so bizarre," Dennis commented. "How can he go from one extreme of totally loathing you to being passionately enthralled with you? Doesn't that only happen in the movies?"

"The answer is really simple," Julian said lightly. "I surprised him and gave him a choice. He decided he did not want his father's dream for himself. He saw an opportunity to express his own nature and he instinctively took it."

"Do you really believe that?" Dennis asked skeptically.

"Dennis, you should have seen him after we finished. He was so different. He seemed so gentle and kind, like he never could have a mean thought," Julian explained. "He asked me to go away with him. He knew I would refuse, but he was not distressed. He seemed to realize there was another world outside this one where he could make his peace. I did not have to tell him where it was."

"How did you think you would be able to let him get away from you so easily?" Dennis asked with some concern. "It seems you were really mad for him."

"I guess I knew he had to find his way for himself for awhile. Anyway, we said something vaguely about hooking up together at a later time. I am not sure what that meant, but it was all I could digest at the time," Julian replied.

"This is some story, Julian," Dennis said, relaxing against the back of the sofa. "But where does the murder fit into all of this?"

"Dennis, he was so happy when I left him," Julian said.

"Obviously, somebody was not happy with him," Dennis mused. "Who wanted him dead, Julian?"

"I really don't know, Dennis," Julian responded with a frown.

"You said the three of you were connected in some way," Dennis said with sincerity. "Surely this must tell you something."

"My instincts tell me that he was caught by surprise. That he did not know it was coming," Julian replied.

"My gut told me the same thing," Dennis agreed. "I felt it at the house."

"The house?" Julian responded with confusion.

"Yeah, the house," Dennis replied deep in thought.

"Whose house?" Julian asked, already fearing the answer.

"Lamond's house of course. You know I had to see the scene of the crime in the purest form."

"Dennis, that was very dangerous. What if you had gotten caught?" Julian scolded. "We're all in enough trouble without that happening."

"Do you have any better ideas about solving this thing?" Dennis questioned, looking into his ex-husband's eyes.

"Yeah, maybe you could question people. Isn't that what lawyers are supposed to do?" Julian suggested half-heartedly.

"You know you can't get the whole truth that way," Dennis scoffed. "You lived with me long enough to know I had to take some risks in my business."

"I always tried not to think about it," Julian explained, turning away from him. He got up and walked to the other side of the room with his back to Dennis. He turned and said softly, "Dennis, I really don't want to go to jail. I wouldn't stand a chance surviving."

Dennis got up from his seat and met him across the room. He took Julian by the shoulders. "Whatever it takes, I won't let that happen." They fell into a light embrace.

Jack came into the parlor. "I'm sorry to break the moment, but Daddy is waiting in his study for you."

"You go ahead," Julian insisted. "I've had enough for now. I trust whatever the two of you decide."

"Tell Pilot I'll be along in a few minutes," Dennis said to Jack.

He turned to Julian. "Go check on your babies and we will talk later."

"Okay, thanks Dennis," Julian gave him a pat on the shoulder and left the room.

Now to get to the photos, Dennis thought.

CHAPTER 18

"What do you have?" Pilot asked as Dennis entered the study.

"A lot," Dennis gushed as he let the pictures fall onto the desk. "We need to look through all of these."

"What are we looking for?" Pilot asked.

"Anything that captures our attention. We should look at even the least conspicuous details."

"This looks like it will take a while," Pilot commented with a sigh. "Shouldn't Matt be looking at these?"

"I doubt he would be of any use. The man is spent," Dennis said, shaking his head.

"Very well. Let's get started," Pilot replied as he took up the first photo.

After awhile, Pilot noted, "Robert kept notes on a *GW*. Do you suppose that could have any bearing?"

"Could very well be," Dennis mused. "There's a folder here somewhere with a tab labeled with that ID."

"Where is it?" Pilot asked, sifting through the photos, "Here it is." He scanned the notes.

"What did you find?" Dennis asked.

"It's strange," Pilot remarked incredulously. "There's an account for many of the events surrounding this household. They are dated."

"Do you know someone with the initials, *GW*?" Dennis asked.

"It could be any number of people, except there are many instances, where some of the help staff would not have privy to these events." Pilot said with thought.

"How about if they made a concerted effort to spy? Would it be hard for those other than the family to gain this information?" Dennis asked.

"No, I guess it wouldn't," Pilot agreed and then added, "Are we assuming that the murder is connected with this household?"

"Well, we aren't ruling anything out, of course," Dennis stated. "But it does seem that Julian is being framed with the murder, which may lead to such a connection."

"You don't believe that he may have been in the wrong place at the right time?" Pilot asked.

"Possibly," Dennis replied thoughtfully. "I don't want to be glued to one area of suspicion, while neglecting an obvious clue. My feeling is that Julian is connected with this murder in some fashion. Let's keep looking and try to come up with an identity for *GW*," Dennis said as he continued to sift through the notes.

"Do you know if Lamond was ill?" Dennis asked.

"I don't know of such a thing. Why do you ask?" Pilot replied.

"In his appointment book, each week there is a date set for a Dr. Garner," Dennis explained. "Do you know of a doctor by that name?"

"No," Pilot answered slowly. "I know most of the folks around these parts, so it must be someone in New Orleans or somewhere far away."

"It could be appointments made for phone calls, but the times have the consistency to indicate actual weekly face to face meetings. Phone calls can happen haphazardly, while face to face meetings obviously need to have more structured time constraints," Dennis guessed.

"Do you think it could mean anything?" Pilot asked himself as well as Dennis.

"I don't know. Can you have it checked out?" Dennis inquired. "It would be nice to question this doctor."

"We probably should have all the people in this book questioned that we can identify. I'll get my sources onto it immediately," Pilot stated like someone with power.

"Do you already have someone lined up to do all of this digging?" Dennis asked with amazement.

"My dear boy, with this family's affairs constantly on the line, I have spies everywhere you can imagine," Pilot said with a grim smile. "Believe me, we'll get to the bottom of all of this mess. We'll have so much information, that it will be impossible not to find this murderer. What my sources can't get, a little arm twisting will render the final results."

"You are either a great friend to have or a very formidable opponent," Dennis said with a nervous smile.

"You are right, young man. You are right." Pilot agreed.

After a couple moments of silence, Dennis stood up from the desk. "I think this is all I can handle for the moment. I guess we can go over this material again once you've had some time to have your people check on these names."

"Very well," Pilot replied as he gathered the material together and placed it neatly into a folder.

Dennis stood to leave, but then turned to face Pilot before he made for the door, "Tell me, if you can thoroughly have people investigated so quickly, why did you not get a dossier of Julian? I mean, you knew very little of his past and yet you let him marry your daughter."

"I never said I didn't have him checked out for his life before he arrived," Pilot replied offhandedly.

"Well, surely you would have had something to say about his eh.....situation had you known," Dennis said with a puzzled look.

"True," Pilot answered. "Lamond had him checked out and obviously he wasn't so thorough, but there were no red flags for me to cause any kind of suspicion. Next, I believe there is nothing that warrants a full write-up of his life. His business is his own private affair, as long as he did not kill anybody, or was some other kind of criminal, which of course, I would have been informed."

"Still......the risks involved," Dennis replied, unconvinced.

"Yes, I did have him checked out to keep a record of past activities and history. However, I never did look at the material. I have it, in case I ever have need for it," Pilot explained. "As difficult as it may seem to believe, I try to let my children and those associated with the family live their own lives. They are left free to make their own mistakes and learn from them, so I leave them to their privacy. My daughter would disown me for interfering in her life. I've meddled, as a father is tempted to do but have always gotten caught. She is not the best person to have mad at me or anyone else."

"That all makes sense," Dennis said, convinced.

"Son, don't judge me too harshly," Pilot ordered in a quiet tone.

"Point taken," Dennis answered, "But you are a powerful man and I'm just getting to know you. Please try to understand."

"Point taken," Pilot said with a smile. "What's next on your agenda?"

"To talk with your daughter," Dennis said with less conviction.

"Well, good luck," Pilot resigned with a sigh. "I wish I could say I'd like to be a fly on the wall during that conversation."

"Thanks for the encouragement," Dennis replied with a frown.

Soon after Dennis left the study, there was a series of knocks to the door. "Yes," Pilot answered.

"It's Elizabeth," she replied.

"Come in, Mrs. Steele," Pilot invited. "Do you need to use the phone?"

"No," Elizabeth replied as she entered the room. "Bernard and I had our own private lines installed, since we have had to work in this part of the country."

"What can I do for you?" Pilot asked, going through another folder containing several sheets of paper.

"I thought I may have a word with you, Mr. Pilot," Elizabeth stated in a firm tone.

"Go ahead. I'm listening," Pilot said with dying patience.

"I just want to say, Bernard and I are holding you responsible for the outcome of this unfortunate situation concerning my son," Elizabeth said, looking directly at Pilot.

"Oh?" Pilot replied, still looking through his papers.

"Yes," Elizabeth said, retaining her resolve, "There would never have been any of this trouble had you sent him home from the beginning of his stay in this dreadful part of the country. You and your family have taken advantage of his good heart and generous spirit. You've led him into a life where he clearly does not belong."

"Your point?" Pilot asked, reading a particular document.

"What I'm saying is," Elizabeth replied slowly in a strong but quiet tone, "There could be some ...consequences for you if he spends even a day in jail."

"I see," Pilot said, unperturbed.

"No, I don't think you do," Elizabeth said, losing patience with his lack of attention. "There appears to be an...indiscretion in Seattle, which you most likely would like to keep secret...."

Pilot turned to her giving his full attention. "I know exactly what you mean and I would not call it an indiscretion, Mrs. Steele. It may offend some people, but I probably do that every day." After a pause, Pilot began again, "Frankly, Mrs. Steele, I am losing patience with you and that miserable husband..."

"Ex-husband," Elizabeth interrupted with a snicker.

"Whatever the case may be," Pilot continued without missing a beat. "When this whole thing is over, you and your husband.... ex-husband are to leave this house and never set foot into it again."

"As long as we understand each other," Elizabeth agreed with gentle confidence.

"No, Mrs. Steele, I don't think we do," Pilot replied, continuing in a normal tone. "It would be in your best interest to encourage that boy to stay here with his wife and family where he belongs. You need to stop badgering him to return east with you.

"I think you are hardly in a position to be giving orders to me," Elizabeth warned with a slight chuckle under her breath.

"Well, let's see," Pilot said, picking up a page of a document that he had been examining. "It appears, Mrs. Steele, you have made a lot of people rich and made some enemies along the way."

"That should be of no surprise to you," Elizabeth replied.

"There have been many people trying to yank skeletons out of your closet with little success. Any atrocities you've created in your life have done little to affect your success or the way your family regards you."

"Making people lots of money tends to make people uh.....forget certain misfortunes," Elizabeth agreed.

"The only one ever to forgive your abusive nature has been your son," Pilot continued.

"This is not anything new to either you or myself. I suggest we conclude our business." Elizabeth made ready to leave.

"No, Mrs. Steele, we are just getting started," Pilot said with a glare. He was taking no pleasure in this conversation. "It appears that Bernard is really not Julian's father." This was the first time that Pilot had referred to his son in-law other than Matt. "It appears that Julian is the product of a brutal rape that lead to his conception."

"That is ridiculous," Elizabeth said with a laugh of disbelief. "He was born 13 months after that incident."

"It's amazing that you can refer to it as if it happened to one of your dreadful clients," Pilot said with pity.

"Well, things happen and then we move on," Elizabeth replied off handedly.

"Well, you did an excellent job of covering it up. There was no trace of evidence to support that this rapist is actually Julian's father. However, Julian's birthday was moved four months later and there is no record to prove that this actually happened. His birth certificate reads the date that you set to have had happened four months later than it actually took place," Pilot said with amazement as he read the document.

"Interesting theory," Elizabeth commented as she sat in a nearby chair. "But as you said, there is no trace of evidence to prove this allegation."

"I said there *was* no trace of evidence, but now there is," Pilot replied.

"That's nonsense," Elizabeth answered back with irritation. "The only person who could have made such a statement is not alive. He has been dead for years. That animal had no way of fathoming such an idea. As you are probably aware, he met an unfortunate accident while in prison years ago. If he had been the least bit suspicious, he would have done the math to dismiss such a thought."

"Mrs. Steele," Pilot said, beginning to initiate a condescending tone. "Paternity tests these days have become so significant that this theory could be easily proven. I understand that this man has been dead for several years, but it was not unusual, even in those days, for the authorities to save tissues samples from offenders of violent crimes to possibly connect these criminals to other crimes. Scientists knew that it was only a matter of time before such determinations could be made."

"Do you think Bernard would agree with your theory?" Elizabeth asked with a light smile. She was enjoying this sport of cat and mouse.

Pilot pursed his lips. "Julian's father, which I have no intention of informing either of them otherwise, could care less when a baby was born. Besides, he was out of the country at the time of Julian's birth."

"I see." Elizabeth sighed with resignation. "Nice work Mr. Pilot. However, Julian might be upset at first that I allegedly lied about his paternity and Bernard as well, but they will see that I only did it to protect them from the awful truth. Besides, Bernard is his father even if it's not by blood. You can see how much my son adores him."

"You may be right," Pilot agreed. "Julian could be upset at first, but he will forgive you as he always has in the past; probably while little time passes."

"So," Elizabeth started with a smirk. "Where does this lead us, Mr. Pilot? As you may have already guessed, my offer still stands."

"As you probably have guessed," Pilot sighed as he sat on the corner of his desk with his hands in his lap, "There is more."

"Yes?" Elizabeth answered with surprise. "I thought you've uncovered everything."

"There is always more, Mrs. Steele," Pilot replied. "It's just a matter of how far one has to go."

"And how far are we going to go, Mr. Pilot?" Elizabeth asked with amusement.

"Far enough to get you back east, with a promise never to return, unless, of course, your son invites you. In fact, a promise to never contact him unless, of course, he wishes to hear from you," Pilot replied. "That is how far we are going to go. I feel you can be persuaded."

"Before I scamper back east, would you mind telling me why I should go with my tail tucked between my legs? Or are you bluffing, Mr. Pilot," Elizabeth challenged.

"Well, let's see," Pilot began once more. "There is a certain trust fund that was bequeathed by Bernard's mother to the first born male child of her first born, as which is supposedly Julian. According to her will, If Julian does not survive her, then the estate is to be handed to the next first born male in Bernard's line."

Elizabeth rose from her chair and paced to the far window. She turned to Pilot. "What does any of this have to do with you and me?"

"Nothing, if you pack your bags and do what you are told," Pilot replied.

Elizabeth sat back down in her chair, "Go on. Let's see what else you have."

"When Bernard's mother died, she made small mention of all of her relatives, except for the first born grandchild. She wanted her first born male grandchild to be in a position to lead the family dynasty. This heir is inheriting a vast estate, dwarfing the other relatives' shares. She assumed it would be Julian that would be able to claim the trust. She believed for years that she was dying. At the time that her will was drawn, she knew that her eldest male grandchild was too young to manage such large holdings. So, she appointed you to manage the trust for a modest salary. When Julian is handed the trust, you will be able to claim one third of the entire estate. She gave you such a large share, because she knew that your work would be over a period of years, and such a potential large payoff would only encourage you to grow the estate even larger. However, it was a slight slip of the pen. If Julian does not inherit the trust, you will lose everything except your modest salary, because if Julian is not the heir, the trust will not be required to hand over the third of the estate to you." Pilot paused as he reached for a glass of water.

"That minor detail can be contested if necessary," Elizabeth replied.

After pausing a moment to think, Pilot commented, "I don't think it can. I think the grand lady made the details exactly as she wanted them. She was said to be sharp as the crack of the whip, right up until the time of her death. During her life span, she was regarded as a vibrant, brilliant woman, and projected a very powerful spirit. I'm sure she had so many legal minds to assist with such a large estate, that an oversight such as this was not possible. She must have had some sort of knowledge or suspicion of Julian's paternity, but loved him just as if he were her same flesh. She probably aimed to protect Julian from the truth. In the case that it ever comes to surface, the rightful heir will step into place."

"This theory seems to be a bit far fetched," Elizabeth commented with amusement. "There are a lot of *ifs*."

"But it fits and makes so much sense," Pilot exclaimed with enthusiasm. "With such vast holdings at stake, an intelligent woman would have checked all the facts. I feel for her. She probably agonized over this entire ordeal."

"I see you've done your homework," Elizabeth remarked with a calm smile. "You have to know she wanted Julian to have all that money. He was the only one who could please that awful woman. Nobody else could stand to be within sight of her. People were often devastated after visits with her."

"What about you?" Pilot asked with doubt. "You don't seemed to have harbored any ill affects from the woman."

"Such things do not affect me, as they would other people, "Elizabeth bristled. "She could say any of the degenerate things she pleased, as long as I got what I wanted from her. I had no trouble dealing with the woman."

Elizabeth continued, "I underestimated you, Mr. Pilot. I can see you are a little bit more than a country farmer."

"I'm sorry I can't take credit for this investigation, as someone else has done it for me. I have just now learned of this, although I've had it in my possession for some time. I don't like to use such things unless I'm forced to it," Pilot replied.

"Well, let's finish the story," Elizabeth said with amusement.

"Sure," Pilot replied. "Another quirk, perhaps to indulge a dying woman, the heir, after he reaches the age of 21 years of age, must come to the deceased's Boston mansion in Massachusetts to be assigned to the trust. Nobody has lived on or near the structure and grounds since the grand lady's death, but a loyal staff has stayed on to maintain it. Upon the signing of the final papers and the transfer of the authoritative powers, the heir is free to live in the huge mansion as he pleases, while governing the family business holdings, politics, philanthropy, and family affairs. Therefore, it's only logical that you would want to get Julian to move back east to push him into the mansion to sign the papers, so you could collect your millions after so many years of hard work before the truth is exposed."

"What is to stop me from just asking Julian to come back east for a visit, and then let him make his way back south, after he has completed his paper work?" Elizabeth inquired.

"I think we both know the answer," Pilot replied with a smile. "Under the terms of the trust, the heir will not take total possession of the family fortune, nor will your share be awarded, until he has been entrenched into the business. He must have lived in the mansion no less than 7 years. You are hoping that once Julian is back east, he will realize that he misses the old life and would find it difficult to return south. Your instincts tell you that he would rather give up the fortune than spend years in that mansion running the family affairs. I believe you feel it will be enough of a struggle to get him back for a visit much less to live. I have to believe your instincts to be correct."

"He may or may not decide to come back for the money," Elizabeth supposed thoughtfully. "What is to stop me from at least asking him?"

"What indeed!" Pilot exclaimed, "If that boy is placed as the heir, there could be a lot of trouble if he is found to be a fraud."

"No one will ever know, unless you decide to tell," Elizabeth deadpanned. "How much of the pie do you want for your silence?"

"This is the deal," Pilot started. "When this murder investigation is completed, you and Bernard are to pack your bags and leave this place, never to return, unless you get an invitation from Julian. There will be no mention of his paternity or his grandmother's will. If he should return for a visit to Washington, you may not present the truth of his paternity or implore him to seek the fortune. If he should decide to remain in the east, you can make whatever pitch you wish to him. That is it."

"And if I'm able to convince him to return at this time?" Elizabeth asked calmly with a bittersweet smile.

"Then he and the world may come across the truth of his paternity," Pilot replied.

"I find it hard to believe that you would be that cruel."

"I am sure he would be devastated. However, he would recover knowing the truth. Eventually, he would prefer the natural chain of events than to be found a fraud in later years. Too many people already know the truth, or at least have their suspicions. Remember, if my sources were able to uncover this material, others may be able to do the same," Pilot explained.

"With this deal, the odds for my success are greatly reduced," Elizabeth deduced.

"You don't seem to be overly upset, Mrs. Steele," Pilot remarked with surprise.

"It is all a game, Mr. Pilot," Elizabeth replied as she got to her feet. "The fun is just beginning. I haven't lost; it is just a minor setback. It is by no means over."

"You are a very complicated woman, Mrs. Steele," Pilot commented. "I would think you would be greatly disappointed, with millions of dollars falling through your hands after so many years of work for mere peanuts."

"I do not have a large fortune, Mr. Pilot, but I have all the money I really need to live comfortably," Elizabeth explained. "However, I still play to win."

"No matter who you destroy?" Pilot asked.

"I'm not killing people, Mr. Pilot," Elizabeth retorted. "I can't be responsible for others' weaknesses. Survival of the fittest, I believe."

"I believe our business is concluded," Pilot said as he dismissed the meeting.

"One more thing," Elizabeth said, ignoring his invitation to leave.

"Yes, Mrs. Steele?" Pilot replied, slightly exasperated.

"If you have all of these sources of power at your fingertips, why are you not using these people to clear my son of these ridiculous charges?" Elizabeth asked with curiosity.

"It is not necessary," Pilot explained, "Your son in-law, or whatever he is to you, will find the killer. There is some unfinished business between your son and him. For Dennis to help Julian get through this unfortunate situation will make some healing for the both of them, before he returns to his law practice in Washington. In addition, this is a family affair and should not be handled by strangers if it can be avoided."

"You seem to have a great deal of confidence in somebody you have just met," Elizabeth observed.

"He is a good boy, with a big heart, and good smarts," Pilot replied. "He will get the killer."

"I guess we all are forced to live with your great hunches," Elizabeth said with distaste.

"Yes, we are," Pilot answered, "Now if you will excuse me, I have plenty of phone calls to make."

CHAPTER 19

Dennis knocked lightly on the door of the children's playroom.

"Yes?" Emily answered.

Dennis opened the door slightly. It had been left ajar, but he was apprehensive as to whether he would be welcomed into the room.

"Is it alright if I come in?" Dennis inquired shyly.

"Sure," Emily replied with a warm smile. She was sitting on the floor reading a picture book to William, while Candy lay playfully on a blanket. Louis was intent with his blocks of shapes.

With a little confidence, Dennis came and sat next to her, curious to see what she and the little boy were reading. With each new picture, he laughed out loud as he guessed the correct animal that Emily asked him to name.

"He's been through this book a thousand times, but each run through is as entertaining as the first," Emily explained.

Sensing the two adults were giving all their attention to William, Louis picked up a book off the floor and plopped into Dennis's lap, as he thrust it into the big hands.

"I'm sorry, but with five of them competing for attention, none of the babies happens to be shy," Emily said with a chuckle.

"No, it's quite okay," Dennis assured her. "What does he want me to do?"

"He'll show you," Emily answered and went back to reading with her other son.

Louis opened the book to the first page and looked at Dennis. "I guess he wants me to read to him."

Emily nodded. "*The Three Little Kittens* happens to be his favorite book of the day."

"Okay," Dennis began. "Here it goes."

After a short time, the two boys got bored with the books and went to look for other toys to amuse themselves.

"Those two are so busy," Dennis observed.

"Short attention spans, but easy to entertain," Emily commented.

"Aren't there two older boys?" Dennis inquired.

"Yes," Emily answered. "Matt's taken them to the stable to see the ponies. He has been putting Jesse on horseback, but I'm worried Jay is still too small. Trouble is, Jesse won't leave Matt alone until he is on the pony's back and then Jay will want to do what his older brother is doing."

"So what will happen?" Dennis asked, bewildered.

"Matt will figure something.... he always does, where the children are concerned. And the animals, for that matter. He's good with both of them," Emily said pensively.

"You seem so sad," Dennis commented with concern. "You know things are going to be alright don't you?"

"I'm sure you and Daddy will straighten out this ridiculous charade, but I know things won't be the same after they settle," Emily said with resignation.

"I don't think any of us will be the same," Dennis agreed. "But we first have to figure things out and reach the truth. I need your help."

"The truth," Emily laughed to herself, "It's funny how it gets lost in the muck at times." She rose from the floor and gestured for Dennis to do the same. They moved to sit into a pair of comfortable chairs, while the children played. At times, one of the boys would stop what he was doing to go over and kiss the baby. Candy would laugh as she got the special attention.

"It's so strange how well they get along with each other," Dennis said with surprise.

"It helps that they're close in age and they spend all their time together. They have a skirmish now and then, but with some guidance, they learn to play well together."

"I need you to tell me what you know of Robert and his relationships between you and Matt. Also, I need to hear your version of the two men's involvement with each other," Dennis said, directly to the point.

"What do you want to know?" Emily asked matter of factly.

"I understand you and Robert grew up together. You can start there and work your way to the present," Dennis instructed.

"This could take a while," Emily warned.

"I have plenty of time," Dennis assured her.

"Well, if you don't mind me telling the story while I change a few diapers and give out a couple bottles," Emily offered.

Dennis was slightly queasy. "I thought you had a nanny for these things."

"We do," Emily confirmed. "But I wanted to spend some time with them myself today. I usually keep so busy with other things."

"Motherhood seems to suit you," Dennis said with a smile. "I can see why Matt cares for you, since the case is the complete opposite with Elizabeth."

"I usually try to refrain from making disparaging comments about people, but I have to agree with you on this point." They both got a chuckle at Elizabeth's expense.

"Ever since I can remember, I've known Robert," Emily began. "We used to play together as these children here do. My first memories are when we were about their age. It's true, I also played with my brothers, but Robert was so much closer in age to me than they were. Still, playing with Robert seemed so much.... easier in many ways. I guess we always related well together."

"It sounds as if you were best friends straight from the womb," Dennis said with a smile.

"Something along those lines," Emily agreed. "However, I think our two families always had grander plans for the two of us. Daddy and Robert's father seemed thrilled that we got along so well. Maybe it due from a standpoint of future business alliances uniting the families, but there were other reasons. The families were close in those days. Robert's mother was alive when we were small. The atmosphere was so lively. I remember being so happy at that time and I believe Robert was just as happy. We grew up thinking that we would get married some day. When we played house, we were married and we used dolls along with stuffed animals as our children. We'd play for hours."

"It sounds like the Camelot years," Dennis said with a big grin.

"Maybe they were," Emily laughed.

"How long did the magic years last?" Dennis inquired.

"Not too many," Emily replied with a smile. "Robert's mother died and along with her, the luster of life between the two families. Robert's father became somewhat removed; spent more time with his business. Or at least, we saw less of them as a family. My nanny would take me to his house to play, or his nanny would do the same, but family get togethers were fewer and farther between times. There would be the standard visits at holidays, etc., but that was it. The fairy dust settled, but Robert and I remained close."

"Was there ever a change in your relationship as you got older?" Dennis asked.

"No there wasn't," Emily chuckled with disbelief. "We would do homework together, play together...we'd even have sleep overs together and they were a blast. We got to eat all the dessert we wanted sometimes. We'd get so sick, but it was still fun."

"You look like you want to cry," Dennis said. He wanted to put his arm around her to give her comfort, but decided not to push it.

"I suppose I will grieve his death when there is time. I know he did horrible things these last few years, but I still love him, like when we were kids. I never stopped loving him," Emily explained.

"So there never was a change in the relationship?" Dennis asked, getting to the point of the discussion.

"During our high school years, we would go on dates and he would kiss me goodnight after he brought me home," Emily said.

"That seems reasonable," Dennis said.

"But don't you see? We did the same things before high school. We'd hang out, play a game or two, eat popcorn watch a movie, or ride horses together. When we said good-bye, we'd give other a kiss goodnight, like we always did. It was a best friends thing."

"What perpetuated the change to 'dates'?" Dennis asked.

"It was our parents. They started to call our get togethers dates," Emily explained. "My nanny would scold me when I telephoned Robert to talk. She watched our activity when we would be together. He was supposed to call me, she said. I thought this was humorous, after all, it was only Robert. At first, Robert thought it funny, but later he agreed that he would be the one to call. He became so serious as we grew up."

"He wasn't always the serious type?" Dennis asked.

"Well, he was and he wasn't," Emily replied. "Robert was always a very good boy as we grew up. He always obeyed and wasn't the least bit adventuresome. He never played practical jokes, but would give me a tease time to time. What I mean is, when we were little, he would always laugh and smile. When he got older, he was always businesslike and much more reserved. His smiles and laughter became slightly forced. I used to tease him about these things, and he would say things like, "I have to behave like a gentleman; we are not kids anymore."

"Sounds like he became a stick in the mud," Dennis commented with a smile.

"He was becoming more like his father, whom he idolized," Emily explained. "But at times, he was the same old Robert. I didn't fault him for who he was trying to be. I understood, in some way, what he was trying to do."

"And what was that?" Dennis asked.

"He wanted his father's approval," Emily answered. "He wanted my daddy's approval; he wanted me to love him; he wanted to be a big success like his father and his father before him. The strangest thing of all is that he already had those things. He really could do no wrong with any of these people even if he tried. Everybody loved Robert and was already proud of him. However, Robert felt he still had to earn these things, like his father's approval, long after his death. I know he died proud of his son, but Robert never believed it. I know he would tell Robert how proud of him he was, but he never believed it."

"It seems he grew to be an unhappy man," Dennis replied

"I'm afraid you're right," Emily agreed. "I thought Robert would eventually find his way." After a short pause, she said with a somber look, "I think maybe he did in the end."

"How do you mean?" Dennis asked with surprise.

"Robert wasn't the horrible man people thought he was," Emily explained. "I know he did some terrible things to this family in recent years, but for the first time in his life, he was asking for help. It doesn't make what he did right; it's just an explanation. Had he lived, at some point he would have understood his reckless behavior and paid restitution for it."

"At some point, we have to get to where you, Matt, and Robert fit together," Dennis said softly.

"This will be more difficult," Emily replied with a strained tone, "For some reason, I've chosen to ignore this trilogy for years."

"It seems you have this in common with the other two involved," Dennis stated to give credence to this short analysis.

"Yes." She hung her head slightly while clasping her hands, "Just another chapter in this year's nightmare. Where should I start?"

"Start when you and Robert began dating, since that was where you stopped," Dennis replied. "There must be some reason you chose to take a break?"

"Like I said, Robert was my best friend," Emily continued. "However, it was time for us to go to college. We went to separate schools. I told him that I thought we should be able to go on dates with other people while at school. He reluctantly agreed, as long as we knew we'd become engaged when we graduated. I thought that was reasonable, because four years seemed a lifetime away at that point. I actually felt I had some breathing room for four years. During my visits home for holidays and summers, we dated."

"Four years has a way of catching up," Dennis said with a smile.

"Yeah, but it wasn't like that," Emily replied. "I had a wonderful time in college and experienced a great deal. I enjoyed seeing Robert when it was time to come home. It was a fabulous four years. I dated some great guys, but they weren't overly impressed with me or I with them. As graduation neared, many of my friends were getting married. I thought maybe that it should be time for me. I knew Robert was expecting us to be engaged, but as long I didn't agree to it, I thought little of it. But then, I thought, 'I've known this man all my life; he is smart; he is handsome; he is the ideal package.' I thought, 'Yes, I should marry this man."

"So, you became engaged?" Dennis inquired.

"Then I met Matt," Emily said in a low voice.

"I hate to interrupt, but it seems the little ones are getting sleepy," Dennis noticed.

"Yes, I better change them and put them to bed," Emily agreed. "Come with me and I'll finish this story. Matt will be along in few minutes with the boys and I'd like us to be done when he gets here."

"Okay," Dennis replied. "You met Matt."

"Yes," Emily said with a smile, "I liked him right away. For some reason, I thought Robert would like him as much as I did and that the three of us could become friends. I imagined Matt thought we could all be friends. It was not like "Love at first sight" with Matt, but I felt so comfortable with him from the start."

"Did the three of you become friends?" Dennis asked.

"Matt and I did, but there were some heavy sparks going on between Robert and Matt, so I did not push."

"Sparks?" Dennis asked, "What do you mean..."

"Sparks...you know...um...." Emily thought for a moment. "It was odd. You would think two nice people would be agreeable, but there was instead friction. I believe it came from both sides, but Robert was more vocal about being uncomfortable."

"Do you think Matt was equally uncomfortable?" Dennis asked.

"As I think about it now, I think he may have been," Emily mused. "My concerns at the time were not about problems people were having with each other. If there were problems, I figured people had the sense to work through them and move on to greater causes. A bit idealistic, don't you think?"

"That would be the most sensible track and the world would get along better if it aspired to something as simple. However, I have to agree with you. People are not simple, but rather dynamic," Dennis replied.

"So, yes. I was young and stupid at the time," Emily said with emphasis. "Yet, I feel it was the wisest choice. Dennis, it really wasn't my battle, because it belonged only to the two of them. If they chose to make me an element of their stress, that does not mean I should involve myself in a situation where I was being seemingly forced to play a part."

"This much is true," Dennis agreed. "But I get the sense you feel you could have done something to help if you took some of the responsibility. You could have been hurt."

"Hurt more than I am feeling at this time?" Emily said with disbelief. "But I see your point. These days, I feel I have experienced the ultimate hurt and then something else happens to put more fuel to the blaze. I see now that I had nothing to do with the conflict between Matt and Robert. However, I hate being the victim of their struggles."

"I think it is time for us to get back to the story," Dennis advised. "I'm losing your train of thought. I really do want to understand."

"Okay," Emily replied. "Something weird was going on with Matt and Robert, but I chose to ignore it. It wasn't my concern, so I decided to take the road where life was leading me, with or without Robert and Matt."

"Understood," Dennis affirmed.

"I decided I wasn't ready to get married," Emily explained. "Call it a whim; something young girls do, but I went with a hunch."

"A hunch?" Dennis said to lead her to more detail.

"Yes," Emily pondered the thought, "I just said it to myself one day, 'Robert will never be my husband. I thought I might be a fool, but had romantic dreams that someday, beyond a shadow of a doubt, I would know exactly the time to get married. I was right, you know."

"No regrets?" Dennis asked.

"None," Emily assured him.

"Let's get to Robert's erratic behavior," Dennis pressed. "When did you start noticing it?

"As soon as he met Matt," Emily answered. "But as I stated earlier, Robert had been slowly changing, since our childhood. Most of us mature, and he did mature. I knew something was different about him, but did not know what it was."

"Do you now?" Dennis asked softly.

Emily finished putting the children down for their nap. Dennis followed her into the bathroom, where she began to draw water into the tub.

"Jesse and Jay will be filthy when they come from the barn," Emily explained. "After they calm from the excitement, they will become very sleepy, so I'll need to rush a bath for them. Second thought, I'll just draw the water; Matt can do the rest."

"That only seems fair," Dennis agreed with a smile. "After all, he is responsible for them getting dirty."

"I'm not sure of some of those things between men," Emily explained. "As I expect men don't know of some of the things between women. I know that's a cop out, but it's the best I can do at the moment."

"I know this is difficult," Dennis prodded, "But I really do need your help."

"Like I said, I stayed away from their problems," Emily said with a defensive tone, "That is...until the night of the murder."

"What was different that night?" Dennis asked carefully.

"Matt hadn't been home from the hospital very long and already he was facing a great deal of stress," Emily explained. "Largely due to his parents staying with us. He was supposed to be taking things easy for a while, to build his resolve for dealing with life issues. There were just so many of them waiting for him when he got home."

" I always stayed clear of the issues between those two, but I could feel the tension reaching a pinnacle. It was so intense. I was afraid of Matt snapping again, so I wanted to protect him, since I'd been so helpless with him since his return. I felt it was time for me to step in to involve myself, to once and for all force a peaceful resolution. Matt had reached the same conclusion, that it was time for this fiasco to end. I thought him to be courageous. However, I was still worried about him. I followed him to Robert's that night. I ended up spying on them, but that wasn't my intention. I wanted to be there in case things got out of hand and to protect my husband."

"So...... how much were you able to observe?" Dennis asked in a slow tone."

"Enough," Emily answered contritely. "I know that house well from my childhood. I had no problem entering the house."

"You were able to get into the house?" Dennis asked, furrowing his brow.

"Yes, of course," Emily replied.

"What did you do once you got inside?" Dennis asked.

"I mostly hid and waited for something to happen," Emily answered.

Dennis felt he was pulling the information from her, but he had to know what she observed that night. "You hid the entire time Matt was in the house."

"Not exactly," Emily fidgeted, "I got curious as to what was happening inside Robert's study. I quietly crept to the door to listen. I was afraid of getting caught. After all, I was not so sure I'd be welcomed. I wanted to be there in case my husband needed me. However, if I wasn't needed, I didn't want to interfere."

"So what did you hear?" Dennis asked intently.

"Not a sound," Emily replied. "I thought I should hear something, but there didn't appear to be talking, screaming, or anything of the sort. I thought it strange, but decided to go to the parlor to wait for them to finish their meeting."

"Did anything else happen, while you were waiting?" Dennis asked.

"Well, I thought I saw a shadow outside the window," Emily said, trying to remember. "I got a peek out of the window and thought I saw a silhouette moving toward the house. It looked familiar to me, but I still cannot place whom I thought I saw. It was dark by this time and I thought perhaps it was a shadow from the trees."

"Think hard, Emily. This could be important," Dennis pushed.

After a pause, Emily shook her head. "I'd have to see it again to gain a clue; I only caught a glimpse."

"If you happen to remember, be sure to tell me," Dennis said with great concern.

"Of course," Emily assured him.

"Are you sure there isn't anything else?" Dennis pressed.

"Well, now that I'm thinking about it," Emily paused in thought. "There was a faint familiar scent in the air at the same time I saw the shadow. Initially, I must have attributed it to the scents of the house."

"But now you are not so sure?" Dennis quizzed.

"The scent is familiar, but I cannot place it," Emily said with concentration.

"Was it a stench or did it smell?" Dennis asked.

"It was a sweet smell, but I'd have to catch it again to have any idea where to place it," Emily said with resignation.

"Okay," Dennis said, deciding to move to another topic. "What happened next?"

"They came out of the study," Emily said gravely. "They sauntered past the parlor toward the kitchen door. They did not notice that I was waiting inside the parlor, so I decided not to make my presence known. I thought I would ask, 'Is everything all right? Is there finally going to be peace between the two of you?' But I didn't. I was in shock."

"What was it that shocked you?" Dennis asked carefully.

"They were laughing and happy with their arms around each other's waists," Emily replied with an astonished look on her face. "They were really quite jovial. I couldn't see very well. I followed just behind them to the door. I was prepared to make my presence known. But I felt while I was inside that I should leave things between the two of them. They appeared to have resolved things. Robert had a disheveled appearance, but Matt looked his usual self. They actually embraced to say good-bye. They actually held it for a short period of time. I thought, 'I should be happy that they became friends.' Like I told you from the start, I felt all of us should have been friends. For some reason, I was not happy. Perhaps the ending was anti-climatic. I did not have to go to the rescue. Things turned out differently from what I was expecting."

"From what you saw, you believe that Matt could not have killed Robert," Dennis surmised.

"No," Emily replied emphatically. "I saw him leave. I had to hurry out the other side of the house, so that I would arrive home before he did. I arrived home just before he pulled up. I rode my horse, so I was able to travel as a crow flies, covering a shorter distance than if I drove a car."

"You mentioned horses early in our conversation," Dennis said reflectively. "You must be quite skilled."

Emily gushed, "I've gotten to be much better, since Matt has worked with me for the past few years."

Julian showed up at the door. "I guess this is their bath water waiting for them." He was holding Jesse's hand with one of his own and holding a sleepy Jay with the other arm. Jay clung to his daddy's shoulders harder as if to say, "Please, no bath, I just want to go to bed."

"We've decided that this is your domain," Emily smiled teasingly as she got up to leave. "But why don't you help." Emily patted Dennis on the shoulder as he started to get up to his feet. They had been seated on the edge of the tub.

"Help?" Dennis answered meekly. Regaining his composure, he answered, "Sure, I'll help. Just tell me what to do."

Jesse walked over to Dennis and lifted his arms. Dennis realized this was a sign to remove the boy's shirt and he obliged. "Nothing to it," Dennis said with a grin.

"Did you and Emily have a nice chat?" Julian asked. The two children seemed to regain some energy as they hit the water. They played peacefully with a couple toys while Julian bathed them.

"She really is a nice girl," Dennis replied.

"Thanks," Julian answered. "I'm glad you like her."

The two men chitchatted a few minutes while the boys finished their bath. Julian put them down for a nap. Since they were older, they would not sleep as long as their younger siblings. They should all wake about the same time.

"Do you know anyone who would be a spy in this house?" Dennis asked Julian as they left the children's room.

"I can't think of anybody offhand," Julian answered as they moved down the hall. "It still could happen. Quite a few people go through the house, except the living quarters."

"That would make sense," Dennis mused.

"What are you thinking?" Julian asked.

"Robert had an informant in this house," Dennis replied in earnest, "He knew of most of what was happening from a seemingly detached source. Someone not necessarily having access to the living quarters."

"An informant?" Julian replied, astonished.

"It has to make sense," Dennis answered, "Robert always had information about events in the house, when he was not here himself. Pilot and I have a folder labeled 'GW' with a transcript of events taking place in this house centered around you."

"What is 'GW'?" Julian asked.

"I was hoping you could tell me," Dennis replied as they moved down the steps.

"Dennis, Robert knew a great many people," Julian said with skepticism. "You are investing a lot of energy in the belief that this murder is somehow connected with me. Surely, he must have had other enemies."

"Julian, the man was obsessed with you," Dennis defended his position. "He had little business activity these last months. Anything necessary to run his farm was delegated to other people. According to his recent calendar, you were the focus of his attention. He had marked on his calendar the events taking place here in the house. He met with this guy Oscar several times. Remember, Elizabeth and Bernard claim a man fitting his description brought them to this place."

"I'm impressed with the information you've gathered in such a short length of time," Julian said with sincerity.

"I want to help you, Julian," Dennis said while trying to stifle the emotion he was feeling.

CHAPTER 20

A few days later.

"You summoned?" Dennis asked as he entered Pilot's study.

"I have a sketch of all those listed in Lamond's notes," Pilot said as Dennis sat in a chair nearby the desk.

"Any notion of who 'GW' could be?" Dennis asked hopefully.

"I'm afraid not," Pilot answered mildly, dejected.

"What were you able to dig up from the names in the files?" Dennis inquired.

"The biggest is an ID of a Dr. Garner," said Pilot as he shifted his chair to face the desk. "The word I got is this doctor is a practicing psychiatrist in Lindsay, a fair size city about 90 minutes from the center of town."

"Lamond was seeing a psychiatrist?" Dennis asked with surprise.

"Well, we know they were meeting," Pilot explained, "But we don't know the purpose."

"Anyway, could you put the squeeze on this doctor to get him to talk?" Dennis asked with a sly grin.

"I don't see why not," Pilot replied. "I placed a call to Julian's doctor at the hospital where he was treated."

"His name?" Dennis asked.

"Hopkins," Pilot replied.

"Was Dr. Hopkins of any help?" Dennis asked.

"He was somewhat reticent at first," Pilot said with a grin. "But he later became more agreeable."

"So you squeezed him to squeeze Garner." Dennis surmised.

"It wasn't so difficult," Pilot responded. "At first he mentioned some mumbo jumbo about patient/doctor confidentiality, but later was brought to reason. It is obvious that his office leaked the intimate details of Julian's condition to Lamond. With threats of law suits and a promise to make a large monetary contribution to the construction of the new wing to the hospital, he became very reasonable."

"What did he have to say about Garner?" Dennis asked.

"You are to meet with Hopkins tomorrow morning to have a heart to heart chat with him regarding the subject," Pilot said with a devious smile. He was very proud to make the doctor squirm. "He promises to have a full report when you meet."

"You've done very well," Dennis commented. "Are there any other names that come to pass?"

"There is Julian's old nemesis, Oscar," Pilot replied, "It appears he's mixed up with Hopkins and Garner to some degree. How much, I don't know."

"Was he the force behind the leak?" Dennis asked.

"I don't know that you would call it force," Pilot surmised. "He took a more cunning approach. Hopkin's secretary was rather a homely sort and Oscar found it easy to manipulate her. The doctor believes the leak started with this relationship."

"I see," Dennis said with understanding. "It may have taken a bit of work, but the secretary mostly like got to the files and fed them to Oscar."

"That's what I think happened," Pilot agreed.

"Where are they at this time?" Dennis asked curiously. "We should put the squeeze on them, as well as the two doctors."

"It seems they've disappeared," Pilot replied grimly. "Does this surprise you?"

"Only if they were not in any way involved with the murder," Dennis answered.

"Yes, I do believe we are on to something," Pilot agreed with hope.

"But why disappear?" Dennis asked, "They could simply deny any wrong doing. Anything we have is purely theory."

"Let's not jump the gun," Pilot cautioned. "There are still pieces of the puzzle to uncover."

The next day, Dennis met with Doctor Hopkins.

"Dr. Hopkins, thank you for meeting with me on such short notice," Dennis greeted the doctor as he was ushered into his office.

"It is not as if I have a great deal to say of the matter, but you are welcome regardless of the circumstances."

"I know that Julian must hold you in high esteem," Dennis said with a smile. "After all, he does owe his life to you."

"Yes," Dr. Hopkins agreed. "Despite what people may think of that man, he does have a great deal of heart. That is what pushed him through his ordeal."

"With that in mind, doctor, I suppose you don't see me in the brightest light." Dennis was trying to narrow any distrust the doctor may have with him.

"As you may have guessed, peoples' thoughts and feelings are highly subjective. I tend to make my own judgements on people, rather than depending on those of my patients," Dr. Hopkins explained.

"And your secretary," Dennis dived into the topic.

"Ah yes," Dr. Hopkins sighed, "Most unfortunate. She seemed to be an honest woman. Even doctors can mistake good character for bad."

"She was probably a vulnerable woman, just ripe for exploitation," Dennis said. He refused to get into a discussion of good guy bad guy with the doctor.

"I suppose," Dr. Hopkins mused.

"Let's start at the beginning," Dennis pressed. "Start talking."

"And where may that be?" Dr. Hopkins raised a brow as he answered slowly. He reached and took a gulp of water. "Could I get you something to drink?"

"You have 15 minutes to tell me what you know," Dennis said impatiently. "At that point, I'll leave and relay the information you give to me into Pilot's hands. He will decide to his satisfaction the content of your report and complete the arrangement he has negotiated with you. Do I make myself clear?"

"Very well," Dr. Hopkins relented. "The sooner the better, I suppose."

"Good. Let's start at the beginning," Dennis replied, beginning to take notes.

"I didn't make a connection between that man, Oscar as Mr. Pilot referred to him, to my secretary. I try not to get too involved with the affairs of the people in this hospital. I already have enough on my mind, without having to worry about the troubles of the people on staff. I saw this man lurking around my secretary for about two weeks. I also noticed my files were not in the exact same position in the cabinet as I would have been inclined to leave them. They were my personal files. Ordinarily, my assistants would not be concerned with the things I may have scribbled about my patients. I attributed the mis-filing to my rushed attempts to catch up with my work, therefore failing to take time for neatness. Not long after the case, she left. I haven't seen the two of them since I noticed the wayward files."

"Fine," Dennis pushed forward. "Let's get to Garner."

"I'm not so comfortable speaking with you about this matter," Dr. Hopkins started.

"Give it a rest and start talking," Dennis deadpanned.

"Apparently, this man Robert was obsessed with Julian and his every action. He would go days with very little sleep. No doctor in this parish would give him medication to help him sleep. He had all the symptoms of a desperate, suicidal maniac. Finally, this man Garner agreed to supply him with some medication to help him sleep, as long as Lamond met with him on a more than regular basis. In a nutshell, no visits, no pills."

"I would think with all of Lamond's connections, these pills would not be hard to obtain," Dennis commented.

"I believe this is my 15 minutes," Dr. Hopkins said with annoyance. "Save the questions for the end."

"Please excuse me," Dennis apologized.

"Very well," Dr. Hopkins continued, "Apparently, Lamond was paranoid about being caught trafficking drugs. He knew very little of the trade and was afraid of blackmail in the likely event he would trust the wrong person. As time passed, Lamond enjoyed venting his rage in Garner's presence. After all, he had an audience to brag of the latest escapades and harm he caused Julian and his family. He would be so loud and obnoxious, the doctor had to schedule the appointments when there were no other people within earshot. Finally, Lamond's plan was not working as he would have liked. Julian and his family did not buckle under the immense pressure he was placing upon them. He was running out of trump cards to play. Only one was remaining. Lamond was becoming distraught. His exterior had become serene, but his insides were still boiling. You see, while he was in hysterics, he was still fighting to gain sanity. Once calamity ended, Garner knew suicide would be the final card to play. He urged Lamond to commit himself to a hospital, but he refused. Dr. Garner and I believe he killed himself and framed Julian for the crime."

"You are finished?" Dennis asked.

"Unless you have further questions," Hopkins replied.

"Where is the connection between your secretary and Dr. Garner?" Dennis inquired.

"Who said there needed to be one?" Hopkins replied.

Dennis thought for a few minutes, "A hunch," he finally answered.

"I'm not one to try and tell you how to do your job," Dr. Hopkins started, now showing the first signs of impatience.

"However?" Dennis prodded.

"The solution that Dr. Garner and I have presented to you is simple. Why make the outcome more complicated than it has to be?"

"Because Lamond was an extremely complex and high strung man," Dennis explained. "There is no simple structure of events where he is concerned."

"Oh well," Dr. Hopkins sighed. "Is there anything else I can do for you?"

"Yes," Dennis replied with a stab in the dark. "How did the alleged murder hit the papers so quickly? It made the early editions, even before the police arrived at the scene."

"My only suggestion is Lamond staged this himself early in the evening before he took his own life," Dr. Hopkins replied.

"I have conclusive evidence that would indicate another solution to your convincing theory," Dennis explained, "Come on doctor, what are you hiding?" He didn't know where this was going but decided to go with it.

"I don't know what you're talking about," Dr. Hopkins replied getting upset, "This is preposterous treatment. I am going to have to ask you to leave. Let Pilot do as he will."

Dennis decided to try a more gentle approach. "I apologize, doctor, for being so direct. I'm trying to get to the truth of what really happened on that overgrown farm they call a plantation. For Julian's sake, can you think of anything else? You don't want to see him railroaded to prison do you?"

Dr. Hopkins took another gulp of water and began to settle back into his calm demeanor. He stared at the ceiling in thought for a few moments. "The only thing I can think of at the moment is the fact that some of the information stated about Julian in the newspapers never reached Lamond's desk, so how could he possibly know that Julian was making arrangements to divorce Emily?"

"Divorce?" Dennis was stunned. After a few moments, he said, "Certainly Lamond would not have acted the way he did if he thought that Julian was going to leave Emily. He would have thought that he had won the war."

"Precisely," Dr. Hopkins agreed.

"How can you be certain? And why didn't you say something about the divorce earlier?" Dennis asked, clearly annoyed.

"Well, it was in the papers," Dr. Hopkins answered smugly.

Dennis scowled. "That's a cheap shot. The papers will print anything. Nobody in his right mind would believe Julian would divorce Emily. Pilot wouldn't hear of it."

"The strangeness of it is, I never put those feelings of Julian's in my notes," Dr. Hopkins explained.

"That has to mean either Oscar or another informant supplied the information to the press," Dennis exclaimed. "That denounces your theory of a suicide note acting as the informant!"

"Yes, that does add another wrinkle," Dr. Hopkins agreed.

"How did the informant find out that Julian was thinking of filing of divorce at one time during his stay at the hospital? Was it a guess, or stab in the dark?" Dennis inquired.

"Now that I think about the report in the paper, there were too many details for supposition. Somehow, the information was leaked," Dr. Hopkins replied. "The report precisely recounted the advantages and disadvantages Julian was juggling at the time of consideration."

"Why did you not include it in your notes?" Dennis asked, puzzled.

"Because, his primary motivation for getting well was returning to his wife and children," Dr. Hopkins explained. "This thought pattern was nixed after one session. I asked him to consider the possibility seriously. He said he would. But you see, I brought the thought process of divorce to his mind at a brief time when he wasn't responding to treatment as quickly as I thought he should be. Meaning, he needed a jolt or push, so to speak, to face these undesirable thoughts and feelings that were lurking inside the back of his mind. You see, he too felt that divorce was not an option. But what if it was? He had to be the one to make the decision; not some dominating father in-law, whom he worshipped."

"So, why the big deal about arrangements for divorce?" Dennis asked, confused.

"This secretary and this Oscar character were not around when the subject of divorce came about as a topic," Dr. Hopkins surmised. "There was this snoopy volunteer we got rid of after she completed a day's work. However, she seemed so stupid and ditzy, I hardly gave her a second thought. It is strange now that I think about it, but she looked vaguely familiar, like I'd know her from somewhere. I guess her ineptitude erased any curiosity. I may have to see her to place her face."

"Would you recognize her if you saw her again?" Dennis inquired.

"Perhaps," Dr. Hopkins said with a shrug.

"She could have overheard a conversation, possibly?" Dennis asked matter of factly.

"Anything is possible, you know that," Dr. Hopkins replied, irritated. "However, I assure you, I am not so careless that it would happen on a regular basis."

"I'm sure that is the case," Dennis conjoled. "When I get a picture, I will ask if you can identify it."

When Dennis returned to the Pilot Plantation, Pilot and he met behind closed doors. He explained to the patriarch what he had gleaned from Dr. Hopkins. He left out the part about the divorce, but made sure to emphasize the need to identify the volunteer.

"I'll get a picture of her and see the significance of her role in this pipeline of information leading to Lamond and the press," Pilot said, writing down his notes.

"What we have here is a pipeline of information leading to Lamond. There is another line leading to an informant to the press," Dennis summarized. "The informant could be *GW*, but we can't be sure. It is likely that some of the details in the newspaper were not included in Lamond's folder of *GW.*"

"There appears to be something missing," Pilot said, scratching his head. "You are assuming an awful lot."

"I'm following a hunch," Dennis explained. "Believe me, the pieces are beginning to fall into place. When we find the volunteer, she will lead us to *GW.*"

"Okay," Pilot relented. "Let's go eat some supper."

"Albert!" Dennis exclaimed as he entered the dining room full of people, "What are you doing here?"

"I thought you could use some help," Bernard explained. "I thought, 'Who other than Julian's brother could really help the situation'."

"Did you have anything to do with this?" Dennis scowled at Julian.

"Of course not!" Julian responded with another scowl. "However, I did have something to do with getting him a return trip fare back to St. Louis tomorrow."

"Papa said it was a family emergency involving Julian," Albert explained. "The return of Julian, who left all of us for dead, and the thought of a *family* emergency, was too much intrigue to resist. With all that in mind, after court this morning, I jumped on a plane and caught a bus to cure my sense of curiosity."

"Well, I won't be able to concentrate with him around, fellow lawyer or not," Dennis howled and then glared at Albert. "*Brother in-law.*"

"I believe that's ex brother in-law, as I see it," Albert replied with a smirk. "It seems as if Julian finally came to his senses when he flipped, and realized that he was wasting his time with the wrong sex."

"Albert, this is my house that you are in now," Julian said quietly but sternly. "You are a guest and will behave as one should around my family and friends."

"Didn't boarding school teach you those things, Albert?" Dennis bellowed.

"Dennis, please," Julian pleaded.

"Julian, how can you let him stay here one night after all the years of hate he rained on you?" Dennis asked with disbelief and emotion.

"I would have thought my two sons would have been able to resolve their childhood sibling rivalry by this time in their lives," Bernard stated in earnest.

"Julian, you do believe your father had your best interests at heart when he sent for Albert, don't you?" Elizabeth said with a sly grin.

"Enough!" Emily said firmly. "No more family abuse for one night."

"Everyone sit down, before the food gets cold," Louisa ordered and then added, "Albert, this is Candace who will be seated between you and Emily. She is the *Governor's Wife*."

As Albert took Candace's hand into his, Dennis bore his gaze into Pilot's eyes. Once Pilot caught his gaze, he did not cast it aside, but continued until Pilot gave him a questioning look. Slowly, Dennis let Pilot follow his gaze over to Candace. He then returned it slowly back to Pilot's eyes. It took Pilot a brief moment, but he then nodded in understanding.

As the families seated themselves, Dennis stared across the table into Emily's eyes. She immediately caught his glance. He looked away, because he did not want to catch attention from anybody else at the table. While the meal was being served, he would occasionally catch a look to Emily's eyes and she would almost instantaneously catch his glance. After he held it a moment, he let it go.

Emily got the sense that he was trying to communicate something to her, so she started looking around the table observing each person. She turned to face Candace and smiled as the governor's wife passed her the mashed potatoes. Then she caught a familiar scent. She could not place it immediately, but realized that it was just Candace's perfume. She relaxed and proceeded to serve herself some potatoes before passing them along to Julian who was seated to her right. Something still unnerved her. The scent stayed with her. She could not seem to will it away from her presence despite the delicious aroma of her mother's fine cooking. The perfume. The eye contact with Dennis. She felt her eyes try to pop from her sockets, but she resisted the impulse. Slowly, she looked across the table to Dennis.

He was there meeting her eyes. He stared hard. Slowly, she moved her head once up and then once down.

Dennis immediately got up from the table and excused himself. He looked over to Pilot. They caught each others' glances and Pilot excused himself shortly after Dennis left the room. Emily grew restless. She felt it impossible to sit still. She thought it would look strange, should another person rise and leave the table. Jack and Louisa were talking and laughing quietly together with Julian at one end of the table, while Bernard, Elizabeth, and Albert were catching up with trivial family matters. Candace was listening intently to the conversation.

She leaned over to Julian. "Keep Candace talking and don't stop." It was not difficult these days to get Julian to talk, but Candace and he did not always see things in the same light. *I guess it is no small wonder.* She rose from the table before Julian had a chance to question her. As she passed through the hallway, she glanced back and saw that Julian had moved his chair closer to Candace. He was engaging in a one way animated conversation with her. She had a look of surprise on her face, but remained intent on what Julian had to say.

"She's been a friend of the family for years," Pilot said emphatically as Emily entered the study.

"Don't you see," Dennis said with excitement, "She could easily be the fly on the wall. She virtually had access to all the comings and goings around this house, as well as many of the family's secrets."

The two men looked over to Emily. "Well," Dennis said seriously, looking into Emily's face. "What do you think?"

"The perfume she's wearing was the same scent I came across at Robert's house that awful night. It very well could have been her silhouette I saw in the moonlight and not an animal's," Emily confessed. "She is a second mother to me, Dennis. How is it possible for her to betray the family and me?"

"Well, did Candace ever like Julian?" Dennis inquired with anxiousness. "From what I understand, she was not always supportive of him."

"Well, not enough to frame him for murder!" Emily exclaimed.

"Let's calm down," Pilot said practically, "Let us suppose she's the informant or killer for that matter."

"Oh, Daddy," Emily sighed as she sat down on the nearby sofa.

"What would her motive be?" Pilot asked.

"Blackmail. A crime of passion. A mistake. It could be any number of things," Dennis explained.

"I agree with Emily, son," Pilot said incredulously, obviously moved, "I find this difficult to digest. She's been like family to us. She spends most of her free time here on the farm. She adores Emily and her children, despite her feelings for Matt."

Dennis started to regain some composure, "I agree that we should act with caution. So, let's set a trap. If she falls into it, we've found our suspect."

"There are so many holes in this story; pieces missing from the puzzle. What will we do if we catch her? We have no motive or proof of a crime committed," Pilot exclaimed, still feeling the effects of emotion.

"Emily and I will set the trap. We will leave you to find the motive," Dennis explained with pumped excitement.

"I am afraid you have more confidence in my abilities than I could possibly deserve," Pilot said evenhandedly.

"Well, consult your dossier and have your sources bring it up to date," Dennis suggested.

"It sounds easier than it really is, but I will give it a shot," Pilot replied, beginning to rein in his emotions.

"We don't need much," Dennis explained, "Just enough to get a few ideas."

"I guess we should plan," Emily conceded softly.

"Yes, but not here," Dennis agreed. "Let's give your daddy some privacy. How about the parlor?"

In the parlor, Dennis and Emily remained standing. They were both too excited to sit and talk.

"I've got an idea," Dennis said with a smile.

"Okay. Let's hear it," Emily said, "And we better hurry up. We're going to be missed fairly soon."

"I'm sure you are aware of the secret compartment in Robert's desk, are you not?" Dennis asked.

Emily smiled. "How did you know about that? Robert and I found it when we were kids, playing in his father's office."

"So, you know how it works?" Dennis asked quickly.

"Yes. Just pop the spring underneath and the top opens," Emily replied.

"Okay," Dennis started. "Somehow, get Candace's attention and relate the story of how you and Robert found the mysterious secret compartment, when you were kids. Talk about how much fun you had finding it. Be sure to say that Robert's late father used to keep things in there that he did not want other people to find...secrets. Make it sound fun."

"Okay, but how is that going to set the trap?" Emily asked.

"The killer wants a file that Robert had on her, which kept an account of her actions in this house. She knows it exists and that Robert had it hidden. However, she doesn't know exactly what is in it. For all she knows, her name could be plastered all over its contents. She desperately wants to destroy this file. I believe it was Candace who came to retrieve it the night Billy and I searched the house. She may have been back to look for it again, but we have the file. It only refers to her as *GW*. I saw her scurry across the yard. She doesn't run well and barely can ride a horse."

"That part sounds like Candace," Emily sighed. "I just can't believe it. So, I guess she will run to the desk to find this file, when she hears of the compartment's existence."

"Right!" Dennis exclaimed. "We'll be waiting for her when she gets to the desk. Okay, let's do it!"

As they turned to go back to finish their supper, Elizabeth stopped them in their tracks.

"The two of you look as if you've seen a ghost," Elizabeth chided as she blocked their exit.

"In a matter of speaking." Dennis glared into her face.

"What have you been doing? Is their something that I should know?" Elizabeth inquired.

"We've been bonding," Dennis answered as he gently moved past her with Emily on his heels. "We have a dinner to finish."

"I'm afraid it's too late," Elizabeth replied, "The plates are being cleared as we speak."

Dennis pushed onward, ignoring Elizabeth's response. She grabbed Emily's arm. "What's the matter girl? Can't you speak for yourself?"

"I've nothing to say to you! Now let me go!" she replied with coolness and gritted teeth.

"I'm warning you," Elizabeth said with ease. "I want to be kept informed with the progress of my son's vindication."

Emily pulled her arm out of Elizabeth's grasp and headed to the dining room.

CHAPTER 21

"If everybody would proceed to the front room, I'll have dessert and coffee served," Louisa said cheerfully.

Animated, family and friends moved freely into the large comfortable room, with many stuffed chairs and a couple of overstuffed couches.

As they entered the room, Pilot took Dennis by the arm and asked, "Why is that brother of Julian's here?"

"I don't know," Dennis answered with irritation. "He has always been a trouble maker. He seems to have a knack for getting in the way of things; particularly mine."

"Well," Pilot said with the same irritation, "Get rid of him. And quickly. We can't have him getting himself stuck in the middle of things. Especially while things seem to be unfolding."

Dennis nodded in agreement.

Since the evenings were getting cool, it was decided that the party would stay in the house rather than go outside to the front porch. Emily and Dennis joined Albert and Candace. Soon, Julian joined the small group, while Pilot stayed close by his wife.

"Can you do a favor for an old chum?" Dennis asked Julian as he pulled him aside.

Julian furrowed his brow. "Chum?

"It sounds better than ex-lover, doesn't it?" Dennis commented and then quickly changed the subject. "I need you to find out why Albert is here and then facilitate his exit."

"I agree, but why the urgency?" Julian asked.

"It's Emily. I can't help but notice that she's under a great strain with another member of your family present. It may be enough to push her over the edge," Dennis explained.

"I'm inclined to agree, but somehow, I feel there is an ulterior motive lurking."

"You're going to have to trust me on this one, Julian," Dennis said, forcing the issue, "You need to talk to Albert right this minute and then hasten his exit."

"Okay," Julian relented slowly. "I've trusted you with more, so the choice is simple."

"Good," Dennis replied as he patted Julian on the arm. The two rejoined Emily, Candace, and Albert.

"Albert, I thought I may have a word with you," Julian beckoned. Surprised, Albert followed Julian to a nearby sofa, where they both took a seat.

"Well, Julian, it seems married life agrees with you," Albert started. "Don't you think you should have started years earlier instead of wasting time with that loathsome pervert?"

"Albert, let's not start about my sexual orientation. I have other things on my mind; like why are you here?" Julian said, guiding the conversation.

"Don't you believe that I came here out of concern for you and how your troubles are affecting Mommie and Papa?" Albert asked with feigned concern.

Julian giggled. "You still call her that? You know she always hated when you called her that."

"That's one reason I do it," Albert deadpanned.

"Well, you evidently are not here out of concern for Elizabeth; you've always hated my guts...." Julian reasoned.

"Julian, you know that can't be true!" Albert said in a shouted whisper. Louisa briefly looked toward them, responding to the harshness of his voice.

"Albert, you tortured me the whole time we were growing up," Julian said incredulously. "All the kids at boarding school teased you for being fat and unattractive, so you elected to take it out on me by beating me daily. It was so cool to make your older brother miserable. You were just as bad as the other boys," Julian said mockingly.

"You are not going to bring all that up again, are you?" Albert sighed. "I thought we had gotten past it,"

"Albert, you may have stopped the physical abuse, but you still beat up on me verbally every time we see each other," Julian exclaimed angrily.

"It is true that I find your previous lifestyle disgusting, but it seems you've turned the corner. You have a beautiful wife and five gorgeous children. You've finally done well for yourself Julian. I am proud of you," Albert said, defending himself.

"Save it," Julian responded. "All your compliments have always been backhanded, laden with insults. Just tell me why you are here, so you can catch the next bus out of town."

"Well, I was hoping for a better time," Albert began slowly. "Besides concern for the family, I have a favor to ask of you."

"There is something you actually want from me?" Julian asked with disbelief.

"Julian, despite what you may think, I have always had respect for you," Albert firmly asserted himself. "You've been able to accomplish a great deal in your lifetime, even with your poor personal choices. Can't that be enough? I can only accept so much from you."

"Get on with it Albert, even though I am totally disgusted with you," Julian said, resigned.

"You know I have two children, a son and a daughter," Albert began.

"The last I can remember, you had a baby boy," Julian replied.

"Well, that baby boy has turned into a 15-year old terror," Albert said with disappointment in his voice. "Julian, I can no longer manage him. His name is Shaun. The summer is several months ahead into the next year. He will be 16 years old at that time. I am not just asking you to take him in for his summer school break; I am begging you to do this favor. I will apologize for anything I've ever done and said to you with my most humblest groveling."

"You want me to take in a troubled teen? Into my house?" Julian asked with shock and amazement. "Albert, you honestly despise me and I know you think I'm some wild pervert. Why in the world would you trust me with your own son?"

"You are my last hope, Julian," Albert replied with his face in his hands. His tired eyes then looked into Julian's face as he pleaded, "If anything can be salvaged of him, I believe only you can save him. I'm convinced you and he have a lot in common and will get along nicely. Like I said earlier, you've managed to do well in your life. When Papa called, he said you were content with your life; he said you were an excellent father and husband; he said you've resolved the confusion in your life revolving around the roles of men and women. You'll be the best role model for Shaun. If you don't take him in..... for just a short while, he will be a hopeless cause. Do you honestly want that on your conscience?"

Julian rolled his eyes. He supposed that Albert was trying to be nice though obviously failing miserably.

"First, my family has to get through this crisis. I have to manage to stay out of prison. Then, I have to think about it. After that, I will have to discuss it with my wife," Julian replied. "I'm making no promises."

"You won't go to jail," Albert said with conviction. "As much as I hate to admit it, the pervert is good at what he does. He'll keep you safe. Just send him home, when he's finished his business."

"Candace, are you enjoying yourself?" Emily asked.

"Yes dear, your mother really knows how to put on a dinner party. But I'm going to have to leave soon," Candace replied.

"I thought you would spend the night," Emily said with disappointment. "It seems over the past year, you have done so less and less."

"I'm in your family's house so often, I don't want to be an extra burden staying over so many nights," Candace replied.

"Candace, you know you could never be a burden," Emily said with a smile. "But I need you tonight. I want to talk about Robert."

"Robert?" Candace said with a forced smile.

"Excuse me ladies," Dennis said. "I'm going to get another helping of dessert. Can I get the two of you anything?"

"Oh no," the two women said, almost shooing him away from them.

"Why do you want to talk about Robert?" Candace asked with a confused look.

"Well," Emily paused. "I can't really talk about it to anyone else, you see. You know what he's done to this family these last few years, yet I still have a lot of feelings concerning him. You know, we grew up together. He was special to me for many years. Candace, I have no one else who would understand, except you."

"Dear, you know you can always talk to me, but do you really want to do it here?" Candace asked. "We...uh...are in the middle of a dinner party."

"Of course," Emily replied, embarrassed, "How could I be so silly? Let's go to the side parlor. We should be able to have some privacy."

"Very well, I suppose we could do that," Candace relented. "I know you've been under a great deal of stress. I can see why you would need to release some of it."

Yes," Emily agreed. "I need to let some of it out." She guided Candace out of the room quickly, before anybody could interrupt them.

They entered the parlor and took seats on a nearby cream-colored camel back sofa. Emily laid out her hands into her lap, while Candace studied her with concern.

"Now, what is it darling that has you so upset?" Candace asked.

"Well.... Uh....," Emily stammered badly. "I can't believe how a person can change so much."

"Now dear, people change over time. Just try to remember the good times when you were children, and dismiss the notion that he turned out to be the dreadful man he became. He can no longer cause anybody pain."

Emily took the lead. "You know you're absolutely right, Candace. I should remember all the good times as children. I'll never forget the time, we sneaked into his father's office. We played a game. He sat in his father's chair behind the desk and talked on the phone, like he was important. He idolized his father and wanted to be just like him. I sat at his side and pretended to be his secretary taking dictation. Robert dropped a pen or something underneath the desk. He bent down below to pick it up. As he came back up, he bumped his head. He must have set off some spring, because the top of the desk popped up and made all the contents from the top slide onto the floor. It seemed to be a secret compartment inside containing just a few things, like papers and such. We quickly shut the hiding place. We were fervent in our efforts to replace the things, just as they were, when his father came into the office. We were so scared of getting caught that we ran right past him without saying a word. That was so much fun." Emily giggled at the thought and shook her head with a smile. "I'll never forget those times."

Candace started to fidget. "I'm sorry dear, I must get going. There's an important appointment, which I must attend. I promise we'll continue with this conversation later, when there's more time."

"Do you have to go so soon? You should really say goodbye to everyone," Emily admonished.

"There is no time dear. Please give everybody my regards. I'll be in touch real soon," Candace said quickly and eased from the parlor.

Frantic, Emily returned to the front room and joined the company of Pilot and Dennis. Elizabeth was nearby, keeping close attention to the three of them.

"You two have to move quickly," Emily said, breathing heavily. She was quite upset, "I did as you've asked and now she's gone."

"So soon?" Dennis exclaimed, "Did you try to keep her a while longer?"

"I tried!" Emily shouted in a whisper. "She was determined to leave. I couldn't stop her."

"Well, we've better get moving," Dennis said under his breath to Pilot. "We don't have much time."

"I know a short cut," Pilot said as he made to exit.

"You can take the horses," Emily advised.

"No time," Pilot replied.

"There is another way. There's a new dirt road, which not very people know exists. We'll take that one."

"Let's go!" Dennis cried. "Emily, do something with Elizabeth. She knows something is up and we can't afford to waste time with her."

As the two men made to leave, Elizabeth quickly made her way over to stop them. Emily intercepted her by slipping her arm under hers. "Elizabeth, dear, I have some late breaking news that I know you are going to want to hear," Emily tried to think quickly, as she lead her mother in-law to the same side parlor where she had conversed with Candace. She didn't know exactly what she was going to tell her.

Julian followed closely behind. "What's going on here?"

"Let's sit down," Emily said, trying to stall.

"Okay," Julian replied as he sat beside her on the camel back sofa. Elizabeth sat in a nearby cane back chair.

Emily let the silence build as long as she could. As she started to speak, Louisa entered the room.

"Is there anything wrong?" she asked. "The food must be bad if everybody is leaving."

"Oh no Mama, everything was simply delicious," Emily assured her mother. "Uh...don't you agree, Matt?"

"Uh.....Yes," he agreed, confused as he looked up to Louisa. "Everything was good as usual."

"Yes, everything was good," Elizabeth said curtly, "Now, on with the news."

Bernard and Albert entered the room. "Is everything okay?" Bernard asked.

"Yes," Julian replied quickly. He could sense that Emily was trying to stall, "It seems Emily may have some important news."

"Mama, perhaps you could order some coffee in here, so we can all be comfortable," Emily suggested.

"Coffee can wait," Elizabeth said firmly. "What were the three of you commiserating about, that your father and that boy had to leave so abruptly?"

"What?" Julian asked, "Did Pilot and Dennis leave the house?"

"It seems that Candace had to leave as well," Louisa commented.

"No more interruptions," Elizabeth demanded. "Now, what is going on, girl?"

"It seems there may have been a break in the case against Matt for the alleged murder of Robert," Emily paused. "Since there is no murder weapon at the crime scene, the case against him appears to be weak."

"We already knew that!" Elizabeth exclaimed in a moderate voice with plenty of edge. Although thoroughly irritated, she maintained her nerves that were tough as nails. "Move on to what is new!"

"What is new," Emily repeated slowly, "Is that Dennis and Daddy are more optimistic than have been the past few days."

"And why are they more optimistic?" Elizabeth asked, coolly.

"Because....," Emily drawled, "There may have been a slight break in the case, so we should have hope. They went to investigate a possible lead."

"And this lead is.....?" Elizabeth prodded with a smile.

Emily began to noticeably squirm. When she saw this pleased Elizabeth, she squirmed with a little more drama. "I can't honestly say..."

"I take it you won't say," Elizabeth accused.

"Leave her alone, Elizabeth," Bernard ordered. "The girl obviously doesn't know a thing."

"I am sorry," Emily said, looking down into her hands with a look of shame. "I guess I just got excited with hope," She looked into in Elizabeth's eyes with meekness.

Elizabeth held her gaze momentarily and then looked to the side. Then she returned, with a smile, "What does Candace have to do with all of this?"

"What do you mean?" Emily replied with a strain of nervousness.

"Well, they obviously left around the same time. Come on girl. We just want to know what is going on and get this mystery solved, so we can go home." She looked to Bernard and Albert.

Taking the opportunity to change the subject, Emily replied, "You don't have to wait for the outcome. Feel free to leave anytime. I'll be glad to send for a limousine, first thing in the morning."

"It seems that if we all put our heads together, we can get this thing over with a great deal sooner," Elizabeth argued.

"I still have not figured out why you are here in the first place," Emily said accusingly. "From what I understand, neither you, your husband, nor your other son, cared about Matt's wellbeing, other than your own selfish motives."

"Well, there are obviously reasons you have trouble comprehending, but let's get back to the point..." Elizabeth replied.

"I don't see this getting us anywhere," Louisa said, rising from a chair. "Emily, I can use some help in the other room."

Emily rose quickly and followed her mother as she exited the parlor.

"Julian, I would think you would be more upset with what has just transpired," Elizabeth accused.

"It is all a matter of trust, Elizabeth," Julian deadpanned. "Perhaps you should try it. By the way, I have not figured why you are here, other than you wanting me to return to Washington with you for some strange reason. Albert has come clean with his motives. Papa is here, because you are here. Perhaps you should confess your true desires."

"Apparently, my explanations have not been satisfactory," Elizabeth replied as she rose from her chair. "I'm going to my rooms. If you hear any news, please don't keep me in the dark."

"I promise," Julian said with a smile.

CHAPTER 22

"It sure is dark out here," Dennis commented quietly, as the truck rambled down the dirt road.

"What's a matter, son?" Pilot said with a friendly smirk. "Afraid of the dark?"

"No, no," Dennis replied, "I never knew a place could be so dark. I'm used to street lamps, lights from buildings and roads signs. The stars light up the sky, but on the ground, it's still dark."

"Well, we might just get you to stay on yet, when this whole mess it done," Pilot said with a soft laugh.

"I don't know about that," Dennis said with a frown, "But this is certainly different from where I live."

After a pause, Pilot asked, "So, what is the plan?"

"Were you able to get anything on her?" Dennis asked.

"It seems Candace was ripe for blackmail, as you suspected," Pilot said with a sigh. "She's in charge of her husband's campaign, which does not amount to much. He gets plenty of funds and is elected fairly easily, despite being unpopular. Candace has not been much of a bean counter, so the record keeping has been in somewhat of a mess. There have been many checks written that have not been accounted for in a long time. In essence, there has been plenty of money coming in and out of the campaign without much of a paper trail. It's easy to suspect fraud."

"Doesn't she have bean counters to take care of those things for her?" Dennis asked, amazed.

"Yes she does, but if things run sloppy at the top, the support staff is somewhat disadvantaged, if you know what I mean," Pilot answered.

"So, Lamond threatened to expose her for fraud if she didn't do what he said," Dennis surmised.

"Well, it's a little more than that," Pilot replied. "He got hold of some of the campaign records and they did not look favorable in Candace's behalf. She also has a big bank account, without much support as to how she got it, which in itself, doesn't mean much, but combined with the other circumstances, looks suspicious."

"Is there more?" Dennis asked.

"A few minor things," Pilot said. "Humble beginnings, of which people have little knowledge; a couple of discreet extramarital affairs; nothing out of the ordinary."

"Meaning, a few things that could cause some embarrassment, but not enough to kill someone," Dennis growled.

"Exactly," Pilot replied. "The campaign mess could have been tidied up a bit, but maybe she didn't know that was possible. Who knows what Lamond could have told her."

"Well, this is going to be interesting," Dennis said as he frowned.

"You have your work cut out for you, boy," Pilot said grimly.

"I know," Dennis said as he sunk into his seat. The two men did not exchange another word, as a plan started to swim in his head.

After a few minutes, they pulled on to Lamond's farm, but kept the truck hidden from view. The main house stood still, as was the case for the rest of the farm. There did not appear to be another person close by the main house as they closed the truck doors, without making an attempt to conceal the noise. Slowly, they trudged forward.

"If she's on her way, it will still take her a few minutes," Pilot advised.

"Well, let's get into the house," Dennis said as he moved forward.

"It shouldn't be that hard," Pilot remarked as he walked along side.

Once the two men were into the house, they started to plan the trap.

"Assuming the bait is taken, we still have to come up with a plan," Pilot said in earnest.

"I've got one," Dennis replied as he moved through the back door entrance, across the depth of the house to the study. Pilot was not far behind him.

"We have the tape recorder?" Dennis asked, looking at Pilot as he moved to the desk.

"Yes, I have it right here with me," Pilot replied.

"Good," Dennis said quietly as he surveyed the room. Nearby to the right of the desk, he spotted a large door, which looked to open into a big closet. He walked toward it. Shelves of books lined the wall to its left. Dark stained wood panels covered the wall to the right, with a few slick oil paintings on the upper panels.

"Let's get a chair for you to sit in here, hidden away with the recorder. I don't think it would be a good idea for her to know you are here," Dennis said to Pilot.

"Are you sure you can handle this yourself?" Pilot asked. "After all, I've known her for many years, so I obviously am more familiar with her."

Dennis shook his head while considering Pilot's suggestion. "Pilot, I don't think she planned to do this killing if she is the one who actually did it. Like you said, you've known her for many years and you were shocked to even consider her to have the capability toward violence. My guess is that if she is the killer, she did it in a moment of passion. So many tragic deaths happen up this way. I don't think she's a raging killer. My thinking is that she would get terribly upset if she knew you were here and very embarrassed while feeling extremely ashamed. As a non-impassioned soul, I will be perceived as less of a threat. As far as she knows, I'm some ordinary man from the east, totally unthreatening."

"If you are so non-intimidating, how are you going to force her into telling you what she knows?" Pilot inquired.

"Is it your supposition, that it will be difficult to make her feel forced to do anything?" Dennis quizzed.

"Yesterday, I would have said no," Pilot confessed, "I'm not sure what to think today."

"I think our guest has arrived," Dennis said he heard some noises from the outside. Pilot moved a chair to the closet and left the door ajar, so he could get the conversation on tape. Dennis quickly set the stage for his plan, then closed the light and sat in a chair off the opposite side of the room. He waited.

Soon, a figure came though the door. It crept lightly to the desk and turned a switch on a small lamp. Dennis could see that it was indeed Candace. She moved to the back of the desk and slid her hands along the base of the top. Suddenly, a spring popped the top of the desk, so it opened like a lid. He could see, to her dismay, that there were no contents in the secret department.

"Are you looking for this?" Dennis said, holding up the folder marked *GW*.

Startled, Candace made to scamper out of the room.

"Hold on," Dennis said gently. "Nothing is going to happen to you."

As Candace grabbed the doorknob to exit, she slumped and gasped for breath. Breathing heavily, she asked, "What are you doing here?"

"I suspected that we might run into each other here, so I thought we'd better have a little chat," Dennis said with a grin, waving the folder.

"I think I'd better leave," Candace said as she continued through the door.

"I don't think you want to leave without this," Dennis said as he continued to wave the folder. "After all, isn't it what you came to fetch?"

Candace stopped in her tracks and turned around. After a brief pause, she replied, "I don't know what you are talking about." Another pause, "Let me see what you mean." She strolled over toward Dennis.

"Not so fast," Dennis teased with a smile, "I want guarantees before I hand it over."

"What are you saying?" Candace replied incredulously, as she leaned against the desk.

"According to what I have here, you've been a very, very busy girl," Dennis said.

"Oh?" Candace said, with a slight waver in her voice.

"Yes," Dennis replied. "I know just about everything you've been doing for the last couple of years. Lamond took very copious notes. I really don't think he missed too much."

"What does that have to do with why I would want those papers?" Candace asked angrily.

"Oh come off it, Candace! Lamond was blackmailing you and both of us know it!" Dennis boomed.

Remarkably calm, or just plain shocked, Candace replied, "What do you mean?"

"I think you know what I mean. I want to hear your side of things before I go to the police. You are a dear friend of the Pilot family and I thought I'd give you the benefit of the doubt before exposing you. Perhaps things can be presented in a different light if you would stop wasting my time and start talking. Do you want to explain yourself to me or do you want me to hand over what Lamond had written and let that be the official story? What will it be Candace?" Dennis said as he ran out of breath.

Candace stood and walked to the far side of the room. If she thought that someone could be listening in the closet, she did not let it be known, "Okay," Candace demurred, "What's the point? I am just trying to protect him. It looks as if I'm not going to be able to do that," she said as she cried softly into one hand.

Why would she want to protect a creep like Lamond? Dennis wondered. "Just do the best you can, Candace, and just take your time. Nothing is hopeless," Dennis soothed.

"Promise me one thing, first," Candace begged.

"I can only make promises that I can keep, Candace, but I'll do my best," Dennis said with a little bit of drama.

"It was not his fault," Candace blurted. "Please do your best not to let anything happen to him. He didn't know a thing about what was happening between Robert and me."

Dennis was lost, but he went with it. "I'll do my best Candace, but you're going to have to be totally honest with me."

"Please, please," Candace begged, "Leave him out of this."

"I'll do my best Candace, but you have to cooperate, or there is no other choice but to implicate him," Dennis said, hoping this scenario would soon play itself out to something concrete.

"Okay, okay; I'll talk, but please...you know he'd never make it alive if the truth came out....please." Candace was sobbing by this point.

Dennis clearly was in the dark but still went along the line of Candace's confession. "Take a deep breath," Dennis said. "I'll do what I can to help him, but first, let's hear what you have to say. When did this mess start?"

"Good. I guess I'll trust you," Candace said, regaining her composure. After stifling a few more sobs, she started her story.

"From the beginning, you know that Robert was not pleased with being passed over for Matt in marrying Emily. At first, I agreed. I felt Robert and her were well suited for each other. We used to talk about this at times. After a short while, it seemed things were working well for Emily and that boy, since she seemed so happy with him. Eventually, I grew weary of Robert's insults of Emily and her husband, and I started to avoid him. He was not pleased, because he got used to me telling him of the comings and goings of things in the house up at the Pilot's. The longer I'd avoid him, the ruder he'd become, when we'd eventually cross paths. "

"One day, a couple of years ago, I got a message from him saying that it was urgent that I meet with him right here in this room. This is when it all started." Candace moved to the adjoining wing chair and sat on its edge with her hands in her lap.

After a sigh, she continued, "We argued. I told him that I would no longer be his spy and that he had to get over his obsession with those two people. But it was too late. I soon came to realize that all his energy was focused on Matt and Emily."

Candace stared at the floor. "You know the rest. What's the point."

"Humor me," Dennis ordered.

Candace seemed to regain her concentration. "Well, he became really nasty. He mentioned some things about campaign fraud and presented me with flimsy evidence about diverting funds to my personal holdings. You see, Dennis, my strengths are working with people, not so much with maintaining accurate financial records. I tend to rely on other people for such things and that was clearly my mistake. Also, I had a few indiscretions over the last few years; my husband had done the same. All of these things were not big concerns other than some potential embarrassment for my husband and myself. I worked too hard to get him through the state legislature and into the governor's office to have our record stained with blemishes. So, I thought, I'd just spend some more time with the Pilots and report what I saw. You know, I liked the family and I saw no harm in telling Robert some of the gossip that transpired in the family."

"Eventually, again, I began to tire of being Robert's puppet in the Pilot household. Once more, I began to see less of Robert, but I continued to spend a great deal of time with the Pilots. You see, this is about the time when things started with Billy."

"Billy," Dennis thought to himself, *"What does he have to do with this mess?"* He tried to mask his surprise, but was finding it difficult. However, Candace was clearly intent with her monologue and did not appear to notice.

Candace suddenly looked up into Dennis's face. "He chauffeured me back and forth between the Pilot's and the bus depot in town. Also, he would take me to the Lamond's when it was warranted. These rides were long, of course. Town is a good distance from the farms, so we had good chances to get to know each other well. We would talk, rather I would chatter endlessly, about unimportant things. It would get my mind off things involving Lamond and the Pilots, as the intensity of the situation began further escalate. Billy would listen to my every word. I was thrilled to have a captive audience. He began to read a few newspapers daily along with other periodicals to further understand all my meaningless chatter of the world's events. He even picked up a book or two to read, which I found to be interesting at one time or another. We fell in love."

By this time, Dennis was speechless. He did not utter a word for fear he would betray himself. Instead, he nodded his head as if to project that he was already aware of the situation, but after a short time, he could not suppress his surprise. "So it really was love?" Dennis said skeptically.

"Yes! It was love!" Candace declared emphatically. "We both knew the situation was hopeless, but we could not help ourselves. We would leave the Pilot's late in the evening, so it would be too late to catch the last bus out of town. Therefore, we had a good excuse to stay overnight at the hotel in town. We stayed in separate rooms on separate floors. Well, he stayed in a room at the basement level, of course. We were so careful. When we thought nobody was looking, he would come to me. The arrangement worked rather well."

"When did Lamond find out about this affair?" Dennis asked, taking a stab.

Candace wrinkled her forehead, "Surely, you must know."

Dennis hesitated. "I want to hear it from you."

"Of course," Candace responded as she continued her story.

"It was just after that Steele woman rode into town. I felt terribly guilty for my part in the horrible havoc Robert was causing. The day after Matt entered the hospital. I paid a visit to Lamond. We argued. I told him under no circumstances would I continue my role in his insane obsession to destroy Emily's family. He was not just hurting Matt; he was hurting those innocent children and my sweet Emily. I was finished with his nonsense."

"He sneered at my tirade. That's when he played a trump card, sealing my allegiance to him forever. He threatened to expose my affair with Billy to the whole world. I feared for both our safety. You know, a young black man having an affair with a prominent white woman would not last long in this part of the country. I could not bear to tell Billy. I wanted to protect him. I thought about us running away somewhere, but I just knew he would never go."

"My conscience was growing heavier by the day, as Robert's madness escalated. I prayed that one day soon he would snap and it would all be over. He constantly threatened me that he would go to the press. He would expose Billy and me if I did not start coming up with some better information. I pleaded with him. I was trying to give him anything to quell him. But this was not possible. Then one night I was convinced that he was ready to expose everything. I had to silence him. I thought if I was to frighten him into thinking that I would kill him, he might would end this mess. You know, like I had fallen off the edge to madness, and would do anything to free myself from him. I packed my gun. I went to his place. I saw he had a visitor leaving the house. It was Matt. When he left, I burst into the house and rushed into Robert's office. He was sitting at his desk. He was smiling so sweetly. He ever so calmly said that everything was over and done with. It made me sick with rage that he teased me with the one wish I wanted. How could it be that everything would be over and there would be no more hostility? I pulled the trigger and he was dead."

"I was frantic. Honestly, I did not really intend on killing him," Candace pleaded sympathy and she was sobbing uncontrollably. Dennis offered her his handkerchief. She took it and blew her nose.

"I had to think fast. I remembered that Matt had just left the house as I was arriving. I figured the police might try to pin the murder on him. It was so convenient to blame him. He was at the wrong place at the right time. I convinced myself that he deserved to be held accountable for the murder, because he had deceived everybody about his horrid past. I quickly left."

"Later, I knew it was wrong to frame Matt for the murder. But I thought if I came clean, the blame might somehow be pinned on Billy. I could not have that at any cost."

Candace looked frantically into Dennis's eyes. "He is innocent. You've got to believe me. He knew absolutely nothing that was going on with this ordeal."

Dennis paused as he quickly digested everything that he had heard. "Your confession seems to fit with everything that I have in this folder. However, your version of the story presents things in a very different light than the one Lamond portrays. For example, there's nothing that explains how the press was alerted and how Matt was so quickly arrested by the police."

"I can see how that would not make the folder, since Robert could not possibly know entirely how the story would really finish," Candace sighed. "I've told you this much, so I guess I can tell you the rest."

Dennis nodded.

"I guess you already know that Robert planned to kill himself," Candace started.

"That is a given." Dennis feigned impatience.

"There was a note on a package left for Oscar. He was to deliver it to the newspaper in town. Searching for anything that could incriminate me, I read through the material quickly to see what it was that was going to the press. It was perfect. Robert was going to kill himself and frame Matt for the murder. I didn't know how Oscar was going to get hold of the package after the suicide was going to take place, so I decided to help things along. I took the package and rushed it to Oscar. I explained Robert's wishes and ordered him to carry through with them immediately. I gave him a great deal of cash with a promise for more if he took that mousy girl with him and got out of town. I threatened him to take the money and run or that I would take him to prison with me for all our crimes. I didn't know exactly what crimes he had committed, but he took the bait and scooted quickly away. He assured me that he would never be found. I still believe him."

"I find it difficult to believe all of your story. I'm not so sure Lamond would agree with everything you claim to have taken place," Dennis said. He was expecting a reaction.

"You can't tell me you believe the ravings of a lunatic over me! He tortured me!" Candace bellowed.

"Relax," Dennis said calmly, "I think something can be worked out that will benefit everybody. Let's CUT THE TAPE here and come to a resolution," Dennis said, signaling Pilot.

"What are you talking about?" Candace said suspiciously.

"What I mean is, I see no reason to include the bureaucrats in our settlement," Dennis explained. "You see, we both want something. I'm not sure Julian will get a fair trial. And I'm convinced that he will eventually get pinned for this murder. I would rather not take the risk before a jury. On the other hand, you do not want to risk involving Billy in this ordeal. Agreed?"

Candace nodded her head with hope.

"Do you have the weapon?" Dennis asked, leaning back into his chair with the folder resting in his lap.

"Which one?" Candace asked as she looked into Dennis's face.

Dennis was dumbfounded. His mind raced. Should he know what she was talking about? How much was he supposed to know? This whole cat and mouse game was getting to be confusing. Hopefully this charade would be ending soon, without him getting caught with all his bluffs. He was close. He could not slip up now.

Dennis sighed. "Come on, Candace. I want all the details without having to constantly threaten you. Which gun did you use?"

" I grabbed his from the desk and shot him in the chest. After I left, I tossed it in a nearby swamp. I wanted to be rid of it and figured it would never be found. I took mine with me, since I didn't use it," Candace replied softly.

"Well, we're going to have to find it," Dennis deadpanned.

"Why do we have to do that?" Candace asked, starting to get upset. Her nerves were exhausted.

"Calm down," Dennis soothed, " Here's the plan. We find the weapon and bring it back into this office. We leave. You use whatever contacts you have incorporating bribery, arm twisting, or anything at your disposal, insisting that this site be searched more thoroughly. Your involvement will seem natural, since you are a friend of the family; you want to throw your weight around in order to help Julian. Between you and the governor, you should be able to push authorities into setting this ordeal up as a suicide. I know this is a difficult task with many contacts consulted, but I believe you can do it."

"You have 2 days before I expose you and Billy, unless all of this plan transpires as directed. Assuming you are successful, you will then leave this country, never to return. I will provide the travel arrangements," Dennis said as he finished unveiling his plan.

"If I refuse this plan?" Candace asked meekly.

"You can take your chances with my threats, which are not idle. I have nothing to lose. At this moment, Julian possesses a first class rail ticket to prison," Dennis said matter of factly. "Who knows what a jury could believe. Maybe it was a proven homosexual that pulled the trigger. A black man taking advantage of a vulnerable white woman may have committed the crime. People make a lot of money trying to predict the minds of a jury. However, I don't see you or I making the jury selection."

"I see I have little choice," Candace said, seemingly relieved. "Can I at least tell Billy goodbye?"

Dennis gritted his teeth to continue his resolve. He grieved for Billy. "I'm sorry Candace, but no. There will not be a soul other than you, Pilot, and myself who will know the truth of this situation. Pilot will see to it that a statement about your abrupt departure is due to some kind of illness. Contacting Billy or anyone else would only place them in danger. You don't want that to happen, do you?"

Candace shook her head, "No, but it hardly seems fair."

Dennis gave a final thrust to the situation. "Candace, I think this deal benefits you the most. After all, you did kill a man."

Dennis felt bad for his friend. Billy did not deserve to be a pawn in the negotiations. He banked that Candace would acquiesce. He did not relish the thought of having to get Billy off the hook for murder.

"What about that folder and the pictures?" Candace asked.

"The pictures?" Dennis replied, mentally kicking himself for his stupid response, but he rebounded ever so slightly. "I'm sorry. My mind was racing somewhere else. I'm going to keep these things in a safe deposit box in Washington as insurance in case you ever decide to return to this country, or make any contact with anyone."

"You are relentless," Candace answered, gritting her teeth.

"Let's go get the weapon," Dennis said, as he stood. Candace stood as well, as they made their way toward the door.

CHAPTER 23

Julian sat on the back porch, looking to the fields in the east. A few small flocks of birds flew close to the horizon. He felt a sense of dread and remorse. It was time to deal with the issues he faced when he arrived home from the hospital, as well as new ones that revealed themselves since that time.

His forgotten family had left. He presumed for good. There was a good chance that he would never see any of them again. One by one, Elizabeth, Bernard, and Albert passed by him, while he sat on the porch staring off into the blazing sun. It was far from a teary eyed farewell. Yes, soon things would be back to normal; whatever that could be.

Dennis came through the screened door and let it slam behind him. Julian did not look to see who it was. Dennis lightly set his suitcase next to him. Slowly, he stepped down from the porch to the ground, holding his coat in one arm. It was cold back east; he would need it to keep warm once he got off the plane.

Julian turned his head to face him, as Dennis stood in front of him.

"Thank you for coming," Julian said finally, without emotion but with sincerity.

Dennis was speechless, so he just nodded.

"It was you, who fixed everything, wasn't it?" Julian said, more of an acknowledgement than a question.

"Things kind of worked out for themselves," Dennis replied softly. He had kept his word to Candace; only Pilot and he worked the details as promised.

"Thank you," Julian said again.

"Are you sure you know what you are doing, Julian?" Dennis asked one last time.

"My place is here," Julian replied softly, "We've been over this."

Dennis paused for a moment, "Julian..."

"Don't," Julian stopped him gently. "I know what you're feeling. I'm going through some of the same things."

"I guess this is goodbye then," Dennis stated.

"Yes," Julian replied quietly and then added, "Dennis, I want you to be in peace. There is no more blame for past mistakes. It's like you said; things have way of working out for themselves. You deserve the best and I hope you get it."

"I had the best once," Dennis said with a shy grin. "Perhaps, someday, I'll find it again somewhere else."

"I hope so, Dennis," Julian said with a little more feeling.

"I will, Julian," Dennis assured him, "I'm in peace. I finally believe I can move on with my life. The memories of the past, your memory specifically, have been laid to rest, but your soul will always be with me."

Dennis placed his hand on top of Julian's, which was set on his ex-husband's knee, "Goodbye, my friend." He bent and kissed Julian's cheek. Then he rose, grabbed his suitcase, and walked toward the truck. Billy was waiting to drive him into town to catch his bus. Julian watched as they rode out of sight.

In a few moments, Emily came through the screened door and set down two suitcases on the porch. She then went back inside for one more.

"Here are your things, Matt, Julian or whoever you are," she said, breathing heavily. "I don't care where you go, but I want you out of this house."

"For how long?" Julian said as he turned around. He had one foot on the ground, while the other rested on the top of the porch. He waited while she plopped the third bag in front of him.

"Not long enough to suit me," Emily said as she gritted her teeth. "I don't know Matt! I can't even think straight right now. I am so angry, I don't know what to do. I just know I have to be away from you for a while. I've had it!"

She went back into the house with the door slamming behind her. After a couple of moments, he sat back down on the porch. After another moment, Pilot came through the screened door.

"I see your wife is madder than a wet hen," Pilot said as he sat next to Julian.

"Oh well, can you blame her?" Julian said with disgust.

"Oh, she'll come around," Pilot assured with a smile. "It may take a while, but she'll come around."

Julian shook his head. "I guess it's the barracks for a while."

"No need for that," Pilot said replied seriously. "There's a vacant cottage, two doors down from Old Bill's place. I figured you'd be comfortable living there for a while. You can be close to some good cooking and your buddy, Billy. Take your bags down tonight, and we'll have it set up for you with a TV set and things by the time you get home from work tomorrow."

"I have the feeling you were expecting my banishment from the big house," Julian surmised.

"There are some things a father.... and a mother can figure out from their daughter at certain times," Pilot agreed, as he crinkled his nose. "I kind of knew what was coming."

After a brief silence he added, "Son, I don't often get to meddle in my children's lives. But sometimes I find it hard not to give advice from time to time."

Julian didn't utter a reply, but continued to listen.

"One day, my daughter is going to forgive your past and accept you for the person you are," Pilot began,

Julian looked at him, "You know what I did with Robert, don't you?" Julian said in a serious tone.

"Some things are hard to keep secret if one is not careful," Pilot explained. "Now, I am not condemning or condoning the methods you choose for living your life. At the same time, I know you cannot deny your true self. Try to have something on the side, and just be discreet about it. Nobody has to know."

Julian turned and looked at his father in-law incredulously. "You would recommend such a thing involving your own daughter?"

"I want my daughter to be happy," Pilot said firmly. "That means you have to be happy. Do whatever it takes to make this happen. It certainly wouldn't be the first time for an arrangement such as this to exist. A matter of fact, it is rather common place. People, spouses, family, tend to look the other way in situations such as these. They are known to exist, but people just don't talk about them."

"I don't think I could do something like that," Julian said with disbelief. "Emily deserves far better. She deserves the best."

"Emily deserves happiness," Pilot deadpanned. "That is your responsibility as her husband. You are *A Pilot by Choice.* In this family there is no divorce and we do whatever it takes to keep us together."

Julian slowly shook his head. "This day has been too much for me. I can't believe all this is happening so soon."

"You're going to have a lot of time to think these things over in your mind," Pilot said as he stood up on the porch. "You can take my advice, or come up with a suitable plan of your own. Remember, you have a wife and five children depending on you. You can't afford to make wrong decisions." He then opened the screen door and entered the house without waiting for a response from Julian.

Julian sat for a few minutes. Unable to process all that was just said, he rose and grabbed the three suitcases, one under his left arm and the others each in one hand. He tossed them into a nearby wheelbarrow and made for the Main Road.

When he came upon the Quarters Road, he saw his new home. *"Will it be temporary?"* he thought. At this point, he wasn't sure he cared. Then he corrected himself. He would not indulge in self-pity. He believed his place was here on the farm. He wondered if Emily would keep him from his children. Certainly she would not deprive them of their father. Perhaps when she cooled a bit, she would let him see them. *Pilot will talk to her,* he thought. It seemed the great man was rooting for him. *"Pilot will help me,"* he thought again. He did not feel so alone. Billy...Billy's family always made him feel at home with them. Perhaps it would be like old times. It will be good to take up with Billy again. It seemed to Julian that his friend and he had gotten away from each other of late. Of course, he had been in the hospital and when he finally came home, there was the other excitement with Robert, which took precedence. Things would be okay, but he already was missing the children.

He came upon the cottage, with the resignation that this would most likely be his home for a while. He went inside the door. It was unlocked. Things did not stay secure in this little village of sorts. People did not think to steal from one another. If someone got an inkling to do so, they usually got caught. There wasn't much that got by the folks who lived in these humble buildings. On the downside, everyone knew each other's business, though there was usually little room for judgement. The folks just let things fall as they fell.

The cottage was clean. It was sparsely furnished, with no rugs, curtains, or decoration. Whoever the previous tenants were, took most everything with them except a three cushioned couch and two stuffed chairs. There was a small empty bookcase beneath the window looking out from of the front of the house which was the living area. It was very similar to Old Bill's cottage. The living area, the dining area, and the kitchen opened into one single room, except for a large counter area separating the kitchen from the dining area. The structure was made of wood; dry enough to easily catch fire. Julian thought he would have to get a couple of fire extinguishers. If he was forced to cook, a fire could happen.

He moved through a very small hallway, which led to three small bedrooms. The far bedroom was the largest, but he chose the back bedroom to park his belongings, because he liked the location of the window over the bed. He thought that the morning light in the east would be nice, even though he was often up and about before sunrise. He opened his suitcase, because he was not ready to settle in for the evening just yet. He thought he might as well make use of the time to unpack and then go for a nice run. He thought of asking Billy to go with him, but decided he needed some time to himself this day. When he got used to things, he would start inviting Billy's company.

When he opened the suitcase, he noticed a letter inside an envelope that was not sealed. Before he made to unfold it, he could tell the handwriting belonged to Emily. Slowly he unfolded it and started reading. On the top of the page, the headline read, *Instructions regarding the children.* He learned that he will be required to pick up the children from the big house each day at 3:00 in the afternoon during the week, when their schooling was complete for the day. He would have to get off work early to accomplish this feat. It would be his job to feed them supper and then return them to the big house for bedtime. On Sundays, he would pick them up for church and return them to the big house for Sunday dinner. He would be welcome to stay, but she would not be in attendance.

Julian set the letter back down on top of his clothes of his opened suitcase and then sat on the bed to digest his latest assignment. It wouldn't leave much time for himself, but the arrangement seemed much better than he originally had hoped. Maybe things wouldn't be so bad after all. As much as he loved his adopted family, it seemed better to be away from them for a while to sort things about his mind and emotions. The bonus would be to spend a good amount of time with his children. He felt relieved that they would not be in circumstance, where they could forget him. He had already missed so much time with them. They were growing up so fast, he wanted to be able to watch them and be a part of it.

Julian decided to forget unpacking for a while, and got himself ready for his run. He knew it would be a relatively short distance, because time had not permitted him this luxury and he was out of practice. Yes, maybe life would settle back into a routine...routine; that was one thing different about Julian's existence on the farm than his past life back east, which was anything but routine.

As he stepped outside the cottage, he saw Billy stretching, getting ready for a run of his own. Julian smiled. *"Maybe some company would be good."* Without saying so much as a word, Julian set to stretch his own muscles. After he started to feel limber, he turned to his friend to signal that he was ready. Without missing a beat, the two men started a slow trot up the Quarters Road, leading to the Cattle Road.

When they finished their run, they stopped in front of Old Bill's place. "You know Mama is going to want to see you," Billy said, as his breathing returned to normal.

Julian knew this to be a dinner invitation. He was in a pleasant mood now that he had completed a good workout. He moved to signal to Billy that he would follow him into the cottage. Jeannette was busy working in the kitchen when her son and friend came plodding through the door. Her face lit up when she saw Julian.

"Lord have mercy, look who it is," Jeannette exclaimed, as Billy reached over to kiss his mother's cheek. She giggled wide-eyed when Julian did the same. He had never before given such a gesture to her.

"Let me look at you," Jeannette said, obviously pleased. "Time has done you some good, baby. Things will only get better for you."

Julian nodded to her with a smile.

She went to a nearby closet and grabbed two bath towels. "You two dry off with these. There is no time for cleanup, before supper is served," she said with a commanding voice. "Now get on out of my kitchen, so I can put some food on the table. Billy, go and get your daddy and sister."

Billy did what his mama told him to do without a word. Julian toweled himself dry as he sat on a nearby couch. Soon, Old Bill came from the back of the cottage into the living area. Billy's sister was not present. It was known throughout the farm that Lisa spent a good deal of time with Jack. The farm's people were not known for gossip, but at the same time, secrets were difficult to keep.

Julian stood as he came into the room. Old Bill immediately set his frame into an easy chair. "You never stood before when I came into a room. I don't expect that you should start now. Relax, boy. We're all the same people."

Manners were not common place at Old Bill's. Other than respect for others present and the absence of rude behavior, all other rituals were not necessary. Julian nodded as sat. He leaned back into the couch and took a deep breath. Soon, he realized that things were as they always had been. At the supper table, Jeannette remained animated, as she went back and forth from the stove, the table, and her chair, while the others ate. Old Billy laughed heartily at all her tales. Billy paid close attention while he ate and Julian did the same. Both were happy to be entertained, while putting aside their concerns for a short time.

This was how things went for Julian over the next few months. There was little contact at the big house, other than when he picked up and dropped off the children each day. Pilot and Louisa had left for their annual trip and stayed a while longer than usual. Last year, they had cut their trip short, since Julian was in the hospital.

On more days than not, Billy would be sitting in front of the television set in his living area when Julian returned home from work each afternoon. Billy would still be there after Julian showered to get ready to head on up to the big house to fetch his children. Jack was also a frequent visitor to Julian's cottage. Jack was able to spend some private time with Lisa, since he started hanging out at Julian's place. However, all were gone by the time Julian arrived with his five children each day. Jeannette would come and leave supper on the stove each day for the little ones and Julian while he was fetching them from the big house. After dispatching the babies back to the big house, he would go to sit on his perch for a while, then head back to his cottage. Jack and Billy assumed their original occupancy that they had earlier in the afternoon. Sometimes, Julian and Billy would go for runs.

Things had settled into a routine for Julian. He could know what to expect each day. It became security for him, allowing him to relax. He started to enjoy life. However, things don't freeze in time.

It was time to start planting for the sugar in the early spring. Pilot and Louisa had returned from their trip. Julian noticed that Louisa looked slightly weary, instead of relaxed, as she usually did each year upon the couple's return. The change was subtle but enough for Julian to notice. He quizzed her about it, but she deflected his comments as meaningless. She said that she caught a bad cold on their trip, but she was about fully recovered. She did not cough, so Julian believed what she said. Apparently, so did everyone else.

Then one day it happened. Louisa collapsed one day in the big kitchen. Quickly, she was brought to her bed inside the big house. The doctor was immediately summoned. She had a serious fever, he said. Pilot wanted to make fervent efforts to get her to the hospital. No time, the doctor said. The fever needed to be immediately reined in, or she would die before they made it to the hospital. Ice packs were applied to her entire body. Still, the fever raged. Pilot was by her side the whole night, as

Louisa fought bravely. The doctor said that the fever could break any moment. The longer Louisa held on, the better the prognosis would be. There was great hope that she had made it through the night, but the fever raged forward.

Julian waited along with the rest of the family in the kitchen of the big house, praying that they would soon hear the good news that the fever had broken. The news never came. Louisa fought hard, but the fever was just too strong. She passed in the early hours of the morning, just as the pitch of daylight settled on the horizon. Pilot was with her when she died.

One by one, each family member was allowed time alone with her, as they said their good-byes in private. She lay in peace, with her eyes closed and the slight glow of the fever made it looked as if she was merely asleep. However, one could sense that the spirit had left her and only her shell remained.

Less than 24 hours earlier, Louisa was bustling about in the big kitchen, making sure the staff got out the lunch meal quickly so everyone could return to work without incurring the wrath of overseers for being tardy. The illness had taken her so quickly, that the family and farm hands had not a notion how to prepare for the confusion of her loss. Pilot immediately declared that all work on the farm was to cease. Only a few of the farm's vital activities were allowed to take place, like the preparation of simple cold food from the big kitchen. The farm's people were stunned.

Quickly, the word was spread in town about the death of Louisa. Although she was perceived as the loving, supportive wife of a great patriarch, her presence and charm would be missed throughout the community. Food poured from neighbors from miles around into the big house. There was so much food that most spilled to the big kitchen for the farm's people. Little of it went to waste.

A grand funeral took place quickly within the next 2 days. There was not a local structure large enough to accommodate the huge crowd that came to pay their final respects. Therefore, one of the nearby hayfields was quickly cleared and set up for the grand event. Several choirs were assembled within a few hours to perform the only instrumentation for this occasion. Pilot knew that Louisa would not have wanted such a grandiose affair to celebrate her death, but he felt the big funeral would be for the benefit of those she left behind. Louisa gently affected the lives of many and certainly all felt the helplessness in dealing with her death. The grand event defused some of this, so all who cared for her were able to move on with their lives.

The farm's work was postponed for a total of 3 days following Louisa's death. At that time, Pilot ordered everyone back to work. However, Pilot himself took 3 more days of seclusion into his rooms. The only people he would see were Emily and Jack. On the third day, he agreed to see Julian.

"Are you adjusting?" Pilot asked Julian as he entered the big man's sitting area outside his bedchamber.

Pilot was seated at a handsome writing desk on the far wall from the doorway. He was wearing a satin tan smoking jacket covering his pajamas. Julian sat in a nearby sky blue shiny love seat. "As well as can be expected," Julian answered softly. "And yourself?"

"Oh, I'll manage," Pilot said as he turned to some papers on his desk.

After a moment, he said to Julian, "My wife left you a few items of jewelry to give to your sons as they grow older; keepsakes from her side of the family. I will have them put in your rooms here in the big house."

"That will be fine," Julian answered. Then he wondered if he would ever set foot into those rooms again, but he kept those thoughts to himself. He was content with the way his life was now at the present time. To be truthful, he could not see living in this house without Louisa's presence occupying it. Again, he kept these thoughts to himself.

"I am hoping that you will be using them again soon," Pilot replied lightly.

"You assured me some months ago of this outcome," Julian surmised.

Pilot looked pleased. "You have been a patient man, Julian. I am very proud of you."

This was the first time Pilot had addressed him as Julian. He smiled approval at his father in-law.

"I can see the time away has been good for you and you have adjusted well after all the chaos within the last couple of years," Pilot stated with a smile.

"Agreed," Julian replied.

Turning his attention to other matters, Pilot picked up several pages of paper. "Lamond's will had been read some time ago."

Julian squirmed slightly and nodded, prompting Pilot to continue.

"To my surprise, he left everything to be divided among your five children," Pilot explained. "These pages state a few of the assets to be transferred into yours and your wife's custody until the babies are able to handle the matters themselves."

"In his own way," Julian started, "He loved those children. At first, because they belonged to Emily and at last, because they belonged to Emily and me."

"So it seems," Pilot answered. "This will carries with it the strong possibility of being contested. It will not be difficult to prove that Lamond was less than stable at the time before his death."

"If you say this is so, than I believe it to be true," Julian replied. "I get the sense that you want little to do with this battle." Julian did not want this battle himself, but it was the children's battle and he knew there was little choice.

Pilot had that look as if he had a plan. "I know you well enough by now that you would prefer to let someone else handle this matter."

"Agreed," Julian replied, slightly ashamed.

Pilot shared his plan. "I have already talked to Jack about taking over the entire Lamond operation. That is, managing the day to day activities. He will be moving into the Lamond household and assuming the responsibility to make a big profit and engage with the farm's people. You will be responsible for managing the children's portfolio, which we know you are greatly qualified to do."

"That will mean an office in the big house," Julian thought.

"This will mean less time in the field for you," Pilot explained, "Because I will also need for you to take more of Jack's responsibilities on this farm. I know you like working with the folks on the farm, but your talents are greatly needed elsewhere. You will still have plenty of time for field operations."

"Who has been taking care of things over all these months?" Julian inquired.

"Robert was doing very little at the time of his death," Pilot answered. "He had delegated to subordinates. He still was able to keep a tight grip on these people, so the operation went smoothly. With him gone, things have gotten sloppy, so it's time for us to move in and take over the farm."

"Have you been dealing with this over the last few days?" Julian asked incredulously.

"No, this is the first I've thought about it in weeks," Pilot smiled. "The time had not been right to move on this, but now it has come."

"If the will is to be contested, what is the sense for following through with the plan?" Julian asked.

"There is a sister. I haven't seen her in a number of years. She and Lamond became estranged a little while back, but I expect her to make some trouble," Pilot explained.

"I guess the scent of money and fortune can erase many memories," Julian agreed.

"Well, it is more than that," Pilot continued. "In his will, Robert named his sister guardian and CEO of the Lamond operations until the children are grown for a salary of $150,000 annually. A good salary, but it would seem meager compared to the value of the estate. It seems to be is a slap in the face to his sister. To further qualify for this position, she would have to pack her bags and move into the Lamond house, which she hates. However, the money is enticing. The estate her late father left her was left virtually penniless, when her ex-husband made some poor financial decisions. So, there's no telling what she might do. I suggest we cut her a deal when the time is right. At that time, we will cut Jack a generous deal."

"How does Jack feel about all of this?" Julian asked skeptically. He knew he loved Billy's sister a great deal and would be very distraught to be so far away from her. However, Pilot could be very persuasive.

"He's still digesting it, but I expect he'll come around," Pilot said without a second thought. "I want this for him. He has trained eagerly for this opportunity all his life. I know it's not the Pilot farm, but I plan on being around for a while and he is needed at Lamonds."

"You don't think I should be the one to go over to Lamonds?" Julian said, trying to stifle a choke.

"My feeling is you, your wife and children are better off here on the farm. Call it a father's intuition," Pilot said with a smile.

"I trust your judgement," Julian replied.

CHAPTER 24

It was still early afternoon when Julian was strolling along the back lawn of the big house after his visit with Pilot. He was walking down the lane coming to the point where the Main and Farm Roads met, when he saw a black limousine coming up the Farm Road toward the big house. He waited as the car made a left turn onto the lane leading to the big house. After a few moments a boy who looked to be in his mid to late teens stepped from the car. He waved at the air in front of his face to try to clear the dust from his eyes. He stood about 5'9" with a very slender frame. His black wavy hair was medium length, parted to the left side of his head. Along with his expensive haircut, he wore tight black jeans and a nylon black form fitting party T-shirt that one might wear to a nightclub. The driver opened the trunk of the long vehicle and produced a large white canvas duffel bag. The boy took it from the driver and slung it over his shoulder. He noticed Julian standing in the road. Immediately, the driver returned to his car and with relative ease, turned it around and receded down the Farm Road. The boy walked toward Julian. When he reached him, he set the bag down in front of him. The boy had an envelope in his hand that looked to be a letter.

"I'm looking for Julian Smith," the boy said. Julian could see some faded freckles on the boy's face. The pale skin looked vaguely familiar. The boy resembled someone that Julian might have known at one time.

"I'm Julian Smith," Julian replied, looking into the boy's eyes. At that time, surprise entered his mind, as he recognized the connection to the boy.

"I'm Shaun Smith," Shaun stated as he extended his hand toward Julian. "I'm your long awaited nephew all the way from St. Louis. I thought I'd never get here. I had to take a plane, three buses and then a limousine to arrive on your door step."

"I thought you weren't due until this summer, when school let out," Julian replied with obvious dread.

"Well, eh.. There was a slight change in plans," Shaun replied "We had to move things up a bit." After a brief pause, Shaun handed Julian the letter. "Here. This is for you, Uncle Julian."

Julian took the letter and opened it: *Dear Brother, I thank you so much for taking young Shaun into your home. I hope the two of you have an enjoyable summer together and really get to know each other. I know his visit comes a bit earlier than expected, but frankly, it could not be helped. I wish you all the luck in the world, but I hope you will not need it. Until September, Albert.*

"Doesn't school start in late August?" Julian said with his brow furrowed.

"Usually," Shaun answered. "Why?"

"It seems your papa is not expecting you back home until some time in September," Julian explained.

Shaun paused. "I don't think he's expecting me back in St Louis at all."

"Why do you say that?" Julian responded, confused.

"Well, he only gave me a one way air ticket with no return date," Shaun said as he shrugged his shoulders.

"Well, let's get you to my quarters. There's a room there where you can sleep," Julian said as he started walking toward the Main Road.

"Don't you live in this big house?" Shaun asked with a confused look. "Papa said you live in a big mansion."

Shaun fell into step with Julian. "Well, I am kind of in the dog house these days," Julian explained. "Until I get out of it, we are stuck living with the farm's people."

"That's okay," Shaun replied. "I'm quite used to the dog house. I've spent many nights in the dog house."

"Are you really such a terror?" Julian asked as they walked along the Main Road. "Am I going to have my hands full with you this summer?"

"I think I'm a good kid," Shaun said with a serious expression. "Papa said you and I would get along real well. He said we had a lot in common."

"He said the same to me," Julian said, remembering the conversation he had with Albert regarding his nephew. "What do you suppose he meant?"

"Well for one thing," Shaun explained, "I'm a gay teen."

"It wasn't too difficult to reach that conclusion," Julian replied. "What's surprising is that you seemed to have figured it out at such a young age."

"I'll take that as a compliment as backhanded as it was," Shaun said with a smirk.

"Well, for starters, you're dressed as if you had just come from a club," Julian said with a small degree of shock.

"Well, that's not far from the truth," Shaun agreed. "I just didn't have a lot of time to change before I got on the plane."

"Is that why you packed so lightly?" Julian asked with a giggle.

"Yes, I was a bit in a hurry, when the time came for me to leave," Shaun replied with a grin. "You may say it was kind of sudden."

"My goodness!" Julian cried with a laugh. "What am I in for this summer?"

Julian and his nephew laughed and talked the rest of the way to the cottage.

Julian was sitting on his perch with a long stem of grass in his teeth with his eyes closed. He was tired. The planting season had begun, so he spent much of the day on the fields supervising the farm hands replacing some of the cane with small portions kept in storage over the winter. Most of the planting had been done last fall, but it was clear that some of the old stalks were not satisfactory, while some of the new seedlings were not going to make it.

Shaun kept him company throughout the day, while he began to learn some of the farm's activities. However, before taking to the fields for the day, they had to slip into town early this morning to buy him clothes and other basics.

Late in the afternoon, they picked up the children from the big house. He thought of getting a baby sitter to get them, since they got a late start with work, but Julian wanted Shaun to meet his cousins. The little ones took to their older cousin immediately. Shaun was a little apprehensive in the beginning, until they started climbing onto him, forcing him to play with him. The brothers and cousin played a little game of hide and seek in the tiny cottage. Shaun pretended he couldn't find them until they reached home base. Baby Candy was able to join them. She wasn't going to be left out of the fun.

Now the children were home asleep and so was his nephew. At least he hoped Shaun was trying to sleep, or least relaxing. The excitement during the last 2 days surely must have made him tired.

Julian kept Shaun close to him since his arrival. His nephew did not seem to mind, as both of them seemed to enjoy getting to know each other. Shaun did not want to speak too much of St. Louis. Instead, he was very eager to learn about the farm and its inhabitants. Therefore, it was easy for Julian to monopolize the conversation, since he had a captive audience. Shaun laughed at all his small jokes and was delighted when Julian lightly teased him. Shaun's presence, so far, had been a joy.

Now Julian wanted some time to himself before retiring for the evening. It was dusk and almost time to head back to the cottage. *"Just a few more minutes,"* he thought as he slumped further back into the fence post.

It wasn't long before he could sense a body approaching. He opened his eyes and saw Emily coming toward him. He closed his eyes. He felt a sense of dread come over him.

"Matt," Emily said. She waited for Julian to respond.

"Hi," Julian said as he opened his eyes and sat up straight. He crossed his legs before him, as he continued to sit on the metal drum. Emily stood before him, holding her hands together at her waist. He smiled sheepishly.

"How are you?" she asked shyly.

"I'm fine," he replied and then after a pause he added, "I am sorry about Louisa. You must be very upset." The couple managed to keep their distance from each other at the funeral. They both were distressed over Louisa's death and did not need the complication of personal interaction. The two had not spoken since Emily set Julian bags on the porch of the big house, banishing him to his present living arrangement.

"I can say the same for you," Emily replied, "I know how much you loved her."

"More than my own mother, that's for sure," Julian quipped, as he smiled lightly.

Emily returned his smile. "I see you've developed a sense of humor, Matt. I guess it's something else I will learn about you." Her smile turned grim as she looked toward the ground.

"My name is Julian," he said very gently. "I know it's difficult for you to accept this truth, but we have to face who I am"

"I know," Emily said as she gazed into his eyes. "I have spent these past months morning the loss of Matt, my husband. As you see, I haven't been completely able to let go."

His wife looked sad. He could feel her pain, with the loss of a man she believed to be her husband, coupled with the loss of her mother. "Emily, I miss him too, but I know he is not really gone. He still lives inside of me. Instead of just Matt in my body, there is Matt and Julian. Julian was always there, he was just hiding," Julian explained.

"How can I see him? All I can see now is a man I don't know, living inside a shell that resembles my late husband." Tears streaked Emily's face. "All I see is Julian when I look at you. How can I find the man I love inside of you?"

"He is the part of me that loves you, Emily. All you have to do is look for him. He is there waiting to be recognized. However, Julian is there as well as Matt. At some point, you will have to accept us both," Julian explained.

"Do you love me?" Emily asked, beginning to get really upset, "Still?"

Julian slumped back against the fence post, "I know I do, Emily, but I feel a lot anger right now. I guess I've been feeling it for quite a while, but it has been difficult to face. I think you're going to have to help me get though it. Maybe we can help each other."

"Anger?" Emily asked bewildered, "What has made you angry?"

Julian collected his thoughts for a moment. He started slowly, "I know I'm responsible for all the turmoil that I have caused you, our family and myself. I feel a tremendous amount of guilt, especially for the pain I have given you. You deserve much better than me, Emily. These feelings of empathy and guilt are easy for me to contend with and harbor."

"Julian, I admit deep down I wanted to punish you for everything that has happened, but at some point, forgiveness is essential to healing," Emily explained earnestly "I am trying."

"I believe I deserve a lot less than you have given me. You could have taken our children away from me with ease. You may have been able to convince your daddy to ban me from the farm. You have done none of that and I am grateful to you for it," Julian said, getting upset. He was angry.

Emily was in disbelief. "You know me well enough to know I could never have done any of those terrible things to you. If not you, then our children. Secondly, Daddy would never have heard of it. You are a son to him. He holds you closer to his heart than some of his natural born children."

"I suppose I knew all of that," Julian said with a sigh. He smeared tears from his own face.

"What is making you angry, Julian?" Emily asked, getting back to the original point.

"It is that," Julian struggled, "I have feelings too. I didn't ask for all these bad things to happen. I'm sick and tired for being blamed for them. Why can't I be forgiven? Why can't you forgive me!"

Emily was startled. Julian had never raised his voice in her presence. He was sobbing quietly.

"Maybe you'd better go," he said softly.

"I think we should continue," Emily said evenly.

Julian said nothing.

"I have forgiven you. I did a long time ago," Emily confessed. "I just wasn't ready to face you, Julian. I needed to sort my feelings. I still have to work things in my mind and heart, but now I need your help."

"Emily," Julian replied. "From the day I met you, I have given and given to you. I would have done anything to make you happy. I only had your feelings to consider. For reasons for which I am responsible, I stifled my own feelings and desires. I solely kept yours to heart. Anything you asked, I did my best to deliver."

Emily nodded.

"Then I made a mistake. Some unfortunate circumstance or the said crisis developed. I was forced to leave my home. I don't honestly know if I'll be able to return to it," Julian said with more tears. "I lost my best friend in you, Emily."

"I am sorry," Emily said softly.

"No," Julian said shaking his head while holding back more tears. "I'm not assessing blame. I'm merely telling you how I feel."

"Do you want to come home?" Emily asked.

Julian let a few more tears fall. "I don't know, Emily. I'm so upset right now, I don't know what to make of it."

"When you are ready, you can come back at any time, Julian," Emily said with a smile.

"Why are you being so nice to me?" Julian asked her, regaining his composure.

"Well, I have had a few losses of late," Emily said, taking in a deep breath. "I lost my mother. In Candace, I lost someone who was like a mother to me. And, as I told you, I lost my husband." Then she added with a shy smile, "Perhaps I can get one of those back."

"Do you really want me back, Emily? Or are you doing it as a sense of obligation?" Julian asked skeptically.

"It won't be easy, Julian," Emily replied. "We will have to get to know each other all over again."

"Maybe we can date," Julian said with a smile. "You know, like we did before we were married."

"That would be nice," Emily replied with a nod.

"After a while, when I do come back to the big house, there will be an addition to the family. At least for a while," Julian said gravely.

Emily looked confused. She nodded for him to continue.

"My brother Albert sent me his son, Shaun, to live with me for the summer. He has been staying with me the last couple of days at the cottage on the Quarters Road," Julian explained.

"Is there any reason for this visit? I got the feeling you and Albert were not particularly close. Am I mistaken?" Emily asked with a touch of amazement. "Is it a favor to him, or were you looking forward to his visit?"

"Actually, I was dreading his visit. Not only that, he arrived over 3 months early," Julian replied with irritation. "Apparently, he's given Albert a rough time. I'm supposed to be the one who understands him and brings him to reason. But you know, Emily, he really seems to be a nice kid. We seemed to have hit it off real well. I've kept a close eye on him since he's been here. This is the first time I've gone off and left him. I guess this is some sort of test."

"Maybe he'll warm up to you better than he did with Albert," Emily said with a warm smile. "Nonetheless, you have my support. Let me know what I can do to help. I think it will be good for you to have someone of kin to you around the house, besides our children. Like some sort of link to your family."

"I guess," Julian sighed, "Hopefully there is a good apple in the bunch."

Emily raised her hands and then let them fall once more to her waist, "I should get back to the house. It's getting late."

Julian bounded off his perch. He wondered if he should at least kiss her cheek. Would any type of affection be appropriate? Without thinking, he held out his hands together in front of his waist, palms towards the sky. She placed hers on top of his and gave them a good squeeze. Then she turned toward the big house.

"Good night, Emily," Julian called after her.

She stopped in her tracks and turned to look halfway back to him. "Good night, Julian," she said softly and resumed her walk to the house.

Julian decided it was time for himself to get back to his little house. He trudged down the Main Road and then made a right down the Quarters

Road. He came upon his home just less than halfway down the road of stones and dirt to his right hand side. He could see the lights in the house through the open window leading to the living area. The dark window to the right belonged to the bedroom that Shaun occupied. It was originally for Billy, but he never did stay in it. Billy was in the house more than Julian was, but he always ate and slept at Old Bill's house. He would come over to read or just to look at television. Julian was often amazed how much Billy read, not to mention the material involved. Julian liked mysteries, where Billy liked to read about politics and famous biographies, which Julian found to be quite boring.

Jack often spent private time in the big bedroom running from front to back of the house on the right side, while Julian stayed in the back bedroom. Julian walked through the front door and was surprised to see Shaun sprawled asleep on the couch with one of Billy's books resting faced down on his chest. The television was playing quietly. Shaun woke as Julian walked across the floor.

"I see one of those books put you to sleep," Julian teased. "It works for me every time."

Shaun moved his feet and sat upright to give Julian room to sit.

"Don't get up," Julian said, patting the boy's leg. "I'll sit in the chair."

Julian sat in the chair, propping his feet upon the rectangle table. Shaun sat up anyway and stretched to wake himself.

"Why don't you go on to bed?" Julian admonished. "You've had a big day."

"That's okay," Shaun replied. "How long have you've been gone?"

"A little while," Julian replied. "I finally managed to run into my wife. It was the first time I'd seen her in months."

"How did it go?" Shaun asked, still waking up from his slumber.

"I don't know if I can call it progress, but at least we are starting to talk," Julian replied. He then mused, "She says we can move to the big house at any time."

"Is that what you want, Uncle Julian?" Shaun asked with a slight frown. "From what I gather from you since I've been here, you've been happy living in this house."

"I've been comfortable," Julian admitted, "I'm not going to do anything for the time being. I will decide when it is time. It's my guess that we will someday be living in the big house. That's what I had originally wanted. It's just that now I feel settled. I haven't cared too much for change these past few years. It's far from the exciting life I used to live," he ended with a chuckle. "But the reality is that things change."

"Can you really consider going back to that house and living the life of a good husband?" Shaun asked with disbelief. "I don't know you very well, Uncle Julian, but Papa tells me you had a previous life before you came to this town. He said you had a partner and an exciting life in the big city with many friends. How did you wind up in this place, so far removed from the rest of the world?"

"I am surprised my brother spoke of me in such glowing terms," Julian replied with a grin. "He was always rude to Dennis. He would provoke both of us into arguments about the way we were leading our lives,"

"Papa didn't agree with the way you were living your life, but he said you did amazingly well for someone so destined for destruction. He admired the way you've turned around your life and decided to live more respectively. He wants you to influence me into doing the same thing," Shaun explained. "It seems to me you haven't made the complete turn. You seem confused about how you want to live your life."

"So, did you come here expecting to be influenced to live a respectable life?" Julian asked with a curious look.

"Not at all," Shaun replied shyly. "I thought life might be easier to live here with someone who at least had an inkling how to deal with a gay adolescent. Granted, I don't need you to raise me. I'm a bit past that stage in my maturity. I was really hoping for getting cut some slack."

"Why didn't Albert ship you off to boarding school?" Julian asked. "That's what our parents did."

"He tried twice," Shaun replied. "They sent me back when they discovered they had a gay boy in their midst. I don't hide what I am. I don't think I could pass for straight, even if I tried. I'm an effeminate male, which I have no regrets about being."

"I wouldn't call you effeminate," Julian disagreed, "Your appearance is on the feminine side, but you carry yourself as any man would."

"You see," Shaun replied, becoming more lively, "I don't care about carrying myself as any man. I should be able to carry myself any way God happened to make me, without prejudice from the rest of society."

"Agreed," Julian said, nodding his head slowly. "I wasn't judging your masculinity as behavior appropriate or unbecoming. I was only saying that I didn't see you as an effeminate boy."

"So, you will not be ashamed to being seen with me?" Shaun asked with a smirk.

"Of course not!" Julian exclaimed. "I'm not some self hating homosexual, if that's where you are going with this conversation. I have made no secrets of my past life as a gay man. It's no secret to anybody on this farm or community at large."

"Weren't you outted by the local newspaper?" Shaun asked with his brow furrowed.

"I see it didn't take you long to get into the loop around here," Julian said with a laugh. "I'm not sure how privy you are to my history here on the farm. I guess Albert would have left a few details out of the synopsis he gave you about me. I'll do my best to fill in the gaps."

"Well," Shaun hedged, "I read all the articles about you. You would be surprised how many of the folks around here kept those papers."

"Is that so?" Julian mused. "Well, here's my story. When I arrived here on the farm quite a few years ago, I was severely depressed. I didn't care if I was gay, straight or where I rated on anybody's scale. I just wanted to find some peace and for people to leave me alone. I don't think I tried to deny my sexuality, so much as it really did not matter what it was to me at the time. Whatever sexual feelings I had were repressed in some illogical way."

"But sexual feelings are just one part of being gay," Shaun said with a frown. "A gay man doesn't view life in the same ways that others do who are different from us. How could you not notice?"

"If I didn't notice, others sure did," Julian answered, remembering how people treated him when he first came to the farm. "Some people were hostile to me for no apparent reason. Others stayed clear of me. I have to say that I was not the most approachable person, as I didn't want to be approached. But people could see I was different. The only people who seemed to care about me unconditionally were Old Bill's family and the Pilots. As much as I wanted to deny that I wanted people to care for me, I was clearly drawn to these two families. Deep down, I was suffering and I did not want to suffer forever."

"I give you credit for not thinking about your sexuality," Shaun said with a challenge in his voice. "How in the world did you see yourself straight, get married and sire five kids?"

"You're still missing the point," Julian explained patiently. "I did not, and sort of still today, think in terms of gay and straight. I concede that if you asked me if I was gay, I would reply, yes, of course. But my mind doesn't work in the way of labels. It's not so cut and dried. People are people and not pieces of furniture with distinct shapes."

"I still don't understand," Shaun replied a little dejected.

"Okay, look at it this way," Julian said, shifting his weight for emphasis. "You said a while ago that you didn't care if people saw you as an effeminate male or something other than a swish. You said it should not matter how you carried yourself, people should accept you for yourself. Agreed?"

"Yes," Shaun answered, following Julian's thinking.

"With myself, it's not so different," Julian replied with a pause, letting Shaun digest some of what he was trying to explain. "Why should it matter if I'm straight or gay. Why can't I live my life the way I want without judgement from others? Why can't I live my life as a good father and husband if I so choose?"

"Because there are other people involved in the choices you make, Uncle Julian," Shaun replied gently. He suddenly sensed the turmoil his uncle had been feeling these last months. Now that his wife said that it was time to come home, Uncle Julian was going to have to make some tough choices.

"Uncle Julian, I'll be with you when you make your final decisions for your future plans," Shaun said with a small smile. "I can see how things are not so cut and dried in your predicament."

Julian felt a sense of relief. He did not want to have to defend actions, but the boy had a few good points. "Some things are cut and dried," Julian conceded. "I think you know I have already made the decision to go back home to the big house. I want to try to be a good husband and to continue being a doting daddy to my children. I just have to reconcile my family life to my private life while trying to stay true to my own person. I haven't figured it out yet. Pilot says I should have some sort of relationship in secret. But I'm like you in that way. I don't do things in secret, but I may have to compromise my values to spare the feelings of those close to me."

Shaun nodded, prodding Julian to continue.

"When I came to the Pilots, I was not thinking so clearly and I made irresponsible decisions. At the same time, Shaun, I don't regret the outcomes. I love my adopted family and my children. I even love my wife in a very dear sort of way. I don't know if it's the way a man should love a woman, but she's a wonderful human being. I can't wait for you to get to know her," Julian said with charged emotion.

"But she made you leave your home," Shaun replied with sadness.

"Her plate was full," Julian replied. "There were too many things that even she could not handle at once. There were all those things said about me in the papers, plus I was unfaithful to her and did not make a secret about it."

"Another woman?" Shaun said with disgust.

"Don't be silly," Julian deadpanned. "I was with Lamond himself."

Shaun started to laugh quietly. "You certainly know how to get yourself into a mess, Uncle Julian."

Julian smiled. "I always have."

A couple of days later, Emily came to Julian while he was sitting on his perch, staring off into space, as he usually did when he was there. Julian looked at her as she approached.

"Hi," she said.

"Hi," Julian replied with a relaxed expression.

"What do you think about when you are out here?" Emily asked with a curious look.

Julian gave a hmmm... while in thought. "You always asked that question."

"And you never answered, other than a light twinkle in your eye," Emily responded.

Julian shook his head slowly, while grinning.

"I see I still won't get an answer," Emily said softly, with giggle, while looking at her feet.

"Do you want to go for a walk?" Julian asked.

"It's funny," Emily replied. "I was going to ask you the same thing.

Julian jumped from his perch and started walking with his wife along the Farm Road. Usually, he let her pick the route and this time was the same. She would move in a direction and he could sense where she wanted to go.

After a few strides, she started to chatter about the children and was her animated self. He would smile and nod as he listened. She had a captive audience and was making the most of it. After a little while and a little bit ground covered, the couple slipped into an old level of comfort.

There were walks and nights spent on the back porch of the big house, where they talked of the loss of Louisa and how much she would be missed. Julian was surprised how good a listener Emily was. In the past, she had monopolized the conversation, only because Julian as Matt had let her. But now, Julian liked to talk at times. To be truthful, he was really as much of a chatterbox as she was. Ironically, they never competed for an audience with each other, as they were equally interested in what the other had to say.

Eventually, the strolls along the farm countryside led to horseback rides along the brooks and fruit trees. Later it would be outings with the children and Shaun agreed to come along at times. His young cousins were starting to take a shine to him and would not hear of him being left behind without protests.

Within a couple of months, Julian and Shaun were living in the big house. On the night they returned, Julian was holding his wife as they drifted off to sleep. Their relationship was never going to be a marriage of passion. It never had been that way. With Emily, coming together gave her a since of security that her husband would always be by her side. For Julian, it was familiarity that allowed him to be close to her. After all, she was his dearest friend. Julian had become a creature of habit through the years and was most comfortable with things staying the same. However, the wise and fools alike know that time does not sit still.

CHAPTER 25

Time came to the later part of summer during Shaun's stay at the Pilot Plantation. He thoroughly enjoyed living in the big house with his Uncle Julian and his family. The little kids were a lot of fun, as long as they got a nap everyday.

The greatest thing about Uncle Julian was that he never told Shaun what to do or how to act. For the most part, he left him alone. Sometimes Shaun would wander from the farm and get back late in the evening. Nobody waited up for him or chastised him for his nocturnal habits. He knew he did not have to sneak into bed, but he was quiet coming in from the night so as not to wake anybody. Occasionally, one or two of the farm kids would join him for some of the late night activities that teenagers like to do.

Even with things going well with the family, Shaun would sometimes find farm life boring. As a gay boy from the big city, he sometimes was homesick for the stimulation that fast paced society brought with it.

Perhaps it was boredom that got him into trouble with Uncle Julian one day.

It was early in the afternoon one August day. The kids were down for their nap and Emily decided to lay down with them. She was usually tired these days, as she tried to make up for the absence of her mother. Julian was taking a break from his new office duties regarding his children's affairs and decided to look in on his family. When he got to the hall to where his family had their rooms, he heard some muffled voices come from the far end. He was curious, because the children's rooms were at the other end with Emily's and his suite, while Shaun's was located at the far end. He found that the source of the noise was coming from Shaun's suite and that the door had been left ajar.

When he looked into Shaun's room to satisfy his curiosity, he got more than what he bargained to find. Shaun was lying on his back on one of the twin beds with his pants down to his knees. His hand closest to the far wall was resting on top of the head of a young black boy that could be around the age of 14, felating him and having a difficult time doing it.

"Not so much teeth," Shaun growled and grimaced, "How many times do I have to tell you." He then caught a glance at his stunned uncle standing in the doorway. With his other hand, he braced the boy's head to make him stop.

"I'm sorry," said the boy to Shaun as he wiped his mouth on his sleeve, while panting to regain his breath. As Shaun pushed him away, the boy realized that Julian was in the room. At that moment, he tucked in his shirt, picked up his shoes and made a hasty exit, brushing past Julian as he squirmed through the doorway.

With his excitement evidently quelled, Shaun quickly pulled up his pants and zipped up his belt. He sat on the side of his bed with his hands in his lap, staring at the floor.

"This is not good," Julian said, closing the door. He paused a few moments, utterly speechless. Then he crossed his arms and leaned against the door.

"Why Shaun?" Julian asked in a normal voice.

"Why what?" Shaun replied, looking up to meet his uncle's gaze. His eyes were very somber, but clearly defensive.

"Well, a couple of things," Julian started slowly, uncrossing his arms, putting them behind his back, still leaning against the door. He could see that the boy's body was starting to tense. He wasn't so much angry with Shaun as he was stunned.

Julian began, "I just don't get why you left the door open. We were lucky that it was me who walked in on you. I'm just glad it wasn't Emily or one of the children."

Shaun gave no response.

"It was as if you wanted to be caught in the act," Julian stated with a puzzled look. "Is that true?"

Still no response from Shaun.

"Shaun, this can never happen again," Julian warned. "Do you understand? If I catch you with something like this again, we will be forced to leave this house. I can't take the risk of the other people in this house seeing you in such a position. If someone other than myself saw you with that kid, we would both be looking for somewhere else to live."

"We?" Shaun looked into Julian's face, obviously distraught. "You mean, that you would not just send me away?"

Julian went to sit next to Shaun on the side of the bed with his hands resting on the edge, "Of course we," Julian exclaimed. "What do you think I would do, just toss you out and forget about you?"

"Well, yeah," Shaun replied slowly with confusion. "I'm bad news, Uncle Julian. I don't always know why I do things, but I usually wind up in trouble."

"You're stuck with me," Julian stated emphatically. "I'm responsible for you. You're not just a kid anymore, Shaun. You're becoming more of an adult. As a parent figure to you, I'm not going to tell you what to do and what your decisions have to be. However, I'm here to help you make those choices, since I may have a little bit more experience than you have at this point in your life. That may sound like a lot of freedom to you, but there is a flip side. If you're going to engage in adult things, like sex for example, you are going to have to take responsibilities and consequences for your decisions. I'm not always going to be there to bail you out when you go out on your own without guidance."

"I am really sorry, Uncle Julian," Shaun said as he started to cry.

Julian put his arm around the boy. Shaun rested his head inside the crook of Julian neck as he cried softly.

"You just have to think about what you are doing, Shaun. Another mistake like this one and we are out of here. I would really miss Emily and the kids. You don't want that to happen, do you?" Julian knew that guilt could be a powerful tool when used properly for parental purposes.

"No," Shaun replied, as he wiped his eyes with the palm of his hand. He sat up straight and sniffed a couple of times, trying to regain his composure. "I don't want to cause you any more trouble, Uncle Julian."

"This is not the first time something like this has happened to you, is it Shaun?" Julian asked gravely.

Shaun gently shook his head.

"Does this have something to do with why you had to leave St. Louis?" Julian asked.

Shaun nodded.

"Do you want to tell me about it?" Julian prodded.

"Well, it is terribly embarrassing," Shaun said as he stared at the floor.

"I'm not going to say you are a bad kid, Shaun," Julian stated. "I would like to hear what happened."

Shaun nodded. "These past couple of years, I've been in trouble. I don't know why I do some of things I do, except I know deep down I can't stand my papa. Sometimes I think I hate him. It's like when he gets angry with me, I get a big charge out of getting the best of him. I think I hate him, because he hasn't liked the way I've turned out as a person. I see disappointment, dread, and distaste in his eyes every time he looks at me. He beats me horribly and I've always been too little to protect myself. The only defense that I have had was to be bad. But even this year, I've been worse than I've wanted to be. It's like I've lost control. I've become this bad person."

Shaun rested a moment while he collected his thoughts. "But I know that I'm not really bad. I only did things to make him mad. I had never done anything bad to hurt anyone else but him, except here today with you. And I swear, Uncle Julian, I really didn't mean for it to turn out this way. I would have felt so terrible if you had lost your family over what I had done."

"It's okay," Julian coaxed. "I'm still listening."

"I learned the martial arts while I was growing up, so I could defend myself against him. I never did use anything like that against him, but the training came in handy when the kids in school started to pick on me. I even read up on some militia offensive tactics to use on kids who beat up on me. I would set some lures to get them to fall into my traps and leave them there for a while before letting them go. Eventually most of the kids got afraid of me."

"So, you are not only book smart but also street smart," Julian surmised.

"Oh yes," Shaun agreed. "I love books, studying, learning and things like that, but I'm also one for fighting back when I'm put in any kind of danger. I may not be very strong, but I definitely am not a wimp. What I don't have in strength, I try to make up in brains and strategy. Most of the time it works. I still get beat up at times, but I think I do most of the damage to my attackers. It's when kids gang up on me that I have a hard time beating them at their own game."

Julian could see that his nephew was a confident boy with a big spirit. He thought the kid would be okay, with a little positive attention to ease some of the confusion he had with parent figures. "What about your mom?" he asked. "What is she like?"

Shaun gasped, "She is just plain dreadful. She does whatever my papa tells her to do. No backbone whatsoever. The only time she helped me was when Papa tried to send me to some sort of reform school. She wouldn't stop crying until he promised her he would never do that to me. She must have cried for 2 days straight. Other than that, she would tell me to try and not make Papa so mad at me. I tried to tell her that he shouldn't treat me so bad, but she refused to consider it. I despise her almost as much as Papa."

"Have you ever had anybody love you, Shaun?" Julian asked with pity. "Have you ever been able to love someone, including yourself?"

"Yes," Shaun replied with a slight nod. "I've had some great teachers who have always been supportive of me. They knew I was different, so many of them were extra protective of me. I wanted to please them in return, so I always studied real hard and got good grades. I was always happiest in the classroom."

"I also knew that all people were not like Mom and Papa. I believed there to be lots of kids like myself who were different than most others. I want to help those kids; take care of them and teach them how to survive in this world. I want to dedicate my life to it," Shaun explained.

"How do you view yourself?" Julian asked.

"I know I do some bad things, but I don't consider myself a bad kid," Shaun answered. "I know that sounds messed up, but I just need to sort some things out, so I don't feel the need to do those things. Once I do that, I'll be okay. I think I can do some real good in this world some day, so I guess I can be an okay guy."

"I'd like to help you, Shaun," Julian said with a smile. "I know where you are coming from these days. I didn't like my parents very much when I was growing up. Like you, I was lucky to have other people around me who cared enough to make sure I got what I needed. Still, it was lonely at times."

"Sure," Shaun replied with a shrug. "I don't really know how you can help. It's really up to me to get myself together."

"Well, you can start by talking to me," Julian explained. "Tell me some of your secrets when you feel comfortable. Tell me what goes on in your head when you get confused."

"Like with what I did before I came here?" Shaun asked.

"That sounds like a good place to start," Julian agreed.

"Well, it's like I said earlier," Shaun began. "Papa and I were not getting along. He was getting madder at me and I was getting to be a very bad boy. It got so he could no longer trust me to be on my own. The night before I arrived here on the farm, Papa had an important dinner with his boss and his wife. Of course, he brought Mom along with him. The boss had a son my age, so Papa asked if I could stay at his house, while the four of them went out for dinner. Papa said the boss's son was the perfect boy and he hoped that I could learn something from him about being a successful young man. After the adults left, I coaxed this guy into sneaking out to a club with me. Curiosity got the better of him, so we went out on the town. I don't drink beer or anything like that, but he decided to have a couple. I could sense he had enough to drink, so I drove us back to his place. In the living room, we turned on the television. One thing led to another and it wasn't long before we were wrestling. I don't know why, but I kissed him and he didn't resist. So, off came our clothes and we started going at it. I was sticking it to him pretty good, when we heard the key in the door. At that moment, I started to shoot and kept going instead of scrambling for some sort of cover. He tried to get away, but I wouldn't let him. The door opened and his parents with mine saw him with his ankles in the air, while I was still plugging away. Papa was beside himself. I really thought he would have killed me if the others did not separate us."

"When we got home, he said I had 15 minutes to pack and that a taxi would be there to get me. He gave me the letter, which I gave to you and some money to take with me. He said a plane ticket would be waiting for me at the airport and it was. He said there would be someone waiting for me at the other end and that too was the case. I was so glad to get out of St. Louis and he was so glad to get rid of me. It worked out well for the both of us."

"That is some story," Julian gasped. "Are there others like it between you and your papa?"

"Oh yeah," Shaun mused. "That was the worst one; the tip of the iceberg. I got caught having sex a few other times. It made him the maddest. I guess that's why I did it."

"Why here then, Shaun?" Julian asked solemnly. "Are you unhappy here on the farm? You seemed to be for the most part content. I know there isn't the excitement of a large metropolis. Is that the problem?"

"No," Shaun said with emphasis. "I really like it here with you and the family. It is true I get bored at times, but it's much better for me here than it was in St. Louis."

"Are you angry with me or anyone else here in the big house, that you would retaliate against us?" Julian asked.

"No," Shaun shrugged.

"I'm trying to understand, Shaun, I need some help," Julian said softly.

Shaun paused and he started to fidget. "It's time for me to go home, isn't it?" he asked softly, "School will be starting soon. Maybe I feel like I'm being sent back to hell. The thought of that doesn't make me happy."

"It's funny you should mention this," Julian said thoughtfully. "I got a package in the mail today. It was full of legal papers giving me custody of you and relinquishing your parents' claim to you. When I called

Albert for an explanation, he said that you were my problem now. If I didn't want you, I had to deal with getting rid of you. He hung up the phone on me."

"What are you going to do?" Shaun asked as he swallowed hard.

"If I sign the papers, Shaun, you will be my ward until you reach the age of 21. On your 18th birthday, you of course, have the option of going out on your own," Julian explained and then asked, "Is that what you would like me to do, Shaun? I will do it, but only if that is what you want. If it is not, then we can look for some other options. I'm sure there are many things that could be done, so that you could be happy."

Shaun took a deep breath and nodded his head. "Sign the papers, please Uncle Julian. I will change. I promise. I won't cause anymore trouble. I'll do anything you ask. You are the greatest, Uncle Julian." He wrapped his arms tight around his uncle's torso. Julian smiled and returned with a light squeeze of his own.

When they parted, Julian looked at his nephew face to face. "There are a couple of ground rules."

Shaun nodded.

"First, no sex in the big house. I understand that your hormones are going, but others living here may not be so inclined to understand. I still have the cottage on the Quarters Road. Pilot made it clear to me, when we moved our things to the big house, that it was still mine to keep for whatever purposes that suited me. You can have all the privacy you want in that house. Don't mind Jack or Billy. They have a few secrets of their own and likely will pay little attention to what you are doing," Julian said, stating the first rule.

"Okay," Shaun agreed. "Thanks."

"Next," Julian began again, "It is the farm's people. Shaun, you have to realize that the people who live in the big house are like God to the farm folks. You have to be sensitive to the way they think. They may say yes to certain things that you want them to do, but they really may not be inclined to want to do those things."

"If you're talking about that boy that was in here, you can rest assured he was doing what he really wanted to do," Shaun replied.

"That may be dandy, but at the same time, be careful," Julian advised. "You have a responsibility to the farm's people, when you live in the big house."

"I understand and I will be careful," Shaun replied.

After a few moments Shaun asked, "What about school? When does it start?"

"Well, we home school here in the big house," Julian explained. "The farm's children have a little school house of their own with a couple of teachers, but Emily is in charge of the instruction in the big house. She's a very bright woman and I'm sure the two of you could teach each other a lot of things."

Shaun frowned. "Isn't there a high school around where I can go? There has to be kids my age going to school in these parts. I'm sure not everybody gets to home school."

"Why would you want to go to one of those?" Julian gasped. "There's a high school in this parish. It's very big and far away from here. Once you get into town, it's an hour's commute."

"Uncle Julian, don't get me wrong. I'm very happy here, but sometimes I get so bored. I don't have so much in common with the kids my age here on the farm. I won't mind the long commute. Can I go to the high school?"

"If that's what you want, Shaun," Julian replied with skepticism. "I'm sure it won't be hard to get a ride back and forth to town. But you will have to get up very early in the morning. Things get going way before sun up."

"No problem," Shaun replied.

After a few moments, Shaun asked, "What about a job for me?"

"A job?" Julian replied confused.

"Yeah, a job," Shaun repeated. "Like I said, I get bored sometimes. Maybe I could help out somewhere."

"Well," Julian started, "With that long commute and homework, when would you have the time?"

"I will have some free time," Shaun insisted. "I won't always be in school and doing homework. Sometimes I'll be here with nothing to do." Then he added, "If I'm at loose ends, I may end up finding a way to get into trouble."

"Say no more," Julian replied quickly. "What type of job do you want? I've taken you on a number of field trips. Did you see anything you would like to do?"

"Sort of," Shaun replied with a shrug. "I would like to learn what Pilot does. You know. How he keeps everything together."

Julian paused for a few moments. "Pilot has lots of meetings. He talks on the phone most of the day. Most of it is gathering information and then making decisions. What did you have in mind?"

"Well, maybe he could use a secretary," Shaun suggested. "Someone to take care of the cumbersome details."

Julian chuckled. "That man has every detail down to the last letter. But I'll talk to him to see what can be done. He is a very busy man, but maybe...just maybe...I'll see. I think it would be great if you could spend a little time with him. He's an amazing human being."

"So, how are things going with you and that rascal nephew of yours?" Pilot asked.

"It's funny you should ask," Julian replied as he sat in the easy chair in Pilot's study. As usual, Pilot was near the telephone and never far from his desk. The mounds of papers were very orderly and Julian had no doubt that the man knew where each page was with each notation marked on it.

Pilot nodded.

"Shaun has a tendency to get into trouble," Julian explained. "He feels if he had more to do with his free time, there would be less opportunity for mischief."

"Like every adolescent," Pilot surmised, stroking the bottom of his chin, while in thought. Julian got the sense that the patriarch knew where the conversation was leading, "Free time for young people trying to find themselves in this world can get them into difficulties."

Julian continued slowly, "Well, when Shaun gets into trouble, he gets into big trouble. He and I have discussed some ways to steer him away from this behavior." Julian paused with a swallow. "He wants to spend some time with you."

Pilot raised a brow. "Isn't he due to return to St. Louis?"

"Well, that's another thing," Julian replied with a shy smile. "We discussed with his papa that it would be better if Shaun stayed with me.... on a more permanent basis."

"You mean your brother will not have him return to St. Louis," Pilot deadpanned. "I figured as much when he arrived on your door step." Pilot smiled. "I also knew that you would be good for him."

"He's not a bad kid," Julian explained. "He has a real good spirit and caring heart. He needs to learn a healthy respect for authority figures and the strange thing about it is, he seems to agree."

"He is a bright kid," Pilot replied as he stared into thought. "I find it odd that he would want to spend time with me. We are so different. I'm the conservative old fogy and he's the liberal upstart. Why would he choose me?"

"He admires you greatly," Julian replied with enthusiasm. "He wants to be like you. He may not have some of the same beliefs as you, but your values, character and ability to influence are attractive to him."

Pilot smiled lightly. "What can I do?"

"He wants to learn about the things you do for the business. Perhaps a job would be suitable. Have you ever thought about getting a secretary?" Julian inquired.

"To learn the business," Pilot sighed. "Well, he is a natural born leader. The children of the farm are mesmerized by him. I guess it would be in my best interests to channel that ability to suit my purposes."

"Do you like him, Pilot?" Julian asked.

"He may eventually be the death of me, but yes, I do find him amusing at times," Pilot replied with a broad smile. "Send him to me at some point soon and I'll have a chat with him."

"Thanks, Pilot," Julian said gratefully as he prepared to exit the room. "You always come through for me."

"That is what papas are for," Pilot replied, dismissing his son in-law.

"Come in," Pilot replied, when he heard the knock at the door of his study.

Slowly, the door opened and Shaun's head peeked inside. Pilot was seated at his desk looking over a few papers. His concentration seemed to be intact despite having another visitor this day. Shaun walked quietly to the chair next to Pilot's desk. He took a seat without making a noise, because he did not want to disturb the big man, who seemingly was engrossed in a particular document.

"What can I do for you, son?" Pilot asked as he turned a page.

Shaun looked directly to where Pilot's eyes would be if the man were facing him. "Uncle Julian said to see you about a job. He thought you may have something for me."

Sensing the boy's gaze, the patriarch turned and faced him eye to eye. He smiled with a glint of laughter in his eyes to put the youngster at ease. Shaun relaxed, returning a small smile of his own. "What did you have in mind?" Pilot asked.

"Mainly, I'd like to learn what you do here on the farm. I'm curious. I don't want to be in your way, so I thought maybe I could help with some busy work you may have," Shaun replied.

Pilot chuckled. "You know, the best way to learn a business is to do the various jobs around the farm. That way, you get the full idea of how the whole farm operates."

Shaun thought for a minute. "Well, I'm not strong like some of the guys, when it comes to working in the fields and fixing fences. I think if I had a great respect for those who do such jobs, the empathy I share with them would transpire."

"I see," Pilot replied in thought.

"I like the details of things," Shaun continued. "I'm good with doting my Is and crossing my Ts. I admit that I'm very stubborn, but I do listen to people. At first, I'm inclined to have made up my mind, but after some deliberation, I do consider what others have to say."

"You are a passionate young man," Pilot agreed. "I hope you will take the time to listen, because three quarters of what I do around here is listen to people."

Shaun nodded.

"Your uncle tells me your stay here is permanent," Pilot stated. "Since you have already been a part of his family here, you will continue to be a part of the farm's family as long as you want to be."

Shaun smiled.

"We have rules and boundaries on this farm," Pilot continued. "I realize, if your reputation stays intact, these boundaries will be tried and you probably will come up with some additional rules for the rest of us."

"I don't understand," Shaun replied with a puzzled look.

"Eventually you will," Pilot surmised, "I was just thinking out loud to my own benefit. Just go easy on us, son."

"I'm really not all that bad," Shaun said defensively, beginning to get angry.

Pilot laughed. "Hold on a minute! I was not being critical of you. I'm just saying that I think you will bring some changes with you to this farm. Change can be very good. You just have to realize that we have been used to doing things the same way around here for a long time. Things may not move along here as quickly as you may wish."

Still non-plussed, Shaun replied, "People can do what they want, they usually do. I'm not here to upset the apple cart."

"Your Uncle Julian did not come here to upset the apple cart, but he has managed to give the folks a few things to think about while he has been with us," Pilot retorted.

"Uncle Julian is a brave man and leads his life the way he thinks he should lead it, despite what other people think," Shaun defended.

Pilot decided to take another tack, "Shaun, what do you see as your life's work?"

Shaun let go of his defenses, while he thought for an answer. "Well, that is a tough question to ask a 16 year old, isn't it?" He thought a few more moments. "I want kids in this world who are different like me to be able to be themselves without living in fear of being abused by the rest of the world."

"I think that's a very noble goal and I am proud of you for having that rest on your heart," Pilot replied warmly. "But Shaun, that type of change will not be easy. Somehow, you will have to alter the way people think about those who are different."

"It doesn't have to be easy," Shaun retorted. "But I still have to try. If I don't, who will?"

"Exactly!" Pilot agreed. "But you have to upset the apple cart a bit to do it. Like I said, try to go easy on us."

Shaun laughed. "Okay, sir, I will try...maybe."

Pilot grinned for a moment and then asked, "Well, how about that job? Do you think you are up for it?"

"Sure," Shaun replied with enthusiasm.

"You see those big boxes in the corner over there by the closet?" Pilot asked, pointing.

Shaun followed his hand motion. "It says on the boxes that they contain computer equipment. Wow! Is that a real computer?"

"That's right," Pilot agreed. "You probably know that Louisa and I take a trip each year just after the harvest. Since she has passed, I decided to leave early this season. I will be back in the spring as things get moving for the next crop. This is going to give you plenty of time to carry through your first assignment."

Pilot gave Shaun a pen and paper to take some notes. "You will have full use of this office. First, I want you to put that computer together for me and set it up for me next to this desk. Next, there's a thick book over by the box, explaining how to write a database on one of the fancy software packages, already installed on the computer. I need you to come up with a database that cross-references all these stacks of papers on my desk and shelves according to date, subject, and the persons' names if they apply. You will need to type a copy of every piece of paper you see here inside that big computer. When I return in the spring, I will be expecting you to teach me how to operate that thing. Understood?"

"This is going to take a lot of time," Shaun said with bright animation in his voice.

"Do you think you're up for it?" Pilot asked feeding the boy's enthusiasm.

"Oh yes! This is the sort of thing that I'm good at doing," Shaun replied.

"Good," Pilot said, obviously pleased. "After reading through all these stacks of my notes, you will have a very good idea of what I do around here on the farm. As you can see, I do a lot of note taking."

CHAPTER 26

Julian and Emily were sitting on the front porch of the big house, when they noticed a small figure walking up the Farm Road. As it approached, they were able to surmise that it must be a man.

The man noticed the two sitting on the porch and made his way in that direction. The man stood around 5 foot, 7 inches and looked to have about 125 pounds on a small thin frame. His hair was red with traces of natural blond highlights. It hung straight with no trace of curl. His bangs were clearly in his eyes and the sides hung over his ears. The style was a bowl cut that a child might sport.

He stopped just short of the porch and let the pack he was carrying on his shoulder fall to the ground. Next, he undid a harness of sorts that had a guitar case strapped to his back. He was careful that it did not fall to the ground but handled it with gentle grace.

Julian and Emily watched as the man sighed and then sat on the edge of the porch as if he had done it a thousand times before in the past.

"Wow!" the man exclaimed as he wiped his brow. He labored gently to catch his breath. "That was quite a hike." He smiled at the two rocking in their chairs and then looked off into the direction he had come.

Julian noticed the man's clothes looked big on him. His short pants were very loose and only kept at his thin waist with a tightly strapped leather belt. His thin nylon buttoned down shirt draped loosely on his shoulders. Its pattern consisted of big colorful flowers. The freckles on the man's face indicated that he might have been exposed to a lot of sun.

"Uh...can we help you?" Emily asked as she stopped her slow rock. She could not decide if she should know this man. He was acting more comfortable than one normally did when they came to a strange place.

"Oh no, not at all," the man replied as he finished catching his breath. "That sure is a long road."

"You walked that whole road off the state highway?" Emily asked with a puzzled look. "That must have taken you most of the afternoon."

"Nah, not a big deal," the man replied. "Actually, I walked from town. It only took me a couple of days."

"Surely, you could have hopped on a ride," Emily answered in return.

"Then I would have had to know where I was going," the man retorted. "I figured eventually the road would lead to something."

"How peculiar," Emily surmised as she slumped back into her chair.

The man, still seated, turned and offered his hand to Julian. "My name is Christopher." After a few odd moments, Julian reached for the man's extended hand.

"I'm Julian Smith and this is my wife, Emily," Julian introduced softly. Like Emily, he was taken back by this man's unabashed audacity.

Christopher smiled and offered his hand to Emily. "I'm very pleased to meet you, ma'am." He held his hand up a good, while waiting for her to grasp it. For others, it may have seemed a sign of rejection, but he just kept smiling as she moved slowly to join her hand with his. Afterwards, Christopher stretched back and leaned against one of the support columns and closed his eyes while crossing his feet.

"Do you have some business here at the house," Emily asked, still feeling uncomfortable with this man's presence.

Christopher opened his eyes and looked toward Julian. "Yeah, I guess," he replied slowly. "I'm looking for a job...somewhere."

Julian did not feel discomfort with this man, but he was slightly awed and amused. "What sort of job do you want?" he inquired.

"I don't know." Christopher furrowed his brow while sitting up looking at his now uncrossed feet. He then looked at Emily. "I've never had one before today." He paused and then added, "I'm sure there is something I could do."

Julian thought it was odd that the man had never held a job. He certainly did not appear to be young. He at least had to be in his late twenties, more likely into his early thirties. But then he remembered his hands felt overly soft, almost like those of a woman's who spent most of her time washing dishes. This Christopher clearly did not have the frame of a man who did a fair amount of manual labor. Perhaps he was one of the desk types, even though he did not carry himself as such a man. "So tell us about yourself," Julian said, amused.

Emily was ready to send this stranger off to Billy to either find something for this man or send him on his way. Billy had taken over many of Jack's responsibilities for field operations, since the latter had taken to task the operation of the Lamond plantation. It was a big step for a man of color to have such a position, but Pilot said it was time to put a black man into a frame of authority. Oddly enough, it was the black folks who had the hardest time answering to one of their own. However, Julian was there to help them through the transition. Pilot was confident that Billy would earn the respect of the farm's people in due time.

Emily believed that Christopher and his feminine nature just did not seem suited to farm work. However, she deferred to her husband. He could be so patient at times. She smiled at him, prompting this strange man to begin talking.

Christopher did not need prompting. He sounded off before Julian could finish the invitation to speak. "I'm from the Walker plantation, which is a couple of parishes off from this one. Daddy's farm doesn't look to be a big as this one. It's probably much smaller. I grew up in a big house like this one. That's why I came up to this house. You know, go right to the top for results, instead of some foreman doling the work. I was never interested in Daddy's business. Mama had long since gone, so I spent a good deal of time by myself. I liked to paint and sketch; play some guitar or other strings. This did not suit Daddy to well, so he sent me to military school. After getting beat up a few times, he let me go to a liberal arts boarding school. Then he said I had to go to college to study agriculture and business, so I could help him run the farm some day. I stunk at it, so I changed my major to art and music. Daddy was not pleased. He then sent me to graduate school to be rid of me for a while longer. After that, he sent me abroad to Europe to find myself. I loved it. I painted with some of the best artists. When he realized that I didn't intend to come home anytime soon, he cut off my allowance and sent for me. Seeing that I had little intention of ever running the farm with him, he gave me my last $100. He told me to go look for work and support myself. I would have stayed on the farm to work, but I'm not very strong to be sitting on tractors and such. I also am terrible with math and can't write very well, except for a few melodies. Would you like to hear some?"

Emily smiled. This strange man now intrigued her. "Not right now, but I'm sure some time soon. I'm sure Billy will find something for you to do. Farm life is hard. Why did you choose another farm? Surely, you would want to work in some music shop or paint store."

"Like I said," Christopher replied. "The road led me here, so I figured this is where I was supposed to be. So, I think I will stay."

Julian rose from his chair. "Come on. I'll take you to Billy. He'll find something for you."

"Thanks." Christopher beamed as he rose quickly to his feet. Hurriedly, he strapped his guitar case to his back and picked up his pack. "It was great meeting you Emily. I hope I get to see you again real soon. We'll have another real good chat."

Emily chuckled, "We'll see."

Together, Julian and Christopher walked toward the Main Road. Julian thought that Christopher kept rather close to him, invading his personal space. It seemed a bit awkward and he had to keep from tripping over this man's feet. When he tried to separate, Christopher would rejoin him.

"Your wife is a real cool lady," Christopher said, slightly animated.

"That she is," Julian replied with a half smile. Emily seemed as mystified by this man's presence as he was, but was not sure if she shared his own curiosity. Suddenly, he hoped Christopher could find a place on this farm, maybe working in the kitchen with some of the farm's women. This place could use someone colorful like this man to brighten things up a touch.

They walked towards Julian's cottage, thinking he would find Billy. When they arrived, he realized it was probably mealtime, so they went over to Old Bill's place.

"Come on in," Jeannette exclaimed as she grabbed Julian and gave him a big hug, "Who is your friend here?

"This is Christopher," Julian introduced as they walked inside to the living area. "He's new around here and I was hoping to find Billy to see about getting this man a job."

"Oh," Jeannette said softly, looking over Christopher. She then gushed, "I am sure he'll find something. He's around back with the others. We're getting ready for some supper. Can you join us?"

"I think so," Julian answered. "I don't think Emily would mind."

Christopher was the center of attention throughout the entire meal. Jeannette could be heard belting laughs at all the silly stories that he had to tell. Christopher was quite a showman. After supper, he played the guitar for them. Anything that he was asked to play, he could do for them with ease. He was very talented.

When it got late, Julian said he had to be getting up to the big house. He told Christopher he could stay at his cottage for the night and that tomorrow he would set him up at the barracks.

"Do you think you could find something for him, Billy?" He asked his friend, as the two men along with Christopher headed outside.

"Maybe he could peel potatoes in the kitchen," Billy replied.

"That is women's work," Christopher bellowed quietly. "I know I am not fit too much for men's work, but maybe I could be some sort of water boy in the fields."

"Well, there's not too much field work going on now, but maybe we could get you something like feeding and watering the animals," Billy replied. "Do you like children? You seem like a guy that they would like. You can work with them. We use children to water and feed some of the petting type animals. Would you like to spend some time with them?"

"That would be great!" Christopher nodded enthusiastically.

"Then, in the spring, you can start being the water boy," Billy said quietly.

"This is the third black eye or bloody lip you've had this month! What do you mean, 'It is nothing, Uncle Julian?'" Julian asked clearly upset.

Shaun fell into the easy chair in the TV room with an ice pack covering his eye.

"This is not what I had in mind when I said you could go to the public school," Julian stated firmly.

"Do you see me complaining?" Shaun argued as he rested his head against the back of the chair. "It's no big deal."

"I'm worried about your safety," Julian said softly, lowering his voice to a normal tone.

Shaun looked up with a smirk. "My safety? You should see the guys who did this to me. They are hurting more than I am. A good swift kick is all it takes."

"How many fights have you been in since school started?" Julian asked gently with concern.

"Oh, I'd say around ten," Shaun replied.

"Ten!" Julian said, starting to get upset again. "Are people picking on you that much? You've only been in school 2 months."

"People are not picking on me at all, except the occasional loser," Shaun explained. "A matter of fact, most people seem to like me. I've got a whole bunch of girlfriends. That seems to impress the guys. They beg me to set them up with dates. I help some of the guys after school with homework. Since there aren't many other brainy guys like me. I'm the logical choice. Their papas do not understand about F grades, so they have to depend on me. I help, because it may not seem the like the case, but I can use some allies. I don't relish the thought of having my face bashed in every day."

"Then how do you explain the black eyes, the bloody noses, and the fat lips? There have to be some people who are out to get you. Is it the gay thing? Are guys ganging up on you to beat up the gay boy at school?" Julian asked, emotion filling inside of him.

"I don't think so," Shaun replied, sitting up. Julian flopped back against the sofa cushion. "There are some of the homophobes who like to show off. They tease and may give me a shove. I slug back and they usually leave me alone. They get the picture that I won't take any of their nonsense. They can taunt all they want, but I just walk away, like it's nothing. Truthfully, I find their ignorance quite funny. They don't like it when I laugh at them, so they punch me, then I slug back. Usually it amounts to one punch and they leave me, the skinny kid, alone. You see, they don't want to get into too much trouble with their papas."

"You're not answering my question," Julian maintained. "Who is giving you these injuries?"

"Well," Shaun hemmed. "Okay, there are some kids that won't stand up to the bullies. They're the effeminate boys, even less masculine than I am who attract the most attention. They're just too weak and less skilled than I am in defending themselves. When they start getting hassled, I get involved and sometimes pay a few consequences."

"Shaun, it is not up to you to police these idiots," Julian explained softly. "That's why there are guidance counselors and the principal to set fair policies to keep the school safe for everyone. Beating up the bullies will not solve anything. I know you have the mind of an activist and want to make statements that intolerance is not acceptable, but there are rules to follow. If necessary, the parents, I'm sure, will get involved."

"Are you kidding?" Shaun asked incredulously. "Has it been that long since you've been in grade school? Come on, get real Uncle Julian."

"Fighting was not tolerated where I went to school. Yes, I admit to some problems in school. If the problems became constant, the guilty parties were expelled from school."

"Yes, but you went to private schools for the rich," Shaun retorted. "If kids misbehave in my school, there's nowhere else for them to go. We're at the lowest ranking among schools. It's either this school for them, or no school. Unfortunately, we're stuck with the bullies."

"This is where the parents and teachers need to work together to iron out the problems. The discipline really should be at home and not at school," Julian said with conviction.

Shaun kept his voice even to keep patience with his uncle. He could tell Uncle Julian was trying to understand. Uncle and nephew were having trouble landing on common ground. "Uncle Julian, try to understand. Grown ups along with most kids don't want to admit that homosexuality exists. They would rather turn deaf ears to it. To meet the issue practically would mean that it actually is a real phenomenon. Teachers and principals would rather believe such issues would work themselves out if they even did exist. As for the parents of these poor defenseless creatures, they think of their girl type boys as sissies. They are ashamed that their sons will never grow up to be mainstream men. They would be embarrassed to show up at meetings to discuss the safety of their feminine sons. Some of these boys don't want to be involved. Their parents blame them for being different and are sometimes cruel in their attempts to toughen up their sons."

Julian shook his head. "I believe you, Shaun. I'm aware of how the world works, even if I'm not in my teen years. I know from experience how cruel people can be toward homosexuals. I will say this. I will NOT tolerate you coming home bloodied up like this. If it happens again like today, I WILL march to that school of yours and make a big stink about this. I don't care how other parents ignore their children's safety or if they turn deaf ears. I will make them listen. It doesn't matter if I am different than the others."

"No, you are not just different, Uncle Julian," Shaun said with a smile. "You're just special." He went to his uncle's side on the sofa and gave him a big hug.

Julian came down the steps into the kitchen of the big house. Emily was keeping herself busy. Without her mama with her, she always had plenty to do. Christopher was sitting at the table, no doubt rattling on about nothing special. Julian found him there often, when he came in from work and chores. Christopher liked his new job but was not a dedicated worker and clearly unenthusiastic about extra duties. His preference would be to sit in this kitchen all day entertaining Emily. She was becoming fond of him and did not mind him sampling her cooking before presenting it to the family. Usually, sampling was all Christopher needed to do to satisfy any hunger he may have. He ordinarily did not eat a great deal of food. He did not dine with the family, except on special occasions, when Emily invited him to stay.

"You ready?" Julian asked, looking straight into Christopher's eyes.

"Oh yes!" Christopher answered brightly. "I can hardly wait." He bounded up from his chair and was instantly at Julian's side.

"What do we need to bring? Worms?" Christopher asked with enthusiasm.

"I got all that taken care of earlier today," Julian assured him. "We just need to pick up the poles which are waiting for us outside."

He looked toward Emily. "We'll be back in a while. Hopefully with some fish."

"Are you going to clean them?" She teased. She asked the same question every time he went to fish.

Julian smiled as he usually did, "Yeah, I'll clean them." Julian didn't usually catch many that were worth eating. If he did, he dropped them off to Jeannette on the way home. Sometimes, she convinced him to stay, while she fried them up in some special batter.

Christopher, along with Julian at his side, headed across the field from the Farm Road away from the big house. It was about a 15-minute walk until they approached the tree line, which would lead to the brook, where he liked to fish.

Christopher was beside himself with joy. He slipped his arm inside Julian's and said with excitement, "You know, I've never been fishing before. Do you think we'll catch a bunch of fish?"

"It's possible," Julian replied with a half smile as he gave his friend a hopeful glance. He did not mind Christopher tugging on him. That is just his way, he thought.

"What is that building?" Christopher asked as he pointed to the right of Julian. They were approaching the tree line. "It looks like an old barn that isn't used anymore."

"Close," Julian replied, "Let's go take a look."

There was no door attached to the structure. They were able to walk inside without deterrence. Christopher clung tighter to Julian's arm. "It sure is spooky in here. Are you sure it is safe? It seems things could fall apart any minute."

Julian let out a chuckle. "It's okay. This place has been here a long time. I think it will stick together long enough for you and I to have a look."

"What are those?" Christopher asked, pointing to their left once they were inside. "They look like giant kettles."

"That's exactly what they are," Julian answered. "They are sitting on what used to be a giant stove. After big rollers pressed sugar juices from the sugarcane, the kettles were used to boil the syrup juices to separate the sugar. This was before the big refineries along the Mississippi were built. The farm had to process its own sugarcane and sell the finished product."

"Why don't we still do it?" Christopher asked.

"It makes better business sense to have someone else do it at a much cheaper price than we could ever do it. It's better for us to keep to the business of producing the sugarcane, than actually turning it into the sugar sitting on the kitchen table," Julian explained.

"If you say so, I believe you," Christopher giggled.

When they got to the brook, Julian tried to explain to Christopher how to bait a hook. However, the strange wiry man seemed distracted by the surroundings. "This place is beautiful," Christopher said as he breathed in the fresh air. He set his pack on the ground and removed a pad with pencils from inside it. "Do you mind if I sketch?" he asked, while he sat and leaned against a tree.

"What about fishing?" Julian asked, puzzled.

"I can fish and sketch, can't I?" Christopher asked with a smile.

"Sure," Julian replied. He kneeled to bait his hook and he supposed he would do the same for Christopher's hook.

"Do you want to cast?" Julian asked as he stood to cast his own line.

"Sure," Christopher replied, as he set down his pad and rose to his feet. "How do I do it?"

"I'll show you," Julian answered as he placed the fishing rod into Christopher's hands. He demonstrated with his own rod how casting should be done. However, with several tries, Christopher could not get the swing of it.

"I never was very athletic," Christopher explained.

"Nonsense. It is just the flick of the wrist. It should be natural," Julian said, taking the reel from Christopher's hands.

"Here," Julian said as he wrapped his arms around his friend. He placed his hands on top of Christopher's and cast a gentle line. Julian let him go. "You see, it wasn't that bad."

"I guess it's not when you're helping me," Christopher replied sheepishly.

After a while of unique silence, Christopher placed down his pad, yawned and stretched. Julian realized his friend had been quiet for a long time, which was very unusual. *Give him a sketchpad and he's quiet,* Julian mused to himself.

"No fish yet?" Christopher asked.

"Sometimes it takes a while and then there are several bites," Julian explained.

Christopher moved slowly over to where Julian was sitting. He leaned backwards, placing his head into Julian's lap. "Wake me when they start to bite," he said. Almost immediately, he was snoozing.

Julian was surprised at the action and at lost for words. *I guess I should let him sleep,* he thought. He shifted his weight gently as not to wake the slumbering man. When he was comfortable, he was able to relax.

What of this man, Julian wondered.

CHAPTER 27

Shaun and his uncle were sitting inside the principal's office, while they waited patiently for the man to arrive. The secretary explained that Principal Mathews was a busy man, and only saw people by appointment. When she realized that Julian had no intention of waiting several days to see the principal, she relented and ushered them quickly into his office. Julian was upset and had begun to throw a small tantrum. Not wanting to cause a scene, she quickly pleaded for them to sit inside the office to wait for the school's leader. Julian agreed, but made it clear that he would not tolerate a long wait.

Principal Mathews entered his office and immediately went behind his desk. He eased carefully into his hardwood chair. The desk seemed to act as a natural barrier to guard against irate parents and unruly students.

"I don't have much time before my next appointment," he stated grimly. "So we are going to have to make this quick. I suppose it was only a matter of time before I was to see one of your parents, Shaun."

"He's my uncle," Shaun retorted.

"What?" the principal replied, lost in his own thought.

"This is my Uncle Julian," Shaun explained. "He is responsible for me."

"Oh, yes," Principal Mathews replied as if he should have known this fact. "Well, Mr. Smith...is it Mr. Smith?"

"Yes it is. My name is Julian Smith," Julian replied.

"Oh yes. I've read about you," Principal Mathew said knowingly.

"I understand your busy schedule and this will not take long. I suggest we get right to the point," Julian said.

"It never is supposed to take long," Principal Mathews mused. "If you can believe it, this is not an unusual occurrence. Somebody always has some emergency. I usually have short breaks between appointments."

"Very well," Julian said, wanting to get to the point. "My nephew is constantly coming home beat up with bruises and such. At first, he played it off as being the hero for protecting some of the other boys. I come to find, while this may be true, other boys have caused my boy harm without him provoking it."

"The other boys.... ah like him.....run away when the bullies come around them. But your...ah...boy seems ready to stand up to them to fight to defend his honor and those he keeps around him. I guess that would make him the hero in these instances. He should just run like the other swishes.......boys."

"Shaun tells me the other boys receive a worse fate than himself, but I want to stick with Shaun as the topic," Julian said, trying to divert a tangent.

"All these boys have to do is act normal and the other kids would leave them alone. Instead, they choose to unite together and form some sort of glee club."

"It's not a glee club," Shaun muttered.

"Whatever it is, I am going to start forbidding it to meet on school premises," Principal Mathews admonished. "It's causing too much of a distraction."

"The absence of dialogue about this issue will only make matters worse not better, Principal Mathews. I believe the boys' discussion of their trials among themselves is actually helping. I'm sure it relieves some of their loneliness," Julian defended. "Besides, these children have a right to associate with whomever they please."

"I cannot possibly use any more of the school resources to baby-sit a handful of limp wrist boys. The staff is over taxed as it is," Principal Mathews said with haughtiness.

"I am warning you," Julian said tersely, leaning forward from his chair. "You better keep my boy safe."

"Are you threatening me?" Principal Mathew asked, starting to get angry.

"If I have to patrol the hallways myself. If I have to drag the sheriff to this school every day," Julian gritted his teeth, "If I have to use my family's influence. If I have to get the governor involved. I will do these things. Keep my boy safe and you will not have any problems from me."

"I will see what I can do," Principal Mathews replied, straightening some papers on his desk. "I guess I should have known you would use the Pilot name."

"But I am warning you as well," the principal said with a coolness in his voice. "If I can find a way to expel all these queers in my school, I will do it."

"Just keep my boy safe," Julian replied, standing up to his feet. He quickly gave Shaun a glance for him to do the same.

"Watch your back, Shaun," the principal said evenly as the boy and Julian went for the office door.

Julian turned back for one last look. "Your days are numbered at this school, Principal."

"That very well may be," Principal Mathews replied with feigned wariness. "But you may get a new principal who is not as sympathetic as I am."

When Julian and Shaun exited to the school hallway, the latter said, "Thanks for sticking up for me, Uncle Julian."

"I meant everything I said," Julian replied, "What is this about your club?"

"It's very informal right now," Shaun explained. "We have lunch together every day. Sometimes the other kids overhear us and make rude comments. The monitor tries to coax us into changing the subjects we discuss. We don't. There is something to be said about strength in numbers. It feels so empowering to have all of us together instead of scattered among the masses."

"We want to start meeting after school. I'd like to organize some socials for us to get to know each other better in relaxed situations. I think it would be great for you to join us from time to time, Uncle Julian. It might help to have an adult figure present to make it more comfortable. Your experience would be a definite plus. Maybe then, some of the other kids that pass for straight would join us. You know, they're struggling inside themselves which can be worse than the struggles the others face. At least we're not alone. Would you consider it?"

"Absolutely," Julian affirmed, as they started down the hallway. "Just be careful, Shaun. Change does not come quickly without some backlash."

Julian, Emily and Christopher were becoming fast friends. Often, Christopher would spend time at the big house during meals and family times. Sometimes, he would wander down with Julian to see Billy's family. He was popular everywhere he went. Everybody seemed to love his colorful personality. He was always uplifting and made people feel good about themselves.

Christopher was learning what it meant to be a dedicated worker. It did not seem so bad after a while. The children were a joy and loved to play with him. He loved to watch them with the animals. Small children and animals were so alike in certain ways. Both loved unconditionally, which was new for him. It became a pleasure to serve them both.

Julian and Christopher got to spend a lot of time together. With Emily doing the job of two women since her mother's death, she often did not have time to accompany Julian on their nightly walks. She was just too tired by day's end. Julian often urged her to acquire some help, but she never seemed to get around to it. With Emily absent, Christopher regularly took her place.

Christopher came to where Julian was sitting perched on his favorite spot. He and Billy had just finished a run.

"Are you ready?" Christopher asked.

"Yeah, I guess," Julian replied, bounding down from his perch to the ground.

"Sweaty," Christopher commented, crinkling up his nose to mock his friend.

Julian slid behind him and gave him a big bear hug. "And now so are you," he said.

"Yuck," Christopher said, trying to free himself. He did not try very hard. He liked the big strong arms folded around him. After a couple of moments, Julian let him free.

"Where are we going to walk tonight?" Christopher asked, pulling Julian by the hand toward the Main Road.

"Let's see," he pondered, "Where would you like to go?"

"I don't know," Christopher replied slyly. "Surprise me. Somewhere spooky,"

"Spooky?" Julian answered with a bewildered look. "What do you mean?"

"I don't know. Somewhere beneath the trees where the birds are beginning to perch, with nature sounds as mysterious things start to bed down for the night, while others wake up to prowl and find food."

"If we catch them in time, we can see the bats leaving their roost for their hunt," Julian offered thoughtfully. "Is that spooky enough?"

"That sounds neat," Christopher replied with a big smile. "Let's go."

They started across a field, east of the big house. This was the opposite field from where they had gone to the brook on their fishing expedition. The expanse had tall winter grass about two feet high underneath their feet.

Christopher took Julian by the hand as they walked. "Are you afraid of getting lost?" Julian asked half teasingly. He did not mind the affection.

"No," Christopher said with a giggle, "I like the feel of your big hands in mine."

"My hands are not so big," Julian laughed with a smile.

"Well, they're a lot bigger than mine, besides, they're warm," Christopher said. "Remember, I'm skinny and don't have much flesh to keep warm. That is where you come in handy."

"To keep you warm?" Julian asked, looking at his friend.

Christopher looked away shyly, "It's not so bad."

When they reached their destination under the trees, the dusk began to approach. There were bats flying through the trees soaring above them to take their nightly flight. Julian and Christopher stopped and stared above to take in the sight. Christopher moved closer to Julian and put both of his arms around his waist. Julian placed one of his arms around his friend's shoulders and pulled him close.

"This feels nice," Christopher cooed, bringing his face against Julian's chest.

Julian stared above, taking in the sight. "Yes, it does."

After a while, Christopher lessened his grip and Julian did the same.

"This was a wonderful idea," Christopher said as he gazed into Julian's face.

Julian brought his gaze down into Christopher eyes where they met with his. "I agree," He whispered.

After a few short moments, Julian lowered his lips to Christopher's lips and brushed them lightly with a gentle kiss. This led to another kiss.

Christopher pushed gently away, but Julian did not let him go very far. Christopher stopped his struggle. "What did you do that for?" he asked softly.

"I don't know," Julian answered, breathing lightly, looking into Christopher's face with a gentle look of awe. "It seemed the thing to do." He let Christopher go and turned away from him.

"Was I wrong to do it?" Julian asked.

"No, I don't think so," Christopher answered softly, still feeling surprised. "It is just that nobody has ever done that to me before." He shrugged his shoulders, "I just.....I don't know......thank you I guess."

"Thank you?" Julian chuckled as he looked back to his friend.

Christopher shrugged.

"Maybe it's time to head back home," Julian surmised.

"Did I do something wrong?" Christopher asked.

"No," Julian answered, starting to walk.

Christopher joined him, sensing the need to keep a respected space.

"Emily says you usually are very bubbly and can't stop your chatter. Why are you not that way with me? You always seem half-serious, almost reserved. I thought that was your way, but she says it's not your way," Christopher inquired.

Julian smiled. "It's because I am always your captive audience. It would be difficult for you to perform if I chatted away the time."

"I guess I can be handful at times," Christopher agreed.

"Not really," Julian assured him. "I have my quiet side. You are just one of the fortunate ones to see it. Emily knows me quite well enough. She just hasn't seen this side of me in a while."

"I think she sees it," Christopher disagreed, "I think she's quite the chatterbox herself...that is, when I'm not around. She just gets caught up in her own chatter, so that she doesn't realize that you are listening."

Julian laughed. "No, my friend. Emily and I compete with each other to see who can get the most talk in our conversation time together. But to her defense, she can be the good listener. Look how she is with you."

"You do love her," Christopher said, making a statement rather than a question. "Very much."

"Yes, I do," Julian quickly agreed with a nod.

"So do I," Christopher said softly.

"I know you do," Julian agreed with a smile.

"Can the three of us always be together?" Christopher asked somberly. "Like a family."

Julian paused in his thoughts. Then, he decided not to answer.

"I just need some time on my own for a while," Julian said, sitting on the bed.

"Fine," Emily answered without emotion. She was dressing in front of the bureau mirror. "You do what you need to do. But I am not moving out of my bedroom. If you want to leave, you can take one of the rooms down the hall."

"That was my intention," Julian answered.

Emily kept herself busy. She was dressing into a pink pastel suit. It was early for spring wear, but the weather had been warming substantially during the past couple of weeks. The cane planting would most likely start early this year.

"Don't you want to talk about this some more before you go?" Julian asked. Her indifference made him uncomfortable.

Emily paused and looked at Julian. "Julian, I decided a long time ago that I was not going to be heartbroken by the tribulations you put yourself through at times. They are your problems and choices. If you want to go, go. But you run the risk that I won't be around when you want to come back to this room."

"Emily," Julian replied, turning to face her, "All marriages go through times when there are inconsistencies in the relationship. Sometimes, one spouse may need a little time to get things into perspective. I think we have been fortunate. In all the years we have been married, we have done well by each other."

Emily chuckled, bemused. "Julian, in our years together, it has been you with the distance issues. I have given as much space as you have needed, without you even asking me. It's not like we have been close in many months. We've shared the same bed and that's been it. I've accepted that about us. You have to understand that I have needs as a woman. I need to be romanced and loved like a woman needs to be treated. If I don't get it from you, I have to explore my options, just as you have done."

"I've been faithful, except for one indiscretion that you know happened a while ago," Julian retorted.

"That may be fine for you, Julian," Emily deadpanned. "But don't expect the same from me. Do what you want."

Julian frowned. *What am I doing?* He thought. *Apparently, I have not surprised her in the least. She has been on to me for quite some time. She probably knows more about, what I'm thinking than I do.*

"Are you going out with that Douglas man?" Julian asked with half interest.

"As a matter of fact, I am," Emily said, putting the last pins into her hair.

"I thought this sort of thing was acceptable around here as long as the parties were discreet," Julian added with resignation. He had noticed Douglas's big Cadillac parked in front of the house on several occasions. Once or twice, he witnessed Emily coming from the car as the man drove to exit down the Farm Road.

"What I do with Milton is my business, as what you do with Christopher is your business," Emily stated without inflection.

Julian frowned again.

"Are you in love with him?" Emily asked. She could not resist asking.

"No," Julian answered. "There is not a cut and dried answer to that one. There are feelings but nothing I can't handle."

"Well, I'm sure you will work it out," Emily said, as she picked up her purse to leave. "I don't want to be late." With that, she made her exit to the hall.

Julian sat dumbfounded on the bed and shook his head. He frowned one more time. He looked around the room. He could not bring himself to move his things into the other room. He decided that he would ask the housekeeping staff to do it for him.

After collecting himself for a few minutes, Julian stood and left the room. Slowly, he moved down the staircase to the big kitchen. Christopher came inside the door about the same time he reached the bottom step.

"How's it going?" Christopher asked lightly.

"Besides my marriage being on the rocks, I guess okay," Julian replied, with yet another frown.

"Things will get better," Christopher said with a half smile. "They always do."

"Well, my wife is off with another man. That's not a good start in making things better," Julian said with a sad chuckle.

"Douglas," Christopher snorted dismissively, "He means nothing to her; just a lot of spit and polish. She will get bored with him."

Julian sighed. "Maybe it would be best if she did not get bored with him."

"You can't mean that," Christopher replied troubled.

"Maybe not," Julian said sadly. "But, I don't know."

After a pause, Julian said, "You know, I am not really up to getting together today. Would you mind terribly if we did it another time?"

"Of course not," Christopher said as he made to leave. "I'll go hang out with the guys at the barracks."

After a few minutes, Julian followed Christopher out the door. He watched him descend down the Main Road.

"I would have figured him to be more my type than yours, but then, he is a little old for me" said Shaun. He was sitting on the steps with a long stem of grass hanging from his mouth.

Julian sighed, "Does everybody think I have this thing for Christopher?"

"Don't you?" Shaun answered, looking at his uncle.

"I don't know," Julian said, still standing gazing down the road. Christopher was out of sight.

Julian broke his gaze and looked down to Shaun. "Would you mind sitting with me on my perch for a while? Just to sit, not to talk. I need some time to clear my head, but I'd like to have some company."

"Sure," Shaun replied. He lifted his hand for Julian to grab. Gently, Julian pulled him up to stand next to him. They started their walk with Julian putting his arm around his nephew's shoulders. He pulled the boy's head close and kissed his crown. He let him go and they walked side by side to his safe place.

CHAPTER 28

"Come on, Shaun, open the door!" Julian said firmly as he banged on Shaun's bedroom door, "You've been holed up in there for 3 days." Julian hammered on the door again.

"Go away!" Shaun yelled feebly. "I'll be out tomorrow."

"What's the problem?" Emily asked. She heard the commotion, which led to the source of the noise.

Julian lowered his arm and turned to his wife, "I think it has been 3 days since I've last seen him. Yesterday, I asked if he was sick and he said yes, that he would be out today. I thought that he didn't want anybody else to catch what he had, like he had quarantined himself. But now, I'm really worried that something else is wrong."

"Maybe he got dumped by a boyfriend?" Emily asked meekly.

"That may be, but enough is enough. I would think that he would be past those adolescent dramas."

"Well, Shaun is a sensitive boy. He may have a tough and vibrant spirit, but he also has a gentle heart. People like that feel the pain more than others," Emily explained.

"That may very well be, but if he doesn't open that door by tomorrow, I'll break it down to get to the bottom of this strange behavior," Julian promised.

Julian turned and once more faced the door. He bent his head and spoke into the door jam with an even voice. "Shaun, I'll give you until tomorrow to open this door. I'll be coming in if I don't see that handsome face of yours." Julian hammered the door a final time. "Come on, Shaun. You at least have to be hungry."

"Go away," Shaun shouted feebly.

"He will be alright," Emily consoled. "Come on. I think we could use a snack before bedtime."

Julian was resigned to the fact that nothing more could be done. He nodded his head and made to follow her down the staircase.

"You know," Emily turned to him with a smile. "You have five more coming just around the corner that will be doing this same thing. That's not to mention that the very last one happens to be your daughter."

"Good," Julian replied unamused, "By then, we will have had lots of practice."

Emily broke into a large grin, as she gently descended the stairs.

Some time during the night, Julian heard a noise in the hall. He was not sleeping very well, because he was concerned about Shaun. What if he was really sick? He thought that he should have insisted that Shaun open the door.

Perhaps one of the children went to get Emily out of bed. He rose from his bed to join in helping her to get the youngster back to sleep. As he padded down the hall, he noticed Shaun's door was left ajar. His new quarters, along with Shaun's, were on one end of the hall, while the children's rooms, along with Emily's were on the other end.

He went to Shaun's room to investigate. When he opened the door completely, he saw that Shaun was not in the room. He went inside. The bedchamber had a foul, stale odor. He sauntered across to the pair of windows just above the twin bed where Shaun usually slept. He threw them open to relieve the stuffiness that had accumulated over the 3 days, while the room had been closed tight.

Julian surveyed the area. The far twin bed was left unmade. There was a small pile of clothes in one corner. School books cluttered the desk. Papers were lined in neat stacks along the wall by the door. He put a shoe on each one, so the breeze coming from the windows would not send the papers in a flurry.

After enough seen, Julian left the room to find Shaun. When he entered into the kitchen, he could see that his nephew had lightly raided the icebox for some left over food. There was a small plate and a couple pieces of silverware resting in the sink.

Where would he have gone this time of night, Julian wondered. At least Shaun did not appear to be greatly injured. He went to tell Emily his latest findings. Perhaps she could help look for him.

"He will come back when he is ready," Emily said rubbing her eyes. She had been sound asleep in her bed. She slept well these nights. The responsibilities of the big house, the big kitchen, and a large family on her shoulders. She was mighty tired by days' end.

Julian sat at the end of her bed. "I'm sorry to have wakened you. You are right. There is nothing we can do at this point." He made to rise.

"Why don't you get under the covers and sleep here tonight. You probably would rest better in your own bed." Julian complied and got into bed. Emily snuggled close to him and within moments, they were both asleep.

Shaun did not return until the following night. He managed to sneak inside the big house without being noticed. There were many ways to get inside the mansion, so one could slip inside quietly if he chose.

When Julian returned home to the big house after spending the day with Billy in the sugar fields, he moved quickly to shed his boots. They were full of mud. Since Jack no longer worked the Pilot plantation and Pilot was away, it was up to him to help Billy organize the planning for the spring sugarcane season. Sugarcane seedlings that did not make it through the winter had to be replanted and the endless task of weeding was reaching top speed. Within the next couple of weeks, the farm would be in full swing with the farm's people once again working the fields. Pilot had informed the family that his trip would be an extra couple of months this year. Therefore, it was up to Julian to manage the farm alone.

It seemed so long since the family had seen the man Pilot. Julian did not realize how much he missed his father in-law until this moment. When Pilot was around the farm, things always had a way of working out for the best. It was nice to be able to depend on someone with that kind of strength. However, Julian knew he would manage.

Once the boots were off and comfortable shoes on, Julian went directly to Shaun's room to see if he had returned. He somehow knew Shaun would be there when he came back to the big house.

The door was closed. Julian made a motion to hammer on the door but restrained the impulse. Instead, he attempted to turn the knob. Surprisingly, the knob turned without resistance.

"Shaun," Julian called softly as he entered the room. Once more, the windows were shut and a slight stuffiness returned.

Shaun lay quietly on his bed in a fetal position with both hands tucked safely between his thighs. He was dressed in a thin dark sweater and a pair of the black coal colored jeans that he liked to wear. He still had on his bright white cotton socks. He was strange about his socks. He never cared too much for clothes except his socks. He always wanted them soft and bright white. He said that they just felt more comfortable than ones slightly worn did.

Julian gently shut the door. His first impulse was to open the window, but decided he should first ask his nephew.

"Do you mind if I crack the window? The fresh air might make you feel better," Julian asked in a friendly voice.

Shaun nodded, keeping his same position.

Julian made his way over to sit on the bed next to Shaun. Gently, he placed his hand on Shaun's side. Slightly startled, the boy flinched, then quickly resumed his position.

"Shaun, what is the matter?" Julian asked with a wave of emotion. He could sense the 16-year-old was deeply troubled and very upset, even if he wasn't expressing it in a tirade.

Shaun rested silently

Julian waited. And waited. And waited. And waited some more.

Shaun let out a deep sigh. Julian did not realize how tense the boy was until he relaxed with the deep breath. Instinctively, he moved closer and placed his hand on his forehead. *No fever*, he thought. He let his hand rest in the thick dark hair.

"How long are you going to stay here?" Shaun asked in a gruffed voice.

"For a while," Julian replied with a half smile, "Do you want to tell me about it? It can't be all that bad."

Shaun did not respond.

"Maybe it is," Julian replied thoughtfully.

"It would hurt too much to talk about it," Shaun answered gruffly.

"It's going to have to come out some time," Julian said, petting his head.

"I would rather it be later," Shaun replied.

"Okay," Julian answered. "I've nowhere to go. I'll just sit right here until you are ready." He continued to stroke his head.

"Do we have to?" Shaun said, getting impatient.

"Yes," Julian answered.

Shaun started breathing heavily as if he was having an asthma attack. Julian realized it was more like dry heaves. He must have been doing some crying earlier. He sobbed gently.

"I am so ashamed," Shaun said, biting his fist.

"Why, Shaun?" Julian, asked starting to really get concerned.

Shaun started making muffled noises, so Julian bent closer to him in order to hear him.

"I'm sorry, Shaun, but I can't hear you?" Julian said, fighting the impulse to cry. Still, a tear managed to escape his eye.

Shaun turned upward and looked into his uncle's face. There was pain in his eyes, "Two boys forced me into the bathroom at school and took turns at me. They said I deserved it for stirring up so much trouble. They wanted to teach me a lesson."

"Oh Shaun," Julian gasped. He gently shook his head. "You did not deserve it and you certainly have nothing to be ashamed about this happening to you." He fought with all his might not to join Shaun in his sobs.

"That's not the worst of it," Shaun started to explain between sobs and chokes. "There were gobs of semen. They were mine. It must have been what I wanted deep down inside."

Tears were streaming down Julian's face. "Oh no, Shaun," Julian said, shaking his head, "That was a physiological response; not one of pleasure."

"You know I never went for that sort of thing," Shaun explained. "But, I thought maybe deep down I was repressing it, you know. And it was just waiting to surface at the right time."

"No," Julian replied again, shaking his head. "That's not what it was."

"Are you sure?" Shaun asked for reassurance.

"Yes," Julian assured, "I'll explain the anatomy of it some other time. Just think that the semen was pushed out of you instead of released from you."

"Pushed?" Shaun said bewildered and slightly relieved, but then said with a pained look in his face, "Uncle Julian, it still hurts, so much," he patted his bottom.

"I probably should take a look," Julian said grimly. "Okay?"

Shaun nodded carefully. Julian stood up to give Shaun some room. "Will you lock the door?" Shaun asked. "I don't want anyone else to come in here with me exposed." Julian complied with the request.

Slowly, Shaun shed his jeans and underwear. Moving slowly, he carefully lay on his tummy across the length of his bed. He was trembling when Julian came to sit beside him, "Relax. It's just Uncle Julian," his uncle said softy. Shaun nodded his head, but remained tense.

Julian gently parted the boy's cheeks to inspect any damage. He held his breath before taking a look. He dreaded what he might see. He wondered if the boy would be severely maimed. What would he do? He tried to think in advance of some comforting words that he should say. He did not want a gasp to escape, if he saw any deformity. He said a quick prayer to keep his stomach calm.

The small fold did not look so bad. It was swollen and very red. There did not appear to be any blood in the area. There was some bruising in the tissue around where the entry was forced. Overall, it could have been a lot worse.

"Were you able to clean yourself afterwards?" Julian asked.

"I took a shower, when I got back here to my room," Shaun answered quietly. "I've taken a couple of them. They make me feel better for a couple of minutes."

Julian wanted to ask if there was any blood, but he did not want to further upset the boy. "Where are the clothes you were wearing?" He asked gently. Shaun lifted his head and pointed to a corner of the room. There was a small pile of clothes sitting there on the floor. Julian stood and went to inspect them. The clothing was soiled. There was some blood, but not a tremendous amount. The important thing was that there was no bleeding at the present time. He went back over to Shaun and sat back down next to him.

"How bad does it look?" Shaun asked with some fear in his eyes,

"Not bad," Julian answered gently with a half smile, "Just a few bruises. It will be healed before you know it."

"My whole insides still really hurt," Shaun said, starting to get upset.

"Have you been able to move your bowels?" Julian asked.

"Are you kidding?" Shaun asked incredulously. "There is just no way."

"Well, that's probably the source of a lot of your aching. Go ahead in the bathroom and we will find away to do it as painless as possible, but it has to be done. I will be back in a few minutes," Julian left the room.

He found Emily in the children's playroom. She was getting their supper. He kissed each one, including his wife.

"I need one of those bottled things you use when one of the children gets backed up inside," he said quietly, making small hand gestures to describe what he wanted. She sensed that he was upset, so she went quickly to fetch it for him.

When she came back, she asked puzzled, "What's the matter?"

"It's Shaun," he said gravely. "He needs it." He didn't want to explain further at the moment, because he didn't want to alarm the children. Also, he wanted to quickly get back to Shaun.

"I know you're busy," Julian stated tensely. "But can you have the car brought around to the house? Also, I'm going to need you to drive it. We need to go see the doctor."

"Okay," Emily answered with grave concern. "Is Shaun real sick?"

"I don't think so," Julian answered, "I think he's more upset than anything, but the doctor needs to take a look at him." He took her further aside and explained briefly what happened to Shaun.

"I'll take care of it. I'll get the nurse to get the children their baths," Emily said coolly. "You better get back to him." She gently grabbed his arm as he made to leave. "Do you think I should call Adam Frank from the church? Shaun seems to like him. Maybe they could talk when we return from the doctor."

"That's a very good idea," Julian agreed

"Do you feel a little better?" Julian asked as Shaun came from his bathroom into the bedroom after showering. Julian was sitting in a desk chair trying to piece things together waiting, while Shaun was getting ready to go see the doctor.

"Well, my stomach doesn't hurt so much," Shaun mumbled while pulling on a pair of clean jeans.

"I don't see why we have to see the doctor," Shaun complained. "I'm humiliated enough without him poking at me."

"We have to be sure there's not any major damage or infection," Julian explained. "It will be over before you know it."

"Why can't he come to the house, like he usually does?" Shaun asked unhappily.

"Well, I figured," Julian started, choosing his words carefully, "he'll be able to give you a better exam at his office." He thought the doctor might need to take x-rays.

"Maybe I'm not in as much pain as I thought," Shaun said hopefully, trying to dissuade his uncle from going.

"Shaun, you can barely walk," Julian said while trying not to nag too much. Then, he gently added with a smile, "We just need to be sure, okay?"

Shaun nodded, with his head down.

"Shaun, I need to ask a few questions," Julian said in thought. He did not wait for an affirmation. "You can barely move. Where did you go last night that kept you away most of today? Seeing that you are so sore, how did you manage on your own?"

Shaun paused. Too tired to formulate an explanation, he started saying whatever came to mind. "A muscle guy that I help tutor came to pick me up. He's the same one that brought me home after all this happened. He feels he owes me a few favors, so he told me if I ever needed anything, just to ask him."

"Where did he take you?" Julian asked. He had a queasy feeling about the answer he was going to receive.

"I had to take care of a few things," Shaun said with an edge to his voice.

"Go on," Julian prompted.

"Without going into a lot of detail," Shaun said evenly, "Those boys will never do what they did to me again or to anyone else. They most likely will never have children. I tracked each of them. I was on my own. My pupil was along for the ride and did not have much of a clue of what I was doing."

"In your present condition?" Julian asked with a frown, "How....did you ah...manage?" He was trying hard not to be upset with Shaun.

"I willed myself to do it," Shaun explained, "I knew it would be better once it was done. I know you don't approve, Uncle Julian. You have to look at it from my perspective. I'm no longer a kid, but I'm not an adult either. I'm caught in some kind of limbo. I have some of the same problems that adults have, but at my age, I'm powerless to do anything to solve them. I have to rely on those older than me to help me work through them or solve them for me. In short, nobody really listens to me. It seems that everybody else knows what is best for me. That was not going to work this time! I...had...to...do...something!"

Julian clutched his hands tight. He stared at them, while he paused to think of the next thing that he was going to say. He realized that Shaun had the need to gain control of the situation. It seemed natural that he would want to recapture from those boys what he lost. He also knew Shaun would eventually have to face the emotional pain of what had happened to him, because nothing he could do would give back what those boys took from him.

"Shaun," Julian started, looking up into his nephew's face. "Look at me," he said quietly. He took a deep breath. "I think those meetings with your friends are important. I'm going to see to it that we'll be able to meet on school property. I'd like to be a member and come to each meeting. Do you think you guys would accept me?"

"Sure," Shaun answered, surprised. "I guess it would be okay if you really want to come."

"Good," Julian replied with a solemn look. "Are you just about ready? Emily is going to drive us. She should be waiting for us outside with the car."

Shaun paused reluctantly.

"It will be okay," Julian assured him. "She's cool."

Shaun almost grinned. "Okay." They headed out of the room.

The drive to the doctors' office was quiet. Nobody in the car cared too much for conversation. Shaun stared out of the window the entire ride. Julian tried to keep an eye on Shaun without being too conspicuous. Emily tried to concentrate on the road, while feeling concern for both uncle and nephew.

The doctors' office was busy. Three or four doctors shared a number of suites. They were all general practice doctors or more succinctly, country doctors. They were famous for sending their patients to specialists to some of the closest cities. Often, nobody went to the specialists and relied solely on the doctors' advice. Their experience was vast, since they often saw a variety of ailments through the years.

Shaun, his uncle and his aunt sat in the waiting room, until the doctor was ready to see them. It was a rectangular room lined with several green leather arm chairs with oak wood frames. On the other long side was the reception table, separated from the room by a piece of sliding glass sitting on top of it. A woman sporting a nurse's uniform motioned for Julian to sign in at the table. Afterwards, Julian regained his seat and they continued to wait.

Shaun was getting restless. Just when Julian thought he was going to insist that they leave, the nurse beckoned Shaun to come through a door.

"Do you want me to come with you?" Julian asked, standing to join him.

"There is no way I am going to go through this by myself," Shaun replied in a disgusted tone.

"I'll follow you," Julian sighed as he ushered Shaun forward. He glanced back to Emily. She nodded for him to go while she waited.

Inside, an examining room awaited them. It was sterile and bright as in any doctor's office. The examining table was covered with the same green leather that covered the chairs in the waiting room, with a sheet of white paper going from one end to the other. It was crinkled, like someone else had been laying on it. Shaun did not know whether he was supposed to sit on it or wait in a nearby chair beside his Uncle Julian. After a short pause, he opted to ease down next to his uncle.

They stared both stared at the floor until Julian broke the silence. "Are you okay?"

"Yes," Shaun said curtly. He was tiring of his uncle asking that question. "Don't worry so much."

Julian nodded.

The doctor came quickly inside the room. He was a pot-bellied middle aged man with a fringe of gray hair circling his bald head. He wore a long white coat over his slacks, shirt and tie.

"Your chart does not state the nature of your visit," The doctor stated. "Am I to assume this visit is routine?"

"You are not the usual doctor our family uses," Julian interjected as he stood to meet him.

"Well, I'm the first available one," the doctor replied. "The chart says that you are in a hurry."

"This is Shaun," Julian introduced, gesturing toward Shaun. He motioned for the boy to stand. Slowly, Shaun eased himself to his feet.

"I can see you are a bit sore," the doctor noticed with a smile.

"You can say that," Shaun answered, looking away.

Julian noticed the doctor's name read the name Carter. Julian put his arm around Shaun, "Dr. Carter, Shaun here..."

"Was raped by two guys in the school's bathroom," Shaun interrupted. He looked at his uncle. "Let's just get this over with."

Julian nodded as he dropped his arm.

The doctor nodded thoughtfully, "That's unfortunate." He advanced the paper on the table and tore off the used portion. "Let's drop your pants and crawl upon the table, so I can have a look at you."

Shaun did what he was told. He winced, as he lay flat on the table with his face pressed hard into the paper.

"Why don't you have a seat, Mr...eh," Dr. Carter pushed his glasses up his nose and searched the chart. "Mr. Smith. You are this boy's guardian?"

"Yes," Julian replied with a nod as he took a seat.

The doctor started examining Shaun. He pulled on a set of rubber gloves and produced a set of instruments. "You know, I had two boys in my office earlier today in pretty bad shape."

"That's too bad," Shaun sneered.

"Let's move on with this," Julian gasped impatiently.

The doctor ignored his remark. He shook his head and added, "Those boys will probably never be the same. Both of them claim to have sustained the injuries by being trampled by the same group of spooked horses."

"I'm sure it was not the fault of the horses. Ouch! Watch it," Shaun retorted.

"Do you happen to know anything about it?" the doctor asked matter of factly.

"I'm not going to claim I do, if that's what you are asking," Shaun replied brusquely. "Can we get this done? You're beginning to hurt me."

"Doctor..."Julian started impatiently.

"I am going to say this one last thing," Doctor Carter said looking back and forth from Julian to Shaun, "If any of you boys had anything to do with each of your injuries, I suggest you make your peace. I see you all are enemies that none of us would like to have. You must realize, of course, that there are two of them and only one of you. Therefore, the burden rests primarily on the party of the minority. This means you, young man. I don't want to see any of you in this office again with such devastating injuries."

Shaun did not utter another word. He lay silently, while the doctor finished his exam.

"You can pull your clothes on, son" Dr. Carter said in a monotone voice as he moved toward Julian. "The damage is not extensive. The bruising is from the initial forced entry. There are some small tears inside mainly made raw from repetition. It does not look like any of the boys were equipped to do sustainable damage. The nurse will give you some pills to take to reduce the inflammation and prevent infection. If the pain pills prove too strong, I suggest switching to aspirin. That will work just fine. If you will excuse me, I have other patients." He started to leave. "And by the way, give your father my regards." He bristled along quickly, letting the door shut behind him.

"So much for bedside manner," Julian said as he waited for Shaun to lace his shoes.

"What does he care what Pilot thinks?" Shaun asked absently.

"Our farm is what keeps this place in business," Julian answered without much thought. He was getting ready to ask Shaun if he was okay but thought better of it. "Are you ready?" he asked Shaun as the boy stood. Shaun nodded. They went to fetch Emily and to fill out the remaining paperwork.

Pastor Adam Frank was waiting in the big house when they returned.

"Hi Adam," Julian greeted with a smile. He gave the good-looking auburn-haired church leader a firm handshake. Emily stepped into the main parlor and extended her welcome.

"Shaun has gone up to his room," she advised. "Can I get the two of you some coffee or tea? We also have snacks."

Adam smiled widely. "Maybe one of those delicious muffins you make?"

Emily giggled, "Coming right up," she said and then whisked herself from the room.

Julian offered a couch, while he sat in a nearby overstuffed chair. The furniture was not overly comfortable. The room was not meant to be a lounge, but rather one of three small stately rooms for important guests. They were all underused as most of the family preferred the single large television room.

Julian relayed the story of the last few days to Adam, as well as the problems Shaun had been having at school.

"He's had a rough year and an awful lot to handle," Adam said in amazement, as he slowly shook his head.

"I should have seen this coming," Julian said with a frown.

"That would be too easy," Adam replied with a smile.

"He's just so passionate about things," Julian said, holding his head in his palms. He then slumped into the uncomfortable chair. "It's like he has this fire burning inside him to ignite other fires wherever he goes."

"It is his spirit, Julian," Adam said seriously, "He has a tremendous spirit. We have to help him channel it in the right direction. He has done some things I'm sure that he has later regretted. But you have to realize that he didn't have a lot of guidance before he came to live with you. We can't try to bridle him. That was what his father tried to do. You have to keep doing what you have been doing with him and show him how to make the right choices. He's not going to learn overnight."

"I feel like I'm blaming him for what happened," Julian said sadly. "This is not what I want to do."

"It's understandable to feel empathy for the pain the other boys must be experiencing," Adam said, trying to comfort him. "There are no winners here."

"It's not so much as me feeling sorry for those boys. I regret the retribution they received. It is just that this may not be over. Their families are not going to forget about all of this," Julian said.

Emily came into the parlor with some muffins. "These are nice and hot," she said with a smile, setting the tray on the cocktail table in front of Adam. She made to leave.

"You can stay," Julian said, "You may want to listen in and solve all these problems."

"I think I'll pass," she declined. "I'm going to bring some muffins to Shaun with some milk. Then I want to make sure the children are sound asleep." She glanced toward Adam. "Tell Nancy I said hi,"

Adam affirmed her request with a quick nod and grin.

Julian let his gaze follow her from the room while distracted in thought.

After pausing, he took a breath to begin his train of concentration. "You know, in my talks with Shaun, I've never heard him say that he retaliated with the vengeance like he has since he has lived with me. In the past, he just seemed to have taken it. Now he is getting into fights in school and now this incident. The violence on the giving and receiving ends seem to be escalating."

"That is why it's up to those who care about him to show him ways of dealing with his problems," Adam replied warmly, "It was only a matter of time before Shaun started reacting to violence with the same in return. For his entire life, that's all he has known. Now he's physically large enough to dish out what he has been taking all these years."

"He wants to go to some camp for the coming summer to work with some sensei for karate," Julian said with a forlorn look.

"What did you say?" Adam asked, looking into Julian's face.

"I said absolutely not," Julian replied, reasserting a firm tone to his voice. "I actually have forbidden it. I don't know much about karate, but from what I understand, it is supposed to be used as a form of art, a form of defense, and a form of competitive sport. I don't think it's supposed to be used for violent behavior."

"Agreed," Adam said in thought. "I'm going to talk to him if it's alright with you?"

"Sure, I'd like that very much," Julian said as both men rose from their uncomfortable seats.

Julian led Adam to Shaun's room, then joined Emily in the children's rooms.

Adam knocked lightly on the bedroom door.

"Come in," Shaun answered. Adam entered and found Shaun sitting on his bed next to a nightstand with his mouth stuffed with a muffin while he washed it down with some milk.

"Hey," Adam greeted him as he sat on the adjoining twin bed directly across from him. "Those things are mighty tasty, aren't they?"

Shaun nodded as he gulped more milk.

"So, things are kind of rough at school, are they?" Adam commented.

"I'm not dropping out," Shaun said flatly.

Adam pursed his lips, "It's probably a good idea to stay in school," Adam mused.

Shaun glanced at his pastor for a moment and then stared at the floor.

"School should be a safe place to go for anyone who wants to learn," Adam cajoled.

Shaun gave no reaction.

"As matter of fact I want to help," Adam said hopefully, looking to Shaun's face.

Shaun glanced briefly to return the gaze. "What can you do? Uncle Julian tried and it didn't help. He talked to my principal to help me. I wouldn't be surprised if the principal organized...what happened to me."

"You won't have to worry about that principal anymore from what your uncle tells me," Adam said, hoping to offer some assurance.

Shaun frowned, "They'll just put another homophobe in his place."

Adam grinned. "That doesn't sound like you Shaun. You've never been a cynical guy. What happened to your ideals to change the world?"

"I'm just a bit down right now." Shaun sighed like an old man. "I'll get them back."

Adam nodded, "Your uncle mentioned a group at school that you formed."

Shaun shrugged, "It's just a group of guys like me who hang out together. Uncle Julian said he would start to come and we would be able to meet at the school."

"I would like to join," Adam said happily. "Do you think you guys can stand another old person?"

"You guys are not so old," Shaun said. Adam was finally able to get a smile from him.

"I even think we may want to consider inviting some friends of yours who are not gay to come," Adam suggested carefully.

"Who would want to come to be with us?" Shaun asked in disbelief.

"Were you not surprised when your uncle and I, your pastor, wanted to join?" Adam asked thoughtfully. "I think there are more surprises coming. We can ask faculty members. We can ask parents. We can ask your friends at school. Others that come forward will make it easier for their peers to feel comfortable to show their support. Perhaps out of ninety of these people asked, only three will join up with us. Maybe later as a result of these three coming, another three will follow."

"I never thought about it that way," Shaun replied thoughtfully. He nodded his head. "It is worth a shot. Why not?"

Adam pressed further. "You know Shaun, when people beat you up and even rape you like those boys did, the answer is not violence in return. There are other ways to change peoples' minds."

Shaun paused without reply. Adam was afraid he had lost him, closing himself off from him.

"Remember what I have said in Church? I taught that revenge belongs to the Lord. When we act in God's place, we take away his power and have to rely on our own."

Shaun replied angrily, "Well, he takes too long! And why did he let this happen to me?"

Adam smiled. "It is true that God lets people do horrible things to us. Remember though, he gives us what we need to overcome these tough trials. I believe that his angels protect us from even worse things happening to us. There are forces of good and evil in this world. Sometimes, it may seem that evil is winning. That's why we have hope. That's why we have faith that good will eventually win. It may not be today or tomorrow. We may have to wait until the day after tomorrow, but all who delight in harming others will eventually pay for their deeds."

"Some of what you say sounds good, but I find it hard to believe all of it," Shaun answered sourly.

"Okay," Adam replied, shifting his weight. "Let's look at your situation. What these boys did to you was reprehensible. You were justifiably angry. Instead of seeking another solution, you decided to return their violence equally. Don't you see the irony? The attention will be turned not to you, but to what you did those boys. You wanted them to pay for what they did to you. It was your ambition to make examples of what will happen to others who try to do the same things. The truth is that others will now believe the infliction those boys bestowed upon you was justified. The reason behind this reaction is because people at large do not like whom you represent. They will think the violent gay boy got what he deserved. In contrast, those boys will receive sympathy for what they did to you. Initially, your internal revenge will satisfy your thirst, but when you do get over your anger and I add that some day you will, there will have been no positive statement made to the world for the harm done to you."

Shaun bowed his head. "You make this sound like all of this is my fault."

"No," Adam answered emphatically, furrowing his brow. "None was your fault. My desire was not to convict you but to show you that there was another, more effective way, to retaliate. Yes, my way is not quick. My ways possibly do not make those boys feel the same physical pain you experienced. However, I firmly believe that God makes all things work together for the good of his people. And Shaun, He has not given up on you or us. He is still going to make good come of all this despair. You just wait to see what God will do tomorrow about the bad things that happened today."

Shaun replied softly in earnest. "The thing I like about going to your church is that you are always so full of hope; that there is unconditional love for me. You speak of people treating each other well, without judgement and prejudices. Sometimes, I think, you're speaking directly to me."

Adam was pleased.

Changing the subject, Shaun asked, "What is your flock going to think of you standing up for the rights of gay kids?"

"I think it will be great for them," Adam answered matter of factly. "We'll be challenging them to accept diversity in people and to practice what I have been preaching. They seem only too wholeheartedly to listen to my words. We will see if they believe the true reality of diversity. Some may leave." He gave a big grin, "For every two that leave, three more will come to replace them."

CHAPTER 29

A few weeks later.

The spring sugarcane season was well under way when it was announced that Pilot would be returning to the farm. He sent word that there would be a big surprise coming when he returned. Nobody had a clue as to what it was going to be. Emily decided to have a grand ball with many of his friends and family present. She even managed to get her two older headstrong brothers committed to come to the festive event.

The ball was going to be the largest that the farm had seen in a long time. Dress was going to be formal. The timing was relatively good, because the nights were still fairly cool. Some good southern cooking from the big kitchen along with extra staff was going to be brought to the big house for the party. Many changes for the night were going to be made at the big house. It was going to be flanked with special antique fixtures used for special occasions replacing the everyday comfortable furnishings. The front room was going be joined with the large TV room, along with the dining room to transform the rooms into one great room to be used as a ballroom. There was going to be a five-piece band with a first class crooner to propel the guests into a fun evening of dancing. The rest of the house was going to contain the fine china accumulated over generations of weddings and anniversaries. These would be dusted off from the storage catacombs underneath the big house for such occasions. The everyday ware would be bunkered for the night. The kitchen in the big house would not be in use. Everything would be coming back and forth from the big kitchen. Palatable small sandwiches, fresh gulf seafood, Russian caviar, mincemeat, along with tasty pies and cakes, with some appetizing finger food would be served all night. Formal draperies with exquisite top treatments would be removed from trunks, lightly steamed and placed on all the windows wells of the formal dining room, the great room and the side parlors. The ones presently standing in place were going to be temporarily replaced.

Why such a makeover of the big house? The big house was built for balls such as this one coming. However, persons that also lived in the mansion desired to have the home-felt presence of everyday life instead living in a museum of extravagance.

Emily was modeling her party dress in the full-length mirror in the sewing room. The seamstress was helping her with the fitting. She was remarkably calm with the comings and goings of the big house on the day before the return of her daddy. It was amazing that the farm's people could make the transformation of the old mansion in a matter of hours. The staff was well organized for the event. Sometimes it would be a few years between parties such as this one on the farm. She decided that it was time for one, since her daddy would be coming home from his longer-than-usual extended leave he took each year. It would be a dawning of sorts for him. This would be the first full season in many years without her mother at his side. This party would be an exceptional sendoff to his new life.

She had nothing to worry or care about for preparations. She had only to dress herself and Candy. This would be the first black tie event for all her children. They were too small to attend the past ones. Julian would bring them into the great room once most of the guests had arrived and return them once everyone had the chance to see them. She reconsidered. She thought they were old enough now to really enjoy dancing and maybe taking their first sips of champagne. Beverages of these sorts were rare on the farm. Only for events such as these were the rules prohibiting alcohol on the farm relaxed. Her daddy forbids the use of any such substances at all other times.

With some help, she was able to get into the dress. She had only worn it once several years ago. Time had been kind to her. Despite having five babies, she was still able to stretch into it. It was tight the last time she wore it. That was the intention. The corset gave the appearance of a flattened tummy while lifting her small but ample breasts. The uncomfortable appendage was not necessary. Her stomach was already tight as a young woman's despite being in her early 30s. She felt her bosom was just the right size. She often thought that she was grateful for average endowment, while other women had their large breasts pressed tightly to their chest, giving that pained smashed appearance. Some people found that attractive. She did not share the feeling.

Emily did not have to worry about making sure her husband looked sharp. He always looked good, dressed to the hilt. She thought it ironic. Here was a man who usually had a day's growth of beard, a pair of muddy boots, and farm clothing that consisted of a white cotton shirt and a pair of tan cotton trousers. This apparel would be accompanied with a filthy straw hat if he had been coming from the fields with beads of sweat on his brow. She still found him handsome in this rugged attire.

A tuxedo was becoming to Julian as was his working attire. His tie was always perfect; shoes always shined; and bleached hair closely cropped, smoothed along his receding temples. Finally, she guessed his studded shirt would be starched enough to make a board. He ironed his trousers himself to make sure the front pleats were firm. Like herself, the years had been kind to him. He held a couple of more years than she did, but he could wear the same cummerbund he did when they were married.

Julian was responsible to make sure that Shaun and their sons were dressed. The boys only allowed their daddy to help them. She giggled to herself that they might come running to her for help if there was too much starch in their little shirts. There was no reason for concern. Their daddy knew just how much he could get away with before they would start to complain.

Shaun was very excited about the party. He was be bringing a date and wanted to look his best. He was counting on Julian for help. She was warmed to that fact he had made a quick recovery from that tragic ordeal that happened a few weeks ago. *They must heal fast at that age*, she thought.

Christopher was another card. He didn't care for the formal fittings. He insisted that he should be able to wear something more colorful and free flowing. Julian told him he could not attend the ball unless he dressed the part. Since he had made a big deal about attending the party, he relented and promised to let Julian help him get ready.

With the dress removed, she had some time to herself. These would be the last moments before the ball. Tomorrow would be the manicure, the pedicure, the facial, and the hairdresser. The hairstyle would be the worst. It would look great once it was done, but with all of her cream-colored hair bound on the top of her head, she knew that she would be destined for a headache. She reminded herself to keep a bottle of aspirin handy.

The day of the ball. Preparations for the ball were nearly complete. The sun was nearly set. Emily was on the front porch, just off the great room. A light spring breeze wafted through the warm dusk air. It promises to be a nice night, she was thinking to herself. Julian joined her on the porch. They stared for a momentary silence toward the Farm Road. It had been doused several times that day with water to keep the dust from rising into the air. It was dusty on the farm, so the extra precaution had been made.

"Got any idea what daddy's surprise is?" Emily asked without taking her eyes off the road.

"Gifts?" Julian offered.

"He's already sent those ahead of him," Emily answered.

"What does your woman's intuition tell you?" Julian asked with a half smile.

Emily smiled less than half. "Only that we will be surprised." She then glanced at her husband while extending her smile to half. "You look handsome."

"As do you," Julian returned with a full smile.

"I haven't seen that nephew of yours in a while. Where is he off to this hour?" Emily asked.

"He went to pick up his date a couple of hours ago," Julian replied. "I told him we'd send a car, but he insisted he wanted to do the honors himself."

"Do you know who it is?" Emily asked, getting interested.

"No. He says he wants it to be a surprise," Julian answered with a full chuckle.

"I guess it is an evening for surprises," she surmised.

"He says he's in love," Julian said. "I've never seen him so excited over a boy."

"Good," Emily stated firmly. "He deserves it."

"You seem to be waiting for something," Julian noticed. "I thought Pilot was not due for a couple more hours."

"I'm waiting for those brothers of mine," Emily answered rolling her eyes, "Daddy expressly said he wanted them to be here for the ball."

"All of them?" Julian asked raising his brow.

"We will see," Emily answered skeptically.

"Are the two older ones getting along with Pilot any better?" Julian asked.

"Not really," Emily answered with a slight frown. "Some things do not change, even with the best intentions."

"Well, I best be getting back upstairs," Julian said with a short sigh. "It's time to get the children ready...including Christopher."

Emily laughed, "Good luck with that one."

"Thanks," Julian said as he went through a pair of open French doors. There were a half dozen sets of French doors along the perimeter of the porch joining the great room. They were locked at times other than for parties and a single door was used to access the porch.

Later, Julian came down the staircase to the great room with Jesse, Jay, William, Louis and Candy, along with Christopher. The children were full of energy with the excitement of the evening shortly coming. A number of guests began to trickle inside and Emily was there to greet them. It was early. There were just a couple of bowls of punch available next to a tray of snacks.

Christopher was quiet for a change.

"Not a word?" Julian asked when they reached the bottom of the steps. The children had already made a run for the punch bowls.

Christopher paused. "I'm afraid I will say the wrong thing," he whispered.

"I thought you would be a hit at any party," Julian teased.

Christopher tried to frown, but broke into a smile. "Just don't go far away from me."

Julian didn't answer but kept smiling.

Soon, Shaun came quickly through the room holding hands with some young man in a black pantsuit. He rushed quickly toward to where Julian and Christopher were standing. Julian thought the type of dress was inappropriate for the boy, but it was, nonetheless, in very good taste. His white silk chemise had a large ruffle front protruding from the jacket. He had dark brown hair, shoulder length, just barely touching his shoulders. His frame was very slender, bordering on frail. His feet were resting on a pair of flat heels. His skin was on the pale side, as if he had never seen the sun's light. His nose was small and lips thin.

Shaun could hardly contain himself, bursting with pride and a big smile. "Uncle Julian, this is Jonathan. Jonathan, this is my Uncle Julian and his good friend Christopher."

Julian met the delicate hand and gave it a gentle shake. "I'm pleased to meet you, Jonathan."

Jonathan smiled, nodding his head once while muttering a short acceptance.

Christopher seemed less than shocked with the boy's appearance and smiled while he exchanged greetings with the boy. "You see," he whispered quietly to Julian, "He's not wearing a tuxedo."

Shaun took Jonathan's hand once more and with enthusiasm said, "Come. I want you to meet my Aunt Emily. I told you how cool she is."

The two boys scurried off toward Emily. More guests started to pour inside.

"Well," Julian said with a laugh. "I guess I shouldn't have been so surprised."

"Surprised by what?" Christopher asked, confused.

"Didn't you think Shaun's boyfriend was very much on the feminine side?" Julian asked.

"I guess," Christopher answered absently. "I thought that's how he liked them."

"I'm convinced," Julian said. "There's nothing wrong with Jonathan. I was just expecting something else. Like a boy in a tuxedo and not in a woman's pantsuit. Shaun is happy. That's all that matters."

"He seems to be a nice guy," Christopher said, distracted. "The boys have left poor Candy by herself. I'll go fetch her. I'll be right back." Christopher was off.

Julian noticed that Shaun had finished his greetings with Emily and that the Douglas man had joined her. He stared in their direction. Their gestures toward each other were friendly and comfortable, not overly sensual. However, Emily did not usually make affectionate overtures.

Julian did not feel jealous. He wondered that he should at least feel a twinge. Maybe it would be a relief if they were indeed more than friendly. Whatever the case, it didn't change the way he felt about her. She was a strong and independent woman who knows how to take care of herself. His admiration for her had never subsided.

Shaun came toward Julian's direction, while Jonathan went off to another.

"Where is your friend going?" Julian inquired as the boy approached.

"He went to the lavatory," Shaun replied with a grand smile. "Isn't he wonderful?"

"He seems very nice," Julian said, delighting in his nephew's happiness. "I especially like the effect he has on you."

"I'd knew you'd approve," Shaun gushed. He then moved closer to Julian and almost whispered, "We are going to wait."

"Wait?" Julian asked bewildered, "Wait for what?"

"You know," Shaun said coyly. "Wait. Until our wedding night."

"Wedding night?" Julian asked beginning to get the picture.

"Yeah," Shaun said with excitement. "When we graduate from high school, we're going to have a ceremony to commit ourselves to each other."

"I see," Julian answered, amused.

"You know, he says he waited all his life for the right one and now he believes it's me," Shaun explained, "So I want it to be special for him."

"I think that's wonderful of you, Shaun" Julian smiled sincerely. "You are worth waiting for as well as he is."

Shaun smiled broadly, "You are the best, Uncle Julian."

"Where did you guys meet?" Julian asked with interest.

"We met at church; Sunday school," Shaun answered.

Julian vaguely remembered the boy's face. It seemed to be familiar. He felt he knew his parents. "What is his last name?"

"Titus," Shaun replied.

"Oh yes," Julian recalled. "They have a farm on the other side of town. I don't recall their name on the guests' list. Did we not send them an invitation?"

Shaun hemmed, "Well, yes. They were not too thrilled about me accompanying their son to this ball. Jonathan did not come right out and say I was his date, but I think they kind of figured it out on their own. I guess they felt too embarrassed to come and be seen with the two of us together."

"I'm sure that was not it," Julian said unconvincingly.

Shaun smirked.

"Well," Julian laughed, "So what. We're having a good time without them."

"Yes we are," Shaun replied, then scurried away to recapture his date.

Christopher evidently lost the butterflies in his stomach. He was conversing animatedly with the governor's cousin. She was a handsome woman and seemed enthralled with the conversation.

Emily's three brothers came through the great room grouped together. Jack was flanked with Lisa, because Marge refused to come. She was dressed in a beautiful yellow gown. *We are stretching all the cultural norms tonight,* Julian thought, *This is going to be an interesting evening.* Victor and Marcus walked in together with no dates. They gave Emily a warm greeting and took a few moments to talk with her. It was not long before Shaun entered the conversation, still holding Jonathan's hand. The look on his face was beaming with excitement to finally get to meet the two mysterious Pilot brothers. While Shaun garnered their attention, Jack, Lisa and Emily, along with Douglas, exchanged pleasantries.

"You don't look very happy," said a voice coming close to Julian.

Julian looked to his right, "Oh, hi Adam," he said with a faint smile, "I was just in thought."

"Come, let's talk," Adam said as he ushered Julian to one of the side parlors. The parlor was much like the others. The exception was the pastel blue decor. Each parlor was outfitted with a different color scheme.

"Well," Adam said, taking a seat on the camel back couch. He noticed some glasses of champagne set on a nearby sofa table.

"Do want a glass?" He asked.

"No thank you," Julian replied, shaking his head slowly, "I think I will pour some water. Would you like some?"

"Sure," Adam answered.

Julian poured each of them a glass of water and sat in an adjacent upholstered chair. He set one in front of Adam on the cocktail table and the other in front of himself. They paused without saying anything.

Finally, Adam asked, "So, Julian, how are things?"

Julian shrugged. "Fine, I guess. Shaun seems to be doing real well; made a quick recovery."

"Yes," Adam agreed.

More silence.

"How about things with you, Julian," Adam pressed.

"I try not to think about that too much," Julian answered as he sighed.

"That sounds familiar," Adam said with a half smile.

"It seems everything..." Julian started while searching for words, "It seems things are out of balance." He paused. "It seems things are changing and I haven't kept up with them." He chuckled lightly. "This refrain is also familiar."

"What has changed?" Adam asked.

"I thought things had changed when Christopher came to us, but I find that things had already been changing," Julian said sadly.

Adam nodded.

"When Christopher came, I started to feel alive again. I didn't realize that a part of me had been asleep. It's a different situation than it was with Robert. I don't feel as passionate. I am spending a lot of time with Christopher and I really enjoy it. I feel close to him without having sex. There is a special warmth in our friendship," Julian said.

"Sounds good," Adam commented.

"I guess that does," Julian agreed, "Then I find myself thinking about him all the time. I think about the time we spend together. I fantasize us making love together."

"How have you and Emily been during this time?" Adam asked.

Julian replied fitfully, "It was during this time that I decided that she and I should have separate bedrooms. We never had a lot going together anyway, but I thought I could use the time alone to sort things out to make sense. Then I figured out that she has been carrying on in some degree with this Douglas man. Things were already changing without me knowing it. I was the last to know about it."

"It bothers you that she's seeing Douglas regularly?" Adam asked.

"What bothers me," Julian explained, "Is that is does not bother me at all. I'm glad she's content. I feel immensely relieved. I just wish it were me who was capable of doing it. I wanted to be a good husband."

"Do you know the extent of their relationship?" Adam asked.

"No," Julian sighed, "We don't talk about Douglas or Christopher. It seems it's understood that we each mind our own business."

"It seems they are friendly," Adam commented. "I really don't know."

"It doesn't matter," Julian resigned.

"What is stopping your progression with Christopher?" Adam asked.

"I don't know," Julian replied, "I haven't figured that one out yet."

"Julian, have you been back to Washington in a while?" Adam asked.

"I've never been back there, since I've come to the Pilot's. I used to think if I ever went back there that I would never come back here," Julian replied.

"Maybe it's time you find out if this is the case," Adam said solemnly. "You have some ghosts to face. I think your heart is telling you that it's time to come to terms with yourself and not feel so bad about it."

"You could be right," Julian agreed.

Adam and Julian joined the rest of the party in the great room. As they passed by the other side parlors, other guests could be seen conversing privately. However, all were being summoned. Pilot would be arriving shortly.

Christopher joined Julian, "Where have you been? I've been looking for you. Your boys and little girl are getting restless."

"They will be fine," Julian smiled. "Their grandpapa is about to arrive and they'll be excited to see him." Jesse, Jay, William, Louis and Candy joined them.

"Daddy, when is Grandpapa coming?" Jesse asked. "When is Grandpapa coming?" Jay echoed.

Julian laughed. "I think he'll be here in a few minutes. And he sure will be glad to see you!" The children were pleased.

There was a loud gasp in the party as Pilot made his entrance. He was dressed in a full tuxedo with black tails with a tall woman dressed in a big blue satin party dress on his arm. The dress was full of hoops and layers of material in full southern classic attire. She was fanning herself with a white-gloved hand. Her hair was the shade of dark walnut, with large curled tresses draping both sides of her neck across her large protruding breasts. The rest of her hair was neatly stacked on top of her head, underneath a small hat that matched her dress. Her skin was the color of alabaster, much the same as Christopher's skin except that it was rich and vibrant as well as free of freckles.

The couple marched down the center of the great room with party guests lining both sides of the aisle. All were in awe of the striking couple. She looked to be slightly older than Emily by a few years. As she passed Julian and Christopher, Julian could see that a big diamond rock was on her left ring finger. A large gold band was used as a buttress to keep it from slipping off her finger.

When the couple came to the end of the row, Pilot signaled to the band to play the evening's first dance. When the music started, Pilot and his lady waltzed easily, counter-clockwise around the dance floor. Mid way through the waltz, there was a signal for the others to join the dance.

"I want to dance, Daddy," little Candy said in a tiny voice. Julian smiled and gathered up his daughter into his arms and whisked her to the dance floor. The little girl giggled in delight.

After a short time, the dance floor cleared, while Pilot stood up from where the band was playing. The lady he was with was off to the left of the platform.

The man Pilot did not have to call for attention. When the masses saw him step upon the stage, all turned toward him to wait to see what he had to say. Within minutes, there was silence in the ballroom.

Pilot smiled and started to speak. "Friends and family, I tell you this is the best welcome home party a man could ask to have upon his return." Everyone smiled with him and gave a short applause. "My leave was extended this year and I am so glad to be coming back home. As many of you or all of you know, I lost my wife of over 40 years last year. This place has not been the same since she left us so quickly. Well, I have some very good news that will perk this place up and send us forward into the future as I am sure Louisa would have wanted it."

Julian moved across the room to join Emily. When he reached her, he gently put his arm around her waist. She returned the gesture with a light squeeze of his hand. She was glad to have him by her side.

Her brothers were within earshot. Victor and Marcus started a heated whispering conversation with Jack. It was Jack who was trying to calm his older brothers and to keep them from leaving the party. When Pilot began to speak, they managed to come to a hush.

Pilot called for the lady off stage and she came gracefully to join him. When she arrived at his side, he began to speak once more. She was smiling properly and surveying the room as if the people were her loyal subjects.

Pilot began to speak. "This lovely lady is Frances Loraine.... That is.... Frances Loraine Pilot. Frances Lorraine is the newest addition to the Pilot family and my new wife. I hope you will join us again for another grand party here at the Pilot house sometime at the end of this year, when we will have a proper wedding and reception. Now, I'm going to stop talking, so that each of you may introduce yourselves to Frances Lorraine. I know you will cherish her as much as I do. Thank you and continue to celebrate."

Pilot stepped down from the stage and immediately started receiving hands of congratulations, with his new wife at his side. The overall reaction was more than surprise. All were stunned by Pilot's latest revelation. Victor and Marcus abruptly left the ball.

After a brief period, the party resumed its normal buzz and the band started to play once more. Still, nobody went immediately to dance. After some discussion amongst themselves, the gentlemen once again beckoned the ladies to dance. Along with the other couples, Shaun and Jonathan joined them on the floor. It seemed that the guests no longer considered them a novelty.

"I have to go after my brothers," Emily said as she broke away from Julian.

He grabbed her hand gently as she started for the exit door. "Are you alright?" he asked.

She paused and then nodded gently. She was obvious consumed with emotion and Julian knew she wanted to be anywhere but in this room. Instinctively, he knew not to join her. She left for the same exit door her brothers had taken.

Christopher made his way to Julian along with Adam. "Where did Emily go?" Christopher asked. "Is she upset?"

Julian gasped and then shrugged, "She has her own way of dealing with things. She will be okay."

"What can we do?" Adam asked with concern. "The tension with your family is mighty thick. Maybe we could do some damage control."

"Can you to see to the children?" Julian asked. "They probably don't completely understand what has happened. If they seem agitated, come and get me then I will fetch them upstairs."

Christopher surveyed the room. "They seem to be okay. They're on the dance floor dancing together. They actually look kind of cute, stepping on each other's feet. They seem to be entertained."

"Regardless, we will check on them," Adam said firmly. "Children keep things to themselves sometimes when they are frightened by something they don't understand."

"I will explain to them later what has happened with their grandpapa," Julian said, looking in the children's direction. "I need to have a word or two with Pilot, so I can get the gist of his mindset. It may be a while before he's free to talk with me."

"His new wife seems to be fitting in very well," Christopher surmised, looking in her direction. "She seems to be taking extra time mingling with the dignitaries of the ball."

Julian nodded, giving the two men their dismissal. Julian stood to the side close to a nearby wall while gazing at the man Pilot, as he moved around the room. Eventually, he made his way to Julian's direction with a glass of champagne in his hand. Julian normally would have chuckled at the sight, since the strongest thing he ever saw his father in-law drink was grape juice. Nonetheless, the glass was near full.

"This is some night," Pilot said, joining Julian while gazing through the crowd, as if he had just walked into the room for the first time.

"Yes, it is," Julian replied, looking in the same direction.

After a short pause, "I take it you are less than pleased?" Pilot surmised.

"I just don't know what to say," Julian deadpanned. "All I can think about is, why, Pilot? Why did you do this?"

"Every man needs a wife," Pilot answered with conviction. "I recall having this conversation many years ago with you. Do you remember?"

Reluctantly, Julian nodded his head. "It's just so soon, Pilot," he sighed. "Maybe not so much for you, obviously, but it is for the rest of us."

"I know there's a period of adjustment coming," Pilot explained, "but the family will come along with this and eventually see that this was a good move."

Julian was not sure he agreed with him, but figured this was not the time to argue. "This is a time of celebration for you. I want you to enjoy yourself. We will all manage with having a new family member. You have to understand this is quite a surprise."

"Agreed," Pilot replied.

"Why did you choose to tell the family this way?" Julian couldn't let the subject go so quickly. "Surely, you could have let the family know what to expect before telling the rest."

"I felt this was the best way," Pilot replied confidently. "First, your brothers in-law most likely would have stayed at home. I wanted them to be here."

"Your relations with them are strained as it is." Julian knew Pilot did not want to hear this about his two eldest sons but thought now was the time to pose the subject.

Pilot bristled. "I have never been able to please those two. However, I would have thought they could put all else aside and be happy for me." Tiring of this line of conversation, he inquired, "Who is that girl Shaun is draped all over? She looks vaguely familiar."

"His name is Jonathan," Julian said with some satisfaction. "He is Shaun's latest beau and obviously is quite pleased with him."

"I see," Pilot replied distantly and then asked, "Who is that young squire that has your heart in a twist?"

"What do you mean?" Julian replied defensively. He was surprised once more by Pilot's perception.

"That little redhead that keeps looking in your direction," Pilot replied, "I sense you are equally aware of his movements, no?"

Julian was not amused with the detachment from the last conversation. Regardless, he answered the question. "He wandered onto the farm a while back and he has become friends with Emily and me."

"It has become a little more than friendship," Pilot stated, seemingly not pleased.

"I didn't think such things mattered to you," Julian replied with an irritated inflection.

"Relax," Pilot soothed. "Normally, they don't, but this one has me concerned."

Julian became distraught. He could not comment.

"This boy is poison to you, Julian," Pilot said gravely, continuing to gaze in Christopher's direction.

"His name is Christopher," Julian growled, "and yes. He does have me in fits."

"He's not good for you, Julian. You need to get rid of him. I suggest you get him out of your life," Pilot said matter of factly.

Julian was astounded with Pilot's audacity. "How can you say so without even meeting him? What harm has he done?"

"I don't hear you disagreeing with me," Pilot replied, continuing to gaze. "It's just a feeling I have. I really don't care what you do with your life. I am not judging, believe me. My concern is for your happiness and," Pilot continued, searching for words for the remaining sentence while shaking his head, "I don't think that boy...Christopher is the one to give it to you."

Julian was now feeling completely depressed. For some reason, he believed Pilot was right. "Will you get rid of him for me? Like assign him to other tasks away from this place? I just don't think I can...."

"Nooo..." Pilot said, emphatically shaking his head, "This is your doing. I can't rescue you every time a wayward lad has you in fits. You have to do it yourself. Besides, I've made that mistake before, remember. I was clearly in the wrong."

Julian chuckled, keeping his thoughts to himself.

"And yes. I do make mistakes," Pilot said as if he was reading Julian's mind. "I'm man enough to admit when I do," He then added with a half smile, "I just don't make them too often."

Julian ventured to another subject; "I am going to be taking a trip to Washington in the next couple of weeks."

Pilot nodded his head thoughtfully. "It's probably time you do. I assume you are going alone?"

Julian took a deep breath and nodded.

"When was the last time you got off the farm?" Pilot asked dryly.

"I get to town every so often," Julian replied absently.

"I mean, really off the farm. I mean to another state or country," Pilot pressed.

Julian frowned, "It has been a long time. There never seems to be a right time."

Pilot paused and then commented, "There was a time I thought if you ever did leave this place, that you would never come back."

Julian responded sadly, "Maybe that's why I never have left."

"You do what you need to do," Pilot said carefully.

Julian nodded.

Later that night.

Julian returned to his room after checking with the children. It was late, but they were still determined to stay awake. *It must have been that extra long afternoon nap*, he thought. He then realized that he too was keyed up. Finally, he was able to get the boys to lie still, after getting their little sister tucked underneath the bed covers. It took a promise to take them camping next weekend if they went to bed without fussing. This only stirred them more, since they were clearly overjoyed. Nonetheless, they complied.

As he undressed, Julian found himself winding down into tiredness. It had been a long day and he was emotionally drained. Soon, it would be morning, but he decided the extra luxury of sleeping late was imminent. He turned off the lights and slid into bed.

After staring at the ceiling for a while, Julian heard a light knock at his door. He sat up in his bed; worried that one of the boys had mischievously wandered from his room. "Come in," he answered.

Slowly, the door opened and Emily padded in close to the bed. "Do you mind if I stay with you tonight?" she asked.

Julian smiled while opening the covers. "Not at all. Come in."

She complied and sidled into his arms. "I didn't want to be alone tonight. I hope you don't mind."

"Of course not," Julian assured her. "You are welcome any night you choose." He lovingly kissed the side of her face.

"I could not stay at the party," Emily said and then asked, "Was I missed?"

Julian answered carefully, "I'm sure you were, but I think the guests could understand. The evening's events were quite shocking."

She seemed to accept his answer.

"What if I don't like her?" she asked not expecting an answer.

"I wondered the same," Julian said softly.

"How are you with all this tonight?" Emily asked with concern.

Julian sighed. "I miss Louisa." He could feel a couple of teardrops on his chest.

"Me too," she said with a light choke.

After a short while she spoke. "Julian?"

"Yes," he answered, softly stroking her head.

She exhaled and then said, "I need you sometimes. Not all the time, just sometimes."

She could feel him smile. "Sure," Julian replied, "I'm here." Then he added, "I get lonely too, Emily. I need you as much."

She hugged him tight and he reached to kiss her.

CHAPTER 30

A few days later.

Julian found Emily in the children's room packing knapsacks for their camping trip with their daddy. She was dressed to the hilt. A light blue suit tailored of thin wool material covered her tall slender body. The attire was far from the southern style, like the ladies wore at the ball. It did not have the conservative look like the suits that Elizabeth wore.

"I can do this," he advised. "You go on ahead with your plans."

"It's okay," she assured him, "I have a little time."

He noticed the camping gear neatly placed by the door. There were a couple more knapsacks along with little hiking boots and two tents.

"Why two tents?" Julian asked. "One should be plenty for us."

She looked up from her packing, "I thought the adults should have their own tent." She returned to stuffing the packs. "I thought maybe you could ask Christopher to go along."

Julian frowned and then slumped onto the bed that she was using to pack. "How about Shaun instead?" he offered lamely.

She looked at him with affection. "Eventually, you're going to have to work things out with him. Maybe this would be a good time. You should be able to get some time with him. Besides, I think you may need some help with four rambunctious boys."

Julian stood and faced away from her while biting into his fist. "Okay, I'll ask him."

The group of two men and four boys set out for a day of fun and games, along with a night of sleeping in tents in the deep woods. The boys kept a short distance ahead with their small knapsacks on their backs. The youngest was struggling to keep up with his older brothers. They constantly asked their daddy which direction to take. Patiently, he would answer to keep moving forward. Occasionally, he would tell them to go to either the left or the right.

Christopher was right by the daddy's side. He too carried a light knapsack on his back, while the daddy shouldered the burden of two tents and a knapsack of his own.

Christopher seemed amused and shared the same excitement that the children carried with them. He was not his usual chatty self. Instead, he reluctantly let the children be the center of Julian's attention. While he preferred to have Julian to himself, he was grateful for the time with his friend. Getting time with Julian has been more of a chore of late. He realized that Julian was a busy man with many responsibilities and family demands. Surely, he felt there should be time for him somewhere. He did not even mind if this meant being by his side while Julian took care of these things. For example, he was pleased to be going camping with the children.

"Have you decided where we are going?" Christopher asked without much expression.

"A short ways down stream from where we fished a few times. It's where the water is shallow and still, so the boys can swim. They'll be able to drop a line and easily catch some small fish, which should make them happy. We'll just have to throw them back if they're too small to keep, which may mean all of them," answered Julian, looking ahead to his sons.

Christopher nodded.

"Thank you for inviting me," he said quietly.

"I'm glad you could come," Julian answered. He meant it.

When they reached a clearing by the brook, interspersed with a few large standing trees, Julian announced that this would be the camping spot. He was relieved to release the gear from his back and arms. Since he had transported the majority of the food, a few dishes and silverware, along with the other items that they would need, his pack was much bigger than those the others had carried.

"Okay guys, it's time to set up the camp site. How about gathering some wood for a campfire, but don't go too far away," Julian said to his sons. He knew the boys would have to keep occupied a while, since he was to set up the tents and dig a pit for the campfire.

"Daddy, can I help you set up the camp?" Jesse asked.

"Sure," Julian answered, smiling at his eldest son., "Do you think you can get your brothers to help?"

"Okay," Jesse agreed. "If they promise not to wreck anything."

"They may need some help," Julian concurred., "Maybe you could give me a hand with them?"

The boy was pleased. "Sure daddy. I'll help them get some more wood and then we will be ready to help." He then paused. "You'll wait to set up the tents for when we get back?"

"You bet," Julian promised.

Julian started digging the fire pit, while Christopher watched.

"Do we have any water left?" Christopher asked.

"The canteens may be empty about now." Julian replied. "Do you mind going down to the brook to refill them?"

"Sure," Christopher answered. He then picked through Julian's pack to fetch a couple of water bottles.

"There are some yellow tablets in the small side pocket. When you fill the canteens, put one tablet in each container. This will make the water safe to drink," Julian said while shoveling some dirt.

Christopher padded down to the brook.

"Okay guys," Julian commanded with a laugh. "That's enough wood. Come over here." The firewood consisted of thin tree branches. He would have to go later to get some bigger pieces.

Finally, it was time to set up the tents. After a long time and a lot of coaching from the daddy, Christopher and the boys managed to erect the tents. It took many times of redoing stakes and lines to get the tents raised. Julian knew at some point that he would have to take the tents back down and quickly reset them, while the children had their attention on something else. He had an idea.

"Okay boys," he said finally, "Good job. I think it's time for a swim. Christopher, can you take them down to the brook?" It was too late. The boys had taken off running to the water's edge and started to strip down to get ready to enter the water. Since they were still young, this would take a few minutes.

"You know," Christopher warned, "I don't know how to swim. What if one of them gets into trouble?"

"It will take a few minutes for them to undress. Another few minutes for them to test the water temperature. Another few minutes after that to get brave enough to get into the water. By that time, I should be down there with you. Besides, it's close enough for me to keep a watchful eye," Julian replied and then added, "You can join the swimming lessons. One of the objectives of this trip is to continue with their swimming education."

"Sounds good," Christopher said and then headed to the water's edge. After a few steps, he turned and added, "Don't be long."

Julian smiled. "I'll be down shortly."

After a day of swimming, fishing, hiking, and some supper, it was time to roast some marshmallows. By this time, it was getting dark and the boys were very tired. Reluctantly and with a few complaints the boys were washed by water's edge. They were glad to get to bed. This left daddy and friend some time alone, sitting by the fire. The night temperature was pleasant, so the fire was not really needed. Regardless, it was still nice to have and it gave a hypnotic, soothing feeling to the light tension between the two men.

They were sitting together on a large log in front of the fire. Christopher moved close to Julian, so that he was touching him. Julian returned the gesture by putting his arm around Christopher's inside thigh, while resting his hand on top of his friend's knee. They sat in silence for a few minutes.

"Is that other tent for the both of us?" Christopher asked.

"Is that okay?" Julian asked, giving him a long glance.

Christopher nodded gladly without trying to show too much emotion. "Oh yeah. It's fine with me."

Julian sat while gazing into the flames. "Christopher." He paused for a half moment. "Do you love me?"

"You know I do," Christopher answered bewildered by the question, "I tell you this all the time."

Julian sighed, "I mean, are you in love with me?"

"I guess so," Christopher answered, "What do you mean?"

"I have a great deal of feelings for you, Christopher. I think about you all the time. Sometimes, so much that it hurts," Julian said. He waited before he wanted to say more.

"I guess some of what you say is good, but I don't want you to hurt," Christopher answered, hugging Julian's strong biceps and triceps muscles.

"I want you so much," Julian said sadly. "But I question if you feel the same way I do. I just have a nagging sensation that you feel differently."

Christopher remained silent for a moment. "I don't know, Julian. What are you wanting to say?"

Julian gave in. "I want to make love to you. I want to shower you with passionate kisses. I want to press our naked bodies together, so I can get into your skin. I want to squeeze your body so tight, that you'll never leave me. I want to shoot so deep inside you, that you'll always have me with you."

Christopher was speechless. After a short while, he replied, "I don't know what to say."

"You can say that you want the same things I do," Julian said with a defeated tone.

"Can you explain again what you want?" Christopher asked.

Julian released himself from him and clasped his hands together between his knees.

"I want to be with you all the time. I want to have a relationship with you that includes sexual relations. I want you to love me the way I love you," Julian said. "I don't know how to spell it out any other way."

"I'm trying to understand," Christopher replied, sensing Julian's frustration.

"Do you ever fantasize about us? I mean, do you think about me being inside you? Or my bluntly stating, do you have the desire for me to put my penis into your bottom?"

"I think about you hugging and kissing me while holding me tight. About making me feel safe," Christopher answered, sensing he was not living up to Julian's expectations. "The rest, I don't know."

"What do you think about when you masturbate?" Julian asked. "Do you ever think about me?"

Christopher hedged. "Well...hum, you mean that warm fuzzy feeling inside? I get that. I dream about you all the time. About you holding me. About the affection I give to you, except, yes, I do dream about being with you without any clothes on either of us. Sometimes, I wake up and there's a mess on my sheets. Semen escapes from me in that way."

"You don't masturbate?" Julian asked astonished.

"Not really," Christopher answered matter of factly. "I don't care for it."

"Have you ever loved anyone else like you love me? Or have you loved anyone more than me?" Julian asked, trying to understand.

"I have been in love with men and women. But no; none more than you," Christopher answered.

"I just don't get it, Christopher," Julian said, shaking his head. "If making love sexually does not make sense to you, what about the simple act of procreation?"

"I don't see what difference sex with men or women has to do with procreation. Making babies is an act in itself. I just don't care for any of it," Christopher said, dejected. "It's not that I hate it or am disgusted by it, I just don't have any feeling for it." After a few moments he added, "But Julian, please don't think that I fail to feel passion for you. I'd be sick to be without you. You have to believe this about me."

Julian nodded. "I'm getting tired. It's time for bed. We can lie naked together and fall asleep. I guess some of our fantasies will come true tonight."

Christopher smiled. He got up quickly and moved toward their tent. After a few moments, Julian rose to his feet to join him. Somehow he knew that one of them would have trouble sleeping.

A few days later.

"Do you have everything ready?" Emily asked as Julian came into the kitchen of the big house. He had just finished packing his suitcase.

"I suppose," Julian answered, "I'm surprised to see you here. I thought your responsibilities have been relegated to the big kitchen and supervising the farm's women. Isn't Frances Loraine supposed to be managing the big house?"

"We're going through a period of transition," Emily explained. "Besides, it has been difficult to let go. She wants to make too many changes. You've noticed the party decorations and furniture have not been put away? She wants to keep all the good silver, china, formal window treatments and expensive art in the big house permanently. This place is looking more like a palace than a home."

"What about the TV room?" Julian asked, slightly perplexed. "Will we at least have it?"

"No," Emily answered. "She wants to leave it transformed as the great room. A huge empty room with no use. She thinks it's an impressive status symbol."

"But family and friends get together in the TV room for informal times of relaxing and enjoying each other," Julian complained. "We should really put our foot down about this one."

"Well, she says the new TV room will be included in the addition," Emily explained.

"The addition?" Julian asked, raising his brow.

"Yes. She wants an additional wing built on the north side of the house to include new rooms for her and daddy on the top floor. Guests suites will be on the second floor with the new family and friends rooms taking the first floor," Emily said without expression. "Daddy wants us to let her do what she wants to make her feel welcome."

"What about the third floor of the west wing? What are we going to do with Pilot's and Louisa's old rooms?" Julian asked.

"Loraine wants to renovate that floor and put us up there in the new rooms. She says they'll be luxurious," Emily said with a smirk.

"Away from the children?" Julian asked. "I won't have it. The second floor suits us fine."

"Don't worry, I told her we weren't interested in moving," Emily assured him. "She said she would build them anyway in case we changed our minds."

"I suppose we can use them as guest suites instead of the ones in the east wing," Julian mused. "That way, the Pilot brothers can have their rooms all to themselves if they should ever decide to bunk here."

"Well," Emily said with a feigned smile, "I guess that's up to Frances Loraine."

"Right," Julian reluctantly agreed. "I think it's time for me to go. Is the car out front?"

"Yes, Adam wanted to take you to the airport," Emily said warmly. "I thought that was nice of him."

"It's an awfully long drive for him. He will most certainly have to rent a hotel room for the night," Julian said with concern.

Emily said with a broad smile. "Nonsense. He'll relish getting away from here for a while. I told him to take his time."

Julian nodded in agreement.

"Is everything ready for you on the other end?" she asked.

"Yes," Julian answered, "Elizabeth is picking me up at the airport in Washington." He kissed her cheek. "I'll see you in a few days."

Emily smiled, "Julian, have a good time and stay for a while."

Julian gave a half smile on his way out the door. As he looked back, he gave her a nod and made his way to the car.

Julian felt remarkably calm when the plane landed safely in Washington. It was late afternoon as the plane taxied itself to the terminal building. He expected to be nervous when he landed into his former home, which seemed to have been a lifetime ago. There was not the sense of dread present that he had been expecting, as the haunting past was awaiting his return.

Instead, Julian was curious. How had the city changed, since he was last here? Was he himself all that different? *Maybe older,* he thought. There was already a feeling of familiarity as the plane landed. He had taken so many business trips and returned home safely through this very airport. Things did not seem so odd.

As he strolled through the jet way, he wondered if Elizabeth would be waiting for him or if she would be at the baggage claim. He was not surprised when he didn't see her as he came into the airport holding area.

Julian proceeded to the baggage claim and retrieved his suitcase. There was still no sign of Elizabeth. It was not like her to forget. Regardless, he headed toward the taxi line. Before he got too far, he saw a man dressed in a driver's uniform with a sign that read "Smith." He thought perhaps that the driver had come for him, since Elizabeth was not present. In fact, it probably made more sense that she would send somebody in her place. Still, he presumed he was not the only Smith in the crowd. Elizabeth had her own way.

"Excuse me, sir," Julian inquired of the driver. "Are you waiting for a Julian Smith?"

"Yes, I am," the driver said. "Is that your only bag? I have a skycap on standby." He signaled for the man to take Julian's luggage. "I'm to take you to Mrs. Steele's home at once. She'll be waiting for you at the house."

"Elizabeth doesn't wait for anyone, but I will take your word, that she'll be there when we arrive," Julian said more to himself.

The skycap and driver saw that the suitcase was safely placed inside the trunk of a long black stretch limousine. "Is this what she travels in these days?" Julian asked the driver.

"Yes," he answered. "Of course until the new one is ready, but I'm sure you'll find this one to be of comfort. Help your self to anything inside. If you need anything, press the call button and I'll answer."

Julian nodded as he moved to go inside the huge car. The driver leaned to go toward the door that was midway from the front of the car to the rear. However, Julian had already opened the door to the rear and made his way inside. He entered what appeared to be an office. He slid onto a leather seat, which was situated in a compartment large enough for a small desk. There was even a phone anchored to the tabletop with a few drawers underneath it. A small beverage bar was off to the side. The office was well equipped to transact business. Butting against the desk, was a set of glass panels that separated the office from a living room of sorts toward the front of the car. He reached to open the door to move to the front. When his hand made the motion, the door slid open automatically. He easily crawled into the roomy area. There were blue leather tufted lounges running up both sides of the car. However in the middle of one side, a glass-stocked bar stood beside a small refrigerator. Directly across from it was a classy stereo system. Julian could see speakers displayed throughout this small room. At the front of the car, a television set was anchored safely in its holder. *This car can keep someone comfortable for a while,* he thought. This one was nicer than any of those used by the farm. He sat and amused himself viewing the world of Washington from the windows.

Elizabeth lived in a small mansion in Northwest Washington. The driver pulled the car up the concrete circular driveway, which came about 500 yards from the street in a quiet neighborhood. The dark brick square front had the beginnings of ivy strands growing up along its sides and facade. It had a manicured look, so it could be assumed the look was of no mistake, but one that had deliberate accents to the sturdy classic building. The landscaping was green with no sign of colorful flowering that was prominent this time of year in Washington. It was vintage Elizabeth: her tastes were classic, simple and expensive.

The housekeeper opened the door to house before Julian could knock with suitcase in hand. He could see Elizabeth in the background. After entering the foyer area, he set his piece of luggage in front of his mother. The inside was exactly as he remembered. The classic large white marble floors radiated though the diamond shaped foyer. Close to the far-left corner, a winding staircase with its polished brass railings beanstalked to the next level.

Elizabeth was dressed in a navy pin strip suit, which was her normal attire from when she rose in the morning until she retired at night. She wore a navy hat, which sat poised on her mahogany hair. It was typically pulled to a bun nestled to the back of her head. She pursed her lips, as she offered no warm greeting. She was never one for any type of affection.

As she pulled on her short white gloves, she began to speak. "Oh, Julian, it's so good to see you. I hate to have to run as soon as you arrive, but you know how things are. I have to go, or I'll be late. Is the car parked outside?" Before Julian had a chance to answer, she rattled forward, "I assume you want to stay at your condominium in Crystal City. Here are your keys and bank book," she said as she dropped them into the palm of his hand. "You will find the place as you left it. Maid service has been coming once a week, regardless to whether it was needed. Your car is exactly where you left it in the garage. It has been shopped once a month, regardless if it was necessary. I believe you will find things in order.

"Let's do lunch one day this week, so we can catch up with things. You need to decide what to do with all the money you and your boyfriend left behind, when you made your exit south. Bye now," she finished as she whirled out the door. Soon, he heard the limousine speed away.

Julian frowned. "Miss," Julian called to the housekeeper who had never left their presence, "Would you please call me a cab?"

"Mrs. Steele has arranged for a car to come and to take you where you want to go. It should be here momentarily."

Julian nodded his thanks. She scurried off to the back of the house, leaving him alone in the vast foyer. As the housekeeper had promised, a few moments later, he could hear another car drive up the asphalt and park outside the door. He picked up his suitcase and made for the exit.

The limousine dropped Julian in front of a tall high rise building in Arlington, Virginia in a section better known as Crystal City. This corner of town was dominated by many towering glass office buildings, hotels, apartments and condominiums, and government headquarters installations. These structures gave the appearance of a tin of packed sardines. The city is conveniently located close to the shores of the Potomac River, which borders Virginia and The District of Columbia. Washington's National Airport lies between Crystal City and the Potomac River. A huge parcel of land sitting next to this glittering mass is the home of all military headquarters better known as the Pentagon. The highway joins the two sections of real estate together. Its travelers cross the Potomac River over the 14th Street Bridge into the city of Washington, DC.

Julian took hold of his suitcase and entered the tall glass structure of a building. He advised the desk clerk that he had arrived from an extended trip and that he would be residing in the building for a few days. The clerk made no mention of Julian's information and advised him that there were no messages waiting for him.

The elevator operator took Julian to the second floor of the penthouse suites some twenty-five stories from the ground. When he stepped off the elevator, he could see that his apartment was the door directly in front of the elevator. The floor consisted of three units, with his being the middle apartment. The hallway was tastefully carpeted with a light neutral color, with some nondescript wallpaper on the walls. Julian paused momentarily before inserting his key into the door to enter the apartment. It had been more than a decade since he had last been inside his old home. *How will the place seem different? What changes have been made? Had anybody other than the cleaning staff been inside since I was last here?* he wondered.

He inserted the key and heard it give a sound of release. He held his breath and plunged inside. The flat smelled fresh as if it had just been cleaned. He stood on the same coffee-colored wall to wall carpet. It left footprints as he walked on it. The furniture was all the same without a speck of dust. The unit was shaped like a capital T, with the living area stretching to the far window. Directly to the right was a large built in entertainment center, with a large television and stereo system. Beyond this wall to the right was a dining room, which opened further into the kitchen. The master bedroom door was to the right of the kitchen and the guest room door lay directly ahead of the kitchen. To Julian's left from the front door, was a set of double doors that led to an office to the left and another one to the right. The one on the left had belonged to Dennis and the other was his. A full bath was sandwiched between the two rooms.

Julian walked to the far wall, which was a full ceiling to floor panoramic window expanding from the wall to the left, to the end of the dining room to the far right. The vanilla sheers were drawn open, exposing an impressive view of the capital city. It was dark and all the glittering lights blanketed the black background. From the view, he could see the United States Capitol just off center. To the left were the Washington Monument, the Kennedy Center, and the Lincoln and Jefferson Memorials. Dennis and he often stood in front of this window looking out into the expanse after a day's work. They would talk about the day's events while holding cocktails in their hands only after loosening their neckties. After a while, they would plan their evening schedule. Those were good times.

Julian left the window after a few minutes of gazing and padded toward their bedroom. The bed was made with the exact same spread that lay on it the last time he had seen it. He opened his closet door. His suits, ties, dress shirts and slacks still hung on their hangers. Several pairs of shoes were neatly laid on the floor, just as he always had kept them. He opened Dennis's closet door and then remembered that it had already been cleaned out before he left. Why did he think its contents might have returned?

He did not bother to look into the dresser drawers. He assumed that their contents were still intact. He did not look inside the top drawer of the nightstand on his side of the bed. *Could the book I was reading at the time of departure still be there?* he wondered.

He left his suitcase at the foot of the bed and made his way back to the living room. He closed the double doors leading to their offices. Dennis's office would be free of all its contents. *Would the papers I was studying at the time still be on my desk?* he asked himself, beginning to feel unnerved.

There was plenty of time to explore the rest of the apartment. He was hungry. He called and ordered some supper or dinner as they called it on this side of the country, to be brought to his suite. For kicks, he told the attendant to bring the same food as he had the last time for dinner.

Realizing he needed a bath, he took a hot shower then wrapped himself in the robe that had been left hanging in the bathroom. When he came out from the bedroom, he could see his food had been set on a cart just inside the door. He did not bother to check the contents. He did not remember what he had eaten all those years ago.

When Julian awakened, he found himself on the sofa in the living room. He checked his watch and it read 12:00 noon. *I must have been really tired. Maybe it was the jetlag catching up with me,* he thought. Some old inkling made him rise and check outside the door of the penthouse. Across the threshold lay copies of *The Washington Post, The New York Times,* and *The Wall Street Journal.* However, other than glancing through them, he did not care to read them.

He thought about calling the farm, but thought better of it. This was his time to be away from it. He decided it was time for a workout. He put his old sneakers and exercise attire in an old gym bag then made his way to the spa. After some time with the weights, a run on the treadmill, a message, and a steam room stay, he made his was back to his apartment.

It was already getting to be late afternoon. He decided to get into some slacks, a button down shirt and nice shoes to go into the city to have a look at things. Even though the car had been properly maintained, he still did not trust that it would drive properly. In the past, he found the European cars to be unreliable, when they were new. By now, his car was probably a classic, when others of its time period had long been left on the side of the road. He thought it best to take a taxi.

Julian found himself walking along Pennsylvania Avenue SE on Capitol Hill. He noticed that the road had probably been paved a time or two and landscape updated since he was last in town. He strolled past an establishment that had been known as a place for gay men to get a drink, where Dennis and he used to meet their friends for cocktails.

He went inside. The place looked the same except the name had changed. So had the bartenders and patrons. He grabbed a stool and had a seat at the bar. He ordered a beer. He was feeling fidgety. He left his beer and went to use the facilities. When he came back, he reclaimed his beer and decided to lean against the rail attached to a wall running parallel to the bar. He began to watch some TV, starting to feel more at ease.

After a short time, a man approached him. He was a few inches taller than Julian and had a lanky figure. He sported a dark bushy mustache that was same color as his dark brown hair, which covered his ears. The man was far from beautiful and was not dressed very well.

"Hi," The man said.

"Hi," Julian said, returning the gesture.

The man stuck out his hand and introduced himself as Gary.

"Julian," he said to the man.

"I don't recall seeing you here before," Gary said with a smile.

"It's been a while," Julian agreed with a half smile.

"Do you live in the neighborhood?" Gary asked, pretending to be interested.

"In Crystal City," Julian replied. "You?"

"Uptown in Northwest," Gary answered. "I work nearby and just got off work."

"I see," Julian said, briefly returning his eyes to the video screen, while taking a swig from his beer bottle.

The man moved closer to Julian. Close enough that he could feel the man's heat touch the skin of his arm. Julian slowly blinked and sighed.

"So," Julian started, "What brings you out tonight?"

"Thought I could use a little company," Gary replied, looking into Julian's eyes.

Julian smiled lightly, returning his gaze. Gary moved closer and Julian met him halfway. They put their arms around each other in a firm embrace. Julian felt himself melting into Gary's arms. It felt so good to be in another man's arms. Slowly Gary started moving a hand back and forth across Julian's back. Soon they parted and looked into each other's eyes. Gary bent slightly and planted a light kiss on his lips. Julian noticed his whole body was on sensory overload. Each touch sent small shocks shooting through his body.

"Do you want to go somewhere?" Gary asked.

"Sure," Julian replied.

The two men made their way out of the bar. Julian stood still, while Gary started moving to the right.

"Did you drive?" Gary asked.

"No," Julian answered.

"Do you want to ride in my car?" Gary inquired.

Julian nodded his head and walked in step with the man.

When they reached Gary's compact car, he unlocked the front passenger door letting Julian into the front seat. Quickly, he whisked to his side of the car and got into his seat. Julian took a deep breath and let his hands rest on his lap, looking straight ahead.

Gary put his key in the ignition to start the car, when he noticed the gold band on Julian' left hand.

"You married?" he asked softly with a smile.

"Yeah," Julian replied with a half smile.

Gary gently let his hand with the key fall into his own lap. "Are you into this?" he asked, sensing a slight change in Julian's demeanor.

"Not really," Julian chuckled.

Gary refrained from making a reply. Then he asked, "Do you want to talk about it?"

Julian brought his hands into a prayer position while touching the tips of his fingers to his lips. He smiled. "I'm supposed to be finding myself on this trip."

"Trip?" Gary said, puzzled.

Julian smiled again. "I used to live in Crystal City...I mean, I still have a place there, but I just haven't stayed in it for a while. I live in Louisiana on a sugarcane plantation. I have a wife and five children. We live with my father in-law along with my 16-year-old gay nephew. My wife is very supportive of me and she may have a lover of her own. There's a man there that I seem to have taken to, but I don't see much hope of it leading to anything."

"Wow," Gary said, letting out his breath.

Julian frowned.

"What seems to be the problem?" Gary asked.

"I'm a mess," Julian replied, "It feels so good to be here, especially since I'm in fits, while I'm at the farm. At the same time, I'm homesick. I miss my wife, children, nephew and father in-law. I miss the farm. I miss my friends. I miss all of it."

"How long have you been gone?" Gary asked.

"Two days," Julian said, starting to laugh.

"Give it a chance here for a few days," Gary advised.

Julian nodded with some agreement.

"You'll come to terms with yourself," Gary smiled, "Take some time and sort things out, so they don't seem so jumbled up in your mind. Then you can go home. It seems that's the place you want to be."

"They do things differently out there," Julian blurted out. "Not in the manner which I agree they should be. They don't talk about things. They go as they please, without acknowledging the truth of the situation. I see a big white elephant in the room, but I'm the only one who sees it."

"I'm not sure I understand." Gary stated with his forehead furrowed.

"It's alright for me to be homosexual if I don't talk about it. I feel like I'm being constantly reminded that if it was known that I had acted on my feelings, that I would be in the wrong. However, my nephew not only talks about his homosexuality, he flaunts it and people act like they don't even notice. I just don't get it," Julian explained with hand and arm gestures full of emotion. "Why is it such a big deal for me?"

"It sounds simple," Gary said matter of factly. "You want to play by the rules and you can't. You view yourself as less than perfect and it's eating at you. It seems nobody is asking you to be perfect, however given the choice, then yes, they will ask you to be perfect. I suggest you take away their choice, then everything will be okay. You need to be yourself. It seems that you have a wonderful family that loves you. Yes, they have a different way of doing things, but it works for that culture. You need to accept it, then you will be okay."

Julian sighed. "You know, I'm not usually so cut and dried with things. I like to think that I let things happen as they are meant to happen. Why am I so concerned about the rules this time?"

"Maybe you feel you have a lot to lose if you don't follow them this time," Gary observed.

"That's true," Julian agreed. "I have never had so much at stake."

"You'll work it out," Gary smiled. "Come on, I'll drive you home."

"You, don't have to do that," Julian blanched. "I can easily take a cab."

"I insist," Gary said.

CHAPTER 31

A few weeks later on the Pilot plantation.

It was mid afternoon, just past the lunch hour. Julian was trudging his way from the big house across to the Main Road to the barracks. He had asked Christopher to meet him in his room.

Julian's mind drifted from the task at hand, naturally deflecting some of the unpleasantness that was to come. The barracks was a large structure. It seemed a lifetime ago when he had taken up residence inside this large building. Not many people were housed there anymore, since most of the farm's people were from generations removed from their forefathers. They lived with their families down along the Quarters Road. Still, Christopher lived there, holed up into one of the compartments small enough to be considered a large closet. He did not complain about his tight living quarters, as Julian had not when he resided there. The barracks always had an eerie feel. Julian felt it would be strange to live once again in a place so large that one could project the image of having the place all to himself.

Julian had to concentrate. He knew what he had to do. This was going to create havoc in his soul. Also, his conscience was feeling a large case of the guilts. *Why did it have to come to this?* he thought. *Surely there must be another way,* he thought again. *Why does Christopher have to pay this price alone? Whose fault was all of this anyway? Christopher's or mine?* The questions kept rattling around in his head. Julian felt that only he had the answers to these questions. He had his answers, but that didn't make him feel any better.

Finally, the 20-minute walk which normally took fewer than 10 minutes had reached its end. He paused in front of the barracks entrance and slowly placed his hand on the door handle. He gave the door a push. His arm felt like spaghetti with little or no strength. He gently gritted his teeth and pushed forward. Briefly, he hoped that Adam had remembered to say a prayer for him as he had promised he would. Julian was going to need all the help he could get.

Slowly, he reached to rap lightly on Christopher's door. *Maybe he forgot about our appointment and went back to his chores after lunch,* he hoped, *No. That could not be. He would have been at the big house at lunchtime if he had forgotten his instruction to stay here in his room.*

The sound on the hollow wood door rang clearly.

Julian could hear an immediate commotion and Christopher had the door open before the third rap.

His face framed a big smile and his eyes revealed the joy he felt. This was always the case with Christopher. Julian sensed that he counted the minutes each day until they would see each other and spend some time together.

Christopher reached and gabbed Julian's hand and brought it to his lips and kissed it. Slowly, Julian drew it back to his side and entered the room. Christopher moved himself to the other end of the room and flopped himself onto his bed, while Julian stayed standing by the door. After closing the door, he gave Christopher a long forlorn look.

Christopher smiled and said, "I'm really glad to see you. It seems we have been just passing each other the last few days. You haven't been around the big house so much." He smiled again, "Does this mean the afternoon is for us?"

Julian nodded.

"Good," Christopher said, failing to notice Julian's somber mood.

Julian brought his hands together just above his waist. He could feel sweat beginning to build underneath his white cotton buttoned down shirt. He could feel the moisture beginning to grow between his legs along the insides of his tan trousers.

"I have some good news, that I hope will please you as much as it has myself," Julian started. His mouth was feeling dry. What he would do for a glass of water. "Congratulations. You are getting a big promotion." Julian was less than enthusiastic.

"Okay," Christopher replied, attempting to follow his train of thought. "That's not necessary. I'm perfectly content with the way things are."

Julian figured as much. He took a deep breath. He was failing. He could not do this thing. It was better to just be blunt.

"Christopher," Julian said, taking a big swallow. "I'm having you transferred to the Wilson Farm up the road. It's a plantation the family took over some years ago. I spent some time there and it's really quite nice."

Christopher started breathing in short breaths. "Why? I like it here right where I am, with you and Emily. I don't want to go anywhere else."

Julian pursed his lips. "I know. I know," he said softly. He then shook his head slowly. "This is the only way, Christopher. I would go myself if I did not have my responsibilities. Since I can't, you'll have to go in my place."

"This does not make any sense," Christopher said, shaking his head, "I love both you and Emily. You are my family. How can you do this? There has to be some mistake."

"Christopher, I can't get away from you. You're always under foot no matter how much I tell you to mix with the other people on the farm and not spend any more time at the big house. You have not listened," Julian said, starting to feel both guilt and anger.

"I have," Christopher insisted. "I've been spending more time with Billy and Jack at their place. I try to catch Shaun, but he's not so easy to find."

Julian put his hand to his forehead. "This is not working," he said. "Christopher," he started again, taking another tack, "I cannot be around you for a while. I try to stay away from you, but you are always before me. I feel trapped with nowhere to go. I don't feel the same way about you as you do me. I told you at the campsite what I needed from you. This need has not changed. In short, you are driving me crazy."

Christopher was speechless.

"This is the only way," Julian continued. "Maybe after a while my feelings will change and you can come back under another set of rules. For now, this is the way it's going to have to be."

"Maybe I can change," Christopher mumbled.

"Christopher, you cannot change an inclination. You have it or you do not have it. You and I have to accept the way things are. I have to find a way to live in this place without losing my mind. When that happens, things will be different with us," Julian explained.

"You are blaming me for your problems?" Christopher said with a sad face.

"I accept full responsibility for my problems. I deal with them the best I can. One, is to make some rules to help me, which you have failed to follow," Julian said evenly as one explains something to a child.

"But I don't like the rules," Christopher said, looking at Julian. "It isn't fair."

Julian softened his expression. He had to fight the impulse to sit next to his friend and put his arms around him to provide some comfort. "I don't like them either," he said, "but I can't accept the consequences. Unfortunately, one of us has to pay the price and since it cannot be me, it has to be you."

Slowly Christopher rose from the bed. He went and stood directly in front of Julian. He reached a hand up to the top button of his lime green nylon silk shirt and undid it. Then he reached for the next one. Julian brought both of his hands up to cup the one Christopher was using. Slowly he brought both down toward his waist. Christopher stood undeterred. He reached once more and undid the next three. Julian shook his head slowly as if to say no, but Christopher ignored the gesture. He shed his shirt.

Julian noticed the thin layer of reddish brown hair on the breastbone of the slender man. He was not the most attractive man, but Julian still found him to be beautiful. Christopher unfastened his thick brown belt and let his cotton trousers fall to the floor along with his boxer shorts. He stepped lightly from them. Julian could not help but examine him. His body was slightly tanned from head to toe. There was very little hair to be found on it, except for a few places below his knees covering his calves and shins. There was a small fringe that was the same color that accented his breastbone protruding from each of his armpits and lightly running along the lengths of his forearms. And, of course, he could not help but notice the soft looking patch nestling his flaccid penis. He wanted badly to touch it.

Christopher waited as he felt Julian gazing at his body. He could sense that his friend was pleased.

Without any words, Christopher went to his bed and descended upon it. He beckoned for Julian to come.

Julian remained standing by the door, fully clothed and slightly dumbfounded. He raised his arm and used his hand to brace the back of his neck. He turned away from Christopher and faced the door.

"Julian, please," Christopher begged, "Come to bed."

Julian turned around abruptly with his eyes growing red. "I can't," he said.

Christopher flung himself back against the mattress, staring at the ceiling with his forearm resting on top of his head. He moved quickly onto his side and propped himself on his elbow to face Julian. Tears were streaming from his eyes and he shot in anger, "What am I supposed to do?"

"I can't have you like this," Julian retorted with a mix of frustration and compassion. "I can't have you do this to appease me. Can you honestly say this is what you want?"

"What difference does it make?" Christopher cried, with tears streaming down his face, "I love you, Julian; more than anything. Isn't that enough?"

"No it's not," Julian said, distraught but without tears. "Do you think that this time would be the last? What about tomorrow? And tomorrow night for that matter? And the next day? This would be only the start. I would be knocking on your door every day, sometimes twice. Would you be able to live this way?"

Christopher fell back against his mattress with his arm covering his eyes. He was sobbing quietly. "If I had to I would."

Julian felt himself deflate. He felt himself reach into his soul to grab a powerful sense of strength.

With full concentration, he began to speak with a clear sense of purpose. "We've done some checking on you, Christopher. It seems that you are a brilliant man. You have a doctoral degree in fine arts and literature from a first class university. Your father knew you for your talent and could not bear to see it go unfulfilled. He let you see the world at his expense, hoping you would find your sense of purpose. When he sensed your resolve to prosper slipping, he cut off your stipend. He agonized over doing this, because he cared for you so much. He felt the guilt for spoiling you to the point that you continue to skirt responsibility. He believed that his intervention in your life was preventing your maturation."

"Now Christopher, I am not one to preach to you for skipping out on responsibilities. I certainly have experienced such failures. I have to fight the impulse to run away from home. As I have the opportunity to resolve my difficulties, so do you."

"You're to report at once to the Wilson farm. They're expecting you there at anytime. Pilot has agreed with me to use that property to open a first class library and center for fine art instruction. You will be instrumental in its setup and inauguration. Once that is done, we want to start sending the gifted children of the farm and many others in the surrounding parishes to you for instruction. This is a great opportunity for you, Christopher and for many of those who want to learn."

Christopher sat up on the side of his bed, still naked, with his head in his hands. He looked at Julian with red eyes empty of tears, "Please reconsider, Julian," he begged. "Being here with you and Emily is the happiest I have ever been. My father is a good man. He tried his best when my mother died, but he was always too busy for me. The two of you are the best family I have ever had."

Julian wanted so much to relent and was pained to maintain his stance, "No," he said evenly.

Christopher started to cry once more.

"You are to report at once," he said, failing. He made a rush for the door and exited as he heard Christopher wail, "Don't go!" His sobs in full swing as they rung through the barracks. Julian quickly found the empty room beside Christopher's. He went inside and shut the door. He leaned back against the closed door and slid to the floor into a sitting position with his knees pressed to his chest. He put the heel of his hands to his eyes and started to sob. Once he started he was unable to stop. He could feel the pain flow through him. Just when he felt that it was unbearable, another sob was released.

All Julian could think about was getting to the big house and then up to his bedroom without being noticed. He thought the chances were good, since nobody was usually inside the big house at this time of day. Pilot would be closed up into his office for the rest of the afternoon. The smallest children would be down for their naps, while the others would be receiving instruction from Emily. Frances Loraine was seldom seen in the big house during the day. She usually spent her afternoons in her rooms. The household help would have finished for the day until the evening meal.

Julian quickly ascended the steps of the back porch leading to the kitchen of the big house. He opened the screen door and let it slam behind him. He hastened to cross the room to the nearby stairwell.

She was wiping her hands clean on a dishtowel when he immediately caught her glance. No use hiding it now. He knew she had seen his swollen red eyes.

"Julian, what is it?" she exclaimed as she instinctively closed the door leading to the rest of the big house.

Knowing he was not going to get past her, Julian slumped down into the closest chair and brought his head near to his knees with his arms cradling his face.

Emily went behind him and fastened the door to the porch. "Julian, what is wrong?" she asked as she approached him from the front. She did not go to him in order to give him the space he needed. Julian did not like to be crowded.

Wanting desperately to mask his pain but no longer having the strength, he cried softly.

"Come on, Julian. If you can't talk to your wife, who can you to talk to?" Emily said firmly.

Julian looked up to her face briefly, and then returned his head to its cradled position. There was silence. He wanted to spare her feelings somehow, but he saw that she was not going anywhere.

She was waiting.

"I sent Christopher away," Julian said between sniffles. Then he could no longer hold back the sobs. Once again, the adrenaline started to flow and so did the tears. "Emily, I had to do it. He was driving me crazy. You should have seen him," Julian said, staring at the floor and slowly shaking his head. "I really hurt him, Emily. I don't think God will forgive me." His sobs continued.

Emily lowered herself on one knee before him and placed a hand on his thigh. "You did what you thought you needed to do, Julian," she said softly, trying to look up into his face. He still continued to cry.

He looked into her face, while tears streaked his own. "Emily, sometimes...I feel... so.....lonely." he cried uncontrollably. "I just don't....know...what to do." More tears. She gently cupped the side of his face with her hand. She did not say a word. "I am so sorry," he said.

"No need to be," she said softly but unwavering.

He again looked into her face. "Emily, I need....." He shook his head slowly. "I need.....I just need......real bad." He cried some more, while she nodded her head. "This pain of loneliness hurts so bad. It's making me crazy."

"He just wasn't the way, Julian," she said, trying to comfort him. "You will find your way. It just was not through him."

"I wasn't fair to him," Julian said, trying to stop the tears, but they kept coming. Just when he thought he cried his last, more leaked from his eyes.

She shook her head as she broke from him. "You did what you thought was best for the both of you. God won't punish you. Let him help you."

Julian nodded, starting to collect himself. Then the emotion flowed again along with more sobs. "Emily," he said, drawing her into a hug. He was still seated and held her in a tight embrace around her waist. "You are my best friend."

She lowered herself and held him tight.

CHAPTER 32

"Come on, Shaun!" Julian cried, pounding the boy's bedroom door with the side of his hand curled into fist. After a pause, he pounded three more times.

"Go away," Shaun replied feebly.

"Shaun, we've been through this, now. Open the door!" Julian ordered, hammering the door with three more thuds.

"Go away," Shaun replied again.

Emily came up behind Julian. "What's the matter?"

"Shaun won't come out," Julian replied, facing the door waiting for a response, "What could be the matter with him?"

"I think his boyfriend dumped him," Emily answered. She then turned around and walked down the hall.

"Come on, Shaun," Julian said into the crack of the door jam. "You've been in there 2 days. It's time to come out."

No response.

"If you don't open the door, I'll break it down. I won't put up with this," Julian warned. "It can't be that bad."

"I'm not decent," Shaun said with a final attempt to dissuade his uncle.

"Well, you have 5 minutes to get yourself together. Then I want you to meet me on the front porch," Julian said.

No response.

"I mean it, Shaun; 5 minutes," Julian warned again. He then headed toward the stairwell and wound down to the kitchen.

He saw Emily fussing with the table. "I don't remember being like this when I was 17," Julian said, scratching his head.

"You probably were not like that at his age," Emily commented. "But I know I probably shut myself up in my room enough times for the both of us."

"Wish me luck," Julian said, moving through the great room without waiting for a response. When he reached the front steps he sat on the top of the stoop and waited. He concentrated on calming himself down to deal with the boy.

After a few minutes, Shaun came through the door and let the screen slam. He then plodded down the first step of the stoop and sat down hard next to his uncle, landing with an exasperated thump. He placed his hands into an upside down prayer position between his knees and bowed his head, staring into the ground.

"Come on, Shaun," Julian exclaimed with a frown. "Don't act like you did something wrong."

"Well, you hollered at me," Shaun said meekly, trying to incite some guilt from his uncle.

Julian bit halfway. "I'm sorry," he replied coarsely. Shaun gave himself a half smile inside without revealing it.

"Tell me what happened with Jonathan. I know it hurts to talk about it, but you got to let me know about these things," Julian said with the empathy returning to his voice.

Shaun loosened up some but still hedged as he started to speak. "Well, it's over."

Julian waited.

"His parents said we were not allowed to see each other anymore," Shaun explained slowly.

"But things seemed to be going so well for you guys," Julian said with his brow furrowed with confusion. "Surely, they must have been pleased."

"They said Jonathan was becoming too comfortable with himself 'in that way' they said. They said I was being a bad influence on him," he said, dejectedly staring at his hands. He then looked to his uncle. "I tried to do everything right, Uncle Julian, and it still didn't work. It's not fair!"

"You are right. It's not fair," Julian agreed. "What did Jonathan have to say about this?"

"I don't know," Shaun replied, "I didn't even get to see him. When I went to get him for our date, they confronted me at the door and told me what I just told you. They said they were not going to go to Adam's church anymore. I guess that means I won't ever get to see him."

Julian tried hard not to relay any cliches like, "You'll get over it in time" or "There will be other guys." He could not think of what to say, so he did not say anything.

"It's so hard to meet nice guys around here, Uncle Julian," Shaun said with frustration. "I thought I finally met someone neat."

"In a couple years, you'll be off to college and then there will be plenty of neat guys," Julian said with a smile. "You'll be bringing some nice boy for me to meet at one of your breaks before you know it."

Shaun frowned and replied somberly, "I don't know about college. Papa will likely cut all funds from me when I turn 18 years old. I won't be able to pay for college."

"Shaun," Julian started, "When I was home last, or in Washington I should say, I moved all the assets that were in my name there and put them into your name. There's plenty of money for you to pay for college and will be some left over for you to live comfortably for a good while after you finish your education. I would be considered wealthy if I stayed in Washington, not like the Pilots, however comfortable enough. It is all yours."

"Why did you do that?" Shaun said with great surprise.

"Well, Emily and I have plenty of money and the children are set for life from what they inherited from Robert Lamond. I didn't need that money for anything, so I gave it to you," he said, glancing sideways into his nephew's eyes.

Shaun smiled. "Thank you, Uncle Julian. You really do take good care of me."

Julian continued, "I have a condominium there that it now yours along with a car, which is probably an antique by now, parked in the garage. They are both regularly maintained and waiting for you when you are ready to take possession. I had all my belongings removed, but it still remains fully furnished."

"So, I can go to college in Washington and be fully set," Shaun said, rather pleased.

"Yes," Julian said.

"You have really made this a home for me, Uncle Julian. Sometimes I think I should change my name to Pilot, just to remove any of my former life from me," Shaun said happily.

"Well, Shaun," Julian said, returning his smile and then added thoughtfully gazing into the horizon, "You and I are the lucky ones. You are *A Pilot by Choice* and so am I. Not many people get to choose their own families."

Shaun smiled broadly and nodded.

Then Julian said gravely, "There's more."

"More?" Shaun asked, curling his top lip. He was not sure he could handle more at the moment.

"Yes," Julian paused to explain, "When I was in Washington, Elizabeth bugged me for days to come to Boston to sign some papers. When she explained what it was about, I refused each time she asked me to go. This is complicated, so you have to listen carefully. I'm not sure I fully understand. I was named, practically speaking, the sole heir of my grandmother's estate. The will was very specific as to the first born of my father who was first born straight up the line to his fathers before him. To inherit the money, I had to agree to satisfy a residency requirement, living for a number years in my grandmother's huge Boston estate. I, of course, refused. Elizabeth was beside herself. She stands to get a healthy commission from the trust only if it is me that inherits the money. This would make her an extremely wealthy woman beyond her wildest dreams. She has been managing the trust in the hopes that someday I would claim it. If I don't claim the estate, it remains in trust until my firstborn is of age to claim the inheritance. If that is the case, Elizabeth gets nothing."

"I tried asking her if I could inherit the money and directly turn it over to you, thus having you satisfying the residency requirement for me. You could do your schooling in Boston. At this time, Elizabeth is fervently working with the lawyers to find a way to do this, since I vehemently refused to have it any other way. After discussion with her people, they said something might be done, since your are of Smith blood and a first born. However, you are first born of a second born. To overcome this, they said I would have to adopt you. This may fly as long as somebody does not contest the will."

"Who can contest it?" Shaun asked.

"Your father is really the only one," Julian said. "It would be a long shot for him, but he could still do it."

"It sounds like something he would do especially where I'm concerned. He hates me," Shaun said with a frown.

"Not necessarily," Julian said with a sly grin. "He would have to go at war with Elizabeth over this one and she would fight to the death. She has a great deal more wealth than he does and she would spend every last dime to fight for what she wanted. Not only that, he would have to fight the legal battle to have me discredited and then fight another one to claim some if not all the estate for himself. The risks are not in his favor."

"I still don't understand how I can satisfy the residency requirement for you," Shaun said, not understanding.

"The ruling would be flimsy at best but possible as long as it's not contested," Julian explained again. "Elizabeth wants this done. She will find a way. There may be a lot of taxes and arm-twisting involved, but your great grandmother holdings are vast. Far more than mine; far more than the Pilots; far more than the Lamonds; and far more than all of these put together."

"How did she accumulate all of this money," Shaun asked.

"Well, she and her family had many kinds of businesses. However, they started out as scientists, developing the power that we use today to make light bulbs work. They started selling power to utilities, which in turn sold it to people like you and me."

"Why did she leave all this to you and not anyone else?" Shaun asked.

"I can only guess," Julian supposed, "Grandmother was very old and could be difficult at times. So much so nobody could stand to be around her very long. Despite her bad points, she was very generous to family members, so naturally all thought they would, at least, get a part of her millions. She behaved differently around me. Perhaps because she knew I was different from the rest, thus shunned regularly by family members. Still, she could be difficult at times. She accepted me, so naturally, I put up with her antics and over time, she became less overwhelming. I know now she must have figured I loved her very much with or without all her money. She always said I reminded her of her late son, Matt. He was our uncle. I never did know him. I just knew that she had loved him very much."

"It seems awfully like a long shot," Shaun surmised, "But I would be happy with what you gave me. I think I could do great things with that money, but it's not really in our hands."

"Would you consider letting me adopt you? I know it would be weird having you as my son, as I enjoy being an uncle to you more than anything," Julian said, letting his vulnerability show.

"Could I still call you Uncle Julian?" Shaun asked hopefully.

Julian smiled, putting his arm around his nephew while pulling him close. "I wouldn't have it any other way," he said.

Shaun drew near to him letting his cheek rest against his uncle's shoulder. "You're the greatest, Uncle Julian."

Epilogue

7 years later at summer's end.

Shaun walked along the Farm Road approaching the big house. He was coming back from looking over the farm to see the state of things, since he was last home. His tour included a visit with Christopher. The boisterous redhead had done a terrific job transforming Pilot's learning institution into a first class facility. The school remained small, but it had a lot to offer. It had become a magnate for international students, because the school's library contained many rare books, many which Shaun had donated. Special professors were on staff specializing in the rare works of literature that the school had collected. As a result of Christopher's program, the farm's children benefited from his knowledge in fine arts and literature.

Christopher was overwhelmingly happy. This had always been the case, since Shaun had known him. *It just doesn't seem natural that someone remained in such an euphoric state,* he thought.

Shaun noticed a wayward woman fawning over Christopher his entire visit. The farm gossip may have some merit to the fact that he had taken up with this girl. *Poor girl,* he thought. *She doesn't have a clue about her asexual boyfriend.* Perhaps they had an arrangement that met both their needs.

Shaun felt that Christopher was still in love with Uncle Julian. Most of Christopher's dialogue had been devoted to questions about Uncle Julian.

Soon, Carmen would be arriving from Boston. They often had difficulties, but even with the shortest of separations, Shaun was still always excited to be expecting their reunions.

Shaun saw his Uncle Julian sitting on the stoop of the front porch next to Adam. He was greatly pleased with his uncle. For some time, he sensed a relaxation about him that he knew had a lot to do with Adam.

Something inside Shaun told him to stop in his tracks. He watched as Adam rose and gave his uncle's shoulder an affectionate squeeze. Shortly after that, he left Uncle Julian to make his way home.

In a moment, he saw his Aunt Emily come and sit briefly beside Uncle Julian. They exchanged a few words and that old familiar stressed look came across his uncle's face. It seemed his jaw tensed and remained frozen in that position. As quickly as she had made her seat, she rose in the same continuing motion. She gave Uncle Julian a similar squeeze to his shoulder that Adam had done just minutes ago.

Shaun resumed his walk and hastened to the front porch. Uncle Julian didn't spend as much time on the cans by the fence as he used to, but he knew that it was probably where he would be headed.

He sat next to his uncle on the porch quietly as if trying not to disturb him. "How are things?" He asked.

"Good," Julian said nodding his head. After a pause, he turned his head toward Shaun. "It looks like you're going to have another cousin."

"What?" Shaun replied, confused. "How is that possible?"

Julian snorted a chuckle. "You got me. Things like that happen."

"Eh...how do you think Adam will feel about this?" Shaun asked.

Julian let out a sigh and pursed his lips. "Adam will be fine. There's no need for concern."

"You know, you can still leave if you want," Shaun said softly. "Things are different around here now. You'd get to see the kid whenever you wanted."

"I know," Julian said with a forlorn look. "I guess I've been feeling that way for a while. I could go at anytime, seeing that the three oldest children have opted for boarding school. The other two are not too far behind. You know very well I can't go. I've been the happiest these last few years than I have ever been in my life. I have everything here that I could possibly want. I guess for the first time, I felt I could do anything I wanted to do."

"It bothers you that the children are leaving at such a young age. I know it hurts you," Shaun acknowledged.

"Oh, they love their mama and daddy, but I understand their desire to get off the farm. It's easy to get cabin fever, especially since there is a big beautiful world out there to see. They needed to go. It's just the time I had with them has gone by so quickly. I didn't expect them to leave the nest so soon."

"You still can go," Shaun said again.

"No I can't," Julian disagreed again. "I love my life here. Besides, I know for some reason inside myself that this child is going to be different than the others. He's going to be a true Pilot and a great man for the people here. I just know he will be the one to stay behind."

"It sounds like he will be a true Smith. The Pilot children have all fled except for Emily. She's more like her mother was. No, the Smiths are the ones to stay."

"Even you?" Julian said looking with eyes of emotion into Shaun's face.

"Even me," Shaun said meeting his eyes, "I'm not going anywhere."

A Note from the Author

It took me 6 years to write this novel. I picked it up and set it down dozens of times. There were periods of 5 or 6 months that I didn't touch it. About half of the writing was done in the last 9 months of the 6th year. A lot has happened to me in the 6 years it took me to write this book. However, the plot stayed the same from the beginning, except for the story of Shaun which didn't evolve until later. If you liked this book, there will be more. I am well into the next book, *Plantation Deceptions*. If the response to *Plantation Secrets* is good, look forward to reading the next one in this series. Shaun is the featured character in this book as is the man Pilot. As the book develops, Dennis (one of my favorite characters) comes back to play a significant role. Don't worry about Julian, he still has plenty to say, as do Elizabeth, Emily, Albert and the rest, along with a few new ones. Send me an email jridout@ix.netcom.com I'd love to hear your comments.

It's difficult to get published at the present time. Even if a new author is lucky to land a publisher, the terms for the writer are less than favorable. We need new authors in the gay and lesbian subject text. You can get published, but it takes a great deal of time and hard work. Feel free to email me to pick my brain. You can also find Patricia Nell Warren at Wildcat Press on the web. She was a big help to me. Look for Pilot Books on the web soon. When the site is finished, there should be plenty of information on it. Good luck! Stay in tune with Pilot Books.